GHOSTWORLD

DAVID BROOKOVER

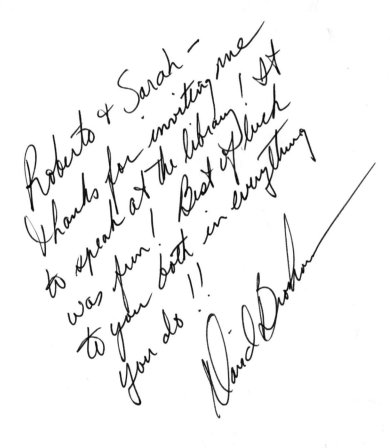

Roberto & Sarah —
thanks for inviting me
to speak at the library! It
was fun! Best of Luck
to you both in everything
you do!!
David Brookover

Curlew Press

Ghostworld
All Rights Reserved.
Copyright © 2012 David Brookover
v2.0

Cover Photo © 2012 JupiterImages Corporation. All rights reserved - used with permission.

Curlew Press

ISBN: 978-0-578-10853-7

Library of Congress Control Number: 2012910796

PRINTED IN THE UNITED STATES OF AMERICA

Prologue

The relentless Atlantic waves gnawed the Indialantic shore, as an ominous fog crept over the Florida beach like a nocturnal stalker silently tracking its prey. The invading mist reeked of death and decay, and drove the skittish sand crabs into their holes.

Like a vile shroud, the fog swirled around a gloomy boathouse suspended over the steep Intercoastal Waterway shore. The modest structure sat on barnacle-crusted concrete pilings like a misshapen stork. A gently bobbing, thirty-nine-foot Sea Ray 390 Sundancer sport yacht, the *Sea Spume*, was docked beside it, rocking and gurgling atop the black velvety undulations.

The teak boathouse was eerily quiet, but inside was another story. The building had been soundproofed by its owner decades ago, and for good reason.

Inside was a torturous, black-magic ceremonial chamber.

Where the victims' screams didn't carry beyond the four walls.

The horrifying ritual that had oft been repeated inside those dead walls was about to commence again. A heavy oaken chair was bolted to the floor in the center of an ancient demonic ceremonial ring and resembled both a medieval king's throne and a modern-day electric chair.

A grotesque series of hand-carved black-magic symbols appeared inside the candlelit circle. Candle drippings from countless past demonic rituals dotted the ceremonial site, and its foul malodor saturated the air and walls.

The profuse black candles cast dancing spirits around the latest victim. A withered elderly man sat slumped forward in a half-conscious state, with only his manacled wrists and legs supporting him. The latest victim wasn't drugged. It was much worse. His life force was nearly depleted.

A man wearing a loose hooded black robe stood stiffly in front of the chair. His face was deeply hidden within the folds of the hood.

"Well, Basil, it's time," the hooded man announced flatly. No emotion.

No remorse. No enjoyment.

The victim struggled to lift his head. His face was gaunt and sunken beneath a sea of wrinkles. "Haven't you taken . . . enough from me!" he snapped hoarsely.

"You know better. I won't be finished with you until I have it all."

"You've lived . . . long enough, Great-grandfather. Don't deny me what little life I have left," Basil implored.

The hooded man stroked his great-grandson's thin blue-gray hair. "Believe me when I say that I'm going to miss you, Basil." He exhaled heavily. "But I need you if I'm going to finally exact my revenge on those that have humiliated us. Surely you can understand that your sacrifice will bring honor back to our family."

"You're always the thespian, aren't you? Melodramatic to the core. Quick with a manipulating word, and every bit as quick to dole out cruelty, especially to your own flesh and blood! I'm warning you, Great-grandfather. If you tap my twin's life force again, I will haunt you till your last breath." The victim was nearly breathless.

The hooded man patted his great-grandson on the head. "Are those to be your final words, then?"

"Evidently, yes," Basil wheezed.

The hooded man stepped outside the ceremonial circle, threw his arms skyward, and initiated a series of black magic chants. The candle flames rose several inches, and then vanished, leaving the two men alone in the blackness.

A cloak of dazzling green energy rose inside the circle like a ghost, and slowly enveloped Basil like an ethereal lover. His shrieks and struggles were futile, as the ravenous aura penetrated his squirming body. After several agonizing minutes, his struggles flagged, then ceased.

A brilliant pure-white beam burst forth from Basil's corpse and struck the hooded man like a lightning bolt, dispelling the abominable darkness. The bolt sizzled and crackled within the hooded man's body until he was overwhelmed and sagged to the floor.

The emaciated Basil was but a shell of life in death, the last of his energy trapped within his great-grandfather.

The lightning flickered out, and the candle flames reappeared. The ceremony had ended.

The hooded man leaped to his feet, fully awash in the vigor of youth. He again touched his hand to the top of the Basil's scalp, and watched as his shrunken form incinerated like a Fourth of July sparkler. Within seconds, Basil's corpse was reduced to a mound of smoking ash, which the hooded man swept into a dust pan and liberated in the Intercoastal waters.

With a lively swagger, the murderer strode rapidly across A1A to his oceanside estate, his twisted mind bent on revenge.

1

It was the week of Halloween. Time for the freaks to show up in costume at the annual kooky-horror *Shriekfest* held at Orlando's Orange County Convention Center. This year the weirdo circus coincided with the grand opening of Orlando's newest and most bizarre tourist attraction, *Ghostworld*.

I would have gladly skipped both events, but my Uncle Jess, the director of the Department of Justice's clandestine Department for Supernatural Investigations (DSI), anticipated trouble at *Ghostworld's* opening and handed me the assignment of monitoring the gala. Since the DSI was my sole source of income these days, I grudgingly agreed, even though he refused to tell me the reason behind his suspicion. But I had a hunch that my dear uncle caught wind of my weekend plans with Kit and torpedoed them out of spite. He was that kind of guy. A first-class prick.

My latest bed partner, Lieutenant Kit Wilson, was a hot-and-cold chick, so we had our share of ups and downs over the years, both in and out of bed. She was a detective with the Orlando Police Department, and got hot under the collar whenever DSI insisted that we work together on a case. To my surprise, she didn't allow those emotions to interfere with her personal life, and we hooked up the night after her sister, Kat, dumped me. Don't ask.

Kat had whined that I spent way too much time with vampires, werewolves, and even trolls, and not enough with her. She moved as far away from me as her pocketbook allowed—Maine. I didn't have the heart to tell her that Maine was Stephen King country, and she might run into more weird shit there than she did with me. Oh well. That was the way the cookie crumbled.

I knew *Ghostworld* was going to be a taxing assignment as soon as I steered my beat-up white Explorer through the back gates. The marbled gunmetal heavens were raining worms on the vast parking lot that stretched as far east as I could see. Not your ordinary garden variety worms, either. These babies were heavy-duty, blobby night crawlers that plopped and exploded like dirty water balloons and made one helluva gooey mess on my windshield. Switching on my windshield wipers was definitely not one of my brightest moves. The blades churned their remains to opaque gore that frosted the glass.

Out of my side window, I saw a skidding, out-of-control limo sliding toward me on the gray ice. I swerved hard right to avoid the VIP mobile that was now ricocheting off every car in its path like a bully bumper car. Finally, the helpless driver ran smack-dab into a concrete light pole, which stopped it dead in its Michelins. But there were other bumper cars loose on the lot, so I quickly parked close to the entrance booths and turnstiles, away from the circular drop-off drive.

Ghostworld's ominous entrance was a gigantic arch populated with Casper-like ghost images, except these Caspers sported malevolent expressions instead of goofy, kid-friendly grins. They gave me bad vibes. I wondered what they'd give the tourist kids.

The sudden night-crawler blizzard pinned dozens of local and state dignitaries inside their blotchy limousines. Things were behind schedule already, so I grabbed the Mickey-D bag on the passenger seat and slipped out a Big Mac and a large sleeve of fries. A man had to eat, and I couldn't cook worth a damn. I even burned water.

The worms continued to fall and burst. I munched the fast food slowly as the accident total escalated. This extraordinary storm was no accident. Somebody had conjured it. My guess was that the person responsible for the spell wanted to put a damper on the grand opening. I wondered what else the sorcerer had in store for the VIPs. As far as a motive, I wasn't going there. I was just being paid to troubleshoot, and establishing a motive went way beyond my assignment description . . . and pay.

I crumpled the thin cardboard containers and stuffed them into the cheerfully printed bag. *Was the grand opening still on?* I hoped not. I was more than ready to ditch this place and rocket over to the Wolfsbane Bar and Grill for a few brewskis. Uncle Jess would understand—not!

I was about to start the engine, when a monstrous yellow front-loader rumbled through the maintenance gates and started scraping the disgusting mess from the drop-off drive. *Damn.* I stuffed the keys back in my pocket. This was yet another example of my rotten luck. There went my excuse for abandoning this ludicrous assignment.

As I awaited a clear path from the Explorer to the entrance, I flipped open the *Ghostworld* promotional brochure that Uncle Jess had overnighted to me. I skimmed through the typical hype and hyperbole and went right to the bottom line: *the owner.*

Jeffrey Stanton the Fourth was *Ghostworld's* majority stockholder. He'd made his fortune the old-fashioned way—he'd inherited it. His great-great-grandfather had cornered the South African market on diamonds. His great-grandfather had invested that pile of cash into oil. The Fourth's father had splurged on several multinational corporations, upping the family wealth to obscene levels. Hell, the Stanton family riches could pay down the national debt and still have enough left to buy a medium-sized third-world country.

After examining the brochure's varnished photos, I saw that no expense had been spared to create a first-class tourist attraction. Not quite on Disney's level, but damned close. *Mansion Macabre. The Raving Revenant Coaster. Specter Splash, the Water Ride. Ghost Town. Wraith Water Park. The Phantom Drop. Apparition Aquatic Park. Spooky Sam's Children's Playground.* And a slew of upscale restaurant "haunts."

I flipped the brochure back onto the passenger seat and massaged my strained eyes. Jeffrey Stanton. His close friends called him "Stan the Man," while the rest of us peons, including the mayor and the local state and federal politicians, referred to him as *Mister* Stanton. What a hoot. The guy was a scumbag through and through.

Lucky in wealth, unlucky in love. Mr. Cash-anova had been hitched six times. The current *Missus* "Stan the Man," number six, was a faux blonde, gold-digging slut with battleship bosoms. Her nurturing father was currently serving a life sentence in the state penitentiary for murder and armed robbery, while her loving mother had bitten the cocaine dust before her daughter, Tandy, had turned her first trick at twelve.

After a few years, the young jail-bait Tandy became a hit with the secretive, wealthy child-molesters. Eleven years later, the used-and-abused prostitute met Stanton at a New York gala where she was "employed" by another high roller. She had blossomed into a high-priced New York call girl with a penchant for big bank accounts. To her, size *did* matter.

An abrasive scraping clamor shattered my reverie. The front-loader plowed the path that I was dreading. Now I had to actually get out there and start earning Uncle Sam's greenbacks.

The worms ceased falling, but the sky remained overcast. Not your typical Florida day. *Were there any more surprises in store for us?* I had a creepy feeling that there were.

A group of overdressed guests fell on the slick and odiferous worm goo. Their clothes would be ripe for the festivities. I gingerly stepped down on the still-squiggling and squirming night crawlers, and my Big Mac and fries flopped and gurgled before settling like an anchor in the pit of my stomach. I allowed the big wigs to pass before I carefully made my way beneath the covered entrance and pushed through the turnstile. I slipped my identification tag over my wrist and moseyed into Jeffrey Stanton's mega-million-dollar fantasy kingdom. I could hardly wait . . . *to leave.*

I dredged up a slew of gross memories and rummaged around for the last time I'd ever encountered a worm storm. My search came up empty. And there was no mention of any such spell in my childhood sorcery and supernatural textbooks, but I knew someone who might know.

I reached for my cell phone, glanced at the park, and froze. *What the hell?* There wasn't a single worm inside the grounds. *What was that all about?* It looked like the sorcerer behind the worm prank had spared the park. *Why?* I wasn't going there, either.

Amazed, I dialed my old family friend as I was swept up by the swelling, smelling crowd and pushed toward the amphitheater. The ceremonies were about to begin.

2

The tumbling clouds overhead reassembled into a menacing kaleidoscope of grays and blacks. I didn't like the looks of it one bit. More trouble was brewing.

My friend answered on the fifth ring. She wasn't as spry as she used to be.

"What kind of trouble have you gotten yourself into now, Joe Luna?" Martha Gibbons exclaimed, foregoing a pleasant greeting.

"None that I'm aware of," I replied, taken aback by her accurate assessment.

Martha owned *Martha's Mojo Magic Herbs*, a popular off-beat potions shop located in Orlando's less-prosperous downtown section on Pine Street. She was a genuine Southern-fried kook with a penchant for concocting unique spells for her clients. Her intimidating appearance scared off half of her potential customers who popped in for a look-see. It was the black patch over her right eye that did it. She claimed that the blind eye could actually *see* into the future, but I wasn't totally convinced.

Her silver-blue hair was perpetually mussed, and her crinkled black dress—as wrinkled as her seventy-something complexion—was shiny and somber. She wielded her crooked dogwood walking stick like a crazed swordsman who wasn't particular about what or who he struck.

"Tell me you're not at *Ghostworld's* grand opening," she said.

The hair stiffened along the back of my neck. "Uh, yeah, I am," I admitted.

"Good gracious, Joe. Trouble is attracted to you like fools to a scam."

She knew me too well. "Not counting the raining worms that fell only in the parking lot, everything is perfectly calm," I quipped.

"Raining worms? Land sakes, I wouldn't call that calm. Sounds like a black magic spell. Now you listen, Joe. Get the hell out of there before something else happens. Something that won't be so easy to survive like the worms were."

Black magic. So she had heard of those storms before. "A few kamikaze night crawlers are no reason for me to play Chicken Little. The sky is not falling, Martha," I insisted, hoping to bait her into revealing more information about the worms.

"Have you ever been in a worm storm before, Mr. Know-it-all?" she demanded shrilly.

I coughed into my hand to hide my reactive chuckle. "Well, no."

"Then I guess they're pretty rare, wouldn't you say?" she continued.

"Sure."

Martha cleared her throat. "I see more trouble comin' for you there, so I'm tellin' you to get away from that place now. I'm not taking 'no' for an answer."

"If you tell me what kind of trouble, I'll take your advice under consideration."

Martha growled, not a pretty sound. "Your parents would turn me into a frog if they knew that I let you stay there tonight," she grumbled.

So much for additional worm info. "So, what kind of trouble?" I persisted.

Another growl. I cringed. "I foresee you entering the gateway to another world—the *real* ghost world."

I chuckled. She was over the top with this prediction. "But *everything* in this place is devoted to ghosts. That's the whole idea"

"Don't argue with me, young man. Everything you *see* in that park is a smoke screen for a legion of real ghosts, champing at the bit to be let loose in our world."

I surveyed the vast park. "That's hard to believe."

"Well, believe it." Her tone was iron.

I tapped my shoe on the sidewalk. Nothing looked amiss. The shrubs and grass were perfectly manicured. The palms swayed. Calypso music played in the distance. Fountains sprayed pleasingly shaped mists.

"So everyone here this evening is in danger — not just me, right?" I queried.

"Not everyone. Just a few of the fat cats."

"So what happens to me and a chosen few who travel into the real ghost world?"

She paused. "Death," she replied soberly. "You'd better beat it out of there while you still can, because once the fireworks begin, you'll be trapped."

My curiosity implored me to ask her about the worms once more. I did.

"Forget the worms. My guess is that they were used to frighten people away from the grand opening," she said. "But it's only a guess."

"Yeah, maybe." I pressed my fingertips against my temples. Uncle Jess's assignment smelled as rotten as the decaying worms, and I categorized it as another *what-has-he-gotten-me-into-now* fiasco. "Uncle Jess hired me to troubleshoot tonight," I stated. "I can't leave."

"You most certainly can! Your uncle would be the first to order you out if he knew what was going to happen to you. Call him and see, but make it quick. You're running out of time."

I didn't like that last part, but her insistence was what scared me the most. I was tempted to blow out of there and grab those beers at Wolfsbane, but my stubbornness kept me rooted to the spot. *What does the real ghost world look like?* And other dumb questions.

My common sense shrank. My curiosity blossomed. Martha's advice didn't stand a chance.

A small group of black-tied dignitaries filed into the elaborately decorated amphitheater across from the looping Revenant Chiller Coaster. They quickly settled into their reserved seats near the stage. It appeared that the festivities would commence with a supercilious speech, followed by the promised VIP champagne tour.

Another seventy or so guests were already seated and ready to go. Suddenly, they all popped up like jack-in-the-boxes and applauded the man entering the stage from the left. Jeffrey Stanton.

He motioned for his guests to sit, and then enthusiastically addressed them. From my position at the right of the stage, I couldn't hear his entire message, but the tone was arrogance personified. The front-row dignitaries all feigned obsequious smiles in exchange for future campaign contributions or political favors from "Stan the Man."

"I'll think about what you said, Martha," I added, but I had already made up my mind.

Martha sighed. "Since you obviously refuse to leave that infernal place, then I hope to God that you've got your wand with you."

I patted my suit coat pocket. "I have it."

"And your magical protective ring?"

I glanced down at the Super Bowl Championship-sized ring with a mega-carat purple diamond mounted in the center. "Check."

"Good. Now you be careful and run at the first sign of trouble. If anything happens to you tonight, your mother will rise from the grave and haunt me till the end of days," she groused.

"I'll be careful," I vowed, and I meant it.

"More important, be *clever*." With that ambiguous remark, she hung up.

Even though I was in an amphitheater full of people, I felt alone. During my phone conversation, the overhead kaleidoscope clouds had become more agitated than before. There was no lightning yet, but I knew there would be. And soon.

I felt cold despite the warm sticky air. *Night.* It was falling fast. No beautiful sunset. No twilight. Just a black curtain pulled over Orlando.

According to Martha, nightfall promised one thing.

Ghosts.

The real McCoys.

3

I edged along the front of the stage and got as close as I could without disrupting Stanton's speech. I listened to his upbeat financial predictions for the park's success, which were pie in the sky at best. The worm blizzard hadn't slowed him down in the least. Must have watched through his rose-colored glasses.

At long last, the windbag ran out of hot air. I moved toward him to warn him about Uncle Jess's safety concerns for the evening's festivities. The enthusiastic applause glued him to the spot. He was eating it up. After it subsided, I was about to hail Stanton, but his burly bodyguard intercepted me.

"You're not allowed near the boss," he enlightened me. "Beat it."

I wasn't in the mood to tangle with one of Stanton's lackeys in front of all those people. "*Nadonu*," I whispered, and the big man froze. I side-stepped him and called out to Stanton as he turned to leave. The crowd began filing out of the amphitheater.

"Stan the Man" stared at his immobilized protector for a moment before shifting his attention to me. "Nice trick. Now who are you and what do you want? You've got ten seconds before I call the cops over here," he threatened. I had to give him credit. Like the worm storm, my magic didn't even scuff his polished veneer.

"The name's Joe Luna and I work for the Department of Justice." I flashed him my identification card. "We have reason to suspect that there might be trouble here tonight that could pose a significant threat to your guests. My advice to you is to postpone tonight's grand opening for a few days while we investigate that threat," I explained. I hoped he'd take the advice. I was really thirsty for beer.

"Joe Luna. Hmmm. I've heard of you," he remarked pensively, then snapped his fingers. "You're that supernatural detective I read about in the newspaper. Fascinating work."

I shrugged. "Thanks."

"So your bosses really believe that we're endangered by some, shall we say, supernatural forces tonight?"

I nodded. "That's about the size of it."

"Let me guess. You're worried about ghosts interfering with our tour?"

I hesitated. *How'd he guess that?* "It's a possibility."

He laughed. "So the almighty Department of Justice has nothing better to do these days than chase ghosts? Is that right?"

"Actually, they're pretty busy with ghosts . . . and other entities."

Stanton's smile flatlined. "You're serious?"

"Extremely. We haven't pinpointed the threat here, and that's why we urge you to delay your shindig for awhile."

"But this place is full of ghosts," he pointed out, gesturing at the park's attractions.

"I'm referring to the real ones, not some genuine-imitation spirits," I shot back. This was getting tiresome. Maybe Martha was right. I should have hit the trail, and let these pompous asses suffer the consequences of their imprudence.

"You know, this place was designed to scare the shit out of our guests," he said.

"That's too bad. I brought only one pair of pants," I quipped.

He laughed hard. "I didn't know you DoJ boys had a sense of humor."

"I'm part-time."

He laughed again.

"Look, I'm serious about the threat to you and the others."

"I can see that, but since things appear normal to me, I'll take my chances."

The guy was as stubborn as yours truly. "That's your prerogative. I've done my job here." I turned to leave. "Best of luck."

He frowned. "Wait—wait a minute."

I made the mistake of my life by stopping to hear him out, when I should've kept walking to the parking lot.

I sighed. "Have a change of heart?"

"No. I have a proposition."

I wagged my eyebrows. "Okay, let's hear it."

"You replace this imbecile bodyguard for the night and watch my tail, and I'll pay you double what the DoJ is paying you . . . in cash," he offered. "Consider it a bonus."

I did a quick mental check of my bank balances and concluded that I was nearly broke. I hated acknowledging my capitalistic shortcomings, but there was no getting around it. *I could be bought!*

I looked him squarely in the eye. "At the first sign of trouble, what I say goes. I'm the boss. If you agree to that, we've got a deal." I fully expected his inflated ego to turn me down, but I had professional parameters to maintain despite my shortfall of cash. No narcissistic amateur was going to manage a crisis situation where my life was at stake.

To my disbelief, he agreed. "Deal," he said and pumped my hand.

My bank accounts cheered me from the sidelines. "Deal."

"Now please release this man from your spell," he asked civilly.

I did, and Stanton immediately reassigned Mister Muscle to another security detail. As the big man passed, he flashed me a hostile glance. If looks could kill, I'd be — well, dead.

Stanton rubbed his palms together. "Now let's see to our guests, shall we?"

With a fervent wave, Stanton directed his guests toward the haunted house, Mansion Macabre, across the park. I hated those places. I detested ghosts that leaped out at me when I least expected it. It was damned unsettling. And, of course, embarrassing.

The procession of VIPs marched behind us like cattle going to slaughter. Being six foot four, I towered over Stanton's five foot eight height, making us an unlikely pair, but it didn't bother me. My imagination was working overtime envisioning the frights that the attraction engineers might have dreamed up to humiliate me inside the mansion, and which of those frights might be the real thing.

And fatal.

4

Bright flares glimmered, followed by crashing thunder. The clouds still roiled overhead, but the lightning was extraordinary. Greens, reds, and blues. Not at all what I expected. I *was* correct about one thing, when I really wanted to be wrong. The person who conjured the worm storm wasn't finished with us. Not by a long shot.

The colorful lightning strobes were extraordinary. The electrical forks didn't appear ... normal, as if the charges weren't electrical, but magical. Another rapid-fire series of shimmering rainbow streaks snaked through the tumbling clouds, a precursor of events to come. Unpleasant ones. The crowd ooohed and aaahed at Mother Nature's beautiful showcase, completely unaware that they were witnessing a potent display of black magic.

Temporarily blinded by the brilliance, I collided with Stanton when he turned to address the group. He looked annoyed, but quickly recovered to reassert his game face for the VIPs, who were still assembling in front of the intimidating Mansion Macabre. Their awe at the lightning spectacle dissipated when they got their first close-up view of the horrifying attraction. Stunned was an apt description. Many appeared to have succumbed to a severe pandemic of cold feet.

The ominous gothic monolith towered in a sea of gloom that contrasted with the brightly lit central park area. The three-story structure confronted us like a menacing multi-eyed monster. I'd already seen one too many of those attractions tonight.

The mansion's numerous steeply pitched gables, black-tiled roof, and thick-paned windows added to its frightening presence. From the roof overhangs, simulated lightning flickered against the mortared stone walls, although they weren't needed tonight. The sorcerer had seen to that. Crooked, leafless trees encircled the structure like petrified centurions, and a densely woven quilt of thorny vines blanketed the arches at the entrance.

The shadowy windows alternately blinked blackness and a ruddy yellow glow. When the windows were illuminated, different shadowy specters glided past the glass of some of the openings, while manic faces peered down at us with exaggerated psychopathic eyes in others. I sensed the group's cold feet plummet several degrees.

Were tonight's specters real, or merely special effects? I couldn't be absolutely positive until I . . . *went inside*, an action that topped my all-time list of idiotic ideas. I puffed my cheeks and exhaled slowly. I was a sorwolf, and we were by nature courageous. And I was. For the most part. Except inside these damned haunted houses. During previous outings, I had morphed into a sor*wimp*.

While Stanton boasted about his creation, this was as good a time as any to introduce myself. My mother was a sorceress, and my father was a werewolf. My twin sister and I inherited a fifty-fifty split of our parental genes. We were—sorwolves.

I was six foot four, muscular, and had Dad's coppery brown hair and eyes. He often bragged that there was an inherent strength in my classically handsome face, but I knew he was a tad prejudiced—we could have passed for brothers.

My fraternal twin sister, Jill, was a knockout beauty bordering on spectacular. She inherited her willowy shape, lustrous black hair, and indigo eyes from Mother. Father contributed his athletic prowess. Jill was currently an aspiring actress and dancer on Broadway, where she attracted more attention for her blossoming performances than for her looks alone. She insisted that her burgeoning fame was crucial for her success, but I disagreed. She was sticking her neck out unnecessarily. We both had dangerous enemies—ones who had murdered our parents three years ago. That's why I took the low road and maintained a discreet profile. Jill refused. We were both stubborn, so we left it like that. A Mexican stand-off.

Jeffrey Stanton was still yakking. The guests were becoming restless, especially with the constant flashes of colored lightning and teeth-rattling thunderclaps. Central Florida was the lightning capital of the world, and I didn't blame them for being edgy. Any of us could be struck by those fierce energy spears any minute. Thankfully, "Stan the Man" gestured toward the entrance. *Come into my parlor, said the spider to the fly.*

"I hope you enjoy your visit to Mansion Macabre, the crown jewel of our park," he crowed, puffing his chest like a proud papa. "A combination of holographic images, robotics, and live actors all working in sync make this one place you'll never forget. Trust me on that."

There was smattering of nervous laughter.

"To make your experience, uh, more intimate, you'll ride through the mansion in cars that seat no more than four—two rows, two across. Each car is computer-controlled by complex communications and relay systems that I had designed specifically for Mansion Macabre. This innovative system can not only decelerate or accelerate your car according to your location, but can also guide you into disguised elevators throughout the mansion that'll take you from floor to floor," he expounded.

I only half-listened as he tooted his own horn. I was anxious to go in and get out as quickly as I could. No more dawdling. No more thinking about how scared I was going to be. Let's get 'er done, son.

During a violent flash, I spied my cancelled weekend date, Detective Kit Wilson. *What was she doing here?* The invitation list was purportedly culled to include only the wealthy muckety-mucks and government brown-nosers. Uncle Jess made it all too clear that I was the sole exception. I can't tell you how much that boosted my self-esteem.

As I slipped through the assembled group to rendezvous with Kit, I bumped into Orlando's chief of police and his drop-dead gorgeous daughter in the second row. Lance Stockard was a tall, burly guy with an unvarying *make-my-day* expression souring his face. He regarded me like I was an irksome insect.

His twentysomething daughter, Gwendolyn, was another story. She was decked out in a slinky flowery-pattern dress with a neckline that plunged clear to China. Her swollen cleavage reminded me of the Grand Canyon. A sunny smile was plastered on her drop-dead gorgeous face, and she greeted everyone like long-lost pals. She was a leggy brunette who had the right connections and the right curves. But I could tell by the way she stared at the master of ceremonies that she was wasting both on that scumbag.

Her eyes never left Stanton as he wrapped up his spiel. I understood her interest in the bastard, but that didn't mean I wasn't a bit . . . jealous. Ole Jeffrey wasn't merely blessed with cash and power; he had the market cornered in the looks department, too. His crisply trimmed sandy hair outlined his pretty-boy face; his ice-blue eyes blazed fire and ice; and his persona radiated confidence, smugness, and an inherent strength.

Stanton searched the group for me and impatiently gestured for me to join him. I sacrificed my quest to make things right with Kit, and marched up the paved walkway like a condemned man. He held the door for me beneath the ominous arches, and waved me ahead. Monstrous latex spiders glowered at us from their gleaming webs spun in each ceiling corner. A shroud of doom settled heavily over my lingering courage. A tragedy was going to befall one or more of the guests tonight. I felt it.

Medieval sconces cast pallid amber light onto the immense *Guest Holding Area* and projected grotesque shapes onto the walls. Holographic paintings were mounted in long rows along the black walls, each depicting rampaging ghosts and demons performing brutal human slaughters. Their scarlet eyes flitted toward us and scowled angrily, while the wails of their human victims were broadcast in nauseating surround sound. *Were the ghosts and demons the real deal tonight?* I was damned if I could tell, so I kept a wary eye on them.

A single recessed track split the gray stone floor and curled into a massive circle at the guest waiting area. Dozens of passenger cars were separated into groups of three, but none of the cars were attached. Three cars stood ready in the boarding zone, presumably for Stanton's VIPs. And his new bodyguard.

Stockard and his daughter took the front seat in the first car, at Stanton's insistence, while Orlando's mayor and his terrified wife slid in behind them. The governor and his wife were joined by a Florida senator and his date in the second car, while Stanton and I climbed into the third car alone. Cozy. Stanton explained that only three cars were admitted into the mansion at a time, and after a two-minute interval, the next trio would follow.

Four gruesomely made-up zombie attendants lowered the security bars across our laps, and Stanton hoisted his fist high into the eerie atmosphere.

"Let the screams begin!" he shouted.

Enthusiastic applause and raucous cheers arose behind us as our three cars moved silently into the next chamber's foreboding dusk. I spun my protective ring around my finger so that the purple gem was on top. I wanted to be prepared for the unexpected.

I didn't have long to wait.

5

The oppressive dark mantle inside the next chamber seemed alive and knocked my typically reliable senses off-kilter. Gross grunts and piercing shrieks assaulted us from every direction, yet we saw nothing. Countless creatures cloaked in blackness swooped down with horrifying swishes and fanned our faces. My instincts were on full alert, and I held my ring finger at the ready, but since the flying critters were coming at us from everywhere, I soon gave up. I refused to act rashly. If I recklessly jumped the gun and unleashed my ring's defensive force against holographic ghoul-wannabes, the diamond's energy might not recharge in time to use against real attackers.

A full moon abruptly appeared and splashed its artificial moonlight down from the cloud-spattered ceiling. Any light in there was good light. Its orangish-gold radiance exposed an enormous Viking Mead Hall right from the pages of Grendel and Beowulf, as well as a plethora of ghastly frights. Wild animal heads, including lions, black panthers, leopards, wildebeests, hyenas, and water buffalo, moved their eyes and haunted the lengthy walls. Ho-hum. I glanced ahead and noted that the tracks eventually guided us toward a vast stone fireplace and its roaring, snapping-and-crackling blaze.

But the yawning hearth and the mounted animal heads were pablum compared to the nasty series of murderous pictures to our left. The track swung us that way, and we got an up-close and personal view of the ghastly portraits. Those deformed and depraved savage slayers didn't just look daggers at us as we passed—they actually brandished their murderous weapons. *Scythes. Knives. Scimitars. Sabers. Cutlasses. Butcher knives. Medieval maces. Double-handed axes. Spiked war clubs.* Metallic clings and clanks spilled out from a host of speakers, forcing us to duck each time one of the lethal-looking holographic weapons flew at us.

I shuddered. *Any one of those ancient weapons might be the real deal, but how was I going to determine which were authentic and which were projected images?* Then the answer popped into the ole brain. A piece of cake, really.

Just watch Stanton. He knew this ride like the back of his hand, and if something out of the ordinary went down, his alarmed expression would immediately alert me.

Despite the barrage of lethal weapons, Stanton was totally composed as he grinned at the hysterical screams coming from the front two cars. The Orlando mayor's booming laughs loudly sliced through the pandemonium; the schmuck was obviously enjoying himself at his panic-stricken wife's expense.

The other riders calmed considerably as we passed the last of the ghoulish violence. The weapon-wielders were all phony. No real killer in the bunch. I was grateful for that. But we had a long way to go inside this shriekatorium, so I had to stay on my toes. Or lose 'em.

Our cars closed on the vicious blaze raging inside the huge stone fireplace. Dazzling yellows, crimsons, and blues. The holographic flames curled up the flue like braided serpents, but they didn't emit the predictable woodsy smell. Instead, our noses were treated to the dank pungency of cemetery dirt.

About the time we began to relax from the harrowing experience with the portraits, a screeching cloud of bats exploded down the flue through the flames and winged directly at us. *Was this the genuine menace Martha had foreseen?* I released my white-knuckle grip on the security bar and shoved my ring finger forward, but a cynical insight suggested that I hold off. I reluctantly did . . . *and hoped that I wouldn't die to regret it.*

Stanton chuckled at my tense reaction, and my face blushed beet-red. I was glad for the fire's dazzling glare, because it hid my mortification. I didn't say a word.

But the bats were holographic and passed through us. While most of us were breathing jumbo sighs of relief, the mayor's wife was still shrieking her head off. And her husband was laughing his ass off. If only his supporters could see him now. His political career would be flushed.

The intense conflagration was another example of *Ghostworld's* sophisticated holographic world. No searing heat. Pre-recorded crackles and snapping broadcast through hidden speakers. Artificial cemetery stench sprayed from well-placed nozzles.

Imagined dangers, but perception is reality to people. Stanton had done a good job designing this place. Judging from the mayor's wife, it was damned effective.

Unearthly groans assailed our ears and spiked our nerves as we were set to enter the flames. Shadowy, ghostly shapes followed the bats from the chimney passage and added more foreboding to our next destination. The scowling specters zigzagged between us, screaming and hissing.

I scrutinized every ghost as it zinged past, looking for signs of an ambush. This would've been the perfect place. The hearth fit snugly around us, so there was little room to defend ourselves. My ring was ready, but I needn't have worried. They, too, were part of the show.

The computer slowed our cars as we entered. The laughing box up front and his hysterical wife had finally quieted. Our merry little band had grown stoically silent, and if I didn't know better, I would've figured they were all dead. I glanced at Stanton, and his bemused smirk was still plastered on his arrogant puss. Things were going as planned.

The 3-D fire surrounded us, hungrily licking, curling, and scaring the hell out of the passengers in the front two cars. More screams. But Stanton and I remained calm.

Stanton tapped my shoulder, and I nearly jumped out of my seat. I wasn't as calm as I thought I was.

"The best is yet to come," he chuckled. "We're heading *up* now." He pointed up at the sliver of simulated moonlight spilling down the elevator-shaft-sized flue.

Unfortunately, "Stan the Man" was dead wrong. There was a back-slamming stop and a breathless pause. . . before our cars sank *down* into the floor!

Stanton's poise exploded into panic. Shit! I realized that he hadn't been joking with me. Trying to set me up. We really were supposed to go *up*. This was the beginning of what Martha had foreseen.

My stomach knotted and double-knotted, and my clenching hands nearly crushed the safety bar.

The others weren't aware yet that our ride was being hijacked, so they sat silently again. Expectant. While Stanton and I tried to fathom what was happening to us.

Who the hell was powerful enough to pull us down through a solid stone hearth as if it were another holographic image?

But that wasn't the most distressing unknown. I didn't even want to think about it as we descended, but the damned question refused to go away.

What was waiting for us below?

6

Stanton grabbed his Nextel walkie talkie-cell combo phone and shouted frantically. "What in hell's going on up there? We're going *down*, you morons! We're supposed to be going *up*! Fix it or you're fired," he screamed. The other passengers heard his ranting, and their fire-reflective eyes widened to proverbial saucers at the shocking news. I wondered what mine looked like.

The flames gradually disappeared above us as we sank lower into God-knew-where. In darkness.

There was no reply to Stanton's tirade. I speculated that there was no cell service down here. We weren't in Kansas any more. Some powerful black force was dragging us down to the Land of Oz. Perhaps the Revenant Realm. Martha's *real* ghost world. The one where Stanton's authority was of no consequence.

My face became dew-damp like sidewalks dappled with April puddles, but the absolute blackness wasn't the only factor straining my wolfen senses to the max. The thick murk enveloping us actually *tasted* rancid. Like year-old black cotton candy.

I couldn't see Stanton's expression, but my amped wolfen hearing detected the ragged thumping of his heart. Our detour from his programmed fright fest staggered his nervous system and deflated his arrogance. He wasn't any more poised than the mayor's wife. Part of me wanted to celebrate his misery with a few whoops, but the other half empathized with the poor bastard.

In reality, our journey to the center of the earth didn't take as long as our stunned minds thought. I glanced at my luminous watch. Ten terrifying minutes. There was no way to estimate our depth, either. Our senses of time and space had been rendered useless by whoever was manipulating our descent.

The air grew inexplicably colder as we dropped, causing Stanton's teeth to chatter incessantly. Click click. Clack clack. He started to get on my nerves. My cold-blooded wolfen system maintained a comfortable temperature.

And still we sank lower.

Faint chanting — or was it singing? — rose like an unheavenly choir, frosting my composure and goose-pimpling my skin. The shrill pitch pierced my entire being like fingernails on a chalkboard. The mayor frantically shouted his wife's name; most likely the stressed-out woman had fainted, which was just as well. I had a bad feeling that some of us weren't leaving here alive.

In the blink of an eye, the darkness was displaced by a blinding light. White night. I'd heard about it from the stories my mother told me as a child, but this was my first encounter. I recalled her words of warning. *Stay out of the white night. If you can't, Joe, run as fast as you can. There are more frightening creatures lurking inside that evil realm than in our own black night.*

That memory wasn't encouraging. There was no place to run down there. Added to my angst was the fact that our attraction cars didn't afford us much protection. They could be crumpled with minimal supernatural force. Then there was my regrettable responsibility to safeguard the prick seated beside me. All in all, it appeared as if I were screwed big time.

The strange chorus grew so loud that I was forced to clap my hands over my ears, but the effort was futile. The four-note melody reverberated through my hands and heightened my pain threshold to the *nth* degree. Like the mythological Sirens' song. Frustrated, I threw down my hands and smashed the safety bar, then I waited for the creatures that my mother warned me about to come a-callin'.

The cars abruptly bottomed out with thuds, and we leaned slightly to the left. Obviously the ground beneath us wasn't level.

Stanton seized my shoulder. "Get us out of this mess, Luna," he demanded. His horrified voice knifed through the infernal singing.

I did what any DSI contract investigator worth his salt would do. I ignored the pompous son-of-a-bitch.

The torturous singing died faster than I could snap my fingers, although it replayed in my head like it was looped. Bad songs had a way of doing that to people.

My body tensed. Creature time. I listened intently, once the ringing subsided in my sensitive ears, and waited for the nightmarish monsters to locate us. I was the only one of our small group who could hear approaching creatures long before they arrived.

One thing we had in common was that we were blind. The light was so dense and bright that I couldn't see my buddy seated beside me.

"What's all this about, Stanton?" the governor demanded sternly.

"Get us out of this soup now!" shouted the senator, while his girlfriend directed a string of expletives at the "Stan the Man."

"Now hold your horses, ladies and gents," Sheriff Stockard yelled. "I've got your backs. I never go anywhere without my gun."

I merely shook my head. He obviously didn't realize that his gun was worthless against the creatures in the white night, but I held my tongue. No use upsetting the women more than they already were.

"This isn't my doing. I haven't the slightest idea of where we are or how we got here," Stanton shot back. "I can assure you that this is not part of the ride *I* designed."

"I'll sue you and your damned park," the governor's wife threatened.

"Now Margaret, don't be like that. I'm not to blame," Stanton pleaded.

Their bickering was getting us nowhere. "Knock it off!" I ordered, despite their wealth and power. To my surprise, they did. "Listen up. I know about this place, although I've never been here. It's called the white night, and people who have experienced it swear that it's crawling with nasty monsters. They might be prowling around and sizing us up for an attack right now. Our sense of hearing is our only defense down here since we can't see, so I want you to remain silent and just *listen*. If we can pinpoint the direction of the attack, the sheriff stands a better chance of hitting some of them. If you don't, we die," I warned them. We probably would anyway. We were unarmed sitting ducks inside our flimsy cars.

"He's got a point," the governor's wife, Margaret, said softly in my defense.

"Who in hell are you to speak to us like we're children?" the governor demanded.

Before I could reply, the senator's date hissed, "Shush. I just heard something."

We stiffened. Alert. Fearful. I swung my ring finger in every direction, but I didn't hear anything but deafening silence.

Then we heard it. A whoosh and rustling to our left.

But the small noise turned out to be a decoy. A monstrous roar jolted the cars and froze our vocal chords. There were no screams this time. Only petrifying terror.

The advancing creature sounded larger than a freight train and more menacing. Stanton struggled against his restraining bar, but it was useless. It was locked tight. Mine was already broken, but where would I escape to? I'd be lost within seconds out there in the white night. Stanton continued to rattle the bar like a madman, his panic generating temporarily insanity. If I didn't stop him, it would spread to the others.

The vague silhouette of a gargantuan creature appeared near the front car. Tall. Wide. Savage. Its dingy white color made it easy to spot in the sea of blinding white. I delayed discharging my ring until it attacked. When it drew closer.

The intimidating creature's foul breath spilled over us, and the senator's date and the sheriff's daughter screamed bloody murder. Two giant steps brought it a stone's throw away from the front car. I stuck out my ring finger, and the diamond fired a laser-like ray into the beast.

Nothing happened.

The gun-happy sheriff fired at the hostile creature, but like my ring's magical force, the bullets proved useless. Neither inflicted a scratch of damage.

Stanton squeezed my arm with his remaining strength and swore at me to save him. Being six foot four, I towered over him, even inside the car. I cocked my free forearm and launched it into his jaw. In the whiteness, he never saw it coming and slumped toward the open side of the car, completely unconscious. I ripped his fingers from my arm and dusted off my hands. One problem solved. Now to the other.

But this problem was massive. The pressure mounted as its clawed hand, the size of a pick-up truck, hovered menacingly above the front car. I was the only one who had the magical means to kill the giant, but how was the million-dollar question.

I'd always heard how acute anxiety halted the thinking process. Solutions didn't materialize in a blank mind.

And at that moment, mine was as blank as the white night.

7

The killer's hand was poised to pummel the front car passengers. I heard a loud noise echoing throughout the white night, and I looked down and saw my feet stamping furiously on the tinny car floor. Before I even considered the risk of attracting the beast to the rear, I pounded the roof supports and shouted gameday cheers. The demon's hand fell to its side as it tromped toward me with its earth-shaking footfalls.

Despite its bulk, the creature arrived in no time flat, and even though I couldn't see it distinctly, I was certain it could see me just fine. I had about five seconds to devise a counterattack before Stanton and I became Panini sandwiches.

I had been mistaken about the creature being dirty white. When it leaned over me, I noted it was a denser white than its surroundings, and therefore appeared darker.

But that wasn't my only lesson. The giant's face was blank . . . featureless. It struck me that our malicious sorcerer didn't want me recognizing the demon and tracing it back to him.

A sea of coal eyes winked open on both sides of us, and I easily identified them—*ghosts*. A dead audience for our slaughter.

I had three seconds left to fabricate a scheme. Make that two. The white demon was already reaching for me, no doubt believing that I was easy prey. I didn't blame it. It sure as hell looked that way to me, too.

The white shovel of a hand was nearly on me.

At the last second, an idea popped into my consciousness like toasted bread. I didn't have any time to question it. I pulled my wand from my belt, repeated the conjuring script displayed in my head, and watched as my drumstick wand became a flashlight.

Not an ordinary flashlight, either. Instead of projecting white light at the demon, my newly formed wand cast *black light* onto it. The reaction was instantaneous. Snarling like a dozen wounded tigers, the demon retreated clumsily in pain and rage, swiping furiously at its body where the flashlight beam struck it.

Our ghostly audience's wide eyes shrank to the size of black raspberry seeds before they vanished. Unfortunately, that shrill, one-note choir started up again for an encore performance as our three cars trembled and then rose toward the Mansion Macabre. At least, I hoped that was our destination. As much that place chafed my nerves, it would be a welcome sight now.

As we ascended, I thought about my flashlight defense. My unconscious reasoning had been straightforward. Sudden bright light blinded people wearing night-vision goggles, because the apparatus magnified the light, so I deduced that black light would affect the creature in the same way, stunning its hidden optic nerves and immobilizing it. *How did I know that it would burn it, too?* Sure, it was a long shot, but it paid off. All was well that ended well—my new credo.

The impenetrable whiteness dissolved to blackness, and I was relieved for once to be deposited into absolute night. Stanton stirred and groaned as he struggled to sit up, but he was too weak. The park owner sagged back over the armrest like a limp dishrag, but he was persistent. He tried again, with success.

He rubbed his jaw and waited for the cobwebs to clear before he spoke. "Did you hit me down there, Luna?"

I smiled. "Something flew past me and zapped you," I lied.

"Oh. What happened down there, anyway? And how'd we get back up here?"

"I made a lot of noise and frightened the big bad monster away." The magic part would remain my little secret. Although the others didn't *see* me project the black light, they did *hear* me raise a ruckus that ostensibly scared away the beast. That was my story, and I was sticking to it.

But my explanation was the least of my worries. The ghosts we saw monopolized my imagination. *What if they abandoned their world for ours? What if the demon came along for the ride? Would the sorcerer who had conjured the demon and transported us into the white night try to kill us again? Or was he or she targeting one person in our group, and the rest of us were collateral damage?* Since the demon attacked the front car, I wondered if one of those passengers was the intended victim. Only time would tell.

The one thing I did know was that I wasn't its target. I was a last minute addition to the VIPs, whom the sorcerer couldn't have planned for. But my assessment of the situation didn't stop there. Maybe everyone was supposed to die down there. If that was the case, then they had to be connected by a common thread. A thread that made them vulnerable.

My clear-cut DSI troubleshooting assignment had abruptly turned for the worse. I felt obligated to these folks to find their would-be murderer, but only if Uncle Jess okayed it. Then there was a little matter of getting paid for that investigation.

At long last, the cars broke through to our world, and we found ourselves at the core of the holographic conflagration once again. After the Meade Hall lights winked alive, the cars locked onto the track and sped in reverse back to our starting point. The portraits and other frights had been switched off. It was obvious that our ghoulish tour had been revised to a rescue mission while we were trapped below.

After the cars braked in the *Guest Holding Area*, Kit was the first to help everyone onto the platform. An army of EMTs and cops immediately whisked the frazzled bigwigs out of the mansion amid four-letter words and a lot of groans. By the time they got to Stanton and me, the place was relatively quiet.

Kit watched as they freed Stanton. After examining my broken security bar, her relieved smile flipped to a scowl in nothing flat. Her expression relaxed a smidge while EMTs checked me over and pronounced me physically sound. Stanton, though, was helped away, so they could tend to his swollen jaw.

Wordlessly, Kit escorted me outside, and we walked from the Mansion Macabre toward the parking lot. I wasn't in the mood to talk about our experience, either, but I realized that sooner or later she would demand a detailed rundown of our vanishing act. This certainly wasn't the kind of date I had in mind a few days ago.

We pushed and shoved our way through a vicious mob of reporters clogging the central park area. Kit pulled me into a small grove of royal palm trees, and we skirted the rest of the ravenous news hounds and sneaked into a medical supply tent that had been hastily erected during our absence.

I checked my watch and saw that over two hours of my life had been wasted inside Stanton's folly. Time flies when you're having fun.

Now that we were alone, Kit broke her silence. "Level with me, Joe. What the fuck happened to you guys inside the haunted house? I mean, where could you possibly hide that we couldn't find you?"

I stuffed my hands into my crinkled sport coat pockets. "I can tell you're not in the mood for the truth, so I plead the Fifth Amendment," I stated.

"Knock it off," she snapped impatiently.

"Oh. You do want the truth."

"Quit being a smart-ass."

"Okay, here's what happened." I sighed, and began telling her, leaving nothing out.

"That's ridiculous!" she stormed after listening to first half of my account.

"You ain't heard nuthin' yet, babe. After we landed, a demon the size of King Kong attacked with the intention to kill us all."

"Uh-huh. So I suppose you saved the day, as usual."

"Well, yeah. I used a little magic to scare the bully away." I didn't realize how tired I was until that moment. I could've done a Rip Van Winkle, no sweat. "You convinced?"

"What a crock! Do you expect me to fill out a report with that cockamamie story? I'd be fired on the spot."

"It's the truth. Take it or leave it. I don't give a damn either way. All I want to do is crash at the farmhouse for a day or two. *Alone*."

She regarded me for a long while before responding. "You must be telling the truth. Nobody in his right mind could fabricate a story like that. Not even *you*."

"Is that a compliment?"

"No way." She thrummed her fingers on the metal folding table between us. "I wonder how the others will describe your side-trip to hell."

"They couldn't see my magic act, but they could see the giant's outline. I guess their version will depend on the political ramifications of the truth."

"What else is new? And if they bury the part about the killer giant, then what? Do you stick to your story?"

Good point. "I suppose I'd go along with *their* story. I'm not too anxious to spend my next vacation inside a mental institution."

"Then what do you expect me to do with *your* report?"

"If the others lie, file it away for future reference in case you and I team up to find the sorcerer behind our hair-raising adventure," I replied, stifling a jaw-busting yawn.

"Well, good luck with that."

I arched my brows. "Are you saying you won't help me?"

"That's about the size of it." She turned and strode out of the tent.

I stretched and followed her, with nothing but sleep on my mind. My love life had just taken a serious hit, and Kit made it perfectly clear that I was on my own again.

I stopped short of the flap and rationalized my situation. Maybe her taking a hike wasn't so bad. I heard somewhere that horny guys were less distracted. Had clearer minds. *Horny was good.*

And the sun might rise in the west tomorrow, too.

8

As I pulled back the flap to exit, I collided with Kit, who was backing into the tent.

Baffled, I stepped aside. "Saw the error of your ways, eh?" I chided her, but her poker face said otherwise. A moment later, I learned why.

Three armed, hooded men burst into the tent, their silenced gun barrels aimed at the two of us. I could've easily neutralized them with magic, but I wanted to hear what they had to say. At the moment, my fledgling investigation needed a jump start.

One of the gunmen positioned himself behind me, while the other two confronted us. Well, mostly me.

"The boss wants to know what happened down there," the short, squat guy demanded with a nasal, East Coast accent.

I shrugged. "Tell your boss he'll have to ask me himself," I retorted. I was in a crummy mood after my escapade below *Ghostworld*, Kit's abrupt brush-off, and my sleep deficiency. "I don't deal with lackeys."

The one behind me kicked the back of my knee, hoping to drop me to the grass floor, but he ended up smashing his big toe. Never wear athletic shoes when kicking a werewolf, even in its human form. My attacker groaned quietly, so as not to attract the attention of outsiders, but he had a rough time gripping his gun while hopping on one foot.

"C'mon, Lenny, quit fucking around!" Short-squat growled at his comrade, and shoved his gun in my face.

"This guy's legs are like cast iron," Lenny griped.

"Who's your Big Bad Boss, anyway?" Kit interjected, distracting frustrated Shorty before he decided to empty his gun in my face.

The bullets wouldn't have killed me, but they sure would've hurt like hell. I owed her one.

"None of your business, copper," he shot back.

"Are you for real? That nickname hasn't been used for eighty or ninety years," she scoffed. "Did you guys just wake up from the Roaring Twenties?"

Shorty shifted his gun to her, which was just what she wanted. Kit's clever diversion afforded me the opportunity to draw my wand before Shorty shot her. I quietly uttered a few ancient syllables, and suddenly our three assailants found themselves holding hostile, hissing vipers.

The pair in front of us dropped the vipers like hot potatoes and rushed toward the tent flap, which I changed from canvas to crinkled iron. The resulting metallic clang bounced them to the grassy floor beside the coiled snakes. They lay frozen, eyes wide, like a pair of poorly sculpted statues.

Before Lenny regained his composure and attacked me from behind, I spun and unleashed a concise uppercut to his nose, breaking it. Occasionally, I needed to have some fun without employing magic spells. Blood spurted from his nostrils like twin fountains. Stunned by the amount of the red stuff soaking his face and hands, Lenny's eyes rolled white, and he toppled backward in a dead faint, launching his gun on a brief flight to a stack of medical supply cartons in the rear corner.

"If you boys want to win an all-expenses-paid trip to the morgue tonight, then by all means *don't* tell me who you're working for," I threatened, as Kit side-stepped the vipers and hustled to my side, her gun trained on the two perps.

For several moments, the only sounds were muffled shouts from the emergency personnel and rapid-fire questions from the reporters outside the tent — and, of course, the hissing vipers.

"Okay, okay, you win. We'll talk," Short-squat agreed, his high-handed bullying voice reduced to a coward's raspy squeak.

"Uh, I'd step on it if I were you. The snakes' patience is wearing thin," I warned.

"Me, Lenny, and Pug were hired . . . ." His voice trailed off as a black cloud rose beneath him, stifling his words and scorching his clothes and flesh. Their throats ignited first, stifling their screams. All Kit and I could do was helplessly watch the two tough guys go up in black flames. In seconds, they were ash and smoke, and my vipers reverted back to guns.

I spun around to save Lenny, but the flames got to him first. All that was left was a steaming ridge of ash. That damned sorcerer again. A surge of dread chased my composure. He had reversed my spell, and that required top-shelf magic from someone who didn't follow the rules.

Thou shalt not reverse a fellow sorcerer's spell. If he was trying to intimidate me, it was working. If he was trying to piss me off, that was working, too.

My brooding was interrupted when someone outside collided with the iron tent flap and swore up a storm. Kit threw me one of her infamous *Now what?* scowls. A crowd quickly gathered outside our tent, and their demanding shouts escalated.

I hastily retrieved the three stooges' weapons, transformed the iron flap back to canvas, and teleported Kit and myself out of the tent a split-second before the cops stormed the place. We cut our escape a little thin. If we'd gotten caught, I hated to think how we would've explained the three cremated bodies, especially to Diaz, who was aware of my magic prowess. I would've been his one and only suspect for the three murders. So much for an open mind.

After we materialized behind the tent, my mind toted some excess baggage that further zapped my sang-froid. My pesky off-and-on sixth sense foresaw more brushes with death during the course of our pursuit of the murdering, black-magic sorcerer.

I can't tell you how thrilled I was.

9

Once we were safely away from the smoldering corpses, Kit's attitude softened.

"Who do you think hired those three idiots?" she raised, stuffing her gun back in its holster. It appeared as if we were on speaking terms again.

Before I answered, I stole a look around the corner and checked out the rowdy mob assembled in front of the tent. The reporters curtly demanded information from the cops as they examined the now-pliable canvas flap. My parlor trick left them scratching their heads. The smoke and ash on the floor left them scratching with both hands.

I faced Kit. "The same sorcerer who sent me down into the white night earlier."

"Larry, Moe, and Curly were sure interested to find out what happened to you."

"Their boss was the one who was nosey."

"Right, but wouldn't he already know what happened?"

I looked out at the restless throng again. I sensed something was amiss, but I couldn't put my finger on it. "Not if the sorcerer wasn't down there with us. I'd bet a million dollars that he went out of his mind when we all showed up . . . alive."

She chortled. "That's a safe bet. You don't have a million dollars," she said, peering around my elbow at the chaotic scene out front.

"Don't rub it in. My lotto numbers might hit next time."

"And I might be crowned Miss America, too." She paused. "So if that big bad sorcerer is so powerful, why'd he send three schmucks to interrogate you? You'd think he'd employ a better class of thug."

I'd considered that, too. "Maybe they were close to the park and had done some grunt work for him in the past. They were a less conspicuous alternative."

Kit's eyes narrowed. "To what?"

"To sending another demon to do his dirty work. Too many witnesses outside to take that chance," I speculated, still searching the area for something out of whack. The more I looked, the more I was convinced that there was something evil hanging around. If it wasn't visible, that just meant it hadn't manifested itself yet.

Kit stepped out from behind the tent. "What the hell are you looking for?"

I sighed. "Nothing."

"Bullshit, Luna. I know you too well to accept that."

I grinned. "I've got a hunch that something's about to happen, but I don't know what."

She groaned. "Great. The usual supernatural stuff?"

"Yeah. I'm pretty sure, anyway."

"Can you remember anything from your white-night experience that might give us a clue?"

I thought long and hard about it. "Nothing."

"Maybe the bastard's planning another attack on his target."

She'd hit the nail on the head. "Bingo!" I exclaimed. "Let's mingle and keep our eyes peeled for trouble."

"Like what?"

"Demons. Shapeshifters. Vampires. Anyone *too* interested in our VIPs."

Kit nodded and we kept to the back edge of the crowd. The approach of my white-night companions immediately caught our attention . . . and everyone else's. The piranha press swallowed them alive, and luckily kept their attention off me. I wasn't particularly anxious to join the VIPs and speak off the cuff to the press until I was up to speed on their version of our Mansion Macabre incident.

"It looks like they're ready to address the reporters," Kit said.

Four OPD cops and three sheriff's deputies stood guard as Jeffrey Stanton, Lance and Gwendolyn Stockard, Orlando's mayor and his pale wife, the governor and his wife, and the senator and his date stepped onto a hurriedly erected dais. Captain Hank Diaz, of all people, spotted us and rammed his way through the expectant reporters like a Pamplona bull.

The swarthy-complected, black-haired Diaz was in his mid-forties, although he looked ten years younger. He hiked his shoulders as he approached, emphasizing authority over stature. My sister, Jill, referred to his conduct as a Napoleon complex; the label described Diaz to a "T."

He was in his usual *teed-off* disposition where Kit and I were concerned. "What the hell are you doing, *Lieutenant?*" he fumed, glowering at her. "Because it looks like a dereliction of duty to me."

"I've been debriefing Joe," she retorted. To say that Kit wasn't fond of her boss was putting it mildly.

He tapped his foot impatiently in the worn grass. "Really? All right, shoot."

"Joe said that it was too dark to see anything, but he thought that one of the passengers might have been targeted for a kill."

My heart started beating again. She hadn't mentioned the giant faceless demon.

Diaz turned his attack-dog glare on me. "That's it? You *think* that one of them might have been a target for murder? What do you base your cockamamie theory on?"

"We were attacked."

"You couldn't see anything. Now you tell me that you *saw* an attack?"

"Let me finish, Captain. I *heard* the attack. A lot of growling and foot-pounding around the VIP contingent."

I could tell from his radish complexion that he hated my guts. The feeling was mutual. "For your information, the others described your darkness as pure *white*."

I shrugged. "Black, white, same difference. We couldn't see squat either way."

He spun in a huff and rejoined the *Ghostworld* celebrities.

"Thanks for not mentioning the monster part of my report," I whispered.

"I didn't do it for you. Straightjackets aren't my idea of a fashion statement."

Stanton opened the press conference with a peppy pep talk. His lumpy left jaw line was grape-purple from my forearm shiver, making it difficult to enunciate clearly, but he had regained his carnival pitchman enthusiasm.

I tuned Stanton out and scanned the area for danger. Kit did the same, but neither of us detected any suspicious people or activities.

The EMTs must've given the mayor's wife a powerful sedative, because she moved like a zombie. Her laugh-a-minute husband's grim expression spelled legal trouble for Pep Boy. The apple-faced senator spoke heatedly into his Bluetooth, and his ashen date looked ready to puke her guts out any minute. The governor, though, stood erect, shoulders back, in complete command. His fear had been brushed aside. He was a pillar of strength for his portly wife, who leaned heavily against him for support. Every one of them was antsy and impatient to bug out. I knew the feeling.

The gun-happy sheriff, Lance Stockard, was the exception. He stood tall, with an air of self-importance, soaking in the limelight. Our nearly tragic experience would make the headlines for months, bolstering his fall reelection campaign.

Then there was beautiful Gwendolyn. She stared at Stanton with stars in her eyes, like a girl with a grade-school crush. It was blatantly obvious to anyone watching that she had the major hots for Stanny Boy, but what threw me for a loop was that she wasn't clever enough to hide it. Tandy Stanton wouldn't give up her sugar-daddy husband and his big money without a fight. Gwendolyn would soon discover that she was out of her league with Tandy. I figured it would be ugly. Maybe hit-man ugly. After all, Tandy had socialized with the dregs of society most of her life.

I glanced up and noticed that the anomalous multicolored lightning show had ended, but the bloated charcoal clouds remained, churning ominously like before. The thick air varnished us with sweat and the unmistakable malodor of evil, a not-so subtle warning that the *Ghostworld* sorcerer had more lethal tricks up his sleeve tonight.

I stole a look at the tent and watched the CSI team enter. I didn't remember Kit or myself touching anything inside, so there was nothing to connect us to those murders. But the predictable Diaz would try.

Kit roughly jerked my sport coat sleeve and gestured nervously at Gwendolyn. My breath caught in my throat.

Rivulets of blood trickled from her eyes, ears, and nose. She carelessly brushed the wetness away, probably believing it to be perspiration. All hell broke loose when the senator's girlfriend let go with full-throated, vein-busting scream and collapsed like a Slinky.

Gwendolyn's terrifying image stopped Stanton cold, and all eyes fell on her.

The murderous sorcerer had struck again.

And I was powerless to save her.

10

The reporters stood slack-jawed. Nobody budged an inch. They were shock sculptures. Too stunned to react. Nothing stirred, including cell phones. After the initial jolt, a few digital cameras flashed and the TV cameras zoomed in on the ill-fated young woman.

I sensed that the supernatural forces were merely getting warmed up. The worst was yet to come. For poor Gwendolyn.

I instinctively shoved Kit back. "Get behind the tent . . . *now!*" I barked before addressing the dazed assembly. "Flatten yourselves on the ground and cover your heads!" I shouted. A handful of people acknowledged me, but didn't respond.

"Get down *now,* or die!" I yelled for all I was worth, and set an example by diving onto the grass and shielding my head.

They finally blinked awake from their trances and moved. All but Lance Stockard hit the deck. He was busily trying to staunch Gwendolyn's bleeding, but it was futile. She bled like a stuck pig. His panicked daughter was a goner. *And he was a dead man.* A black aura wafted around both corpses.

Without warning, Gwendolyn's head exploded like a tripped landmine, and her headless body flew backwards toward the tent. Fragments from her shattered cranium pummeled us like grisly shrapnel. I winced as a sharp bony shard pierced my exposed side. As I rolled and yanked it out, the sheriff collapsed face-first into the grass, most of his face sliced away. His glory days were finished.

The place erupted into pandemonium, with reporters and guests alike running helter-skelter, terror-stricken at the crimson gore freckling their clothes, hair, and faces. But the worst wasn't over. The gray matter and bony scalp fragments that had been propelled skyward like a Fourth of July skyrocket came raining down to earth like a foul hailstorm, showering us yet once again with her stomach-retching remains.

A slew of reporters and cops vomited loudly, while others shrieked like asylum inmates, clawing at their hair like rabid monkeys. Television cameras lay abandoned on the red-puddled lawn, while several newspaper photographers plucked clumps of gooey gore from their lenses and flashes.

Without warning, jagged cobalt lightning bolts fractured the agitated sky and struck the ground thirty feet from the dais. The earsplitting explosion staggered a mob of retreating reporters, and the violent black energy dispersed like a cluster bomb. Their clothes and flesh were instantly ignited, incinerating them in seconds. Cremated exactly like the three thugs inside the medical tent. *Ghostworld* rapidly became a hushed crematorium.

The rest of us were reeling from the blast. Some ears bleeding. All stunned and deaf. Because of that, the maniacal screams failed to create mass hysteria. No one could hear them. I was among the first to recover enough to move with a purpose, but the ringing in my wolfen ears was intolerable. Kit stumbled toward me like one of the *Walking Dead*, with red teary eyes and an agonizing grimace. I took her trembling outstretched arms and pulled her gore-dappled body against mine.

During our hug, I felt a sticky wetness ooze through my fingers on her back, and I discreetly took a peek at the wound so as not to upset her even more. A slender bone splinter shaped like a warped arrowhead had pierced the skin between her shoulder blades . . . an inch from her spine. She was lucky.

"C'mon, we're leaving," I said firmly. I could fix her up just fine, but not in front of an audience.

Kit protested, but it was a feeble attempt. The horror and pain glazing her eyes said it all ... "Get me out of here."

"I should stay and help with . . . ." Her knees buckled before she finished her halfhearted objection. I hoisted her off the ground and carried her through the exit to the pungent parking lot. Like a stomach-turning mist, the rotting malodor was so dense and rank that I choked after one whiff. The stench was much worse than the ghostly choir down in the white night, and that was just plain awful.

Kit came to her senses as we reached the Explorer. I opened the passenger-side door and propped her against the frame. Her unstable body threatened to topple at any moment.

I said, "Hold tight while I get rid of your pain. Face the inside of the car."

Kit nodded gratefully and turned, but since she was still a bit groggy, I wasn't certain that she understood what I was about to do. So I waited until she relaxed. I didn't want her to panic, draw her gun, and put a bullet between my eyes. Stranger things have happened to me.

I waved my wand and spouted a few familiar words. A dazzling burst of cinnamon light arced from the tip to the wound like a welding torch, and a small brilliant blaze masked her injury. Kit moaned, but didn't move. After an agonizing several minutes, her back was completely healed . . . *without a scar.*

"All done," I announced, tucking the wand back under my belt. "Dr. Luna declares you to be fit as a fiddle and scar-free."

Kit whooshed and released her white-knuckle grip on the door frame.

"Thanks," she managed softly and pecked me on the lips. They were dry but soft.

"Any time. Got another one of those for me?"

This time she pressed her lips hard against mine and kissed me for all she was worth. I estimated a cool million. After another half-dozen more, the color gradually suffused her pallid cheeks, and her legs steadied. I sure felt a helluva lot better, too. Despite the prevailing worm stink.

"Care for a ride into town?" I asked her.

"Uh, I'd better not. I'm assigned here until further notice. No time off for good behavior." A bloody fragment of gristle fell from her bangs. She grimaced as it landed next to her shoes. "I hate this place!"

"Join the club."

"God, *Ghostworld* is a nightmare!"

"And that nightmare includes murder," I added.

She reclined on the edge of the seat. "Murder?"

"Sheriff Lance Stockard and his daughter."

She mulled it over. "That's a little farfetched, even for you."

"The sorcerer killed them both, and I want to know why. I need your help on this, Kit."

"I agree that Gwendolyn Stockard's death looked supernatural, with her head exploding and all that, but using her to kill her father is a stretch."

"Trust me, that's what happened. There's a supernatural imprint on his corpse. I saw it. You've got to trust me on that. I actually saw the black-magic aura."

"Let's say I believe you. I still can't get away tonight. I'm on *duty*, Joe."

I said, "I'm taking you to the ER for medical assistance. Don't forget about your back injury. It needs some medical treatment."

She crossed her arms. "It's gone, and you know it."

"I can always put it back."

She contemplated my argument. "You would, wouldn't you?"

"To save your career, yes. But it won't be necessary. I just know these things."

"You think that your magic's the answer to everything, don't you?"

"Pretty much."

"You're impossible. All right, I'm game, but make sure I don't get caught."

"Deal." After she scooted across the seat, I shut the door, climbed behind the wheel, and started the car.

"So why are you so sure that Gwendolyn Stockard was murdered?"

"For one thing, if she wasn't killed by a spell, she'd be the first in recorded history to die from an exploding migraine . . . and kill her own father in the process."

She feigned a grin. "Cute. Real cute."

I ignored her sarcasm. "The way I figure it, when the giant demon failed to kill the Stockards in the white night, the sorcerer must've been damned desperate to make sure they died tonight, because he orchestrated it in front of a live crowd and a TV audience. Why it was so important that they had to die tonight is another mystery."

She looked puzzled. "Then who was his target? Gwendolyn or her father?"

My expression clouded. "My guess is both. But until we know more, it's just a guess."

She gnawed her bottom lip. "Are we going after the murderer now?"

"No, because I don't have a clue as to who we'd be looking for. I want to drop in on a friend, and hopefully she can point us in the right direction."

"I see. If you don't mind my asking, who's your friend?"

"You'll see when we get there."

She clenched her teeth. "You can be so exasperating!"

I nodded. "Thanks for the compliment."

11

A pesky rain fell as we drove into downtown Orlando. At least it was *real* rain. No night crawlers this go-round. The mercury vapor *streetlights* cast an eerie salmon haze over the streets as we turned left onto Pine Street. We couldn't seem to shake the spine-chilling atmosphere no matter where we were tonight.

An EMT ambulance appeared out of nowhere behind us and zoomed past, sirens wailing and lights flashing. It nearly side-swiped the Explorer, forcing me to bounce over the curb. *Who'd he think he was, Richard Petty?* My anger quickly subsided and we drove until we saw the peeling, painted sign for *Martha's Mojo Magic Herbs.*

The *hell-bent-for-leather* ambulance driver scattered the curious crowd ahead of us like they were pigeons in Rome. He screeched to a stop in front of Martha's shop and leaped out with his stone-faced partner. They secured a gurney and wheeled it through the entrance. *Now what? Had something happened to Martha Gibbons?* She was my destination.

Blue and white lights blinked hypnotically atop the three police cruisers parked at odd angles beside the fluttering yellow police crime scene tape separating the crowd from the shop. Kit slapped the dashboard with her palm and swore.

"I take it that you wanted to question Martha tonight?"

I nodded.

"Great. Now it's a sure bet that Diaz will find out I'm here instead of *Ghostworld.*"

"We've still got your injury for back-up," I reminded her.

"We're not even close to a hospital."

Nothing was working out for me tonight. I wanted to punch the steering wheel, but I realized that I'd break the damned thing off. "Tell you what. Stay here and I'll check out the shop. That way no one from the force will know you're here," I volunteered.

Kit scrambled out the other side. "Oh, no you don't! *I'll* do the checking. That's my department. If Diaz finds out I'm here, he finds out. I can't let you go barging in and get arrested."

"I thought you didn't want to get caught?"

"You *do* want to know what's happening with your friend, right?"

"You're damn right I do."

"Then I'm the one who can get through the barricade. You don't stand a chance."

I raised my hands in supplication. "Maybe your buddies have softened their attitudes toward me."

Kit shook with frustration. I had that effect on women. "And maybe your POS Explorer is a sweet ride. Now get back in the car." She marched toward the commotion.

Ooooh. Calling my SUV a POS was hitting below the belt. That hurt.

So of course I didn't return to my semi-sweet ride. I tagged along at a discreet distance until I reached the back edge of the gathering of curiosity seekers. Kit ducked beneath the tape and greeted her fellow detectives.

Being six foot four created a major problem when I tried to blend in with any crowd. I more or less stood out like an unruly cowlick. As Kit chatted with one of her fellow doughnut eaters, Sergeant Jim Fisher, his gaze drifted my way, and he frowned instantly. For a connoisseur of bakery specialties, the sergeant was surprisingly gaunt, with a sour face shaped like those elongated African tribal carvings.

He stood there conversing with Kit, but kept one eye glued to me the entire time in case I tried to crash his party. Then the lecture, Miranda Rights, and handcuffs would come out. I wasn't going there. I'd wait for Kit to give me the lowdown.

With a parting scowl, Fisher escorted Kit inside. I figured they weren't going to extend me the courtesy of giving me a Get-into-Martha's Free Pass, so I'd have to enter the old-fashioned way—*break in*. I made a beeline for the side alley that dead-ended at a service road running behind all the stores on the block.

As I jogged, I glanced up and recoiled at the identical roiling kaleidoscope clouds that had been present over *Ghostworld* during the murderous bedlam. I instinctively growled, and it wasn't indigestion, either. That damned sorcerer appeared to be following me.

Lightning flickered overhead—an orangish-green horizontal web—and I picked up my pace. I paused at the pitch-black service road to get my bearings, then I zig-zagged between toppled garbage cans and clusters of slick, stinking garbage to Martha's back door—*locked* back door. I checked out both directions before waving my hand over the corroded doorknob and three deadbolts. They clicked open. No muss—no fuss. I cautiously forced the creaking steel door open so as not to alert any roaming cops inside.

But running into an entire battalion of cops would've been more desirable than what greeted me inside the storeroom. My wolfen hackles sprouted and bristled along my neck.

The entire place was painted in blood.

Russet gore and clumps of animal hair and flesh were splattered across all four walls, the floor, and the high ceiling. Scorched, broken skeletons the size of small ponies littered the floor. Thin strips of charred flesh and sinew were sparsely woven between the blackened bones, a sure sign of intense fire. I sniffed the stale decay and detected an otherworldly presence. The battle here wasn't over.

There was a demon lurking somewhere in the gloomy, poorly lit area.

I surveyed the carnage and wondered what had happened. *An invasion?* But more importantly, *was Martha all right?* I'd find out soon enough, after I dealt with the otherworldly presence.

A savage snarl resonated from the far front corner and startled me out of my reverie. A pony-sized, four-legged silhouette peered out from the far side of a stack of pallets. A single fluorescent light dangling from the ceiling barely illuminated the vast space between us. Gradually, an elongated muzzle appeared, followed by a pair of spiky ears, coal-black eyes, and two front legs. The devil dog's flesh glistened smoky green and clung to its skull and neck like cellophane wrap. Its soulless button eyes drilled me with a slayer's glare.

I didn't break eye contact, because doing so would have automatically conveyed my trepidation to the creature, and those hellish brutes feasted on human fear. If this one expected a fright feast from me, it would definitely starve to death.

After a protracted stand-off, the killer pooch moved from the shadows and revealed all of its three hundred pounds of bony ugliness. My wolfen genes escalated to DEFCON 1, alertly awaiting its initial move. The devil dog crouched, preparing to attack me, but that was as far as it got. I raised my wand, sighted it like a rifle, and launched a white-hot fireball at it. The demon monster jumped toward me and immediately burst into a blossom of crimson entrails and flaming flesh. The explosion was far enough away that I was spared a costly dry-cleaning bill.

A myriad of fluorescent lights blinked to life, and the menacing gloom vanished. Kit shoved open the inner shop door and panned her gun barrel in a half-circle before spying me in the rear doorway.

She lowered her gun and crinkled her nose at the pungent foul smell. "Jesus, Joe, what the hell happened in here?"

I raised my index finger, lowered my eyelids, and leaned against the block wall. My body jerked as the past horrific visuals filled my mind. Martha was busy battling a surge of devil dogs leaping through a circular portal of bright white radiance like circus lions jumping through a fiery ring. The supernatural portal was a conjured rift in the dimensional fabric separating our world from a very familiar one—the *white night*.

Despite her years, the old girl wielded her magic wand and its spewing fireballs like a young King Arthur brandishing Excalibur. She mowed down the invaders as they emerged from the rift, splashing blood, innards, and slabs of burnt flesh and hair everywhere. After the first wave of hellions was annihilated, the next wave was cleverer. This time, they used their fallen brethren as shields from Martha's fireballs.

The first devil dog leaped safely into the storeroom as the corpses exploded behind it. It darted toward the rear exit as a decoy to draw my friend's fire. Meanwhile, two more appeared through the smoking corpses and attacked Martha from the side. The dimensional portal radiance shrank away.

Martha was caught off guard when the two hellions pounced. One of the brutes clawed the wand from her hand and knocked her flat to the floor, but she muttered a breathless chant that launched her attacker like a skyrocket toward the ceiling, where it detonated into an umbrella of bloody body parts.

The second was in a mid-air leap and would've torn Martha's throat away if Jared, her son, hadn't appeared in the doorway and killed it with his own fireball. At extremely close range to his mother, the demon burst into flames and blanketed her in crimson gore, making her unrecognizable. What bothered me was that Jared was completely unruffled by his mother's close call with his fireball. He could've killed her with his reckless magic.

Police sirens wailed in the distance, and the decoy stole along the wall and hid behind the pallets. Jared conjured a bathing spell that removed the bloody mess from his mother before helping her back into the shop.

The next thing I heard was the cops' excited voices as they charged through the front door. I mentally sniffed the atmosphere. Although the rift had vanished, its imprint remained, and it was an odd blend of scents. Brimstone. Sea-breeze saline. Dune grass. A hint of motor oil. *Motor oil?* I vaguely remembered smelling motor oil as we descended below Mansion Macabre, but amid the panicked riders, it had been just a footnote at the time.

When my streaming visions ebbed, I was jolted back to the present. I squinted into the harsh fluorescent lighting at Kit, who hadn't budged an inch.

"Well, what did you see?" she demanded impatiently.

"An amazing battle between Martha and a bunch of devil dogs. If I'm right, the attack here is connected to what happened at *Ghostworld*."

She appeared disgusted. "That's pretty farfetched, even for you. Now why don't you tell me exactly what you saw, and I'll draw my own conclusions."

So I did, including the motor oil smell and the white-night portal.

12

Kit regarded me skeptically after she listened to my description of
Martha's battle with the devil dogs and my rationale for connecting
it with the *Ghostworld* events.

"Well?" I demanded, rushing across the gore-slick floor to meet her.

"I'm still trying to see the connection. I'll let you know later." Typical
Kit. A one-way communicator at the strangest times.

She waited for me, and we stepped into the shop together. Two
police detectives, Jared, and a twenty-something Goth chick were the
only people inside. I did a double-take at the stand-offish, wide-eyed
extremist as she browsed the assortment of magic candles on an end-
cap display. Her greasy black-dyed hair fell in clumpy strands across her
shoulders, and her lips, eyes, and cheekbones were highlighted with
smears of black make-up. Her formless raven linen dress fell loosely
to her ankles and partially concealed a pair of scuffed military boots.
Definitely not my type of woman.

I surveyed the quaint interior. Someone was missing. "Where's
Martha?"

Kit spoke softly to one of the detectives, then looked at me. "Your
buddies in the ambulance drove her to the hospital."

"Is she all right?" I thought about her close call with Jared's fireball.
That kid needed his magic license revoked.

"Just shaken, but the EMTs were pretty tight-lipped before they left."

I swung my gaze toward Jared. He was his customary vacuous self.
His brown-eyed stare was fixed, dull, and *out there*. If he wasn't doing
drugs again, I'd eat my fishing hat. He'd seen the inside of several rehab
centers over the years, but he'd been bounced out of every one for
continuing his cocaine habit behind their backs. What a loser. I felt sorry
for Martha, who had put up with his shit for the past seven years. The
kid was twenty-five now, and it was past time he grew up and kicked
his nasty habit. But Jared was weak in every sense of the word—except

for his inherited magic. I cringed. A hopped-up magician could be big trouble.

His hairstylist colored his ragged auburn hair a shoe-polish black and added a stark white streak in the front for good measure. Sadly, that was the zenith of his appearance. The band of his green boxers peeked over his baggy shorts, his flip-flops were worn, and his skull-printed shirt was two sizes too big for his slight frame.

Kit followed my disgusted line of sight and tapped my shoulder.

"How about focusing on the investigation instead of Jared?" she reminded me sharply. "Remember, it was *your* idea to come over here and jeopardize my career."

"You're right. What's the story here?"

"Some witnesses called 911 and reported seeing an unmarked van pull up at the curb. Three ski-masked gunmen jumped out and stormed inside. The van was green and didn't have license plates. They watched the men aim their weapons at Martha and demand cash. She opened the cash register, but then the store filled with smoke."

I arched my brows. "Smoke?"

"Yeah. The smoke cleared after a couple minutes, and the three men were gone."

"They didn't run out the back way, because I would've seen them in my vision."

"And they didn't leave through the front door, either." She paused as a violent clap of thunder rattled the windows. "Their van's still parked outside."

"So what happened to them?" I muttered, but I wasn't as stumped as I let on. *Did Martha cast a spell on the would-be thieves, or did Jared?* I moved toward Jared, who stood behind the hickory check-out counter. He shrank against the wall.

"Tell me about the smoke," I commanded gruffly. Just the sight of the cokehead rankled me. "And keep your voice down. I don't want the cops to hear."

"We didn't conjure the smoke, if that's what your thinking," he whispered.

I was. Dammit! "So where did it come from? Tell me before I forget the cops are here and rip your lungs out."

His faraway expression sharpened to utter fear. He took me at my word, because he knew I was a werewolf and very capable of carrying out my threat.

"Look, the smoke came out of nowhere, and like Kit said, when it left, the crooks were gone, too. Me and Mom didn't see what happened to them, but we did hear snarling in the back room. We looked and saw these great big demon dogs jumpin' outta thin air." He studied my unwavering glare and added, "That's all I know. Honest."

"First of all, you wouldn't know 'honest' if it smacked you in the face, but your story better be the truth . . . *for your sake.*"

Kit overheard the kid's story, even though she was pacing across the shop. She possessed incredible supernatural powers, too, but no one else knew about them but me.

Jared nervously licked his lips. "It . . . it is. I *swear.*"

"Save it," I barked and rejoined Kit.

"Do you believe him?" she asked quietly.

"I shouldn't trust anything that skinny shit says, but I do this time."

"I'm not totally convinced that he or his mom didn't conjure the smoke," she noted.

I had an idea about the crooks and the smoke, but I wasn't about to share it at the moment. "You might be right. I'll ask Martha about it at the hospital."

Goth Chick meandered to the counter and struck up a quiet conversation with Coke Boy, while the detectives were still busy collecting evidence, which at this point would require only a thimble to transport to headquarters.

But I kept my gaze glued on Jared while I spoke to Kit. "I firmly believe that the crooks' appearance was a matter of bad timing. Maybe the sorcerer didn't want them interfering with his planned devil-dog attack."

Kit shook a glass jar of bat-wing flakes, cringed, and quickly returned it to the shelf. "That makes sense, *if* your mysterious sorcerer caused that portal."

Before I could reply, Captain Diaz strode into the shop, breathless and flushed. The guy was a heart attack waiting to happen.

He froze when he saw us. "What the hell are you two doing . . .?" He saw the two detectives and rapidly reined in his temper. "We'll have that chat later. Right now I've got bigger fish to fry."

Kit inched closer to me. "What fish?"

"The ambulance taking Martha Gibbons to Orlando Regional Medical Center was T-boned by a dump truck a few minutes ago and totaled. The EMTs bailed at the last second and escaped with slight injuries, but Ms. Gibbons is . . . ."

"Is what?" I spoke up. I hoped he wasn't about to say *dead*.

"Is *missing*."

A lightning sizzler and a cannonade of thunder ripped through downtown, and the shop's lights blacked out.

13

Seconds after our black-out, a terrific shock wave pummeled us like an NFL linebacker, scattering us among Martha's inventory. My airborne body collided with shelves of straw dolls, and I slid unceremoniously to the floor with the dolls tumbling atop me. I brushed them away and listened to the crashing of bodies and the tinkling of shattered jars. *Had another rift broken through our dimension?*

Dazed, I tried to raise my ring to ward off any evil presences, but I found that my arms and hands were pinioned against the wall. I struggled to free them; it was no use. I was a sitting duck for whatever was coming our way.

A gleaming white apparition materialized out of the blackness in the center of the shop, and floated along the walls until it came to me. It stopped and dropped right in front of me.

The ethereal form was thin and crooked, as if God had welded lightning bolts together, but its sheer brilliance prevented me from defining its face. What I *did* manage to detect chilled me to the core. Its indistinct wings fluttered slowly, clanging and creaking as if they had been crafted from metal. When it leaned closer to my face, enormous, lethal viper fangs and keen, spiky boar tusks filled my eyes. It appeared to be studying me, although I couldn't make out its eyes.

"Joe Luna?" The deep feminine voice reverberated like we were inside an echo chamber.

I shrank from it, but the wall stopped me cold. My bestial instinct pressed me to become a werewolf and defend myself, but the ghostly figure appeared to control my wolfen genes as well. *What on earth could accomplish that feat?*

"How do you know my name?" I replied huskily.

"Don't speak aloud. I can read your thoughts," it cautioned me mentally.

Oh, that was just great. A mind-reading demon.

"I am *not* a demon," it snapped, obviously offended at my remark.

"Then what are you?" I thought.

"Later. First, I require your help."

My help? It had to be kidding!

"I assure you that I am not kidding," it said. "And I am a *she*, not an *it*."

Oops.

"How could I possibly help *you*?" I asked her telepathically.

"I want you to investigate the place called *Ghostworld* and discover who is behind the many violent murders."

"There have been only two murders there," I reminded her.

"There will be more."

"Oh." This was shaping up to be a really fun case. "Am I going to be one of the murder victims?"

"Not if you're clever enough."

She sounded like Martha, but their collective advice wasn't exactly reassuring.

The shop was dead quiet. No one moved or said a word, but I heard their breathing. Fast and irregular. Outside the windows, the world was black, too. No streetlights. No lightning. It was as if we'd dropped off the face of the earth.

"All right, I'll do my best to find the killer," I conceded. *What choice did I have?*

She leaned even closer until we were practically cheek to tusk. "I will hold you to that promise, Joe Luna."

My body temperature dropped below freezing. *Was that a threat?*

"Yes," she answered. "If you abandon this investigation before you locate the murderer, you will suffer my curse."

I didn't bother asking what kind of curse. Hell, a curse is a curse in my book, and they're all bad news. "Look, I gave you my word. I'll do everything I can to find this guy." I paused. "Our bargain doesn't include my killing him, does it?"

"No. I will make that decision when the time comes."

Like a hummingbird on a caffeine binge, she flew across the shop and fastened herself to the wall above the check-out counter. Gravity wasn't a big deal to her. The ghostly bully cocked her right arm, conjured a brush, and began sketching with what looked like violet DayGlo paint. Fascinated, I watched the drawing take shape.

It appeared to be a symbol, and from studying the history of magic with my mother, I pegged it as an ancient one. The rough outline quickly swelled into a detailed shape, but before I could analyze it further, I was yanked to my feet like a rag doll and repositioned where I had been standing when the lights went out.

Suddenly, the shop was illuminated again, and our intimidating visitor was gone. We checked each other out, but we were none the worse for wear from our extraordinary experience. Even the shelves, inventory, and ruined jars and bottles were back in place, as if nothing had ever happened.

"Holy shit!" one of the cops whistled, his gun drawn. "What the hell was *that*?"

The front door flew open and a disheveled Captain Diaz stumbled inside, his wiry black hair singed and cork-screwed.

Kit advanced to her boss. "What happened to *you*?"

"I got the shock of my life, that's what!" he ranted. "After the lights went out in here, I tried to open the front door to find out what the hell was going on. When I grabbed the goddammed door handle, I got the electrical jolt of my life!"

I noticed that Kit held back her laughter, but it was a consummate struggle. I was glad she did, because we didn't need Diaz flying off the handle again.

"After I got my ass fried," he continued, "nobody touched that fuckin' door again."

"Sorry to hear about your tough luck, boss," Kit empathized, tongue in cheek.

The panicked detective holstered his gun. "There was a frickin' ghost in here after the lights went kablooie, Captain, and it drew that graffiti on the back wall."

Like an out-of-control tea kettle, Diaz was close to blowing his top at the absurd remark, but Kit stepped in and gestured toward the wall. The symbol retained its piercing glow, despite the illumination from the shop lights.

Diaz combed his splayed fingers through his frizzed hair, but it remained spiked. He scrutinized the drawing. "Jesus, what's that supposed to be?"

"Some kind of symbol," Kit speculated. "We haven't had the chance to examine it yet." She glanced at me, and I nodded my agreement.

"I want to know *what* drew it!" Jared piped up, his face a terror-stricken mask.

All eyes shifted to me, except Goth Girl's.

I pumped my shoulders. "You got me hanging."

"Well, the ghost was parked in front of you the whole time," Jared pointed out. "We could see you and it just as plain as day, man."

One of the detectives chimed in. "Yeah, how about it, Luna? What was so special about you?"

"Nothing. It just stared at me, that's all." I bent to Kit's ear. "I'll explain later."

"You'd better," she whispered.

I stalked toward the counter, and Jared instinctively backed away again.

"Ease up, Coke Boy," I said gruffly and gestured up at the sketch. "Does anyone have any idea what that symbol means?"

The others closed in for a better look. The drawing consisted of an unbroken circle surrounded by three coiled vipers with a triangular heads. The serpents' eyes were crystalline grids of fractured lines that glared menacingly out at the world. As I thought, it was a symbol I'd never seen before.

"I'm beginning to think that the whole lot of you went loony tunes during the blackout," Diaz thundered. "And, *Lieutenant Wilson*, if you expect me to repeat that ridiculous ghost story to the chief, you've got another think coming!"

After all our past supernatural investigations together, I was ticked that Diaz questioned our account — but hey, like the man already told us, he was fried. But that didn't stop me from reminding him of that fact.

"It's one thing to admit there was a ghost in here to you, Luna, and it's quite another to expect the chief to swallow it," he grumbled.

"So leave out that part. Blame the whole incident here on a lightning strike. If I remember correctly, there was a big one seconds before the lights went out," I suggested. "And the lightning would explain your fried appearance, too."

"Watch it, Luna."

"I was just quoting you."

He frowned, loathing advice from anyone. "I suppose," he agreed begrudgingly, then turned to Kit. "Since you're the fiction writer in the department, create your usual bullshit report and have it on my desk first thing tomorrow."

Kit looked hesitant.

"If it's on my desk *on time*, I won't bother to ask why you abandoned your assigned post at *Ghostworld* to go shopping with Luna." With that parting shot, the fricasseed captain marched outside, got in his cruiser, and sped away.

Both detectives nodded their empathy at Kit before exiting the shop. The outside crowd was history, no doubt frightened away by the earlier lightning strike. I couldn't blame them. Curiosity had its limits.

Kit looked up at me. "Now what? You've really gotten me into hot water this time. I'll never hear the end of this from Diaz."

"At least I'm good for something," I quipped, as I snapped a few pictures of the symbol with my cell phone camera.

She disregarded my wisecrack.

When I finished, I said, "So I guess a couple of stiff drinks, some romantic music, and soft candlelight at the farmhouse are not in the cards for us tonight."

"Ooooh," she managed through clenched teeth. "You are . . . *incorrigible*."

I grinned, then turned serious. "You asked me what the ghostly creature wanted with me. Still want to hear about her?"

"*Her?*"

"Yeah. She wanted me to find out who's responsible for the *Ghostworld* murders, both present and future. Or else."

"Future?"

"Yeah. It seems she looked into the future and saw more murders there."

"That's swell. Did you agree?"

"What part of *or else* didn't you understand? Of course I accepted. It was either that or be cursed for all eternity."

Her face blanched. "You're putting me on, aren't you?"

"I wish I were. But I've saved the best for last."

She rolled her eyes. "Oh, God. What's that?"

"You're going to help me find the killer sorcerer."

She appeared skeptical. "Did the ghost threaten to curse *me* if I didn't help?"

"Uh, not exactly. I kind of read between the lines."

She relaxed, and her cheeks reddened. "You're a real piece of work, you know that?"

"That's what my mother always told me."

She brushed her blonde hair behind her ears. "You want to drag me along on *your* investigation so I can piss off Diaz some more. Is that your brilliant plan?"

"When you put it that way, it sounds like a bad idea. But, hey, it's your call. While you're making up your mind, I'm going to find Martha."

She snorted a laugh. "My people are already turning Orlando upside down looking for her. What makes you so sure that *you* can find her when they can't?"

"Because I know where to look," I replied smugly.

"You can be the most arrogant . . . ."

"Do you want to find Martha or not?"

Kit chewed it over briefly, then propped her folded arms across her chest. "It depends on where're you're planning to look. I'm not up for a wild goose chase."

I shifted my gaze to Cokehead and Goth Girl. "I'm not planning to look any farther than this shop."

14

I approached Jared and glared at him with alternating copper and fiery orange eyes. His jaw dropped when he saw that I was on the brink of changing into a werewolf.

"Where's your mother?" I demanded thickly, my hands and face sprouting hair.

To my surprise, he was angry and combative. I never would've guessed that the kid had it in him. "Shut up, you fool! They're watching us. *Listening*," he hissed.

I weighed Cokehead's warning, found it to be rational, and backed off my werewolf transformation. It made sense that whoever had instigated the brutal attack on Martha was spying on us like SPECTRE in a James Bond novel. But I had the perfect solution for our problem. I cast a simple yet effective spell around the four of us.

"There," I announced, "now no one can understand a word we say or read our lips. To anyone listening, our conversation will sound and look like chipmunk chatter."

Kit eyed me cynically. "You're shittin' me, right?"

"No, I'm on the level. For once." I faced Jared. "All right, hotshot, answer my damned question."

He glanced nervously at Goth Girl and then back at me. "What makes you so sure that I know where Mom is, when the cops can't even find her?" he replied evasively.

I felt my wolfen hair sprouting again like spring weeds.

Kit grabbed my elbow. "Not now, Joe. He can't tell us where Martha is if you make sushi out of him. Remember, they're watching—whoever *they* are."

I reigned in my trigger-happy hormones, but I now needed another way to persuade the kid to talk. I didn't have one. The longer I mulled it over, the more I rejected violence as an edge. *How about logic?* It always worked on me. *What the hell.*

"Jared, I'll tell you why I'm dead certain that you know where your mother is. When I employed my "sight" to see what happened in your storeroom earlier this evening, I saw you save your mom's life with a fireball."

Cokehead shrugged. "So? What does that prove? Nothing."

"It *proves* that the woman you saved wasn't your mother!" I asserted, pounding my fist on the counter to punctuate my contention. In my peripheral vision, I watched Goth Girl at the end of the counter, and she didn't flinch an inch from my violent fist thumping. *She couldn't be that stoned, could she?*

"That's crazy, Joe! You're not making any sense."

A sanctimonious grin creased Kit's mouth. She undoubtedly believed that Jared had me cornered, and that my argument was about to go up in flames. Well, I had news for her—I was about to spring my Lincoln Lawyer closer on him.

I pressed on. "You practically killed your mom with that fireball."

"Bullshit."

"Really? Your fireball came within inches of incinerating her, along with the devil dog, and yet I saw from your nonchalant expression that you weren't real concerned whether she burned or not. That's when I was positive that that woman was not your mother, no matter what she looked like," I announced triumphantly.

"That doesn't prove anything," he mumbled, pouting like a three-year-old.

I really had the urge to knock his belligerent block off, but I mustered enough patience to stay cool. Kit was right. Dismembering him wouldn't produce Martha.

The two detectives who witnessed the glowing ghost reentered the shop.

"Our crime scene crew just showed up from *Ghostworld*. You want 'em to start in front, or out back?"

"Don't talk!" I warned Kit quietly. "Remember, we sound like chipmunks."

Kit opened and then quickly snapped her mouth shut. Instead of speaking, she jerked her thumb toward the rear.

"Right. Anything else, Lieutenant?"

Kit shook her head "no." The pair exchanged odd looks, but vamoosed without further comment.

"That was a close call," she exhaled heavily. "Thanks for the heads-up."

"No problem." I waved the tip of my wand in Jared's face. "If you don't want to talk like Chip and Dale for the rest of your life, I advise you to come clean. You've got five seconds to think it over. *One*."

He checked out the Goth chick.

"*Two*."

She gave an imperceptible nod.

"*Three*."

His mouth opened and closed like a breathless guppy.

"*Four*." My grip tightened on the wand as I prepared to unleash the spell.

"All right, all right, I'll tell you!" he rasped.

I lowered the wand a notch. "I'm listening."

"Promise not to look at her when I tell you where she is."

"I'll give it some serious thought," I retorted.

Kit groaned. "C'mon, quit being so damned mule-headed, Joe."

I frowned. "All right, I won't look."

Jared anxiously shuffled from side to side. "Mom's right next to us at the end of the counter."

Goth Girl.

Just as I figured.

15

I kept my promise and didn't look at Goth Girl.

"Why'd you disguise yourself like this?" I posed.

"I saw the devil-dog attack coming yesterday in my blind eye, but I didn't know exactly when. So I hid my doppelgänger in the closet until it was time," she explained.

Kit was clearly bewildered by this turn of events. "A whatsit?"

"A doppelgänger is a ghostly double of a living person," I responded. "Sorta like a supernatural clone."

Kit looked puzzled, as if my definition was as clear as mud. "Hmmm. Clone. Double. Like an android?"

"Pretty close."

"Okay, I think I have it now. So, Martha, the EMTs actually wheeled your doppelgänger out of here, not you?"

Martha hesitated. "I reckon it was a devious thing to do, but it had to be done, dear. My life was in real danger. Still is, for that matter."

Kit was upset. "And what about the dump-truck accident that nearly killed the EMTs? Was that part of your plan, or just an unlucky coincidence for those guys?"

Martha chortled despite Kit's indelicate accusation. "I made sure those two boys stayed safe. When I arranged the accident, I planned for them to be magically removed from the ambulance seconds before impact. I had no choice. My doppelgänger had to be destroyed before it reached the hospital, and the doctors discovered she wasn't human."

"Since the cops can't find her—it—then what happened to it?" Kit pressed.

"Like any obedient spell, she vanished," Martha revealed. "No one will ever find her." She looked up and noticed that the symbol on the back wall was gone.

"I saw that the symbol has disappeared, too. I say good riddance. We've got enough on our plates tonight without playing cryptographers."

Kit backed off, appeased. "Thanks, Martha. I feel better about your ruse."

Martha moved along the counter and touched my arm. "But you saw right through my little deception, Joe. You always were a bright boy."

My face flushed warm. "Thanks, but all the credit should go to Jared. His recklessness gave you away when he saved your doppelgänger from the devil dog."

She scowled at her son. "You've got to be more careful in the future."

He kneaded his hands. "It all worked out, so don't make a big-ass deal about it."

My hand shot over the counter and corralled his arm. I yanked him tight against the hickory. "Don't ever let me hear you backtalk your mom like that again," I snarled. "Next time, they'll be your last words."

My harsh breaths spilled over his face as he contemplated my warning. I saw by the fear distorting his face that I'd put the fear of God into him.

Jared tried to wrench his arm from my grasp, but I held firm until he apologized.

"I got the message. I'm not stupid, ya know. Now let me go."

"Don't you have something to say to your mom?" I persisted.

He lowered his face. "Sorry, Mom."

"That's better." I slowly released my grip. The smart-ass picked a bad night to rub me the wrong way. My tolerance was threadbare.

Kit squinted, a familiar sign that she was ready to slip into her interrogation gear. "Martha, you said that a vision tipped you off about the devil-dog attack. Is that right?"

"Afraid so. When that damned smoke showed up and those three crooks vanished in it, I knew that my vision was on the mark. I didn't wait for the smoke to disappear before I changed my looks and ordered my doppelgänger out of the closet. If I had waited till the smoke cleared, the killer would've known what I did.

"But what surprised me, though, was that the doppelgänger actually fooled the black-magic sorcerer. Maybe the guy's an amateur."

I drummed my fingers on the counter. "I don't think so. It'd take more than amateur to create a rift in the fabric between our world and the white night."

"The Emerald Zone," Martha corrected me.

Her correction threw me for a loop. *Emerald zone? Was white the new green in supernatural-ville?* I'd heard of that hellish place somewhere in my past, but I never had any idea that the Emerald Zone *was* the white night. Live and burn.

Jared shook his head. "The killer might not be a very powerful sorcerer, so he could've used someone else's magical force to amplify his own weakness."

"How's that possible?" Kit asked.

"Simple. The sorcerer uses *his* magic to suck the energy from another sorcerer —like he was a battery."

"There's another way," Martha chimed in, her Goth face grim.

Jared and I exchanged mystified glances.

"Our killer could've murdered a powerful sorcerer and stolen his powers," Martha offered.

"Yeah, that's a possibility, too," Jared agreed.

I skipped the theorizing and tried to stay focused on the situation. "So you really believe that's what happened, Martha?"

"Maybe, maybe not — but it's something to consider. Let's face it. At the moment, none of us has a clue about who we're dealing with, and until we do, we'll be easy marks."

More good news.

"So what do you think happened to the three would-be thieves?" Kit asked.

I piped up. "I'd bet the farm that they were hijacked by the white . . . I mean the Emerald Zone, and joined the ghostly choir in there."

Goth Girl managed an almost imperceptible grin. "Maybe, but with all that smoke, I couldn't say it was one way or the other for sure."

The air suddenly spun like a micro-burst around us, creating a turbulent rip current that hurled us in every direction. It was déjà vu . . . *all over again.* Like before, we crashed landed in various spots around the shop as several walnut-like objects materialized in mid-air. Slowly, the ominous objects cracked open and gave birth to six floating black cantaloupe-sized orbs before vanishing.

I attempted to speak, but my words warbled and died inches from my mouth, as if I were speaking underwater. "He's broken my chipmunk spell," I shouted, but no one heard me.

The glowing orbs merged like a high school atomic model and began spinning furiously. When the rotating blur stopped, the orbs had formed a *large* black beach-ball-like object. Without warning, it abruptly flattened like someone had deflated it with a nail, and swiftly slipped under the door to the storeroom where Kit's CSI team searched for evidence. Shaken, we managed to stand and regroup at the back door.

"Joe, let's get out of here," Kit implored. "My heart's just about had all the black magic it can handle for one night."

I held up my hand. "Hold on a second." I turned to Martha in her Goth Girl disguise. "Are you positive that you don't know who's behind this?"

"I wish I did," she lamented, and then glanced uneasily up at wall.

The mysterious symbol had returned.

Martha looked worried. "I hope that's our ghostly visitor's idea of a cruel joke."

Kit stared fearfully at the glowing sketch. "Why?"

"So it doesn't mean what I think it does."

Anxiety knitted Kit's brow. "What do you think it means?"

"That *they* are somehow involved, which is about the worst thing I can imagine."

I was getting a bad case of the willies myself. "Who're *they?*"

Martha's good eye thoroughly roamed her shop before answering. I'd never seen her so jumpy.

She finally whispered, "The *Gorgons.*"

16

orgons? Before I could get the words *You're out of your mind* past my lips, spine-chilling screams erupted in the storeroom where the deflated beach-ball object had gone. Kit's CSI team shrieked for help. Their voices were beyond panic. The poor cops pounded frantically on the door, but none opened it. Bodies or body parts bounced hard off the back wall with dull, sickening thuds. Kit reached for the doorknob, but Martha grabbed her arm and pulled her away from the commotion. Blood seeped beneath the closed door and swelled into a surging, dark-red puddle. Then silence. *Dead silence.*

An enormous boom shook the entire building, and Kit fell against the counter. That boom wasn't an explosion. It was something else.

Like Kit, my first reaction was to charge into the storeroom like Sir Lancelot and rescue the CSI team. But now I was pretty sure there was no one left to save. And even if there were, Martha didn't want Kit going back there, and I figured that was a good enough reason for me to stay put, too.

After the boom, a savage bone-rattling roar sent numerous glass jars vibrating off the shelves and crashing on the floor. Dust trickled from the ceiling like Christmas snow, but this was no holiday. It was déjà vu for me. That roar was too damned familiar, and it wasn't a pleasant memory. More like a nightmare.

The Emerald Zone giant demon had returned. Live on our stage.

I had chased off that white bully once tonight, but I wasn't one to press my luck. The damned fiend could have the store—it was insured. It just wasn't getting us.

"Let me go, Martha! I've got to help them," Kit pleaded, coming close to slugging the old woman to escape. "They're my team . . . my family. I can't just stand here and do *nothing.*"

But Martha refused. "They're beyond help now. Don't you hear the silence? They're all dead." Kit finally twisted out of Martha's grip and bolted for the door. "Don't be a fool, dear. Stay away from there."

"I'm going inside, and that's that." She drew her gun and aimed it at me. I just happened to be standing between her and the storeroom entrance. "How about it, Joe? You going to try and stop me, too?"

I shrugged. "You're a big girl. Do what you want. But for what it's worth, Martha's right. They're all dead." I gallantly stepped aside with a sweep of my arm.

The next roar nearly brought the ceiling down. Sawdust and plaster flakes cascaded down on us like a choking blizzard sans the tempest. Another *boom*—a weighty footfall—rattled our teeth and shuddered the old building to its rafters. Jared vaulted the check-out counter like an agile gymnast and sprang out the front door. I didn't know the kid had it in him.

Kit's hand hovered above the doorknob; she apparently was having second thoughts about her rescue plan. Before she made her final decision, a white glowing liquid oozed through the door. Not under or around it, but *through* it, as if the door weren't there! Like door sweat. The ominous substance expanded so fast that it enveloped her hand in the blink of an eye.

"The Emerald Zone!" I hollered, as lightning flashed and exploded on the sidewalk across the street. I saw Jared shriek and dance a little jig as if his pants were on fire.

"Goddammit, somebody help me here!" Kit shouted, dropping her gun and using that hand to try to free her other one from the menacing substance.

Martha hobbled toward Kit, but I warned her away. "Go out front with Jared. We'll be out in a second." At least, that was my plan. Sometimes I was too optimistic.

The milky luminous liquid had absorbed the door, Kit's entire arm, and the back wall—including the glowing symbol. The movie *The Blob* came to mind. There wasn't a second to waste. If that stuff smothered the rest of her body, she was a goner.

I brandished my wand at the swelling evil and earnestly chanted. When the wand was warmed up, I thrust it into the white ooze at the point where it held my on-again, off-again lover.

As I waited for my spell to do its thing, gusty invisible breaths rustled our hair. The giant was close. Too damned close. I mentally kicked my spell into high gear and launched a potent wedge of black light into the center of the ooze, like I had beneath the Mansion Macabre. The big guy bellowed in severe pain and retreated from the toxic darkness in two long flatfooted steps.

My dark light opened a narrow chasm in the ooze covering Kit's arm, and I hurriedly pulled it out. There was a loud sucking sound, which I considered appropriate for a substance that sucked in the first place. I stuffed Kit under my arm like a rolled-up newspaper and ran out the door into the night. *The dark night.*

The jittery Jared and his Rock of Gibraltar mother met us outside the front door and took Kit from me. Her eyes stared blankly straight ahead. Martha said that they'd take her to a tearoom a few doors down where she'd receive magical, not medical treatment. Relieved, I promised I'd be right down after tidying up a few loose ends.

First, I warned the cops away from the shop, claiming that it might explode any minute. I knew they wouldn't believe my story about the advancing Emerald Zone. I also advised them to call in the SWAT team for back-up; more trouble was on its way.

When I finished with the cops, I felt real uneasy about being seen in a dainty little tearoom. My image would take a hit for years. After my grueling day, what I really needed was a pitcher of beer with a few whiskey chasers. Not a tea bag and hot water.

Stay cool, Joe, I told myself. *You can do this. Just sit way in the back behind a potted fern where no passers-by could possibly see you.*

I trudged down the sidewalk like a doomed man toward the hoity-toity tearoom. When I got there, I stalled my entrance by checking out the flowery sign. I exhaled sharply and stepped in. *Goodbye, alcohol relief. Hello, tedium.*

17

The SWAT van skidded to a screeching stop in front of Martha's place and blocked Pine Street. I saw them and stepped back outside. Their arrival was my governor's pardon. I had escaped a fate worse than death: tea. The black-garbed SWAT cops leaped out the back doors, and four of them jogged toward me. *Now what?* I knew their leader, and he and I got along all right. Sergeant Moses hailed me.

"What's up?" I asked, shaking his hand.

He wanted me to describe what had gone down inside Martha's shop, because he didn't trust anyone else's account. I was flattered.

My gaze wandered inside the tearoom. My three comrades were nowhere to be seen, which I took as a good sign. Kit was hopefully in the back receiving magical help as I spoke. I turned back to the sergeant and gave him my edited version of the events.

"Who ambushed the CSI team?" Moses pressed.

"I honestly don't know. The back door was blocked from the inside, so I didn't see anyone."

Sergeant Moses was baffled. "How's that possible? You said you were back there earlier."

"I was, but whoever attacked your people must've blocked it from their side so we couldn't interfere."

"Where's Lieutenant Wilson?"

"She's been taken to the hospital," I lied. "I'm not sure which one."

He curled his lip. "What happened to her?"

"She got hurt at *Ghostworld* and didn't tell me. She fainted inside the shop, and after I saw fresh blood on the back of her shirt, Martha and her son drove her to the hospital." If my story got back to Diaz, he couldn't be too upset about her absence. But then again . . . .

The sergeant got a call over his radio and stepped away to take it. When he returned, he said, "My men can't break into the storeroom, either, and they tried both entrances."

Another SWAT team cop ran up to us. "Sergeant, the radios don't work."

"What the fuck are you talking about? I just used it a few seconds ago," Moses bellowed, then tried his own shoulder-mounted radio again, but it was dead now, too. I suspected the killer sorcerer didn't want any more interference with the next act of his murderous production, so he knocked out all police communications.

A white flash from inside Martha's shop lit up Pine Street like high noon. The Emerald Zone oozed through the windows and door, gobbling up real estate like there was no tomorrow. My muscles knotted. *Who was it after? Martha, Kit, me, or all three?*

The cops beside me gasped at the strange glow but stood their ground. The shouting detectives hanging around the shop beat a quick retreat across the street. Their hysteria was contagious and infected the three who came with Moses. Only the sergeant remained impervious to the rampant fear. He was about to levy an ass-chewing to his three subordinates when the cops down the street started shooting into the light.

"Dammit!" Moses hissed. "C'mon, you pussies, let's get down there before the street beaters shoot themselves." They didn't move. "Now!" he shouted so loudly that even the detectives stopped firing.

The sarge and his guys warily approached the Emerald Zone where it had camped in front of Martha's place, and I shook my head. I knew where this was going. Been there—done that. Their plan to attack the light would only end horribly. They'd be flattened by the invisible hellion. SWAT pancakes.

Damn! I was the only one who could protect them, but I wasn't happy about it. I'd escaped the white night twice tonight, but the third time might be the charm—for the Emerald Zone.

Some days it didn't pay to get out of bed.

A sudden roar silenced the shooting, blowing out the shop windows and propelling Sergeant Moses and his small group into the street. Their whirling bodies crumpled against the police cruisers like Humpty-Dumpty's, despite their Kevlar vests. They lay still. The others ducked into a shadowy alcove, where they plucked glass shards from their bloodied uniforms and lacerated faces.

The Emerald Zone began creeping forward again like an ominous sea fog, whiting out our dimension as it moved toward me. The tearoom. And my friends.

The concrete quaked and cracked from the giant's unseen footfalls. I had a sneaking suspicion that the approaching giant might somehow have armored himself against my black wand ray, so I beefed up my defense. I conjured a massive searchlight like businesses rent for grand openings and strategically positioned it on the sidewalk between me and the zone. I was confident that it would knock the big guy for a loop and quickly end tonight's madness, so I could go home and catch some Zs.

The searchlight flickered to life and shot its broad black beam into the whiteness that diffused its edges and outlined the demon. It was time to lay some serious hurt on the murderous bully.

But the dark beam proved ineffective this time. My worst fears were realized. Both the Emerald Zone and the giant continued to advance. There were no agonizing bellows and retreating footfalls. My confidence waned at this monumental setback. *How could I possibly defend myself against such overwhelming odds?*

Worried, I retreated a few steps, but the Emerald Zone followed like an alabaster predator. Its forward movement quickened, camouflaging the giant's hostile white hand until it burst into our night. The sinewy fingers curled into a wrecking ball and pummeled the magic searchlight into sparkling dust.

I shielded my face from the fine debris as my failsafe wolfen genes instinctively exerted their predatory dominance and kick-started my physical change.

Were they nuts?

The demon would pulverize me. Tear me to hairy shreds.

I tried to stay calm, but it was tough. I managed to keep pace with the white night's relentless pursuit, while I endured my painful werewolf transformation. Normally I could walk and chew gum at the same time, but my backward steps failed me when my heel snagged a raised sidewalk block. I fought to maintain my balance like a flailing tightrope walker , but gravity won, pulling me down with a thud onto the concrete. Despite my wolfen strength, I felt like I'd taken a tumble onto a bed of nails.

To add insult to injury, the white giant's fist appeared directly above my prone body, poised to smash me into a threadbare wolfskin rug.

I got in one mournful howl before that wrecking ball descended with the speed and silence of an avalanche.

18

My werewolf reflexes were much quicker than my human ones. I rolled away from the crushing blow and hopped onto its plunging wrist. The ground shook as the fist mashed the sidewalk and sank another two feet into the sand below before stopping, but I miraculously held on during the impact. I came within a whisker of being half the man I used to be.

I was a werewolf now, prone to violence and primitive thinking. Instinct trumped reason. I growled savagely at the giant while feverishly slashing at a single area on the thick wrist. Its white blood spewed over my mahogany fur from a severed artery, and its delicious scent boosted my primal brutality and spurred me on to greater fury. But I wasn't ready to claim victory yet, because I hadn't reached my ultimate goal. Kill the son-of-a-bitch.

Its other hand emerged from the brilliance, and King Kong punched me with a single finger. Momentarily dazed, I managed to hold on with my sharp claws. An entire galaxy of stars appeared in my head, as if I were the Hubble telescope, and my weakened body sagged beneath its thumb. The giant's wounded fist was still embedded in the ground, and although the demon attempted to free it by pulling and twisting, it only weakened his crippled wrist. That bleeding fist was going nowhere fast.

My hybrid animal mind recovered quickly, which was a good thing. After ditching my internalized galaxy, I glanced up and saw the giant's other hand headed toward my exposed head, with murder written all over it. This time it was no finger punch. My dilemma had just escalated to a four-alarm emergency—one for each knuckle of its plunging hand.

I ducked beneath the creature's trapped wrist and missed the blow, but the sidewalk didn't. More of it was pulverized to dust and gravel. With a quick slash, I opened up a nasty gash in the demon's other wrist, and the creature yanked it back with an ear-popping yowl. I dropped a few feet as the giant finally tugged his first fist free, and more concrete fragments flew everywhere, imploding the Well's Florist display window beside us.

I couldn't see its featureless face in the light to get an idea of what it was going to do next, so I packed up my attitude and bounded down the sidewalk. I'd had enough.

But the injured giant didn't agree. Wailing in torment, it staggered after me, anger pulsating from the white night like an emotional beacon. I crossed the street to lead it away from the tearoom and my friends, but my change of direction appeared to stump the big guy. It remained motionless in Pine Street, uncertain of which way to go.

I growled and snapped at it, charged and retreated, trying to get it to resume its pursuit, but the damned thing just stood there outlined in the bright light like a petrified tree. My theatrics were getting me nowhere, so I rolled the dice. Crouching on all fours, I slowly stalked it, preparing to attack the demon in its own backyard—the Emerald Zone. *Risky?* Yes. *Suicidal?* I hoped not. But I couldn't let the giant demolish the tearoom where my friends were tending to Kit, without doing my best to protect them.

I moved within *fifteen feet* of the white night's boundary, and there was still no movement from the giant. *Ten feet away*. It didn't budge. *Five feet*. Saliva splashed over my fangs in anticipation of the attack (a revolting wolfen habit). *Two feet*. The point of no return, but the giant's immobility persisted.

Suddenly, its hand emerged from the Emerald Zone and lashed out at me. I was quick, but that hand covered a lot of real estate and was impossible to dodge. The hand scooped me into the air as the fingers curled tightly around me and sealed out all light. I found myself trapped in a living, breathing dungeon.

The tree-trunk fingers closed in, squeezing me into a fetal position. I clawed at the hairless flesh of its palm, and white blood spilled out and splashed over me like the Canadian Niagara Falls. In my limited space, I started choking as I gasped for air.

And still the damned fingers closed.

Weakened, my clawed hands fell limply away. I was dying. Choking on its thick, disgusting blood.

A muted thunderclap struck nearby and shook the giant demon.

For an instant, it lost its balance and tottered, but it rapidly regained its stability and continued its slow, tortuous kill. During that instant, I peered out from the sliver of space between two of its fingers and witnessed a faint flicker, followed by a serrated black lightning bolt. I felt it strike my captor inside its home base. With an excruciating bellow, it withdrew its hands from our night into the Emerald Zone, dumping me from its grasp in the process. I fell two stories, but I managed to land safely on my feet. All four werewolf feet.

I high-tailed it down an alley, morphed back to my human form, and backtracked to my Explorer where a fresh change of clothes awaited my nakedness. When I glanced down the street at Martha's place, the white night was gone, along with the demon bully.

The cops were slow to react, conflicted from what they'd witnessed and their dogged disbelief in the supernatural. Martha's stretch of Pine Street resembled a war zone in a third-world country, but even that didn't motivate the SWAT team to action. They were reduced to mindless zombies seeking any truth other than the one they'd just experienced.

I wasn't about to help them. I slipped past Martha's shop in front of the cops' shell-shocked gazes and continued down the glass-littered sidewalk to the tearoom. This time, I didn't hesitate to enter. Any beverage tasted better than demon blood. Even . . . *God help me* . . . tea.

I glanced back at the clearing sky and wondered who'd conjured that black lightning bolt that had saved my bacon. Like my father used to say, "Don't look a gift horse in the mouth." So, instead of driving myself crazy hashing and rehashing the mystery in search of an answer, I decided to follow his advice.

And relax with a spot of hot tea.

19

I paused beneath the tinkling bell and scoured Maya's Tearoom for my friends, but there was still no sign of them. I advanced to the center of the place and scoped it out.

Yellow-flowered linen tablecloths and matching napkins draped the wicker tables set with dainty cups and saucers, tiny spoons and forks, and a slender leaded-glass vases sprouting single yellow roses. There wasn't a frosted beer mug in sight.

South American water colors portraying exotic rainforest plants, tropical villas enveloped by white verandas, and reddish-orange jungle sunsets adorned the quaint restaurant's bamboo walls. A vine-smothered lattice fronted the cash-out/take-out counter, and two back exits were framed in the back wall—one doorway was masked by a black velvet curtain embroidered with half moons and pentagrams, and the other by a sturdy oak door. I guessed my friends were hidden beyond one of them, but which one?

"You must be Joe," a sultry feminine voice remarked behind me.

I swung around and confronted the woman. An alluring, raven-haired lady in her late thirties stood there, decked out in a strapless orchid-pattern dress that seemed appropriate for the tropical-themed restaurant.

"Who are you?" I demanded, my left hand drifting toward my wand.

She smiled. "You won't need your wand," she said. Her deep sable eyes never wavered from me. "Your friends are in the back room."

I pointed at the two doors. "Which one'll get me to the back room?"

When I returned my gaze to her, she was gone. Poof! What a creepy chick. *What other magical surprises awaited me here?*

My animalistic side screamed danger, so I rechecked the interior, but found nothing to fear . . . except for the endless rows of teas. The lights suddenly dimmed to candle brightness, and the hackles rose on my neck. This restaurant would be a perfect fit for *Ghostworld*.

I crept stealthily to the back, wary of yet another Emerald Zone ambush. My sensitive wolfen ears and nose probed the doorways for the sounds and scents of my friends. I alternately inspected one opening, then the other, until I zeroed in on Kit's familiar scent and Jared's muffled voice.

I pushed through the mystical velvet curtain, descended four steps, and wandered into a rainforest-motif banquet hall. It looked so real that I got the distinct impression that I actually was in South America, and not a quaint tearoom in downtown Orlando.

Martha, Kit, Jared, and a brunette woman with her face buried in her cradled arms occupied one of the tables. As I approached, I noticed Kit's pasty complexion and the faraway sleepwalking glaze coating her eyes. Her eye sockets were sunken and accentuated by purplish-black bags, and her cheeks were cadaver craters.

A large porcelain bowl, filled to the top with steaming water, sat in front of Martha, still sporting her Goth Girl disguise; Jared stared into it like he was reading a book. Martha glanced up and nodded at me.

"Did you chase that monster off?"

"You could say that," I replied. There was an emptiness in the pit of my stomach from Kit's zombie appearance.

Martha patted the seat beside her. "Sit down and look into the water."

The scalding water bowl trick was as old as the hills. We were about to glimpse a remote place. I gestured at the brunette. "Who's she?"

"Just never you mind. Keep your eyes on the water," she directed.

She chanted and waved her hands over the bowl, and the steamy surface changed to ice. I watched as a vivid picture of her shop's backroom appeared in the frost. My jaw dropped two feet. The place was neat as a pin. The grisly devil-dog remains were gone, as well as those of the slaughtered OPD crime scene investigators. It must have all been swept away into the Emerald Zone, leaving OPD with a murder mystery that would remain a cold case forever. Diaz would be beside himself, but he'd get over it.

"I figured as much," she lamented.

I leaned back. "Is that image in real time?"

"What'd you expect?" Jared chimed in. "A look into the future?"

I refused to be drawn into another heated exchange. For one thing, I was exhausted. For another, I was concerned for Kit. "What's the matter with her?"

Martha's expression saddened. "I'm afraid Kit's contact with the Emerald Zone seems to have wiped her memory as clean as my back room."

The news stabbed me through the heart. "Her mind's blank?"

The raven-haired witchy owner of the place popped into the room carrying a tray of small teapots and a single china cup. "Don't worry, Joe. My teas will bring her back to us. You must have patience."

"And who exactly *are* you?" I inquired suspiciously.

"Maya, of course. This is my restaurant," she retorted, as if that fact were common knowledge to all the male beer drinkers in Orlando.

Martha patted my hand. "This might take quite a while, so why don't you skedaddle home and get some sleep. I'll call you the minute she's back to her normal feisty self."

"You sure I can't help?"

"You'll be more of a hindrance than a help," Maya added, without Martha's tact. "Go home. Come back when Kit's better."

I pushed away from the table. "If you're sure that I . . . ."

"We're sure," Martha and Maya spoke up simultaneously.

There was one question that had been nagging me. "Why was the white night named the Emerald Zone?" I asked Martha. "I mean, it's not green."

Martha chuckled. "Its nickname was inspired by the movie *The Wizard of Oz*."

I scratched my head and stifled a yawn. "I don't see the connection."

"The magical Emerald City," Martha continued, "with its notorious wizard."

"Weird logic." I wrung my battle-weary hands. "And another thing . . . ."

"Yes?"

"You wouldn't have any idea who conjured the black lightning bolt awhile ago that collapsed the Emerald Zone, would you?"

Martha guffawed. "I shore do. You're lookin' at her."

"I had a hunch you were the one. Thanks for looking after me." I glanced at Kit and the unidentified brunette again and left the room. "Good night."

I couldn't get away from Pine Street fast enough. I was about ready to drop. I nearly fell asleep at the wheel twice on the way home, but each time I pictured Kit's wan expression, and it shocked me awake.

I punched in an XM radio oldies station and sang along to one of my favorite songs, *Bad to the Bone*. My singing was off key, but I made up for it by singing louder. My fingers tapped to the blaring drumbeat, and that helped me stay alert, too.

So far, the entire night had been one maddening nightmare. My role at the grand opening hadn't exactly gone according to script, and to add insult to injury, that hideous ghostly fiend forced me to undertake a seriously dangerous investigation.

And now I chalked up another addition to that sinister list. Someone was watching me. I sensed it to my core.

I shuddered to think what tomorrow might bring.

Hopefully not Martha's mysterious *Gorgons*.

20

The late-night air was thick with humidity and fog. I cruised warily along the two-lane blacktop road leading east to Osteen, a stone's throw from my farm. The Explorer's headlights barely dented the proverbial pea soup, so what I'd hoped would be a cushy trip back home turned into a daunting drive. I boosted my wolfen sight and plowed ahead.

A large hazy splotch appeared out of nowhere in front of me, and I tromped the brake pedal, sending the SUV into a screeching slide. I spun the steering wheel sharply left to keep it from slipping into one of Volusia County's mile-deep drainage ditches. With a whiplash jolt, the Explorer stopped inches from the shadowy gully. *What in hell was in the middle of the damned road? Another friggin' ambush?*

My heart jumped into my throat at the near miss, and my fatigue was history. I was fully awake now, and ticked off at my rotten luck. I powered down the side window and squinted into the cottony curtain shrouding the low rural region, but the indistinct shape was gone. My irritation dissolved to vigilance. I smelled a trap and quickly raised the window.

A cold sweat seeped through my pores, drenching me in seconds. Eighty-eight degrees and one hundred percent humidity did that to Floridians from even the slightest exposure. I mopped my brow and fought my rising paranoia. Something was out there, and it wasn't a coincidence that it blocked my side of the road. It was planned.

The obscure stain in the fog reappeared, and the closer it drifted—not walked— toward me, the more it looked like a swarm of bees. *Bees? Out here in the middle of the night?* I reached for my wand and reflexively shielded my face as they were about to crash into the windshield. *Was the Ghostworld murderer trying to kill me again?*

But there was no collision. I sat there frozen to the spot as the swarm *passed through* the glass on the passenger side and slowly materialized into a . . . woman! *What kind of black magic was that?* Finally, I stirred from my trance and tilted my protective magic ring at the still-forming apparition, wracking my addled brain for a counter spell.

When the woman was fully shaped, I pinched my forearm to check if I was dreaming, but the prick of pain told me I wasn't. The person seated beside me was an impossibility.

The woman was none other than Gwendolyn Stockard . . . *with her head intact.*

"Hey, don't point that ring at me," she blustered, staring at the windshield. Her hands fastidiously pressed several wrinkles from the dress she'd worn at the *Ghostworld* grand opening ceremony. Her cleavage still bulged from her plunging neckline, and despite her incredible entrance, it still excited me. *What could I say in my defense?* I was part wolf, after all.

"But . . . but . . ." I sputtered like a babbling idiot, but I refused to drop my ring defense until I understood what this was all about. Supernatural logic dictated that my passenger was a demon disguised as the deceased Gwendolyn Stockard.

She laughed. "Pull yourself together, Joe. I'm not here to hurt you," she said between chuckles. "I'm here to warn you."

"Warn me?" I said, still stunned by her presence. *I watched her die, didn't I?*

"You seem really surprised to see me."

"Of course I'm surprised!" I nearly shouted. "I saw your head explode and kill your dad in the process."

"That *was* gross."

"Of course it was. Do you have any idea who killed you?"

She shrugged. "I don't have, like, a clue. But you know, I don't *feel* dead."

Didn't feel dead? Remind me never to come back as a ghost. "Is that a fact?" I didn't believe her. She *had* to know who killed her. She was covering up for someone.

"Poor Father." There wasn't an ounce of remorse in her declaration. Pure chill.

"There's sincerity if I ever heard it," I stated sarcastically.

She finally turned and faced me. "He was a terrible father, but it wasn't my intension to kill him." She paused thoughtfully. "And it wasn't my intention to die in the process, either."

"And yet you're sitting here in my car, seemingly alive. How's that possible?"

"Powerful magic."

"Whose?"

She grinned. "That's for me to know and you to find out."

I felt like I was conversing with a smart-ass middle-school kid. Enough with the frigging games. "Are you a ghost?" I asked point blank.

"No."

"Then how do you explain your being here?"

"I guess somebody snatched my soul seconds before I died and let me watch my head blow up. After that, like, nasty sight, I was flown away to a place where it's dark all time. All I can hear is, like, one voice. A woman's voice."

"And she told you to visit me tonight?"

Gwendolyn bobbed her head.

"And told you to warn me?"

"Well yeah, or I wouldn't be here, 'cause I don't even know who the hell you are," she snapped.

"Are you in the habit of taking orders from strangers?"

"Don't be a shit. Of course not. You know, I don't like you very much."

Big deal. I wasn't in the market for any new ghost friends. "So if that female voice ordered you to make love to me right now, you'd do it?"

"Not on your life!" Gwendolyn retorted, but her face crinkled with uncertainty.

Whoever had magically grabbed her soul was pulling her strings, and I was curious to see how her handler directed her to respond to my baited statement. I exhaled heavily.

"All right, warn me and then beat it. I need some goddamned sleep."

"You're pretty ungrateful," she huffed. "I came here to warn you as a favor."

"Favors always have strings attached, as far as I'm concerned, you can forget the warning and hit the road," I sputtered, anxious to find out how her boss reacted.

Gwendolyn's eyes rolled back to white as she contemplated her response. After a long moment, her brown eyes returned. "My warning comes with no strings attached. I don't want you to investigate my murder. It's too dangerous, and you'll only get, like, involved in things that don't concern you. Trust me, you don't want to end up in the middle of this. Your magic isn't strong enough to protect you from my murderer."

I bit my lip thoughtfully. I had to know more. "Like the *Gorgons?*"

A flash of recognition blazed, then died in her eyes, while her expression remained impassive. "Are you like referring to the mythological women with snakes for hair?"

"No."

"Then I'm afraid I've never heard of anyone else with that name."

She was lying, but I couldn't prove it. I just *knew.*

"All right, you've delivered your message. I'll give it some serious thought." Of course, there was no way that I was quitting this case. I didn't want to be cursed for life, and the *Ghostworld* murderer had already targeted me as another one of his victims—two very good reasons to stay the course.

Gwendolyn reached for my ring hand, and before I could yank it away, she grabbed it. Physically *grabbed* it! My blood ran cold. *How could this ghost be physical?*

"Goodbye, Joe."

With that, Gwendolyn dispersed into a bee-like swarm and escaped through the windshield again, leaving me wide-eyed and terrified. The girl had actually touched my skin. *What kind of black magic allowed spirits to make physical contact with the living?*

I sat staring at the swirling fog where the swarm had vanished, pondering my frightening experience, when blinding lights appeared behind the Explorer. Several shadowy figures leaped out.

A low wolfen growl rumbled in my chest.

What now?

21

My uninvited guests surrounded the SUV before I had the chance to mull over the phantom Gwendolyn's warning. I fully expected these highwaymen to be more challenging than Shorty, Lenny, and Pug had been in *Ghostworld*, so I was close to changing into a werewolf once again. This was getting old. And so was the night.

Several fuzzy figures strode up to my door as I stepped from the car. I wasn't going to be trapped inside when the fireworks started.

But it turned out there weren't going to be any fireworks.

"What's up guys?" I asked the teenage boy standing closest to me.

"Hi, Mr. L," he hailed. "We saw your SUV angle parked across the road, and we sorta figured you might have some kind of emergency, like a flat tire."

I recognized the voice rather than his fog-smothered face. The Good Samaritan was Jason Hollinsworth. His dad, John, rented and farmed the southeast corner of my forty acres, charmingly referred to as Moccasin Wallow. That little piece of hell was eight acres of mucky swamp; John grew celery and radishes there. I never set foot in that gloomy cesspool, because it was crawling with mean-tempered water moccasins that would love to sink their poisonous fangs into yours truly. They didn't bother John, though, which was pretty embarrassing for me when we discussed his crops.

"Actually the old rust bucket's fine, Jason, but thanks for stopping," I smiled, relieved that these teenage joy riders weren't a bunch of nasties getting paid to take me out. To be quite honest, Gwendolyn's bizarre visit fried what little was left of my composure, putting me at a disadvantage if I'd had to fight them off.

Jason cocked his head as if he didn't buy my story. I looked at the way the Explorer was parked across the road. Hell, I wouldn't have believed me, either. He probably thought that I'd had a few too many drinks down at the Wolfsbane. I was about to reassure him, but he figured it out on his own. "Okay, Mr. L. See ya 'round."

"Wait a minute," I said. "Are you guys planning a few Halloween pranks this weekend?"

The boys laughed in unison. That sealed it.

"You never can tell," Jason replied, tongue-in-cheek.

"If my house gets egged, I'll know who to come after," I threatened in mock-seriousness.

"You don't have to worry. My dad would kill me if I did anything to your farm."

I wished that he'd sounded happier about his dad's decree. "Well — have fun, guys, but drive carefully in this fog. I don't want to read about you in tomorrow's newspaper."

"Will do."

"Thanks again."

The boys piled into Jason's lifted Ford 250 pick-up and roared past me down the road. So much for being cautious. After I headed for home again, I chuckled at the pranks my sister and I had played on Halloween. Eggs. Smashed pumpkins. Soapy screens. Ahhh, the good old days.

My housekeeper, Tillie, left all the lights burning in and around my country home, and the welcoming beacons pierced the eerie fog and marked safe harbor for me like a friendly lighthouse. Behind all that fog, my two-story wood-frame farmhouse was ornately trimmed, and had four gabled roofs and numerous porch posts that extended around the front three-quarters of the first floor. That generous porch added a homey touch to the century-and-a-half-old house's exterior.

Home had never looked so inviting, even though I could see only its lights.

The sturdy iron gate spanning the road entrance slid back silently as I drove past. Without much guidance from me, the Explorer clung to the driveway's contours and braked in front of my capacious barn.

I pressed the remote on my visor, and a pair of steel-reinforced doors swung away to reveal the yawning entry to what was cleverly disguised as a ramshackle outbuilding. Never judge a book by its cover. The barn was heavily fortified with bulletproof and fireproof walls that protected it from a human invasion. I conjured an invisible shield to provide further protection against supernatural enemies. Thanks to Uncle Sam and

Uncle Jess, the barn was stocked with beyond-sophisticated electronics and communication gadgets every bit as good as the FBI's equipment.

I parked the rank worm-mottled Explorer in its usual inside space, but before getting out, I cleaned the Explorer with magic. Even the rust sparkled—for now.

The barn was sectioned off into two areas. My office, a shower and dressing room, a furnished living room, and my state-of-the-art magic workshop shared the space with the Explorer. The windowless half was the black side and could be accessed only by magic—*my* magic. Sort of a one-person combination lock. I was too tired to check on my pride and joy stored in the black half of the barn. It was time to hit the feathers.

I locked up and tramped through the pesky fog toward the back of the farmhouse. My eyelids were lead-weighted and my mind was downy-dense. I was halfway to the promised land when I collided with a fog-cloaked car in the driveway. I swore vigorously and checked out the model. Chevy Yukon. Black. Government. I was steamed. A painful throbbing nearly immobilized my kneecaps where they had smacked the bumper. I bent and briskly massaged them. *Wouldn't I ever get any damned sleep tonight?*

I cautiously circled around the ghost ship of a car and limped hell-bent-for-leather like Super Gimp toward the house. My visitor was either FBI or CIA. I groaned. Or worse . . . my uncle's Department of Supernatural Investigations.

The welcoming glow of the burning lights faded, along with its aura of hominess. Now it held all the warmth of a concrete Washington DC office building.

What I desperately needed was a Holiday Inn.

22

The café curtains drawn across the kitchen window diffused the light and created a dull sunspot in the fog. As I climbed the back steps, I watched a pair of muzzy silhouettes chat and gesture like ill-formed apparitions. One of them was Tillie. My anxiety subsided. She was an intuitive ghost who was a great judge of character . . . after she died a hundred and fifty years ago. During Tillie's life, her human insight had been iffy at best—how else could she explain her ready capture and neck-tie execution for being a witch? Her list of pre-death boyfriends had been terribly questionable, too.

Since my late-night visitor had been admitted, then he or she couldn't mean us any harm, because I'd cast a protective spell over the farmhouse, like I did with the barn. Any malevolent intruder would be instantly disintegrated on the spot. It hadn't failed me yet, but I now had my doubts. My magical *Ghostworld* adversary was extremely powerful.

My irritation escalated a notch into an incensed mode. If this wasn't an emergency, and it sure didn't look like one by the way the two women were gabbing away, then why didn't the government wait until morning to send someone out here? When I stepped inside, Tillie was babbling with a woman I'd never seen before beside the kitchen sink. Our visitor held one of my UCF football team mugs filled with steaming coffee. A holstered 9mm semi-automatic lay on the kitchen table's glass top.

When Tillie saw me open the door, she smiled and excused herself from the room. The woman turned to me after Tillie scooted into the front living room.

"You must be Joe," the stranger greeted me with a voice that was silk-edged and amazingly strong. She was slender, tanned, and fiery with round cocoa eyes that sized me up as she spoke.

"Do I know you?" I asked, trying to place the face, and failing. She appeared to be in her late twenties, and although she was attractive, I sensed storm clouds, not seduction, lurking inside those piercing eyes.

She smoothed her pixie-cut, jet-black hair. "Look, we both know we've never met before, so let's dispense with the chit-chat," she stated bluntly. "My name's Dana Drake." She offered her hand.

I admired her sturdy grip. She certainly wasn't a prairie flower.

I settled into a chair at the table. I motioned for her to join me. "Who do you work for?"

She sat next to her holstered gun. "Your uncle. I imagine you're wondering why he sent me out here."

"It's crossed my mind."

She shifted uneasily. "I gather that he didn't bother to tell you that I was coming."

"You might say that, but to give him the benefit of the doubt, I've been unavailable all night in case he tried." Which I seriously doubted. "Look, uh . . . ."

"Dana."

"Right. Sorry. Look, Dana, I went past dog-tired a couple hours ago, and I'd rather continue our meeting in the morning when I can actually think."

"It *is* morning."

I threw her a withering glance and stood. "This conversation's over. I take it that you're planning to stay here tonight?"

"That was the plan, but if you'd rather that I find a motel . . . ."

"Yes, I'd rather you did, but it's too foggy tonight to be out there hunting for places to stay. You can sleep in the downstairs guestroom."

"Thank you," she said, but there wasn't much gratitude attached to those two words. She was typical DSI. Arrogant . . . and irritating. I nearly changed my mind about staying.

Tillie motioned for me to join her in the living room, so I bid Dana good night with a quick nod and limped into the front of the house. My knees still hurt like hell, but my wolfen system would soon mend them, hopefully before I hit the sack.

A fire roared in the fireplace, burning away the humidity and making the place homey again.

"Thanks for letting Dana stay tonight." Tillie was forever the eavesdropper.

I sighed and brushed off her compliment. "I just didn't want Uncle

Jess blaming me if anything happened to her."

Tillie harrumphed. "You're too modest . . . and too tired. Get some sleep, and I'll see to our guest."

"Sounds like a plan." I would've kissed her cheek, but she had returned to her ethereal form. Which immediately reminded me of Gwendolyn Stockard's bone-chilling touch in my car. Suddenly, I found myself surrounded by the dead, though that was far better than being surrounded by the *undead*.

"I don't want what's-her-name anywhere near me until I've showered, shaved, and checked her out with Uncle Jess."

She chuckled. "I understand. Sleep in for a change and forget about getting up with the chickens . . . or at least wait until the cluckers are in the oven," she quipped.

I smiled, but couldn't quite muster an all-out laugh. "Good night, Tillie. You're the best."

I don't remember stripping off my clothes before my head plowed the inviting pillow, a stone's throw from Dreamland. The last images that played through my mind were Gwendolyn's outrageous behavior inside the Explorer, and an imagined glimpse of Dana Drake's naked body. An intriguing blend of human curiosity and wolfen fantasy.

Moments later, the ponderous forty-winks mantle snuffed out both.

23

I awoke with a start from a corker of a nightmare. Metal-winged creatures with snakes for hair chased me through downtown Orlando, but I didn't know how it ended. The morning sun spilled through my bedroom window and bailed me out.

I rubbed the crusty sleep from my eyes, jumped in the shower, shaved, and slipped into a pair of khaki cargo shorts, a green Polo shirt, and a pair of white New Balance running shoes. It was time to meet with my uninvited guest and find out what the hell she wanted.

My satellite phone rang before I could escape the bedroom, and I immediately recognized the caller—the bane of my existence, Uncle Jess Luna.

I snatched the irritating instrument on the first ring and greeted him coldly.

"Scramble," I snapped. I activated my own scramble button on the phone while Uncle Jess did the same.

"Why the secrecy?" he sputtered, unused to taking orders.

"A stranger spent the night . . . *downstairs*," I added before he jumped all over that provocative statement.

"Dana Drake?"

So he did send her to see me. "That's what she said."

"Medium height, thin, black hair, and scrappy?"

"Yeah, that's her," I replied. "So why'd you sic her on *me?*"

"Because you can use some back-up on that *Ghostworld* case you volunteered for. From what I've heard, she's perfect for the job."

"So you heard about my accepting that case already. Bad news sure travels fast," I grumbled. "What's so special about Drake?"

Uncle Jess was speechless for several moments, a new world record for him.

"She's a contractor, like you, and comes highly recommended. The guy who referred her swore up and down that she could handle herself . . . and then some."

It sounded like she didn't work for DSI. "Is Drake a werewolf?"

"You'll find out when the time comes. I don't want to ruin the surprise."

Oh, great. Just what I needed—another bombshell.

"I received a preliminary report on the *Ghostworld* incidents from my agents in Orlando, but I'd like to hear your side," he said, avoiding further discussion about Dana Drake.

I ran my fingers through my damp hair and related the *Ghostworld* events in chronological order. The narration took awhile, and for once he listened with minimal interruptions. When I finished, he reflected on my report.

Uncle Jess cleared his throat. "This morning Senator Kane demanded an official investigation into the mansion ride's dangerous mechanical defect, citing his concern for public safety."

"Of course," I interjected sarcastically.

"Furthermore, Kane's insisting that the FBI investigate Gwendolyn Stockard's unusual death."

"What a congressional blowhard," I grumbled. "He's stumping for the undecided votes in his tight re-election race."

"That's about the size of it. His hot air will inflate headlines right up until next week's vote. If he wins, he'll drop the *Ghostworld* issue like a hot potato."

"Yeah. You know, someone tried to kill Martha Gibbons last night."

"I know. She phoned me this morning and told me. She also wanted me to call Hank Diaz and tell him that Kit Wilson's taking an extended official leave of absence. Seems she's working for DSI now." He chuckled. "Hopefully not for long."

"She's in pretty bad shape," I added. "It might be longer than you think."

"I'll make sure she gets as much time as she needs to recuperate. Martha's working to bring her back now, and that certainly gives us hope."

Uncle Jess was showing a softer side, one that I've never seen before. I wondered what got into him.

He continued. "I sent a team over to Maya's Teahouse, where Martha said they were hiding out until you track down that rogue sorcerer. I don't have anyone like him on our books here in DC, so he must be way underground. Hold on a minute, I have another call coming in."

When he came back on the line, his easy-going manner vanished. "Dammit, Joe, my men just reported from that teahouse and told me that there was no sign of Martha or Kit. They searched the entire place. Even the Maya woman seems to be conveniently out of town."

My empty stomach somersaulted a few times. "They were there last night. I saw them myself in the banquet room out back." I was suddenly anxious about both women.

"I'm looking at the recon photos as we speak, and there's no banquet room in the back of the place."

I slumped on the bed. "When I was there, I got the feeling the place really was in South America. And, that Maya woman's a witch. You don't suppose . . ."

"That's she in cahoots with the *Ghostworld* murderer? It could be. Or maybe Martha conjured them away to a safer location."

Uncle Jess was grasping at straws. "No — I don't think she would do that without letting one of us know. Even if Martha didn't tell us their exact location, she'd let us know they were in hiding, so we wouldn't worry or waste valuable time looking for them."

"I suppose you're right. She's in trouble."

"There's one other thing I forgot to mention that might or might not have anything to do with their sudden disappearance."

"Shoot."

I described my run-in with the ghostly figure and its drawing on the wall. "Martha thought the sketch symbolized the *Gorgons*, whoever they are." An electric tension zapped me across our connection.

"Oh, God! This is worse than I thought. Martha didn't mention them. Anything else you didn't tell me?" he asked, redirecting the subject from the *Gorgons*.

"Yeah. Gwendolyn Stockard showed up in my car on the way home last night, head and all."

More electric silence.

"Don't leave out a single thing, you hear?" Uncle Jess was back to his typically gruff self again.

I detailed my entire encounter.

"This is bad. Real bad," he muttered. "I should take you off the case. There's powerful magic involved here—more than you can handle, I'm afraid."

"You know damned well that I can take care of my self!" I argued.

"So far, yes, but it'd be better to let more experienced agents handle it."

I slammed a fist into the mattress. "I gave my word, and now that Kit and Martha have vanished, I'm even more determined to find this guy." I massaged my aching temples.

"You don't have any idea of who you're up against."

I was about ready to blow my stack. "Are you referring to the *Gorgons?*"

Uncle Jess hissed, "Don't ever speak their names out loud. Believe me, you don't want to attract their attention."

"Why? Who are they?" I demanded.

"I don't know for sure, but they've secretly wielded their ultra-strong magic for centuries."

I'd never heard of anyone intimidating Uncle Jess, and that concerned me. But on the other hand, if no one had seen the *Gorgons* for centuries, they could be dead.

"Remember, I didn't go looking for the *Gorgons.*" I enunciated their name slowly just to throw another scare into my dear uncle. "They were responsible for drawing their symbol in front of me, so I guess they wanted me involved."

"You're as bullheaded as your father," Uncle Jess protested, his voice ice. He had protested my parents' marriage from the get-go, and his action had strained the Luna family relations ever since. He'd considered his brother foolish for marrying a sorceress instead of another werewolf. Talk about bigotry.

"Yes I am," I retorted. "But don't forgot, you sent me that hotshot Dana Drake to watch over me," I reminded him with a syrupy dose of sarcasm.

Uncle Jess was nearing his wits' end. "There's your physical contact with Gwendolyn Stockard's ghost to consider," he pointed out.

I stared thoughtfully out the window at two squirrels playing tag in the front-yard live oak. "So why's that such a big deal?"

"Because there's never been a single reported incident like it since I've run DSI. Without a precedent, we can't create a counter spell."

"You mean a spell that would zap her away?"

"The spirit you saw was definitely not a ghost, since she physically *touched* you. This is bad," he repeated for the umpteenth time.

"So you're saying that I'm entering uncharted magic territory."

"Exactly."

I recalled Kit's blank expression, and it reinforced my resolve. "I'm going to see this case through, Uncle Jess, come hell or high water."

He exhaled heavily in defeat. "Since there's nothing I can say to dissuade you, all I can offer you is . . . whatever support you may need later."

How about wishing me *good luck*? But that wasn't Uncle Jess's style. After he hung up, I stood and marched out of the bedroom. My knees were completely healed. As I descended the stairs, gunshots cracked the early-morning stillness behind the house. I flew down the rest of the steps and heard more shots.

What kind of trouble had Uncle Jess's superwoman, Dana Drake, gotten herself—*and me*—into?

And all before breakfast.

24

I pushed through the screen door and flew off the porch, landing on the paved sidewalk between the house and barn. I checked my workshop fifty feet behind the house, but Dana Drake wasn't anywhere out there. My old workshop was a single-story rustic wooden structure reminiscent of Amish architecture. The small windows were shuttered with an exotic space-age, bulletproof and bomb-proof titanium alloy developed by the Department of Defense, and Uncle Jess had it installed gratis last year to protect my rare magic inventory. The door was shut and locked.

I shielded my eyes from the low sun and surveyed the dense jungle to the north. The prickly brush, scrub palms, vines, and assortment of pine trees stretched east and west. Birds flew in and out of the foliage, and scrawny gray squirrels leaped between thin branches like circus daredevils, but that was the extent of the movement there. No Dana. The wooden swing bridge that spanned the breadth of the two-acre pond behind the workshop was also empty. I was getting nowhere fast. *Where in blazes was she?*

I mopped away sweat from the escalating heat and humidity. The scene was eerily silent except for the mockingbirds' melodic songs and the Carolina wrens' raucous tweets. There were no more gunshots to guide me to her, and I didn't know where the previous ones had come from.

It would take quite a while to roam the entire farm, and Dana might not have that much time. She could be lying some place bleeding to death. I pulled out my wand and crossed the bridge that led to a small private cemetery and Moccasin Wallow—my favorite place. I could've changed into a werewolf and used my hunting prowess to locate her, but I wouldn't have had full control of my actions. I didn't want to be the one who killed instead of saved her.

The cloudless tropical setting was perfect for golfing, sailing, and beach trips, but seemed incompatible with murder. After I crossed the bridge, the faster I walked-ran, the slower I went. It was akin to running in muck. A black magic spell impeded my progress. Someone didn't want me finding Dana.

The path continued through a sparse copse, where I paused to inspect the ancient cemetery that was dead center (no pun intended) in the large clearing beyond the tall ragged pines. Still no sign of the damned woman. I should've kicked her out of my house and life last night, but I was too exhausted to think straight. Now, instead of reading the sports page and sipping a hot cup of Tillie's special-brew coffee, I was out here tramping around like Jungle Jim in sweltering ninety-degree heat. Life could be obscenely unfair.

I shrugged off the negativity and moved on. Whatever or whoever had attacked Dana was probably on the farm because of me, but why kill her when she was the secondary target? *Why not come after me?*

I stepped into the clearing and approached the white-picket fence bordering the cemetery. I meticulously maintained the hallowed grounds, because it was the home of my ghostly friends and advisors, the GPS—the Ghoul Philosophers Society. Although it was much too early for them to make an appearance, I sensed that they were watching and cheering me on. At least I hoped so.

I stepped over the low fence and advanced through the spell's resistance toward the other side.

"Get down, for heaven's sake," a crotchety male voice hissed at me.

I ducked and glanced around for the source of the warning. I finally spotted a grizzled, bearded face in one of the weather-beaten gravestones. It belonged to none other than the crankiest GPS member, Captain Harley Watterson. The eternally fifty-year-old ghost had been the sea captain of an English Merchant Marines ship that had been sunk by a Spanish frigate over a hundred years ago. He was sharp as a tack, all business, and quick on the uptake.

"What's going on out here?" I whispered.

"Pop-ups," he replied.

I frowned. I'd heard of Pop Tarts, but not those. "What's a pop-up?"

"Annoying little demons that pop up out of nowhere, materialize long enough to inflict some physical damage, and then vanish to pop up again where you least expect them. They've been doing that to your girlfriend for the past half hour," he explained.

"She's *not* my girlfriend," I snapped.

"Whatever you say, Joe," he said cynically.

"So how do I get rid of them?"

"You don't. Either you kill them or they kill you, matey."

"How many of them are there?"

"I saw seven."

"How come they haven't attacked me yet?"

"Hey, I'm not a psychic, Joe," he growled.

"Okay, okay, I'm sorry." My nerves were on edge, awaiting the first attack. "So how do I kill them?"

"I'm not a witch, either. But I will say this . . . they can't kill what they can't see." He grinned and winked at me just as the first little demon appeared behind me and clipped me hard on the back of the leg. Before I could turn and defend myself, it was gone. I thrust out my ring finger, but my protective ring wasn't there. In my haste, I'd left the protective ring back in my bedroom.

"Son-of-a- . . . ."

Another demon appeared at my left side, leaped, and nearly tore my ear off. This time, I got a quick look at it before it disappeared. The pint-sized pop-up looked like a miniature horned Satan, complete with brown flesh, bulbous blood-red eyes, razor-sharp claws, pointed yellow teeth, high-ridged cheekbones, a horrifying scowl, and a pair of curved skull horns. Their only contrary features were their thick, club-like feet that were used to kick and pound their quarry between bites and abrasions. I envisioned Dana's shredded body and winced. Sushi . . . on bone.

Three more of the two-foot-tall gravity-defying demons appeared simultaneously, and by the time I raised my hands to defend myself, I was missing three chunks of flesh—one from each of my legs and one from my shoulder. I howled my frustration and spun to fend off more pop-up attacks, but the effort was futile. They would eventually wear me out.

What I desperately needed was an invisibility spell like Harley suggested, but the problem was that I didn't know one that didn't require throwing together an exotic herb recipe. But even if I decided to go that route, the little bastards would slice and dice me into stew meat before I made it across the pond.

It looked like my only option was to go down swinging, and that didn't excite me one iota.

25

I might have gone a bit over the top in my argument with Uncle Jess, but he always found a way to provoke me into saying things I later regretted. This was one of those times. Now I wondered if I had been too hasty in my judgment to continue the *Ghostworld* investigation, when I could've taken a good long vacation on some Caribbean island with a rum drink in one hand and a tanned beauty in the other. I hated to admit it, but Uncle Jess's assessment of my long odds might've been on target. I *was* in over my head, and the carnivorous pop-ups pretty much proved it.

"Where's the woman?" I asked breathlessly

"The one who's *not* your girlfriend?" Harley quipped.

Another two demons flashed into view and slashed more meat from my unprotected legs.

"Dammit, quit being a wiseass! Where is she?" I bristled. I swiped at two more pop-ups like they were vampire mosquitoes, but missed each time.

"She's lying under that fan palm just inside the jungle on a straight line from Rupert's headstone," he replied.

Rupert O'Neal was another ghostly member of the GPS, and I quickly spotted his weather-worn headstone and the broad fan palm. I shot up and sprinted through the tall bahaia and timothy grasses as fast as I could against the black magic resistance. I headed straight for Dana's jungle location, trying my best to dodge the little cannibals, but they seemed to be everywhere. One chomped my hand and caused me to drop my wand in the unruly grass near the jungle's edge, but I didn't retrieve it. In this impossible situation, the wand was useless anyway.

I belly-flopped into the shade beneath the monster fan palm and came face-to-face with Dana. Her clothes reminded me of Tarzan's Jane—barely there. Her black shorts, white shirt, and bra were tattered fragments of bloody cloth.

Despite my new location, the pop-ups assaulted me mercilessly, but they had a tough time reaching Dana in the confined space at the palm's base. I wriggled into the low area beside her and batted the aggressive little beasts away from my face, but it was a losing proposition. I was much taller than Dana, so I stood out like the proverbial sore thumb.

My knuckles and the backs of my hands took a beating, and I worried that there'd be no flesh, muscle, or tendons left to maneuver them in my defense. There was only one thing left to do—change into the quicker, faster-healing werewolf. Without waiting for logic to kick in, I crawled back into the clearing.

Dana was shocked. "Do you have a suicide wish? For godsake, get back under here where it's safe."

"It may be safe for you, but I'm too . . . ." I swatted at the offending pop-up and made contact for the first time. But it was too little too late. Four more appeared and took their pound of flesh. Blood flowed freely from my wounds and stained the grass red.

There was no time to argue. I was already feeling lightheaded from the blood loss and numb with raw searing pain.

I began my wolfen transformation, but the constant attack made it impossible for me to concentrate, and my physical change became stalled at the starting line. The pop-ups' attack mode ramped up to fast-forward, and they chomped and slashed my flesh with the lightning speed of a school of piranhas. The bright morning light waned to twilight.

I collapsed to one knee, my body afire. The excruciating sensory overload short-circuited my transformation, and I remained human. I was a breathing cadaver.

"Joe! Dammit, get under here before it's too late!" Dana screamed.

Her urgency was lost to my dazed mind. My hands, which had valiantly protected my face during the entire assault, were reduced to fleshless bones that toppled off my hands into the grass one by one. My exposed face was totally vulnerable.

The demons took advantage immediately, striking my nose and cheeks from every angle. I crumpled to my fingerless palms and skinless knees in the grass, bellowing desperately. Like a punch-drunk boxer, I stubbornly refused to go down for the count, but my life force was rapidly ebbing.

One pop-up cruelly ripped away an eyebrow, and another worried the closed eyelid below it. I didn't have long to live.

I rolled on my side, stripped of flesh and drained of blood. My breaths were ragged, and my heartbeat barely registered in my chest. My lucidity wilted to incoherence. My lingering consciousness was immersed in the serenity of a cool tropical beach, where I found peace from the carnage.

My wolfen senses detected a thin ribbon of living essence inside my skeletal remains, but it was shriveling fast.

As far as I was concerned, the *Ghostworld* case was closed.

26

My lungs wheezed their last, then shut down like a punctured bellows, eclipsing my wolfen immortality. The steel-drum band fired up its haunting, echoing music inside my Caribbean reality getaway, and I moved my imaginary sandaled feet to the Trinidad beat while sipping my icy piña colada and enjoying the light briny breeze.

Suddenly, the overhead sun swelled to such outrageous proportions that its burning brilliance engulfed my tropical paradise, and cast me into blackness again. After what seemed like an eternity, light dawned on my unconsciousness and grew brighter by the second. *Was this the light at the end of the tunnel I'd heard so much about?* I stared out with my lidless eye to see if I'd made it to Heaven. I hadn't. Instead, I witnessed an extraordinary spectacle.

My wand was levitating three feet above the meadow grass and was the source of the incredible radiance!

My pain-stricken brain cells didn't catch on immediately. Comprehension was beyond their current capacity. Gradually questions formed, a good sign that my thought processes were regenerating just fine. *Who was manipulating my magic wand?* Then trepidation rejoined comprehension on my mental bench. Each magic wand was personalized for its sorcerer owner so it couldn't be utilized by anyone else. And yet someone was manipulating mine.

The wand's dazzling glow soon masked the jungle and cemetery, and I felt the presence of a stalwart apparition beside me, but I couldn't see or hear it, or judge its intent. It was just there.

The presence revived a primordial reaction—fear, but I was too frail to shiver. Or panic. Or defend myself.

Another spark stimulated a far better sensation—hope. Hope that the unseen presence wasn't hostile. Hope that it might heal me.

It probed the deepest recesses of my feeble mind, cleared away the painful memories, and jump-started my full complement of mental faculties. My outer body's exposed, raw nerves regenerated rapidly and jammed the neural highways with their operational statuses.

A drastically greater brilliance pierced my lidless eye like a red-hot branding poker, and I screamed . . . or at least I did in my head. My jaws and lips were hyperextended, but all that escaped my mouth were shallow breaths. I was breathing again, but it hurt like hell.

Why was the spirit torturing me?

Gradually, the inferno in my eye was extinguished, leaving a thin veil of flesh draping it. A new eyelid. I worked it up and down like a kid with a new toy . . . and it worked like a charm. *Who was the apparition and why was he or she healing me?* I wanted to mail them a thank-you card.

The bright yellow glow steadily diminished to a soft shade of buttermilk, and then vanished altogether with the spirit. The smoldering Florida sun displaced them both. Its soothing warmth had never felt so good.

I sat up with care and noted that I was seated in the same grassy place where I had collapsed earlier. I warily scanned the meadow for pop-ups, but none of the cannibal demons was in sight. I examined my regenerated body, especially the fingers. They were completely restored, including the most minuscule scars and lines. *How was that possible?*

What was even more amazing was that my cargo shorts, green shirt, and running shoes had been returned to their original condition. *What had happened to me in the strange yellow light?* I was brand-spanking new. No harm done. *Who could've possibly pulled this incredible miracle off?*

"Joe!" Dana hailed me from beside her savior fan palm.

She hobbled weakly from the jungle shade into the meadow sun. Her clothes were as I remembered them—bloody rags. The rest of her mostly exposed body was pockmarked with raw sores that oozed blood and pus. *Dammit!* They were already infected.

She staggered like a Saturday-night drunk toward me, and I caught her quivering, depleted form with surprising ease before it hit the ground. My physical strength had been totally restored, too.

"Get me back to the house," she cried into my chest. "It hurts . . . like hell."

I spotted my wand where it rested in the tall grass. *Could it have cast the regenerative and healing spells for me on its own, or had I just imagined its levitation and glow?* I stared at it, suddenly hesitant to reclaim it. *If the spirit had hijacked its powers, would it respond to my commands anymore?*

Dana yanked my shirt sleeve. "We have to get going *now*," she sobbed.

I desperately wanted to ask her if she'd watched my miracle from her front-row seat in the jungle, but she was in too much pain to think rationally. I knew the feeling. I had just gone through it myself. So I simply nodded, slipped my arm around her waist, and supported her on the trek back to the farmhouse, grabbing the wand along the way. I needed it to heal Dana's wounds, but I had my doubts.

And I had my doubts about Dana, too. Uncle Jess hired her to be my protector, but she appeared as vulnerable as any normal woman. *Had he lied to me?* I was nearly convinced to throw in the towel on the *Ghostworld* investigation. It was flat-out too dangerous. But if I were a betting sorwolf, I'd place my money on my insatiable curiosity.

It wouldn't allow me to bail out on this one, no matter how detrimental the case was to my health.

27

Tillie O'Neal, my live-in cook and housekeeper, ushered us in through the back door and greeted me grimly.

"Land sakes, Joe. Put Dana in that chair real easy," she ordered in her typical heavy-handed manner. Long strands of reddish hair broke across her shoulders with wispy ringlets curled over her forehead. Her face was austere, her manner wise and knowledgeable, and her eyes green lightning. She was tall, curvaceously slender, and domineering. Oh, did I mention that she was also a *ghost witch?*

Tillie had the uncanny ability to materialize in human form so she could cook and clean for me and take care of any of her old business. Convicted of being a witch before the Civil War, she found herself sitting on a skittish horse with a noose tightly fitted around her fragile neck. It was then that she'd cast two spells. The first had cursed the families of the religious hypocrites responsible for her conviction, and they'd been afflicted with boils and blackening skin before dying long-suffering deaths.

Her second spell had summoned a demon—I'm not certain which one, and Tillie refused to name it—that gave her three hours of daily physical presence in this world in exchange for her soul. For a witch, that was a no-brainer. The demon granted her the freedom to vary her daily physical time, which these days usually accommodated my fluctuating timetable.

Tillie changed one of the kitchen chairs into a soft recliner, and Dana slumped into it. She shut her eyes and dropped her arms to her sides as Tillie administered a magical anesthetic to block the pain. I took that opportunity to appraise Dana, because I'd been too tired to notice much about her last night. She was wiry and athletic, had small perky breasts and boyish hips that some guys would find sexy. Not me, but some guys.

Tillie clucked her tongue. "Joe, I'm so sorry I didn't help you fight those nasty demons, but to tell you the truth, I don't know any spells that would stop them," she said sympathetically.

"Really?" That was hard to believe, because she'd been closely acquainted with a lot of powerful sorcerers over the past one hundred and fifty years.

"Yes, really. I don't pretend to know everything about magic," she huffed.

I scratched my chin. "Well, fortunately for Dana and me *someone* knew the right spell to eradicate them, or you and I'd be talking ghost-to-ghost right now. Who do you think saved us?"

Tillie hesitated. "I wish I knew. I was standing under the pines by the cemetery when I saw you go down in the meadow. Quite honestly, I thought you were dead, but then your wand levitated from the grass and threw out a blinding yellow light, and the next thing I knew, you were standing and completely healed."

"How much time expired when the wand floated to me standing?"

"Only a few minutes."

"God, I thought it was *hours*," I said, amazed.

"Like you always say, time flies when you're having fun," she quipped with a quick wink.

I smiled at her attempt to cheer me up, then sobered. "Do you think it's possible that my wand acted on its own?" I realized it was a silly question, but I had to know.

She glanced thoughtfully out the window. "No, that's not possible."

"Then who could have gotten rid of the pop-ups and healed me? It sure looked to me that my wand was responsible," I persisted. I had a gut feeling that Tillie was hiding something from me.

"I already told you that I . . . don't have a clue." Her use of modern slang was attributed to her many afternoons of watching television soap operas.

Her edginess confirmed that she was withholding information. Information that she must've considered dangerous for me to know. So, I had no recourse but to unleash the mega-bombshell in my arsenal.

"Could the *Gorgons* have saved me?"

Fear varnished her eyes. "Where'd you hear about them?" she demanded, her eyes flitting around the kitchen like a sparrow flying in a hawk's shadow.

Dana lifted her head. "Hey, guys, do you mind? I'm sitting right here in front of you bleeding to death while you guys shoot the shit." She sounded drunk.

"Don't get your knickers all in a twist, dearie," Tillie admonished her. "Joe'll have you fixed up as good as new in a few minutes."

Dana groaned and rolled her eyes as her head fell back against the headrest.

I quickly told Tillie about the apparition that sketched the Gorgon symbol on Martha's shop wall. "Uncle Jess clammed up when I mentioned them this morning and told me to never repeat their names again. And now *you're* reacting the same way. What's up with you two, anyway? What's so special about the *Gorgons?*" I spluttered, frustrated by their refusal to disclose what they knew about them.

Tillie cleared her throat. "They . . . they're the most powerful magical forces on earth."

"Yeah, that's how Uncle Jess described them, but that information really doesn't tell me squat," I grumbled.

She sighed. "They're very private, um, beings, and people who have interfered in their business in the past have disappeared or been murdered."

"Hmmm. So why would the *Gorgons* want to save *me?*"

Tillie wrung her hands anxiously. "No sorcerer that I know of has defeated the pop-ups, no matter how strong their magic is. So, the only ones powerful enough to kill the pop-ups and bring you back from the dead are the *Gorgons*, but I have no idea why they'd do it."

Another question without an answer. "Do you have any idea how I can get in touch with them?"

Tillie shuffled her feet. "No, and don't even think about it. It's much too risky, even if I knew how. If they want to contact you, they'll do the contacting. Not you."

"This damned *Ghostworld* investigation is driving me nuts, and it's not even twenty-four hours old," I carped, then focused my attention on healing Dana's wounds. With a spell similar to the one I used on Kit's wound last night, I hesitantly raised my wand and directed the cinnamon arc to Dana's entire body. It formed a bubble around her like a transparent eggshell, and slowly healed the raw bites and the infection.

I studied my wand. It seemed to be in perfect working order, so I must've imagined it healing me on its own. But still . . . .

"Well, the only things you know for certain about your new investigation, Joe, is that somebody wants you dead and somebody wants you alive," Tillie stated somberly.

I shot her a withering glance. "You make it sound like I'm caught in the middle of a magical tug-of-war. Now that's a real cheery thought."

28

Dana looked a little more at ease after showering and slipping into a new pair of creased black slacks and white shirt than she did after I healed her, but that wouldn't take much. She still had a bit of that deer-in-the-headlights look that gave me the creeps as I ate my oatmeal. She sat across from me at the kitchen table and stared dully at me, blighting her pretty freckled face.

As an excuse to escape that hunted look, I walked to the counter and turned the television on to the Brighthouse twenty-four-hour news on cable Channel 13. Tillie served me a stack of pancakes and mounds of scrambled eggs and cheese, sort of an oatmeal chaser. I dug in and kept my eyes glued on the headline stories: Gwendolyn's exploding head, the sheriff's freakish demise, and the ruckus on Pine Street last night.

The station played the recording of Gwendolyn's ruptured head, its bone fragments piercing her father's face, and the subsequent gory rain over and over. That stuff was too graphic for the morning news, in my humble opinion, and certainly did nothing to fuel my appetite.

The next recorded video showed last night's Pine Street crime scene, and the camera panned the demolished sidewalk in front of the shop where the demon giant had me trapped for a while. Fortunately, I was long gone before the news crew made its appearance. Uncle Jess wanted his employees to avoid the media at any cost—short of killing the reporter and cameraman, of course. DSI operated off the national radar, and exposure of any kind threatened its survival. Not even our country's president knew of our existence.

"Turn that horrible shit off," Dana grumbled. "I'm trying to eat, here."

I agreed, so the flat screen went black.

I attempted to make polite conversation. "How're you feeling?"

"Like I've been to hell and back," she blustered, without glancing up from her plate. She plowed into the sumptuous fare like a starving refugee.

Dana was even more contentious than Kit. *And Uncle Jess had the temerity to insist that she partner up with me on the Ghostworld gig?* The last guy he sent me seemed more qualified than Jungle Jane here, and *he* had been murdered the same day he arrived. She nearly bit the dust after a mere nine hours, which would've been a new record.

After I completed my gluttonous breakfast ritual, I sipped my coffee and admired the pastoral view through the back window. I didn't like leaving the serenity of the farm to investigate violent vampires, werewolves, or trolls — but hey, it was a living.

Dana gulped down three cups of Tillie's special-brew green tea, and then wiped her mouth.

"So what's on the agenda today, *boss?*"

I definitely detected a hint of hostility in her tone, as I turned from the window and put my empty coffee mug on the table. Her attitude pissed me off, so I let her have it. "I thought we'd try contacting the *Gorgons* first."

Her creepy stare dissolved instantly. "C'mon, Joe, get with it. You heard what Tillie said—that's impossible."

"Are you always this cheerful in the morning?"

"You want cheerful?" She feigned a smile. It was hideous.

"Forget it," I muttered. "If you want to stay angry, go ahead, but you're not working with me. I'll call Uncle Jess and have him send you on your merry way within the half hour."

Her expression flipped from riled to dread in no time flat. "You know I don't have much to be cheerful about, after nearly being eaten alive by those pop-up things. That doesn't exactly make me the happiest camper in Orlando at the moment. So give me a break, huh?"

I rolled my eyes. She was going to be difficult to work with, hands down. "Okay, I'll cut you some slack, but remember that I went through more than you did out there, and I'm not climbing all over you."

"You went through *more?*" she disputed, astounded.

"Yeah. I died out there," I said tersely.

Dana immediately realized that I was right, and she reached across the table and held my hand. "Sorry. I got carried away with my own self-pity. Now let's try this again." She pulled her hand back and straightened, looking official. "What's the first thing on today's agenda, boss?"

I couldn't help but laugh. "Better. Much better. I figured we'd check into who wanted Gwendolyn or her father dead. I . . . we . . . need a motive if we're to track down the murdering sorcerer. Sound fair enough?"

Dana begrudgingly went with the flow. "The sheriff's death was a long shot. Who could've predicted that his daughter's exploding head would strike him just the right way and kill him? What are the odds? A million to one? Ten million?"

"The killer manipulated the entire series of events with magic. He or she saw it turning out that way ahead of time."

"Okay. How about starting with Gwendolyn Stockard? She died first."

"That's going to take a lot of leg work." I abhorred leg work. It was too much . . . well, work.

"I was thinking we should take the car."

I laughed again. Maybe she wasn't such a hard nut after all.

Dana idly tapped her short, nicely manicured fingernails on the glass tabletop. "I got the impression from watching the news video of Stanton's speech after your trip below the mansion that he and Gwendolyn had a thing for each other."

"I think everyone there got that impression, but we can check it out. Let's start with Stanton's wife, Tandy."

Dana chuckled. "You really do have a death wish, don't you?"

I smiled. "After that, I'd like to arrange a chat with Senator Kane. He's been getting an awful lot of campaign publicity from their deaths. It may be a coincidence, but I don't really believe in them, myself."

"Neither do I. Political motivation." She pondered the notion. "Good idea."

"He comes off as an innocent ride victim, but that might've been his plan all along."

"You mean he might be a closet sorcerer?"

"Could be. He might've arranged the whole Emerald Zone bit, but the giant let him down. So he went to Plan B."

"It's plausible, but if anything had gone wrong down there, the senator would've been in the same boat as the rest of you."

She grasped the case logistics quickly, I'll give her that. "True, but there's another possible flaw in my theory. If Kane was the sorcerer responsible for our side trip, then why would he need to send those three thugs to question Kit and me in the tent?"

Dana frowned. "I hadn't heard about that."

I described our run-in with the three stooges.

"Yeah, that's a major sticking point for your Kane theory," she agreed.

"Jeffrey Stanton could be a person of interest who wanted Gwendolyn dead."

"Hmmm, it's a long shot." She hesitated. "Let's say he attempted to end his affair with Gwendolyn, but she got angry and threatened to tell his wife about them. So Stanton applies a little hocus-pocus, and presto, she's out of his hair for good."

I asked Tillie for some more coffee, and she brought some green tea for Dana, too.

"What if the killer's someone you don't know?" Tillie chipped in.

I took a sip of the steamy stimulant. "I'd say that's very possible. I plan on asking Uncle Jess's research department to research *Ghostworld* from inception to grand opening. Who are the investors? Were there any property purchase snafus? Does Stanton have any enemies who are capable of powerful magic?" I presented my questions.

Standing and stretching, Dana gestured to me to get moving. "Time's a-wastin', Joe. Do you want me to schedule an interview with Tandy Stanton, or do you want to?"

I wasn't listening. I was hashing over another detail as I drank my coffee.

"Well?" she pressed.

I snapped out of my stupor. "What? I'm afraid I didn't hear you."

She repeated her question and examined my expression. "What's eating you?"

"Boy, is that the wrong question after this morning," I quipped.

She blushed. "Sorry, let me rephrase that. What's on your mind?"

"When I was inside the Emerald Zone the first time, I smelled a weird combination of scents."

I had her full attention. "Like what?"

I finished my coffee.

"Brimstone, a salty sea breeze, dune grass, and motor oil. No, now that I think of it, the motor oil smelled more like marine engine fuel."

"As in boat marinas?" she asked.

"Yeah," I agreed.

She bit her bottom lip. "Maybe they'll lead us to the killer."

"I hope so, especially if Tandy Stanton and Kane don't pan out as suspects."

With that, I rose and headed for the back door.

"You coming?" I asked, mirroring her own eagerness. "Thanks, Tillie."

My ghostly chief cook and bottle washer waved as I rambled outside.

Dana fell in step beside me, and we marched briskly toward my barn office. The sun was still shining and the sea breeze injected coolness into the scorching heat and humidity. It appeared that my new partner would be all right. But then again, I really hadn't spent enough time with her to know for sure.

Dana Drake might turn out to be my worst enemy.

29

Dana gawked at the surrounding opulence as we passed through the ornate, vine-choked security gates of Orlando's premier community, Isleworth. The vast mansions were home to countless stars of the NFL, NBA, PGA, and LPGA, as well as executives and doctors.

"This place is something else, isn't it?" I commented while listening to the female Garmin GPS voice call out turn-by-turn directions to the Stanton estate.

"I suppose," she replied nonchalantly.

Before we left the farm, I asked Uncle Jess to research *Ghostworld* from concept to the finished product. He promised to get right on it. Dana arranged a two o'clock afternoon appointment with Tandy Stanton, but didn't have any luck locating the elusive Senator Kane. Like my FBI counterparts, I planned to drop in at his home unannounced.

I was troubled that Martha had yet to contact either Uncle Jess or myself about her location and Kit's condition. I thought the world of Kit, and the not-knowing was driving me up a wall. I wanted her back in the worst way.

The massive Stanton mansion appeared on our right and resembled a European castle with its four parapets, beige stone and marble exterior, and enough lined Corinthian columns to support Orlando's downtown arena. The base of each column reminded me of a stack of welded rings, while the top motif was elaborate scrollwork with flowers and leaves.

Dana didn't seem impressed with the architecture or the arrogant attendant who opened the gate for us upon our arrival. Maybe she was jealous of all this wealth. I parked in front of the oversized portico, and we trotted up the chestnut-brown stone steps to a tall pair of steel-and-stained-glass doors.

The blonde Tandy Stanton answered the doorbell herself, apologizing that she'd given the help the afternoon off. She was casually dressed, wearing cut-off jeans, a light blue tank top with no bra, and a deep tan.

Her bare feet flaunted her meticulously manicured toes, and she caught me staring at them.

"I hope you don't mind my bare feet, but I despise wearing shoes in the house, Mr. Luna." Knowing her background, Tandy Stanton probably hated wearing clothes inside, too.

Dana hadn't told her the reason for our visit, or else she might've slammed the doors in our faces. Our petite, curvaceous hostess examined our identification and guided us through the maze of rooms to the Florida room in back. We had an excellent view of the charming Lake Islesworth. The furnishings were expensive, but gaudy. The odd assortment of colors didn't complement each other, and the furniture was a mish-mash of styles. She had money, all right, but no taste.

A tray loaded with a variety of finger pastries, a silver coffee pot, and a jar of sun tea sat in the middle of a wicker and glass table, surrounded by costly china cups, saucers, and crystal tumblers. I helped myself to the goodies, but Dana begged off.

The walls were crowded with Tandy's portraits and framed pictures, but in person, her appearance wasn't as young or beautiful. Crow's feet radiated from the corners of her eyes, her complexion was pie-crust flaky, and without make-up, her eyes and eyelids were nondescript. But, I was pleased to see that her bodacious breasts were as tantalizing as advertised, stretching her cotton tank-top to onion skin.

I should've been on edge, because if Tandy were the one responsible for Gwendolyn's murder and the conjured Emerald Zone, she was capable of dispatching us without breaking a sweat. But my gut instinct hinted that she wasn't the murderer, and for now, I was a believer.

After Tandy filled her plate, and Dana finally accepted a tumbler of sun tea, I started the conversational ball rolling.

"I imagine you heard about Gwendolyn Stockard's strange death," I stated.

She nodded grimly. "Such a tragedy." Her gaze hardened to ice.

"Were you aware that Gwendolyn was infatuated with your husband?" Dana blurted out without regard for the suspect's feelings.

I nearly dropped my china plate. My partner unquestionably lacked the subtlety of an interrogator. Her style was more like . . . the Russian KGB.

Tandy nodded.

"And because of Gwendolyn's aggressive advances, I suppose you were jealous of her," Dana pressed.

Tandy's eyes narrowed. "Wouldn't you be?" she shot back.

Dana nodded. "I suppose, but I wouldn't kill the woman over it."

Tandy sat erect, her nostrils flared. "Is that what you think? That I wanted to murder that little bitch?"

"That's what we're here to find out," Dana stated.

"Sure I wanted to kill the conniving home wrecker, but I didn't blow up her head," she fumed.

I quickly re-entered the conversation. "But you planned to kill her?"

"Hell, no. I made arrangements to pay her to go bye-bye next week, but obviously she died before our meeting, which turns out to be a stroke of good luck for me."

"You saved your money and got your husband back," Dana summed it up.

"Yeah. Ain't life grand."

I put my empty plate on the table and took a long pull of tea. "Did Gwendolyn have any enemies that you're aware of?"

Tandy shifted in her chair, and her breasts bounced to the beat. "Honey, I can't help you there. I really didn't know her personally."

Like your husband did, I thought. Her answers left us at the starting line again, so we were finished there. I stood and thanked Tandy for her hospitality and candor.

Once we exited the Isleworth gates, Dana said, "That was a big bust."

"They sure were," I agreed.

Dana bristled and threw me a disapproving frown. "You're such a pig, Luna. You know I didn't mean it *that* way."

Our visit was strike one in the relevant information department, but at least we had narrowed our field of suspects to the rest of the world's population.

"You know, Tandy might be a sorceress who killed Gwendolyn to save the money," Dana suggested.

"Tandy's not a sorceress. If she was, I would've felt her magic. But she might've hired one. Let's keep her on our suspect list for now."

"Agreed. It's still early. You want to drop in on the senator?" she asked.

"Why not."

"You think he really did it?"

I shrugged. "Hey, anything's possible, but . . . ."

"But what?"

"I don't think he's smart enough to pull off a double murder."

"Besides, we've got our other two Kane theory-busters to consider."

"Right."

As I punched in Kane's local address in the Garmin GPS, I still had the feeling that someone was watching us. I couldn't shake it.

I braced my nerves for another attempt on my life.

30

A winding palm-lined driveway led to Kane's hacienda-style manor that nuzzled a veritable jungle of tropical plants that separated it from its neighbor to the north. The reedy shoreline of a glistening lake adjoined the property's south edge and cast its glittering reflection on the flaxen-and-rust-colored home.

As we pulled up to the front of the estate, we saw a dozen black FBI SUVs parked at the entrance. Before Dana and I exited the Explorer, we found ourselves surrounded by several granite-faced FBI agents wearing the tried-and-true blue polo shirts and slacks. Identification lanyards dangled from the necks of the two agents who approached us.

"What's going on here?" I asked civilly for the sake of DoJ interdepartmental harmony.

"None of your business, sir."

"We have an appointment with Senator Kane, and . . . ."

"Cancel it. The senator's not entertaining any visitors at this time."

"Says who?" Dana demanded.

"Says *us*, lady," the agent beside her window retorted.

"Now back up and leave the property immediately," the one identified as Special Agent John Browsky tersely ordered. He was tall and lanky, and his dark hair was neatly trimmed in a military-style brush cut.

I flashed him *my* identification. "Get away from my car and let us out," I snapped, reaching for the door handle.

Browsky shook his head and grinned humorlessly. "This isn't your branch's crime scene, uh, Joe. The FBI's got this one covered, so take your business elsewhere."

"Listen, butthead . . . ."

Dana grabbed my elbow. "Hold on a second," she said, and then hit a speed dial number in her cell phone. She spoke in hushed tones with her hand cupped over the microphone. When she finished, she snapped the cell phone shut and gave me a thumbs-up.

"Just wait a minute, Agent Browsky," she advised him.

He stood there cooling his heels in the sticky fall Florida heat, while we waited comfortably in the Explorer's air-conditioned interior.

The agent on Dana's side of the car flashed her a flirtatious grin. "So what's a *cutie* like you doing with a second-rate Department of Justice guy?"

Dana ignored his banter, choosing to admire the violet flowers and blossoming crepe myrtles in the front of the hacienda instead.

"Hey, babe, I'm talking to you," he said angrily, and lightly nudged her shoulder.

This time, she responded. Twisting her head toward the open window, Dana glared at the jerk. "You touch me again, and I'll break your goddamned arm."

"Ooooh, I'm really scared," the man laughed, pretending to be frightened. The other agents laughed, too.

My temper was about to explode off the charts, but Dana softly advised me to wait. I reluctantly backed off.

Browsky drew his gun and stuck its lethal barrel between my eyes. "I ordered you to leave, hotshot, but you ignored it. So now I'm placing you both under arrest for violating an FBI crime scene and refusing my order to vacate."

Before I grabbed his gun and taught him a lesson about interdepartmental courtesy, an agent raced from the house waving a sheet of paper like a white flag. The winded, red-faced agent shoved it at Browsky. A sneer creased his face as he read it.

"Damn!" Browsky muttered and wadded the paper. The shoe was on the other foot now. It was his turn to control his temper. "We gotta let 'em inside," he snarled. "Direct orders from the top dog."

"You sure?" the other agent groaned.

Before Browsky answered, Dana rammed her open door into Agent Flirty, and I heard a few cracks in his chest from the impact. He tumbled backward and landed on his side, holding his fractured ribs.

"Bitch!" Browsky shouted. He shifted his gun toward Dana, but I launched my door into him with such force that he flew ten feet into the manicured foliage. He didn't get up.

I was impressed by Dana's action. My bodyguard exhibited more spunk and strength than her petite frame implied.

I slammed my door shut, and the remaining agents flinched. "Anybody else want to try and stop us from seeing Senator Kane?" I challenged. They reholstered their guns and backed away.

Dana drew her Smith and Wesson 9mm handgun with Old West quickness and joined me. The two fallen agents would survive, but it might be a long, painful process. Oh well, that's life.

We strode along the driveway and up the steps to Senator Kane's open front door, wondering what the FBI was doing here. They had mentioned that it was a crime scene, but nothing else. We were about to enter when Dana froze and looked to the right. I saw him, too. What appeared to be another agent was spying on us from the corner ornamental garden, but when he saw that we'd made him, he slipped around the side of the house.

"Let him go," I told her, but she ignored my advice and warily approached the garden. I followed her.

The earth was black and still wet from last night's rain. She bent and examined the shaded area.

I stood watch. "What are we looking for?"

"Footprints."

I scratched my head. The soil behind the oleander and azaleas was undisturbed. "There *aren't* any prints," I observed.

"Exactly," she agreed, then frowned. "This means trouble."

No footprints. What could manage a trick like that? About a hundred demons or vampires that I knew of. "What kind of trouble?"

"C'mon, hurry!" she exclaimed, and sprinted toward the house as if it were on fire.

I ran after her, covering our flanks. I had a real good idea of what we were dealing with. An assassin demon. If I were right, then maybe the *Ghostworld* sorcerer had summoned it to off Kane. *But why?* I couldn't think of a single reason that made any sense.

I sprinted faster and hoped we were in time to save him.

31

As we neared Kane's front door, the hacienda's hulking twilight shadow enveloped us with abrupt coolness. Its steep tile peaks and profuse ornate arches were awe-inspiring, but we didn't take time to dwell on their structural splendor.

I'd never encountered an assassin demon before, but I'd read about them as a teenager during one of Mother's sorcery lessons. That knowledge was a wee bit hazy now. Okay, maybe a lot hazy.

Dana stopped short of the entrance. "We should split up. Surprise it. I'll go 'round back, and you go through the front," she proposed, as we inspected the shrubs and flowers for demon eyes that would reveal its position.

It could've disguised itself as anyone or anything, and I wasn't taking any chances. I'd lived through enough surprise attacks in the past twenty-four hours, and I wasn't anxious to test my luck again.

Dana moved away from the porch. "It's after Kane, isn't it?"

"That'd be my guess. Now get a move on before we're too late."

After she vanished around the corner, I entered the sprawling house and met another blue boy. I shoved my ID in his face, and he stepped back like I had the plague.

"We've got a hostile on the grounds," I announced gruffly, shoving him aside and storming into the foyer. "Where's Kane?"

The young agent scowled and looked like he wanted to kill me, but his surly attitude didn't faze me in the least. I've had that effect on law enforcement since I began cleaning up supernatural messes for Uncle Jess.

The ground started shaking, and the massive crystal chandelier began vibrating in the foyer above us. It felt like a minor earthquake. The tinkling grew louder and more agitated.

"Where is he?" I repeated.

The agent looked terrified. "He's . . . he's in the family room," he stammered.

DAVID BROOKOVER

I seized his shoulders, lifted him off his feet, and shook the bejesus out of him. "Which way's the damned family room?"

He pointed lamely toward the end of a long hallway that split the hacienda in half. His mesmerized gaze never drifted from the boogying crystals. These new FBI recruits were pathetic.

I hurried down the hall, sneaked a peek at the plushily appointed living room and a grand piano that probably cost more than my entire farm, and continued into the deep shadows near the hall's end. The place was so large that I could've used my Garmin GPS to navigate it.

The quake worsened, and I had to lean on the walls for balance. As I closed in on the light at the end of the hallway, I heard muffled, excited voices. I hoped I wasn't too late, although the world might be a better place without the pompous Senator Kane. *But who was I to judge?*

The voices grew louder. Actually, they were shouts and haughty commands that weren't being obeyed. The senator sounded like he was in the midst of a booming tirade, but I couldn't make out his words over the groans and creaks of the shuddering house. Sprinkles of plaster dust burst from the ceiling and clogged the air, creating a choking fog that slowed my progress.

I was about to explode into the family room, but my progress was blocked by a familiar swarm of black bees. I slid to a stop on the dust-coated floor, and Gwendolyn Stockard materialized in front of me. She raised her hand like a crossing guard.

"Don't go in there, Joe," she warned, her brows pinched with concern. "It's a, like, trap."

"I don't have much of a choice. My partner's coming in from the back," I exclaimed impatiently. "I can't strand her like that."

"Dana can take care of herself." She paused. "Like, Kane's already dead."

"I don't believe you. I just heard him," I argued. "But if you're right about that, then it means the FBI is helping the demon spring its trap, and I'm not buying it."

Gwendolyn grinned—or rather a soulless, humorless facsimile. "Not all of them are FBI, Joe. They're, like, conjured reproductions that aren't alive, at least not how you and I define living. They're under the command of the demon assassin who's, like, waiting for you right now around the corner."

121

"But Dana . . . ."

Gwendolyn laughed. "Believe me, she'll be all right."

I wondered what made her so sure. "Is Dana part of the trap?"

Gwendolyn sobered. "She's definitely on your side, but that's, like, neither here nor there. To put it simply, the assassin doesn't want to kill her. It's, like, after *you*."

Oh, great. How much luckier could I get.

"Why, for godsake?"

Gwendolyn pumped her lifeless shoulders. "That's for you to find out. Now if I were you, I'd, like, run back to your wreck of an SUV and drive as fast as you can back to your farm. The assassin can't, like, touch you there."

"Why not?" I coughed from the dusty air. I was so white that I looked like a thinner rendition of the Pillsbury Doughboy. Strangely, none of it clung to Gwendolyn. Another damned mystery.

She stomped her foot. "Because that's, like, just the way these demons are! Look, I didn't make the rules. I was sent here to, like, warn you, and I've done my best to make you leave. Now the ball's in your court, buddy. Live or die. Your choice."

"Who sent you to warn me?"

As before, my question went unanswered. Gwendolyn's form dissolved into that buzzing swarm again and vanished, leaving me alone in the shuddering house. *What should I do?* Kane's angry voice still reverberated in the hallway. *Was he alive, or was it an evil deception like Gwendolyn claimed?*

Growing up, my mother harped at me for being so obstinate. She swore that someday it would get me into big trouble.

I spit out a glob of pasty dust. Today was that *someday*. Despite Gwendolyn's warning, I was going in. I couldn't let Dana walk into an ambush alone.

I grabbed my wand, positioned my protective ring in front of me, and wished that I'd remembered to bring my more powerful mage staff along.

Oh, well. It was just one of those days. Pop-ups before breakfast and demon assassins before dinner. I didn't even want to think about a midnight snack.

32

The family room windows imploded from the conjured quake's force as I rounded the corner. The plaster fog thinned, so I inhaled deeply to clear my mind and settle my jumping-bean nerves. My wand and ring were ready for instant combat.

But there was no sign of the demon in the large rectangular room with six white leather sofas scattered throughout, an eight-foot flat HD television screen, and a stone fireplace the size of Texas. Four glassless patio doors overlooked the lake and reed-populated wetlands, a large wet bar spanned the opposite wall, and African wildlife trophies lined the wall next to me—a taxidermist's dream. Black wildebeest, white rhinoceros, male lion, brown hyena, and plains zebra heads hung on the polished teak.

But the most tragic trophy of all lay below the TV. Senator Justice Kane was spread-eagled on his back, a gaping crater the size of a softball where his chest used to be. There was little blood on the white polar bear rug beneath his fallen corpse, and I realized that the raw injury had been cauterized upon impact. This I knew about. The cause of death was an assassin's fireball.

Two bodyguards, the senator's girlfriend whom I'd met at *Ghostworld*, and three blue boys lay horribly contorted around the vast room, their lifeless muscles petrified with intense fright. Not even the rumbling quake could loosen their arched backs, crooked arms, and twisted legs. Their dead eyes bulged like dull red marbles, their warped mouths imprisoned their silent screams for eternity, and the edges of their hollow chests were blackened and smoked meat.

Fireballs again.

So where was the assassin? And, for that matter, where was Dana? I was relieved that she wasn't among the dead, but she should've been here by now. The hacienda was big, but not *that* big. A lump of concern lodged in my throat.

The sunny room darkened suddenly as storm clouds rumbled and tumbled on the western horizon. *Was this just another summer sea-breeze thunderstorm, or one that was home-brewed by the demon?* I voted for the latter.

After Gwendolyn's dire warning, I figured the demon was still waiting around to finish me off, so I concentrated on the crime scene. Cautiously, I advanced deeper into the family room and examined every nearby object for the assassin's eyes. Fiery orange demon eyes. It could've taken the form of anything, so it was easy to overlook. And die.

I closely inspected exotic vases. Trophy heads. Sofas. Lamps. Tables. Sound system speakers. Bar stools. Liquor bottles. Knick-knacks. Nothing.

I moved slowly, one step at a time, not wanting to rush into its trap. I figured that I was about halfway into it as it was. The house ceased shaking, and the atmosphere grew deathly still. The clouds became blacker as they drifted toward the hacienda, casting the room into early darkness.

Lightning flared, followed quickly by deep rolling thunder. A cool breeze fluttered the vertical blinds dangling over the patio doors like clattering skeleton bones. An icy dread crept up my spine and embraced the back of my neck, but I had to keep my cool if I planned to get out of there alive. Which I did, of course.

Without warning, one of the bodyguard corpses sprang to its feet, its orange eyes blazing. It shed its human features and mushroomed to a monstrous nine feet of electric green energy that devoured every shadow in the room.

"You fool, Luna. You should've taken the ghost girl's advice and lived to face me another day," it chastised me with a super-bass timbre at the fringe of human hearing.

My protective ring projected a vivid purple shield around me. "Do your worst, you murderous son-of-a-bitch!"

It spread its fiery hands a foot apart and cooked up a sizzling, crackling fireball. My eyeballs nearly slipped from their sockets as I watched the floating fireball grow in size and intensity between its clawed hands.

The assassin's green-flamed lips parted again, revealing black flames beyond—demon fire. "So long, Luna."

With a hollow laugh, it launched the fireball at me and scored a direct hit. The ring's field protected my chest from the magical weapon's penetration, but the impact knocked me into the teak paneling below the rhino head. The mammoth trophy slipped from its wall mount and nose-dived toward me. I shielded my head, but I needn't have worried. The horned skull careened off the shield and rolled toward the assassin.

But the demon didn't waste time bemoaning its lost opportunity. It had already created a larger fireball by the time I glanced its way.

"You were lucky last time, but this one will put an end to you. Your weak magic can't survive two of my death balls in a row." With that, he threw his new and improved sizzler.

The bastard was probably right, but I wasn't ready to throw in the towel just yet. I swiftly produced a counter fireball and chucked it at his. I turned my face away from the blinding explosion that showered the entire room with white-hot sparks. The walls, trophies, and furniture caught fire immediately from the supernatural embers, and soon we stood at the edges of a raging inferno. Neither one of us was touched by the flames.

My wand's finish blistered from the collision's energy bounce, and soon my loyal magical instrument was a smoldering black matchstick. It would be useless until it regenerated, which could take days. Its demise rendered me defenseless against the demon's vicious attacks. One more fireball ought to do the trick, and I'd be toast.

Without Dana's help, I was a sitting duck. I desperately needed back-up, but it looked like my earlier spirit healer had taken the afternoon off.

The situation called for a clever Plan B, but I was out of time. The demon pitcher was already starting his wind-up for my strike-three pitch. I shut my eyes and muttered a chant as he released the fireball.

33

I escaped Kane's family room with a second to spare. I felt the fireball's heat, and then all of a sudden I found myself inside my barn office. No blaze there.

I wasn't planning to stick around Kane's place and be the assassin's next victim, so I transported myself to my barn and crumpled into my comfy leather office chair to think. I carefully placed my fried wand on my work table and examined the burns on my hand. They were already healing. My wolfen genes never slept.

I wasn't giving up the fight; I was plotting a strategy for my return. And I didn't have much time to do it. The demon would leave soon or demand its pound of flesh from Dana. I planned to finish our battle this afternoon . . . on my terms . . . before there were any more collateral victims.

I grabbed my mage staff from the closet and stroked its smooth wood, recalling the day when my mother presented one each to Jill and me. She told us about their wood composition and the talismans at the tip.

The staffs were magically produced from two tree sources: a eucalyptus and a haugtrold. The eucalyptus wood bound us to the moon and water and possessed the magical powers of protection, purification, and healing. The midnight-blue haugtrold timber was obtained from the monstrous world of *Trolldom* and channeled the supernatural forces in our atmosphere and that of the Otherworld for our bidding.

A collection of enchanted talismans was fastened to the tip of both staffs. One talisman was identified as Celtic Knots, consisting of rings created from interwoven bands. Its prime functions were to protect us against wicked plots, evil spirits, and demons. A silver pentagram was included to repel evil energy back to its sender. A Sheiah Dog, a Celtic symbol, protected us from the run-of-the-mill black magic, while the final talisman was fashioned from a pair interlocking triangles and dubbed the Seal of Solomon. It invoked the considerable powers of the hallowed spirit world to protect us against the blackest, most powerful magic spells.

The phone rang and ruined my musing, and I snatched the aggravating landline phone from its cradle.

"Yeah," I snarled, not bothering to check the name on the caller-ID display.

"Having a good day?" The sarcastic remark belonged to none other than Uncle Jess.

"No, thanks to your assignment."

"Well, I did try to talk you out of it, remember?"

Me and my big mouth. I'd completely forgotten our argument this morning, so I clammed up. "Gotta go. I'll call you later." I hoped.

"But . . . ."

He wasn't used to being blown off like that. "I'm in the middle of a fight with a demon assassin. Senator Kane's dead. Bye."

As I put the phone down, I heard him shout one word. "Water!"

Hmmm. Not a bad idea. *Why didn't I think of that?* I transported myself back to the late senator's burning hacienda and confronted the demon. It was still there. Waiting for me to reappear, and I didn't disappoint it.

As soon as I showed up, it spotted me and began working on another deadly fireball.

"You're back!" it growled in its deep, rumbling pitch. "I'm going . . . ."

A teeth-rattling thunderclap clipped the tail end of its message, but I got the gist of it, and it wasn't a cordial invitation to the Demon's Day Ball.

Before it finished its murderous task, I hurriedly chanted a spell in our family's ancient, mystical language, tapped my staff on the tile floor three times, and waited.

The fire and its searing heat were insufferable, but that was nothing compared to the heat generated from its fireball, especially if it hit me dead on. I watched the demon put the finishing touches on its weapon of mass destruction and waited for my spell to take effect. If it didn't soon, I was history. I started to worry.

Maybe in my haste I'd screwed up the spell. Said it wrong. Left out a word. Haste makes waste when people are addled and rushed. All I knew was that my spell was MIA and the demon assassin was alive and well and favoring me with a hideous, fiery scowl.

It targeted me and fired off a sizzler, but I batted it away with my staff. It blew out the fireplace wall. The assassin roared its frustration, and charged.

Where was my spell? What had I done wrong? I needed about three seconds to rectify my error or become a crispy filet mignon.

I rapidly repeated the spell and discovered my error—I'd left out a word.

It was tough to differentiate the demon's fiery body from the swirling, licking flames devouring the hacienda—except that it was green. I retreated from its approach until my back smacked the wall. Dead end. The assassin grabbed at me with its blazing outstretched arms, but I slid aside. It recovered and came for me again. *Where was my spell?*

Suddenly, a violent whirlpool appeared in the floor below the demon's feet and sucked its writhing form into its frothy depths. The hissing assassin uttered one mournful howl before disappearing from this world.

The magical whirlpool shriveled to a gurgling eddy before vanishing into the floor. Uncle Jess's advice had saved the day, but I wouldn't tell him. I'd never hear the end of it.

The storm's gale-force winds whistled through the glassless patio doors and fueled the ravenous blaze. It was time to vacate the premises.

The blowing sheets of rain battered me as soon as I appeared on the patio wedged between the lakeshore and the burning hacienda. I shouted Dana's name into the storm, but it was immediately swept away by the buffeting gusts.

Sirens whined in the distance, and I realized that I had to find Dana before the cops showed, and I became their number-one suspect for murder and arson. Telling the cops that a demon assassin was responsible wouldn't strike the right chord with their realities. One thing I learned about cops a long time ago was that they suffered from acute imagination deprivation. Kit was the lone exception.

I chanted and tamped the mage staff on the wet patio blocks, and a protective field appeared around me, shielding me from the rain. I utilized my wolfen sight to look into the maelstrom and search for Dana, but she wasn't out there. *Where was she?* I had a nagging feeling that something bad happened to her. But then again, she might have run for the hills when she saw me losing the fight against the demon assassin. From her gilded reputation, it didn't sound like Dana's style, but I really didn't know her *that* well.

The sirens drew closer, so I was forced to leave without her. I transported myself to the Explorer and fired up the engine. The headlights clicked on, and my mouth gaped.

Dana surfaced in my headlight beams, drenched and shivering, while three other women who were nothing but trouble stood behind her. A guttural werewolf growl quivered my ribcage as the red-eyed scowling threesome escorted Dana to the SUV.

Vampires.

God, I really hated vampires.

When would this nightmare end?

34

The storm pummeled the four sodden women as they tramped through the driveway puddles to reach the Explorer. I rolled down my window and my shirt was instantly drenched.

"Let us in, Luna," the tallest vamp threatened, "or we bite your friend."

They'd put Dana in one of their trances—her face was utterly expressionless.

"What'd you do to her?" I demanded, ready to attack the vile bloodsuckers.

"We drugged her. Don't sweat it. Your latest love interest'll be completely fuckable by morning. Now are you going to let us in, or do we initiate a new member into our little vampire troop?" the tall spokesman replied curtly.

Love interest? What a joke, but I kept my mouth shut. No use confessing that we're merely working partners, until I discovered why they'd taken Dana hostage.

I didn't believe the tall vamp's lie about giving Dana a drug, because a partial vampire bite paralyzed humans, too. I did, however, believe they weren't bluffing about turning Dana into one of the undead.

"Get in," I relented and rolled the window up. It was surprising to see vamps out this early in the afternoon, but the sun was thickly shielded by the storm clouds.

The tall one slipped into the seat beside me, while the other three scooted across the rear bench seat. I felt wolfen bristles sprout on my back. Centuries of inbred hatred between our two species couldn't be vanquished that easily.

I made a u-turn in Kane's driveway and sped away from the firestorm before the cops and fire department arrived. I missed them by thirty seconds. Close call.

The list of *Ghostworld* guest murder victims was growing by leaps and bounds. Sheriff Lance Stockard. Gwendolyn Stockard. Senator

Justice Kane. And it appeared that my name was on that hit list. *What possible motive could he have for eliminating us?* I couldn't fathom our shared connection, but I had a hunch that Orlando's mayor, the governor, and maybe even Stanton himself were targets, too. Something was rotten in *Ghostworld*, and I vowed to get to the bottom of that bloody quagmire before The Grim Reaper caught up with me.

The howling tempest was equal to a violent tropical storm. Even with my super-charged wolfen vision, the visibility was close to zero, and it was impossible to avoid plowing through the surface-street lakes and crossing a few center lines. I maintained a white-knuckle grip on the steering wheel during our entire trek to who knew where.

"What's this all about?" I asked Tall Vamp, keeping a sharp eye on both my unwelcome guests and the treacherous road. At the first sign of aggression toward Dana, my werewolf persona would rip them apart so fast they wouldn't know what hit them.

I was acquainted with these vamps, but I didn't brag about it. I had run into them years ago when I was working one of Uncle Jess's cases. These three were affiliated with an all-female vampire bunch called *The Druids*, and each of them sported a gaudy tattoo depicting a nude, long-horned vampire with blood dripping from its razor-sharp fangs. The gang boasted that its design was both intimidating and exotic, but I considered it sick and twisted. Then again, I was old-fashioned when it came to classical vampires and bizarre tattoos.

All of my undead guests were knock-out gorgeous, if you liked your women pale and frigid to the touch. Flavia was their tall blond leader, who carried herself regally, but had a gutter-snipe mouth and a volatile temper. The petite one was Sabina. Her black hair flowed past her shoulders from a center part, and although her sumptuous body was thin and curvy, I'd seen her easily dispatch a three-hundred pound-attacker. Cara was the feisty one. Always belligerent. Always offensive. Never took the high road during a confrontation. Her strength, aggressiveness, and stamina were at odds with her slender, ethereal body. Of the three vampires, Cara was the most dangerous.

"Are you going to tell me what this is all about?" I repeated irritably. Between the abominable weather and my smug ride-alongs, I was in a foul mood.

"It's about you driving us to your farm," Flavia replied brashly.

I gritted my teeth. "And why would I do that?"

"Because your little piece of ass back there will never see the light of day again if you don't."

"Did Drusilla put you up to this?" I pressed. Drusilla was the leader of *The Druids*, and a beauty and seductress in her own right. But she was no fool. Men who crossed her came away missing vital body parts.

"That's none of your business."

I had a sudden inspiration. "Gwendolyn Stockard's ghost didn't arrange this reception, did it?" I asked.

Flavia and her pals laughed.

"*Us* take orders from a fuckin' ghost? You've got to be kidding me," Cara asserted, super-sizing the sarcasm.

"Shut up and drive," Flavia barked, flashing her big red eyes at me.

The explosive gusts shoved the old warrior SUV around like a lightweight, but somehow I managed to stay the course toward the farm without summoning my magic.

"So when we get to my place, are you guys planning an orgy?" I persisted, hoping one of them would leak vital information to my case.

Flavia reached over and stroked my thigh. The talismans atop my mage staff jangled when she bumped it. "Whatever you want, Joe. Just as long as you stay . . ."

"Be quiet!" Cara shouted over the storm's din. "Don't tell him anything. Remember Drusilla's orders."

"So Drusilla *is* behind this kidnapping!" I exclaimed. "So now I wonder who put *her* up to it. Must've been somebody important."

Flavia's hand tightened and drove her bestial nails into my skin. I growled.

"If you ever touch me again, you'll have to clap with one hand," I threatened her as my eyes blinked to wolfen orange.

She swiftly withdrew her hand and scooted to the far edge of her seat.

Cara hissed at me, and Sabina ordered Flavia to knock it off.

"I'm to ask you one more time, and if I don't get an answer, I'm pulling off the road and ridding the world of three vampires," I snarled. "Now . . . what happens when we get to my farm?"

"Don't forget your friend," Sabina hissed, a tinge of fear rattling her soft voice. "If you change, she's a goner."

"You can have her," I lied, knowing full well that I could eliminate Cara and Sabina before they had a chance to put the death bite on Dana. It would be close, but as a werewolf, I had a long lethal reach. But I was betting that they'd answer me rather than face an uncertain future.

The vamps exchanged angry scowls, and then Flavia spoke up.

"Okay, you win, Luna. When we reach your farm, we're going to cozy up inside your car for the night. You and your friend will be set free just before dawn."

"Really?" It was obvious that someone wanted us bottled up for the night so he could pull off another murder. I told them so. *But who?*

"If you're so clever, figure it out. We're not telling you jack," Cara sputtered.

With that biting remark, Cara made the top five on my all-time shit list.

"I'll tell you this," Flavia said with a crooked grin that eclipsed her beauty. "Someone's going to die tonight . . . someone you know . . . and there's nothing you can do to stop it."

Frustrated, I clenched my teeth and drove. No more questions. I had the answer I sought, even though I didn't like it. *Was the target someone else from the Ghostworld case?* Possibly. *Was it a personal friend of mine?* I doubted it, since Martha Gibbons and Kit were safely hidden and my other close friends were already ghosts.

Lightning continued to fracture the turbulent skies on a regular basis and hurl ground-shaking thunderclaps our way. I quit thinking about possible victims. It was fruitless. Flavia was right. Even if Dana and I escaped tonight, we wouldn't know where to go and whom to save. The vampires had me over a barrel, and there wasn't a damned thing I could do about it.

35

I parked in front of the farmhouse instead of the garage, and shut off the engine. The barn and back property were definitely off limits to our vampire captors. The less they knew about me, the better.

The front of the house was eerily dark, and I was worried that something terrible had happened to Tillie. Even though she was a ghost and technically dead, I wasn't confident that she was beyond the reach of the powerful *Ghostworld* murderer.

It was a dark and stormy night . . . whoever had written that clichéd line hadn't spent it with three vampires. Lucky putz.

I massaged my aching temples. My brain was close to blowing a breaker from contemplating a slew of escape proposals on the drive over, but each violent scheme jeopardized Dana's life and wouldn't afford the vamps enough undead life before I dispatched them to provide me the name of tonight's targeted murder victim. Discouraged, I leaned back against the worn seatback, lowered my eyelids, and sighed heavily. I shouldn't have surrendered to the vamps so easily, because I had an abundance of supernatural powers at my disposal. It was flat-out embarrassing.

The Druids remained silent and motionless in the dark, which was a blessing. Lightning struck nearby and we all jumped—everyone was on edge. I recalled last night's black lightning and wondered if this last strike had been natural or conjured. Since there was no way of knowing for sure, I erased it from my thoughts. I had more important issues to ponder.

The rain fell in buckets, and the pounding raindrops on the roof were hypnotic. I felt myself drifting off to sleep. Suddenly I jerked awake. I didn't know how long I'd dozed, so I quickly surveyed the group. Everyone was still in the same position. The vamps were leaving Dana and me alone . . . for now.

"Anybody up for a walk?" I asked gamely. My stiffening legs demanded exercise.

No response. I drummed my fingers on the steering wheel. I could've used some conversation to lighten the mood and keep me sane, which sounded schizoid since I wanted them to shut up earlier. But my mind was churning out an endless stream of "what if" scenarios and I couldn't turn it off. The moral of my predicament: *be careful what you wish for.*

It was getting stuffy inside the Explorer, and the inside windshield was fogged. Without fresh air, Dana and I would fall asleep and possibly asphyxiate, but the lack of oxygen wouldn't bother our non-breathing guests. Maybe that was their plan.

There was only one remedy. I threw open the door, and the whipping rain soaked the rest of my clothes in seconds flat. But its coolness felt refreshing. Reviving.

"I need some air," I said flatly, and stepped outside. Cara shouted after me, but the tempest drowned her words.

Flavia joined me and didn't look happy about standing in the rain. "Are you crazy, Luna?"

"That's not exactly a news flash," I yelled into the gusts.

"Go back inside the car," she ordered, pointing to the Explorer.

I faced her and mopped the rain from my eyes. "Go to hell."

She smiled cheerlessly. "Already been there."

Before we continued our lame battle of wits, another blistering lightning bolt struck close by and illuminated a leaping, snarling silhouette. It hurled itself at Flavia.

Unsure of the shadowy beast's identity, I backed off, but the vamp screamed bloody murder. Another flashing strike displayed the beast's thick form as it plunged right *through* Flavia. Then I knew what it was.

Tillie's ghost mastiff, Merlin.

The poor disillusioned dog's failure to take down Flavia didn't deter him at all—he bounded through the SUV's rear door and barked and growled viciously. Muffled screams melded with the squall, and the doors were quickly thrown open. Sabina and Cara bailed from both sides and hurriedly joined us, their expressions terrified masks.

"What the fuck *is* that thing?" Cara demanded, her vamp eyes piercing the watery gloom like red-hot embers.

"My guard dog," I replied simply, looking past her toward the house. Tillie must have sensed trouble and had come to our rescue—indirectly.

If she had another trick up her sleeve, I hoped she would use it soon, because the three vicious vamps looked ready to put the bite on me.

The large mastiff sat erect by Dana's side, baring his considerable canines in our direction. I blinked and cleared the rain from my face again. Suddenly, I knew what Tillie was up to—she had separated Dana from her captors.

About the time I got the picture, the vamps did, too. Cara turned and ran down the flooded driveway toward Dana and Merlin, but before she'd managed five splashing strides, the Explorer's doors slammed shut and locked. She stopped and screamed her anger, but she should've waited for the main event. A pair of invisible hands seized her and flung her into the Explorer's side. Her body caromed flaccidly off the steel, with most of her bones shattered.

Her crushed body landed in a heap in a shallow puddle, but Cara wasn't finished. Leaning heavily against the SUV, she painfully inched her way up to a standing position, and I realized that her body had already begun to heal. I didn't have much time to deal with Flavia and Sabina before Cara joined the fray. Two on one I could handle, but three-to-one odds were too steep to guarantee the outcome in my favor.

I was so absorbed in my thoughts that I never saw Flavia coming. She tackled me and slashed at my face with her claws. She was strong— much too strong for me to fend off for long. We rolled off the concrete drive onto the mushy lawn, each of us vying for a kill hold.

I instinctively transformed into a werewolf, as I did every time my enemy was stronger. I held tightly to her arms as I endured my physical change. The conversion didn't take long. It never did, unlike the movie transformations filmed in slow-mo. But it did hurt like hell.

My bones cracked, muscles, tendons, and cartilage shifted, and my skull reshaped itself into a fierce wolfen countenance with saliva-splashed teeth and fiery orange eyes. My black nostrils pulsated wildly at the close proximity of my adversary. My reconfigured brain grew primal. Ferocious. Hungry. Nearly uncontrollable.

Flavia tried to pull away, but it was too late. I lifted her up and threw her hard into the mud. Her face and body were buried a foot beneath the puddles.

I quickly leaped up and confronted Sabina, who had altered her features from human beauty to her savage vampire persona. Her skull was hairless, black and leathery, her forehead was blunt above her slanted crimson eyes, and her lips were tightly curled back, revealing her lethal white fangs. Her spiked ears twitched as she prepared to attack.

Flavia freed herself from the sucking muck and transformed herself into her predatory profile. She and Sabina book-ended me, and Cara was rapidly regenerating.

Three-to-one odds again.

I didn't like my chances.

36

They both attacked at once. I growled fiercely and swung an arm at the leaping Sabina. I pummeled her ribs in mid-flight, deflecting her attack. She snarled and flapped her arms like a wounded duck before landing hard with a muddy splash beside us.

With my other arm, I snagged the charging Flavia and clamped it around her neck with a vise grip. She struggled violently, spitting and hissing. Her free claws dug into my hairy back and extracted clumps of bloody flesh. A murderous howl rent the maelstrom as I increased the pressure on her neck.

But Flavia wasn't a quitter. She seized my arm and buried her claws to the bone. I wailed like a dying coyote from the intense pain, loosened my grip around her neck, and wrenched my arm away from her disabling grip before she did any more damage.

The powerful Flavia massaged her neck and helped the dazed Sabina off the ground. I swung around and confronted their next assault. Sabina was still too woozy from her crash landing and broken ribs to initiate a frontal attack, so she and Flavia circled me like vultures, their saber fangs exposed and ready to rid the world of one werewolf. I tried my best to ignore my wounded arm, and bared my teeth whenever one of them moved in too close.

I chanced a quick glimpse at the Explorer and winced. Cara's healing had proceeded faster than I'd anticipated, and I realized that once she rejoined her blood-sucking comrades, I was history.

What the hell was Tillie waiting for? I needed her magic now. Then it hit me. Maybe Merlin had gotten loose on his own and did what came naturally to him—attack! Maybe Tillie was inside sound asleep. Two too many maybes.

Out of the gloom, a wild scream pierced the air, and I glimpsed an airborne figure gliding over the driveway gate and heading in our direction. I growled loudly, envisioning another *Druid* flying to its sisters' defense.

But I was wrong.

My acute wolfen vision made out its features despite the torrential downpour, and I shivered . It was one ugly son-of-a-bitch.

Its gaping mouth was crammed with spiky teeth, and its emerald eyes returned my stunned gaze. The flying creature's skull was triangular like a billiard rack, its forehead wide with four horns, and its chin chiseled to a bony point. A satin-like hooded cape fluttered in the wind behind its flowing black gown, and the short sleeves exposed its long talons. I'd never seen any supernatural being like it. Hoped I never would again.

The creature swooped down at Sabina and decapitated the hissing vamp with a single slash of its lethal claws. Cara ran at the flying killer, screaming like a banshee, and jumped up to intercept the creature's freefall glide at Flavia. The two collided with a wet smack, then Cara fell lifelessly back to earth, closely followed by the splash of her leathery head. The killer levitated above her vanquished foe and stared angrily at Flavia and me.

I wasn't easily surprised by anything vampires did—their violent actions were somewhat predictable—but I was totally blown away by Flavia's next move. She ran at me, fangs retracted, and reverted to her human form.

"Help me, Joe! I'll tell you everything. Just keep that *thing* away from me."

My werewolf alter-ego didn't fully grasp her meaning. Its brute brain was programmed for survival at all costs. Kill or be killed. Rip out Flavia's throat and save the hideous creature the trouble.

But the way the killer looked at us stirred understanding in the depths of my brain. Two against one. A vampire ally was better than none at all this time. There was no second guessing for a savage mentality, unlike my human one. A decision was made. Period. No going back. No regrets.

Keeping a wary eye on the hovering creature, I growled and flashed my teeth at Flavia. She stopped short, nearly slipping on the slick grass. But the vampire got the message. Not too close.

My sluggish bestial mind envisioned one solution to our problem, but it would render me extremely vulnerable. I was about to go for the gusto when the front porch light snapped on. The cavalry had arrived.

37

The mysterious decapitator hovered ominously in the air above the Explorer, and Flavia stood terrified as I entered my painful transformation back to a vulnerable human. Through the steady downpour, I saw Tillie's ghostly contour step onto the front porch and assess the situation.

Seconds later, she waved at me like a madwoman, but I couldn't react. I was incapacitated at that moment, being half-wolf, half-human. I managed to peek at the flying, wingless creature to see if it was attacking us, but it was still hovering in place.

I stuck out my freakish human-wolf arm and called for my mage staff. The driver's door flew open, and the staff zoomed into my open paw-hand. I hugged it close until my metamorphosis ended, which took all of twenty more seconds.

As it turned out, I was worried about the wrong creature. I should've been watching Flavia. The sneak had changed back to her primal vampire form while I was de-wolfing. She snarled once and pounced, but Tillie came to my rescue. My live-in ghost reared back and flung both arms at Flavia's back. A dozen silhouettes shot forward at blurred speed and pummeled the vampire's back. I stepped aside and let her smack the driveway, face first. Multiple wooden stakes protruded from her back like pins in a pincushion. I was impressed with Tillie's magic. Flavia burst into purplish-black flames.

Dammit! Though Tillie had saved my life, the last of the vamps was dead, and so was my hope of discovering the name of tonight's pending murder victim. Now I'd have to wait for the announcement in the morning paper or TV news.

The unearthly blaze reduced Flavia to a modest pile of muddy ash. As the cool rain soothed my acute disappointment, it also reminded me that my clothes lay scattered about the lawn. I quickly retrieved what was left of my shorts, wrapped the dripping fabric around my waist, and cinched it tight with my belt. I waved my thanks to Tillie, and she entered the warm, dry house.

My makeshift Tarzan look would get me by while I dealt with the hovering creature, but when I glanced above the Explorer, it had vanished. I spun a 360 just to be certain that it hadn't repositioned itself, but there was no sign of it anywhere. Gone was good, but the creature left without giving me some kind of sign whether it was friend or foe. I sighed. From now on, I'd have to watch my back for that ugly flier.

Cara's and Sabina's headless bodies burst into flames and were reduced to powdery ash in no time. Good riddance. I'd bury their heads later.

I sprinted to the Explorer where Merlin stood—or more accurately *sat*—guard on the back seat next to my unconscious partner. I jumped behind the wheel and sped into the dry barn. After the SUV lurched to a stop, I carried Dana over to the central seating area and deposited her and her purse on one of the three sofas arranged in a horseshoe configuration.

That accomplished, I shuffled into my office, stripped off my skimpy jungle wear, and hopped into the shower. The steamy spray stung my injured arm, but revived the rest of my wet, iced parts. I felt my wolfen regenerative genes hard at work with the healing process. By morning, there wouldn't even be a scar.

After toweling myself dry, I felt like a million bucks. Totally refreshed and relaxed. My next project was reviving Dana, and I hoped it went faster than poor Kit's recovery. I checked my voicemail for messages, hoping to hear about my friend's condition, but there were none. No news was good news. I tried to stay optimistic.

It was a typical sultry Florida fall, so I slipped on fresh summer clothes and athletic shoes. While the Northerners were shivering from the October cold, we Floridians were still in our sweating mode.

Dana hadn't moved from where I'd propped her head up on a pillow at the end of the sofa. Her expression was a picture of angelic serenity, betraying her frightening, near-death encounter with the three vampires. I wondered how much she'd remember when she awoke.

I flicked on the fifty-inch flatscreen TV mounted to the wall behind a pair of pegboard cabinet doors, and switched to the local cable news station. I yawned and stretched after viewing twenty minutes of the crime and flood stories. The only notable exception was the "Breaking News" segment concerning the fire at Senator Justice Kane's Windemere mansion. Since there was no mention of recovered dead bodies, it was obvious that the ruins were still too hot to inspect. But the night was still young.

I dozed off, and when I awoke an hour later, Dana stared at me with red-rimmed eyes. Angst had erased her angelic serenity.

"Where am I?" she said, her voice groggy and thick. "And where are the vampires?"

"Whoa, take it easy. The vampires are gone and won't be bothering you again. *Ever*." I paused. "You're inside the barn behind my house."

She surveyed its vast interior. "Some barn. Where're the animals?"

I smiled and patted her hand. "Uh, they would be you and me."

She struggled to a sitting position. "You're always making with the jokes."

I nodded. "A little humor makes the bad times easier to swallow. That's my personal doctrine."

"Humor *and* sarcasm," she corrected me.

"Hey, nobody's perfect."

Dana sobered. "What happened after I blacked out?"

I described my vampire adventures, the run-in with that mysterious flying creature, and concluded with Tillie's heroics.

She smiled. "Thank God for my guardian angel."

"Your what?" I asked, dumbfounded.

"Tillie and my real guardian angel. And I don't consider her ugly at all. She is what she is."

"Uh, I'm sorry about that. I had no idea."

She chuckled. "I just hope she didn't hear you."

I vividly recalled the creature's decapitation skills. "Yeah, me too. I've never seen anything — er, anyone — like him."

"*Her*. Her name's Agatha, and she has feelings. So if you should meet her again, be gentle . . . or you might have to face the consequences."

I massaged my neck. I was well aware of those consequences.

"So why aren't you out there looking for the killer's next victim?" she asked, all business again.

"Searching for a needle in a haystack would be easier." I wrapped my good arm around her shoulders. "And besides, I had to stay here and take care of my new partner." I pecked her cheek.

"Thanks. I didn't think you liked me very much."

"That was then; this is now. Let's just say that you're growing on me." I laughed. "How about we go back to the house and get a good night's sleep?"

"Not yet." Dana opened her purse and pulled out a pack of smokes and a lighter. "You don't mind, do you? When I'm nervous, I get the urge to smoke."

I empathized with her. I got the same urge after sex.

"Knock yourself out. I might join you." I tapped a butt out of her pack and lit it. It didn't taste the same without a sexual entrée.

We sat silently, enjoying each other's company.

"Thanks for staying," she said softly, blowing smoke toward the high ceiling.

"My pleasure."

She suddenly was transfixed by the television news. *Now what?*

"Did you see *that*?" she cried excitedly.

"See what?" I replied, cocking my head toward the screen.

"There's trouble at *Ghostworld*. The reporter on the scene reported that Jeffrey Stanton's trapped inside his office."

"Now?"

"They said it was a *live report*," she answered, snuggling against me.

We stared at each other, wordlessly sharing an identical thought. *Stanton was tonight's intended victim.*

I got up and rushed toward the wall that separated this side of the barn from the other side—the *black area*. It was time to boogie.

There was no sign of a door in the high, broad wall; the area could be accessed only by magic. *My* magic. I pointed the tip of my staff at the wall, and a blue arcing energy stream instantly created a doorway in the solid surface. I strode into my secret area, which housed stores of state-of-the-art weaponry, a varied collection of disposable black clothing, and my pride and joy.

I wouldn't let Stanton fry like Senator Kane, but I'd have to move fast. Because of the crowded fire scene, I couldn't magically appear out of thin air. There'd be too many witnesses, and Uncle Jess would have a fit. So . . . I'd have to travel the old-fashioned way—in my customized black beauty.

38

Dana followed me through the blue magical radiance to my secret universe.

"Ugh! You drive a hearse?" she groaned, checking out my pride and joy.

"Not just any hearse. This baby is a 1947 Silver Wraith Rolls Royce hearse," I corrected her, disappointed by her lukewarm reaction. But I wasn't totally surprised. It had that effect on women. Kit Wilson always referred to it as the "meat wagon."

My black beauty's sweeping fenders reminded me of the rolling surf at the beach, and its abbreviated rectangular cab and storage sections flowed above those graceful lines. Years ago, I swapped out the long glass panels and door windows for bulletproof glass. While I was at it, I added an armored hood, doors, bumpers, and quarter panels. I'd replaced the original engine with a specially customized Dodge Hemi, which then required a complete suspension and transmission overhaul and update. Unlike the raucous roar of youthful performance cars, I had the hearse outfitted with a super-stealth exhaust system.

For obvious reasons, I switched the original Rolls Royce flying lady mascot hood ornament with a silver wolf head. Since I used the Silver Wraith for clandestine night missions, I installed vintage ultraviolet fog lights which, with my wolfen vision, afforded me a terrific after-dark view.

I had a detailing buddy of mine paint a skull and the phrase *Dying Breed* above both rear fenders. It was a shrewd touch, considering that the werewolf population in North American was dwindling. Sort of an ironic public service announcement.

I didn't waste time explaining all that to Dana. I had to shake a leg if I planned to save "Stan the Man." I waved Dana back to the gray area, and was about to climb in the hearse when Tillie materialized behind me.

"I'm sorry for ruining your plans," a feminine voice said, startling me.

I swore as my injured arm slammed into the driver's door. "How many times have I told you not to sneak up on me like that?" I thundered.

"Obviously not enough," she shot back. She frowned at me with her favorite *Joe look*—exasperation.

But Tillie had her moments. She was a throwback knockout dressed in her curve-hugging black cotton and lace dress that rustled impishly at her ankles and exposed a generous crease of cleavage. It was her only dress. Her hanging dress.

"Consider this your last warning," I sputtered. I shouldn't have been so hard on Tillie since she'd just saved me from the vamps, but I was in a hurry, and impatience made me irritable. "Now if you'll excuse me, I've got a life to save."

She held up her hand. "Not so fast." She watched way too much ESPN college football Gameday with me.

My hand lingered near the door handle. "What?"

"Are you going after Stanton tonight?"

I eyed her suspiciously. "Have you been eavesdropping again?" I accused her.

"That's beside the point. I came out here to your precious fortress to warn you Stanton's not in his burning office. It's a trap . . . for *you*. He's somewhere else on the property, suffering a slow, torturous death.

"When you walk into *Ghostworld*, you'll have to deal with black magic that's more formidable than any you've ever heard of," she explained.

I propped my good elbow on the roof of the hearse. "Exactly how would you know that?"

She fidgeted with the lace adorning the waistband. "Because I've known witches who went up against such magic, and I never heard from them again. I don't want that to happen to you."

"So you're advising me to watch my step?"

"Haven't you been listening? Forget about saving Stanton. He's a dead man walking—he can't be saved. They'll see to that."

"Who're *they*?"

Major fidgeting. "No . . . no one. Forget I said that."

"Are you referring to the *Gorgons*?" I asked boldly.

She was panic-stricken. "Shhhh! Don't ever say that name again unless you've got a death wish!"

I shrugged cavalierly. "No death wish here."

Tillie managed the faintest of smiles and hugged her breasts between her upper arms, inflating her cleavage. "Don't go. Humor an old ghost and stay here tonight."

She was purposely throwing in a little erotic cheesecake to entice me to stick around, and although I believed her about the *Ghostworld* sorcerer's incredible black magic, I at least had to *try* to save Stanton. After all, if anything happened to him, I wouldn't get paid for my bodyguard work yesterday.

"I'm going, and that's that. The *Gorgons* be damned," I said mulishly. I thought Tillie was going to faint from my outburst.

She mouthed something that looked like *stubborn fool,* and vanished in a huff.

"Do you make a habit of talking to yourself?" Dana had reappeared in the magic rift.

"I was having a conversation with my housekeeper," I replied defensively.

"I gathered you're not afraid of the *Gorgons?*"

I stiffened. Another eavesdropper. "What do *you* know about them?"

"Enough that I don't want to go out of my way to tick 'em off," she replied.

"Why's everyone suddenly so concerned with them? They sound like mythical hobgoblins to me. I'm going to do what I have to do, and not worry about people I haven't even met. Okay?" It appeared as if everyone connected with magic knew about the *Gorgons* but me. Apparently I had to get out and socialize more.

Dana trotted over. "I'm going, too," she stated firmly, as if "no" wasn't an option.

I'd already wasted enough time, and I wasn't about to spend more arguing the trip's dangers with Dana. I gruffly gestured for her to climb in, and the inner wall rift disappeared behind us. Another rift opened to the driveway, and we rolled out of the barn and into the raging tempest with the grace and power of a world-class sprinter. After we cleared the front gate, I floored it, and our heads slammed back against the headrests.

We hadn't gone more than a half-mile when Dana screamed, "Look out!"

I stood on the brake pedal. The rear-end fishtailed, and the frame swayed like we were trapped inside the cradle from hell. Breathing hard,

I peered through the silvery curtain; the ultraviolet fog lights penetrated its opacity.

My heart sank. As far as I could see, the Emerald Zone's pristine whiteness had displaced the land outside my farm. We were virtual prisoners, locked away within my farm's boundaries. Stanton was now officially a dead man . . . unless Dana or I conceived a brilliant plan of escape real soon. But that was easier said than done. *How could we possibly slip past the white night and its monstrous inhabitant?*

The answer was as plain as the nose on my face.

We couldn't.

39

I smacked my hand against the steering wheel. "We're basically screwed," I exclaimed in a surly tone. For some inexplicable reason, the *Ghostworld* murderer was bound and determined to keep me on the sidelines tonight, but I couldn't fathom why. *I mean, what did he have to fear from my puny magic?* In a one-on-one confrontation, I couldn't stop him from nailing Stanton. I smacked the wheel again. It just didn't add up.

An earth-shaking rumble shook the Silver Wraith, followed by another. And another. The Emerald Zone giant was headed our direction . . . and fast.

Dana hadn't responded to my theatrics and succinct gripe, so I turned to see what was on her mind.

She was gone!

My nerves flittered and my gut soured. I checked out the casket bed in back, but Dana wasn't there, either. *How the hell had she exited the Silver Wraith without using the door?* Uncle Jess was right on target with his ambiguous assessment of her talents, which reinforced my earlier thought. Neither one of us really knew much about DSI's new hired gun.

Could the Ghostworld *sorcerer have spirited her away?* I was considering that frightening angle until the Emerald Zone brightened like an old light bulb about to blow and redirected my train of thought. I tried to see past my fogged breath on the windshield into the blinding whiteness, but I struck out. No giant silhouette. Nothing.

Another round of teeth-rattling thuds jolted the hearse, and I hit my head on the rearview mirror. I readjusted it and massaged the pain in my scalp. More thuds inside the white night. But this time they were interspersed by earsplitting, dolorous howls that engulfed the storm's rage.

Suddenly, the giant's arm plunged into our night. I slammed the hearse into reverse before I was a sardine in a tin can. Sure enough, the damned thing crashed where the front end had been seconds before.

The arm was blood-black from numerous wounds. Before I left the hearse to examine the nature of the injuries, its thick elbow cocked like it was about to swing its fist at someone, and disappeared in a blur. *But that was impossible, wasn't it? Who in their right mind would challenge that killer on its home court? Someone suicidal, that's who.*

Almost immediately, there was a thump that would've shattered the Richter-Scale record, and I heard a death wail that curled my toes. The ghostly Emerald Zone choir fired up, and its high-pitched melody surfed the gusts. I winced. But the torturous singing didn't last long. After reaching its crystal-breaking crescendo, it abruptly died out. So did the giant's wails.

The hushed white world flickered a couple times before it was snuffed to black like a spent candle. I exhaled loudly and collapsed back in my seat. *Was the giant dead?* Common sense dictated *no*—but hearing was believing. *If so, who could've killed it? The Gorgons?* I doubted it. I knew I was ecstatic about the big guy's demise, but they didn't have anything to gain by vanquishing it. *Or did they?*

With the formidable Emerald Zone gone, I could head down to *Ghostworld* and rescue ole Jeffrey. Except for one small detail.

Dana was missing.

It was déjà vu. The last time she vanished, I found myself mixed up with three nasty vampires, which started me thinking that I might be better off without her. After all, she'd taken up too much of my precious time already. More of a hindrance than a help.

But I shook my head and grimaced. I just couldn't bring myself to drive away without at least making an effort to find her, so I pulled up my wet shirt collar and shoved the door open.

"Where're you going?' Dana asked sharply . . . from *inside* the Silver Wraith.

I slammed the door shut. "Where the hell have you been?" I demanded, relieved but perplexed.

"Miss me?"

"Well yeah, but you didn't answer my question."

"I was scouting out the Emerald Zone to see if there was any way around it. There wasn't."

I noticed her bruised face and arms and was genuinely concerned.

"God, you look like you picked a fight with a Mack Truck. What happened?"

"I ran into a couple trees in the dark, that's all. The bruises'll heal," she said apathetically.

I got the impression that she was lying. *Had she slain the giant?* Nah. Impossible. "Did you hear the fight inside the Emerald Zone? I think the giant's dead. It sure sounded like it, anyway," I told her.

She grinned. "You couldn't miss it with all that racket. If it's dead, I'm glad. Now we don't have to worry about the vampires or the giant from now on."

I refused to burst her bubble by enlightening her that I was always on the look-out for vampires. We weren't exactly kissing cousins.

"I've got a first aid kit back in the barn," I offered, but she stoically declined.

"I thought we were on our way to *Ghostworld*. Have a change of heart?" she asked. When I didn't answer, she added, "Or are you afraid of the *Ghostworld* killer?"

Another maddening partner. What a lovely pair of taunting personalities. Kit and Dana. Surly and sarcastic. I must have been cursed at birth.

But for once, I kept my mouth shut, and started the engine. The hearse shot down the road like it was in hyper drive, but before we traveled a mile, the Silver Wraith disappeared into thin air. Our delay forced me to exploit the supernatural shortcut.

The teleportation highway.

40

Peering through the teleportation fabric, I located the perfect place to re-enter reality, and park—behind the deserted Mansion Macabre. This time I remembered to bring my mage staff along. Dana and I hiked to the edge of the daunting attraction and scrutinized the chaos near the front of the park. Tall flames licked the sky as six fire-hose plumes cascaded down upon it. But the firemen's luck had run out—the rain ended.

"Time to get Stanton out of there," I alerted Dana as I readied my staff for our mission.

She gripped my wrist. "No, don't. Tillie said he's not in there, and I believe her," she insisted, mesmerized by the untamed conflagration.

I pulled my hand away. "Look, everyone in Orlando knows Stanton's in there," I argued. "Why else would the park staff tell that to the cops and reporters?"

"To throw them off the scent," she replied. "Maybe they were under a spell at the time."

"I don't buy it. If we don't get him out now, it'll be curtains for him."

"It's a trap. I feel it," she warned me. "I'm sure the murdering sorcerer had a back-up plan in case you got past the Emerald Zone and showed up. Trust me. Stanton's somewhere else on the property, and we've got to find him fast before he dies."

My stubbornness surfaced, as it often did. "Nice try, but I'm going to pull him out right now."

I cast my retrieval spell toward the blaze and watched the blue energy stream shoot from the staff's tip into the distant burning building. Within five seconds, a smoking figure emerged from the energy stream.

But it wasn't Stanton. It was another orange-eyed assassin demon! Dammit. Tillie had been right.

It sucker-punched me before my shock wore off, and I went flying into the mansion's hard stucco surface. I bounced away like a racquetball and fell into the drenched shrubbery below.

For his second and final act, the demon produced a typical murderous fireball and readied it for launch. T minus three seconds and counting.

"So long, Luna. This is payback for killing one of my brothers."

Demons had brothers? Hmmm. As with most bad guys, it wasted time talking—gloating over its control of the situation. Now I wasn't certain whether this assassin was blind or just plain stupid, but it totally ignored Dana standing off to the side. Until it was too late. When he finally noticed her, she simply vaporized him. No muss. No fuss. Child's play.

The stars receded in my head and I stood painfully. My staff was still attached to my hand, and I wished that I'd had enough presence of mind to notice that a minute ago. I could've dealt with the demon myself. I liked the idea of teamwork when I was on the rescuing end, but I wasn't so keen about being saved. It must've been a man thing.

I repaid her with a silly grin. "Thanks; I owe you one."

"Consider us even," she said, aware of my manly discomfort.

I nodded. "How'd you manage that vaporization trick?" The casual manner in which she dispatched the demon bothered me. *Was she a government assassin?* I'd heard about those people working for the CIA.

She arched her brows. "You didn't see her?"

"See who?"

"My guardian angel. She was right behind me."

I hadn't seen anything clearly except the Milky Way. "Musta missed her."

"Now can we look for Stanton?" she asked, all business again. End of subject.

I swallowed a sizeable wedge of humble pie. "Yeah, sure. Sorry about not believing you about the trap."

She nodded her acceptance of my foolishness and pointed toward the south section of the park. The large sign proclaimed Ghost Town. "Well?"

"Looks as good as any place to start." I wasn't about to argue with her again.

She promptly set off for the neon-lit Western ghost town, and I hurried after her like a chastised puppy. I rubbed my jaw and neck. This investigation was certainly a ball-buster.

She and I hopped the abandoned turnstiles and silently entered the

19th-century replica of an Old West ghost town. Without tourists milling about, the place was flat-out eerie. Ominous. Gloomy storefronts, hitching posts, water troughs, gas lampposts, and plank sidewalks lined the central cobblestone street. The shop windows exhibited old-style fashions and mining-town hardware. Honky-tonk piano music spilled into the street from an elegant saloon, *The Silver Nugget*, and I pictured myself downing an ice-cold mug of beer and mingling with seductively dressed saloon ladies. Man, that sounded good right now.

Several holographic horses whinnied, snorted, and stamped at the hitching posts when we stepped onto the street. The horses were a nice welcoming touch for tourists. Unfortunately, we weren't tourists.

We hadn't walked fifty feet when a cloud of bats swooped down from one of the buildings at the end of the street and headed directly at us. Holographic bats again. Stanton and his engineers had redundant imaginations.

Dana froze. "The bats are real!" she hissed.

Real? I hated bats. I took a second look at the hard-charging fliers and saw that they weren't the garden-variety insect-munchers. These were larger than fox bats, with a four-foot wing span, smoldering red eyes, and stalactites for fangs. Supernatural bats! There were at least a hundred of those ugly carnivores. As they flew closer, I focused on their hooked claws that would make short work of their prey. Like us.

I quickly tapped my staff three times on the cobblestones, and a green bubble shield encompassed us and repelled the attacking creatures. We winced from their piercing squeaks as their leathery wings scraped our force field.

When the last one winged around us, we turned and saw them circling for another attack. *Why?* They couldn't penetrate our defense. *It was useless, so why keep trying?* I soon had my answer.

Their dagger-sharp claws penetrated the shield and came close to skewering us, but the force field refused to wholly yield. The bats finally disappeared over a storefront.

Dana clapped her hand across her mouth to stifle a scream. "Oh God. Look!"

An army of killer daisy-like flowers with spikes for petals sprang up at the far end of the street and propagated within the cobblestones at a tremendous rate. The killing field expanded toward us, and at the rate they reproduced, we had five minutes until we were pushing up daisies. I redirected the staff's magic to halt the homicidal flowers' progress, but in doing so, I had to sacrifice our defense shield.

The advancing spikes were stalled for the time being, but the bats now had a clear shot at us. We faced two grim prospects—be sliced and diced by murderous claws, or be bludgeoned by flower spikes. The mage staff quivered in my hands. It was up against some damned strong magic, and I felt my spell on the flowers weakening.

It looked like it was going to be another fun night at *Ghostworld*.

41

The bats reappeared.

Even as a werewolf, I'd be no match for a squadron of flesh-eating bats with claws the size of Joan Rivers' nails. Our only chance to live rested solely on my magic versus *his* magic. *Could I pull it off?* I recast our green protective bubble a breath or two away from the squadron's arrival. Not having time to swerve away from us, they crashed into the bubble, one after another, mangling their bodies and severing their arteries. Blood spurted everywhere. The gore-covered shield held, but unfortunately a few bats survived to claw another day.

On cue, the daisy-spikes began reproducing and sprouting again, and advanced like a tsunami.

In a perfect world, I could've maintained the shield *and* halted the spikes' progress, but my magic wasn't usually strong enough to walk and chew gum at the same time. However, I was never one to admit defeat, so I rolled the dice and conjured both. The protective bubble materialized as a watery green film, and the spikes' progress slowed, but neither spell operated at an optimum level. Behind us, the surviving bats returned and clawed at the weakened force field. One of the winged bastards broke through and raked my shoulder, agitating my wolfen genes. Hair sprang up on my arms and neck.

Dana's firm grip on my arm arrested them. "Don't," she advised.

This time I trusted that she had a better plan, and I mentally shut down the transformation. I exercised my arm a few times. It tingled where Dana touched it. Talk about your magic touch. That got me wondering. *Could her limited magic complement my own to defeat these enemies?*

Another bat clung to the force field and plowed three furrows in my back. This time I grunted and looked over my shoulder. They had clawed a small hole in the bubble. My magical endeavors, though valiant, were failing us big time.

"Joe!" Dana shouted and frantically gestured at the advancing spikes;

they'd closed within ten feet of us.

"Concentrate!" she yelled above the bat squeals. The creatures smelled blood—my blood—and redoubled their efforts to penetrate our dwindling defense.

"I'm doing the best I can," I shouted, but I struggled for a hundred and ten percent. Gripping my trembling mage staff for all I was worth, I shut out the pain and focused solely on our defenses.

Dana seized the staff with both hands, closed her eyes, and muttered something under her breath. Suddenly, I pictured broken bat carcasses and exploding spikes. *Was it all a dream?* When the vision vanished, I noticed that my staff had calmed . . . after Dana had grabbed it. *What was up with that?*

"Concentrate, dammit!" she growled, her eyelids squeezed tight.

I hastily recalled the destructive visions, and as they intensified like high- definition video, a tremendous surge of energy coursed through the staff. A crimson light blossomed throughout Ghost Town, and my arms suddenly felt like Popeye's after downing a can of spinach.

I cheated on my half of our focus bargain and chanced a look around us. The bats disintegrated to powdery vitriolic guano, and the daisy-spikes burst into red dust. It was just the way I imagined it. I shivered. Scary stuff.

Our shield paled and vanished, and the mage staff, although still a bit warm, settled down. Dana's eyelids gradually rose.

"What just happened?" I asked her suspiciously. "You've got more magic skills than you let on. C'mon, come clean."

She shot me a coy grin. "What you don't know won't hurt you."

"Dammit, Dana, we're partners. We shouldn't keep secrets from each other."

"Okay, I know a little more magic than I let on. Satisfied?"

That was it? The big confession? Oh, boy. "I guess it'll have to be."

"Good. Let's find Stanton."

I stuffed my hands in my shorts' pockets, and we sauntered along the now-red cobblestone Main Street and scrutinized every storefront for suspicious activity.

After we'd passed four stores, Dana asked, "Which business would you try first?"

The saloon sounded damned good, but the place didn't fit the bill . . . not yet, anyway. *Where would the sorcerer most likely have stashed Stanton?* I mentally reviewed the store names for a clue. Lee's Laundry. Kelly's Medicine Shoppe. The Silver Nugget. Como's Barbershop. Frank's Fine Meats. McCain's Hardware.

I stopped in mid-review.

Dana studied my face. "What is it?"

"If we were going to torture someone before putting them out of our misery, a butcher shop's the perfect place, with all those lethal tools and knives," I explained. The fake business appeared deserted, but the torturous action could be happening in the back.

"How about the jail?" Dana nodded toward the Tumbleweed Jail.

"Too obvious," I objected. "C'mon." I climbed the steps to the raised wooden sidewalk and tentatively entered Frank's Fine Meats. I wondered what a pound of ground Stanton cost. My fingers curled tightly around the mage staff.

As Dana stepped inside, the holographic horses started their entertaining routine and several holographic tumbleweeds cartwheeled through town.

"This place gives me the willies," Dana said, scanning the butcher shop's interior for danger.

I halted. "Did you decide to search the Ghost Town first because you sensed Stanton's presence here?" I asked, trying to determine how strong her magic was.

"Yeah, a little bit."

"No major vibes, then?"

"No major vibes. Let's take a quick look around and get out of here."

She wasn't the only one with the creeps. I regretted my search choice. Damn logic, anyway! Out of the blue, I imagined what Dana looked like naked. Dangerous situations occasionally affected my sexual libido that way.

"Get your mind out of the gutter," she snapped, glaring at me.

Dana shock #2. "You read minds, too?"

"Only when we work together, and right now I'm the only one concentrating on Stanton's whereabouts."

This time I was the one feeling naked. "Only when we work together, huh?"

"Yep. Trust me, I wouldn't venture into your low-life mind if I didn't have to."

"Very funny," I grumbled.

"Not to me. Now can we get back to searching this place?"

"Yeah, sure." I felt invaded, but I was sure she'd heard that thought, too.

The butcher shop door slammed shut behind us. We both jumped a foot.

My upper lip instinctively curled back like my wolfen counterpart, exposing my teeth. Someone knew we were here, and I didn't relish that one bit, especially with those lethal knives on the premises.

Dana and I exchanged anxious glances, and against our better judgments, cautiously walked deeper into Frank's butcher shop.

42

The bittersweet odor of fresh meat assailed my nostrils as soon as we reached the glass display case. *Was it Stanton, or another one of Ghostworld's manufactured smells?*

A spotless white counter sat atop the display case, equipped with two vintage balance scales and boxes of wax paper. Our approach must have triggered a sound show. The beef in the case mooed, the lamb baaed, and the chicken clucked. Cute. If we were elementary school kids, we'd get a kick out of it. But we weren't.

Holographic customers, a husband and wife and their two small children—a boy and a girl ten to twelve years old—shopped at the far end of the case, while a rotund, jolly butcher waited behind the counter, his apron splashed with bloody smears.

He smiled at our approach. "May I help you? The rib steaks are on special today for 29 cents a pound."

"Not interested, meathead," I muttered, while Dana ignored him altogether.

His smile flipped to a frown, and he bared his thick, finely honed teeth. "How about some ground Stanton-burger then, *shit*head."

I couldn't believe my ears. *Had this holographic butcher just said what I thought he said, or was my exhausted, overwrought mind imagining things?* Dana swung around toward the counter; she'd heard him, too. One look into his globular black eyes told us that this guy wasn't part of the daily tourist show.

Before I could think of a clever retort, he flew at me over the case and tried to rip the mage staff from me. For an airy ghost, it was damned strong.

I kept my cool for a change and reacted with a quick chant. My staff jolted the assailant with a bolt of ethereal electricity. Mr. Butcher howled, a haunting unearthly sound that played on my nerves like a screechy violin, before he vanished in a puff of acrid smoke.

GHOSTWORLD

I coughed and turned. "We must be . . . ." The rest of the message froze on my tongue. The innocent-looking family of shoppers was attacking Dana.

The husband shredded the back of Dana's shirt, while the mother went for my partner's neck with her long spiky teeth. The young daughter brandished a thick cleaving knife above Dana's face. The razor-sharp blade glistened beneath the fluorescent ceiling fixtures.

I quickly conjured a protective shield around Dana, but the ghosts invaded it as if it wasn't there. Quickly withdrawing the spell, I swung my staff at the deranged family, but the staff swooshed right through them. But their ghostly punches connected and drew blood from my lip. Not exactly fair. I kept my wolfen persona at bay. Brute force wasn't the answer.

The father floated above the counter and secured a larger, more menacing meat cleaver. I cast another electrical blast into dear old dad, and he writhed and shrieked in its crackling web before withering to a short-lived smoke ring. Poof. Gone.

When I spun around, Dana was lying on the floor, blood oozing from her flailing hands. *Where was her guardian angel?* There was no sign of her. What a weird arrangement.

So, I guessed that it was up to me to defend her.

I blasted the young girl with an identical charge that had worked so well with the butcher and Shopper Dad, and she went flying ass-over-applecart through the wall into Never-Never Land. Shopper Mom glowered at me after watching her ghostly daughter vanish, and rapidly freed Dana. With a shrill war-whoop, she charged me with bullet speed.

Her teeth parked themselves in the back of my hand holding the mage staff, peeling away strips of flesh like I was an apple. *How was that possible?* Powerful magic, that's how. My fist flew open from the agonizing assault, and my lone weapon bounced twice on the floor before rolling to a stop against the display case. No matter how hard I shook my hand, Shopper Mom held on with the ferocity of a pit-bull.

I directed my protective ring at her and unleashed its purple force, but it was ineffective. Further incensed, she dropped down and sank her chompers into my calf. She worried it like a rat with cheese, splashing blood over me and the display case glass. I kicked my leg, hoping to shake her off—but being a ghost, she had no substance, except where her teeth ripped into my flesh. But even when I struck her face, it became ethereal for a brief instant. The pain in my calf was unbearable, with no end in sight . . . until I bled to death.

Dana screamed bloody murder, which I supposed was appropriate considering our one-sided battles, but Shopper Mom kept me so occupied that I couldn't see who was coming at her now. To be honest, I couldn't have protected her even if I saw her attacker, because I was too preoccupied with mommy dearest and her fangs from hell.

Dana scrabbled backwards from her assailant on her hands and feet. As she came into view, I saw that her cocoa eyes were terrified. A moment later, I saw why.

The wraithlike Shopper Son emerged from behind the counter shadows wielding an axe. Its blade was poised to separate Dana's head from her shoulders.

43

Shopper Boy took his sweet time floating above the counter to Dana. He savored her vulnerability and terror. The little bastard. Dressed in airy denim shorts, a Deadhead tee shirt, and black sneakers, he grinned maliciously at his victim-to-be.

His mother, meanwhile, gnawed my calf clear to the bone. She wore a blood-free yellow summer dress and designer sandals, but there was nothing fashionable about the way she devoured me. *Dressed to kill* was more like it.

My staff was my last resort. I stretched my hand toward the display case and summoned it. It vibrated and hammered the floor, but couldn't budge. The *Ghostworld* sorcerer's magic prevented it from obeying my command. That guy played for keeps.

Discouraged and frightened at our seemingly inescapable predicament, I dragged Shopper Mom along the blood-smeared floor toward Dana and her axe-wielding assailant, but before I reached them, my head spun like an out-of-control carousel, my vision blurred, and my knees buckled like rubber.

I stared helplessly as the bratty kid raised the axe above his shoulder, primed to chop through my partner's thin neck. His mouth stretched cartoon wide, and his eyes glistened like a polished pair of onyx gemstones. After he descended beside Dana, she kicked out at his closer leg, but her strike continued through his ethereal body. She screamed, and the kid's expansive smile nearly swallowed his ears.

I punched my attacker's head again, but it was no go, too. We were goners.

A black gauze fell across my eyes from extreme blood loss, and I was about to call it a life when another pair of ghostly forms shot through the front door. *Reinforcement shoppers? Weren't these two enough?* My vision was so muzzy that I couldn't make out the new players. I toppled to the tile floor and rested my head on the cold, hard surface.

Suddenly, a dog barked inside the shop. A big dog. And it didn't sound happy. I blinked away a layer of haze and lay there shocked at what I saw. Merlin, the squirrel-chasing wonder dog, flew into Axe Kid, knocking him and his non-ghostly axe to the floor. With one vicious chomp, Merlin tore out the ghost kid's throat, and the would-be killer vanished in a puff of acrid smoke, just like his ghost father.

Meanwhile, Tillie took the high road—no gory, unladylike violence for her. Thrusting her arms out, she growled a magic spell that changed mommy dearest into a harmless ghostly spider. Tillie glanced my way, winked, and brought her ghostly foot down hard on the scurrying spider. I fell back limply, laughing and moaning simultaneously.

I had just discovered that it took a ghost to kill a ghost. Live and learn.

"You get yourself into the damnedest scrapes, Joe Luna," she chided me lightly, and I could tell she was pleased with herself for saving our skins.

"How . . . ." My consciousness started slipping away again.

Tillie clucked. "Here, allow me." In her ghostly form, she cast another spell, and my leg was good as new.

Dana stood stiffly and shambled unsteadily to my side. "Thanks to you both," she said hoarsely, and helped me off the floor. Her complexion was corpse-like, but her spirit was revived.

I looked questioningly at Tillie. "How'd you know that we were in trouble?"

"Why, that was the funniest dang thing I ever saw. A young woman materialized out of a swarm of bees in the kitchen and told me that you and Dana were about to be murdered. Unless Merlin and I skedaddled over to *Ghostworld* to save you."

Stunned, Dana and I stared at each other for a moment. "That was Gwendolyn Stockard, and she's pulled that dog-and-pony show on me a couple times before."

"Strange is all I got to say in the matter," Tillie said.

"Did Gwendolyn tell you anything else?" Dana queried.

"Oh yeah, I almost forgot. She told me to git out of the butcher shop like it was on fire after Merlin and I were done saving you." She nervously scanned the place. "I reckon we'd better take her advice."

"I agree. Time to go," Dana said and started for the door. She grabbed me on her way. "You heard the lady . . . let's go before more ghosts show up."

Tillie and Merlin vanished into thin air, while I bent to retrieve my staff, but it wouldn't budge. It weighed a ton. I threw up my hands and headed for the exit. Ghostly wails drifted from the closed door behind the counter, and I sprinted double-time outside.

"Son-of-a-bitch!" I growled. "I couldn't lift my staff off the floor."

"What are we going to do without it?" Dana asked.

I shrugged. "I'm not going back inside, that's for damned sure," I groused. "It'll find its way back home eventually."

She scowled. "In the meantime, how are you going to protect us?"

"We'll use *your* magic?" I shot back.

"It's gone . . . like yours."

Sirens wafted on the slight breeze. More fire trucks arrived at the fire site.

"So where could Stanton be?" I murmured, more to myself than Dana.

Dana looked past my shoulder. "Oh my God! Forget about him. Run!" she exclaimed, her voice breaking.

I couldn't believe what I heard. "What are you talking about?"

But she ignored me and took off running toward the jail.

My alarm bells rang and I pivoted. Prickles compressed my spine. Stanton stumbled out the front door of McCain's Hardware, his face a swollen bloody pulp, his clothes tattered strips, and his body bruised and battered. But that wasn't what chilled me.

He wore a dynamite vest and stumbled toward us, his expression begging us for help.

"Wayland!" he shouted hoarsely. "Wayland!"

That didn't sound like help to me in any language.

"I'm coming!" I shouted after Dana, and raced down Main Street away from Stanton as fast my legs would carry me.

I had just passed Dana, when she looked back and dragged me down to the pavement.

We bounced and skidded, scraping skin and bruising bones on the cobblestones.

A cataclysmic explosion rocked the entire park. Hot air rushed over us, and we chanced another glance back.

A surging, searing firestorm was bearing down on us like a flaming tidal wave.

We both ducked our heads under our arms.

44

S tan the Man was history, blown to smithereens.
We were next.

The shadows were wiped from *Ghostworld's* Old West storefronts as
if it were high noon. The wall of fire rushed toward us, crackling the hair
on my head and arms as it neared. We coughed from the choking black
smoke that preceded the firestorm by seconds. No time for prayers. No
time for flashbacks. We were about to become crispy critters.

Dana screamed, and I was about to join her when we were suddenly
blanketed by darkness instead of flames. The painful cobblestones
beneath us were gone, and I found myself sitting behind the Silver
Wraith's steering wheel as if we'd never left. I blinked repeatedly to
convince myself that what I saw was real, and not some heavenly way-
station setting designed to comfort me after death.

But it was real.

The bitter smell of my singed hair permeated the interior, but that
seemed to be the extent of my injury. I chanced a peek at the passenger
seat and met Dana's amazed gaze.

"How'd you pull it off?" she asked, her voice weak, tremulous.

"I thought *you* were the one who got us out of there in the nick of time."
She appeared confused. "No."

"Then maybe your guardian angel pulled us out of the fire." *Literally.*
Again, "No."

My fingers played across the bristly tufts of singed hair on my scalp.
"Then who?"

She slouched into the generous leather seat. Her slumping posture
reminded me of how I felt—wasted.

"*I* saved you guys," an all-too-familiar voice announced from the
casket bed.

I nearly had a heart attack. "Gwendolyn!" I exclaimed. I saw her prone
form in the rearview mirror, stretched out on her side and resting her

head on her elbow-propped hand. The casket bed was a perfect resting place for a ghost.

"I . . . I didn't know you had . . . you know, magic powers," I stammered. Seemingly, everybody I bumped into these days had acquired magic.

It was beyond difficult to fathom Gwendolyn's pulling this ghostly savior bit off by herself. It had to have been her manipulator. *But why save us? What was his/her motivation? Could our savior be the Good Witch of the North?* Strike that last question.

"It looks like I've got magic powers now," she answered with a wry grin. "Being dead's not as bad as I thought."

"What do you mean?" Dana pressed, quickly recovering from her numbing bewilderment.

"Like, uh, popping in wherever I please, any time I please. And, like, doing magic is so fun." Her Crest toothpaste smile was etched into her naïve face.

"So why *did* you save us?" Dana persisted, arching a single brow.

Gwendolyn's smile sagged to half mast. "Actually, I was told to save Joe, but I thought, hey, why not save the wise-ass's girlfriend, too. Sorta like two for the price of one."

Gwendolyn might have had big boobs and an alluring presence, but she was still very immature. But then again, nobody was perfect.

I could practically *feel* the heat radiating from Dana. That last comment had sent her temperature soaring

"Thanks *sooo much*," Dana remarked with clenched teeth, her steamy sarcasm thick and unmistakable. But the cynicism went right over Gwendolyn's, like, head.

"You're welcome," Gwendolyn replied nonchalantly.

I placed my hand on Dana's trembling fist to convey my empathy, but she yanked it away and buried it in her lap. She was pissed to the max.

More sirens sounded, but closer than before. I glanced over the trees at the Ghost Town blaze. Those poor firemen were getting a real workout tonight.

"Time to go," I stated flatly." I didn't want the cops to discover us anywhere close to the new fire. Kit wasn't around to prevent her cohorts from taking me for a ride down to the 33rd Street Jail and booking me as a suspect.

I twisted the ignition key, and the kick-ass V12 engine roared to life.

"Where to?" Dana asked me as she kept her eyes on our ethereal guest.

"Anywhere but here," I replied. Before I put the hearse in gear, a fist knocked loudly on my window and a flashlight beam blinded me. I shut off the engine.

"Get out of this . . . whatever it is, Luna," a frowning Captain Diaz commanded.

We were caught.

"She's gone," Dana hissed, referring to Gwendolyn. That was one serious problem gone. Now to explain our presence there.

I got out and confronted Diaz, who stood there holding a flashlight in one hand and his service pistol in the other.

This obviously wasn't a social call.

45

Hank Diaz's olive complexion blended with the night beyond the glare of his flashlight. He was dwarfed by five burly detectives standing behind him. These guys I liked. I knew half of them, but I realized that our prior working relationship wouldn't cut me any slack tonight.

"Evenin', Hank. What can I do you for?" I asked, keeping my greeting light to make me appear above suspicion for the Ghost Town explosion.

"Don't give me that crap. I know you're up to something out here," Diaz shot back.

"Just watching the firemen do their thing," I replied. "What's up?"

The breeze carried the Ghost Town smoke to us.

He jerked his head toward the Ghost Town inferno. "That's what's up, and I have a hunch that you are involved somehow."

"I'm sorry to disappoint you this time, Hank, but we got here right after the explosion."

He played the flashlight beam across my head. "Then how'd your hair get burnt?" he growled.

I patted my hair. "Oh, that."

"Yeah, that."

"I put a tad too much charcoal lighter in the grill earlier, and I nearly went up in flames when I lit it," I lied. I nodded at Dana. "I was preoccupied at the time." I hoped he bought my story. It was the only one I could think of.

Hank exhaled slowly. "I can't picture you as an outdoor chef," he muttered, holstering his gun. "What was the occasion?"

I jerked my thumb in her direction. "Her birthday."

The detectives chuckled.

"When we went inside to eat, I heard about Stanton on the TV, and we cruised over here after dinner. I hope he's all right, because he owes me money for a security job I handled for him." That part was true, of course.

"I wouldn't bet on it."

"Really?"

"Really, but I don't know anything concrete yet."

"Looks like I'm out a grand."

"Yeah. That's the way the cookie crumbles, Luna." There wasn't an ounce of sympathy in his tone.

He turned to the detectives. "Okay, let's break it up. Head over to Ghost Town and see what you can find out. I'll be there in a few minutes."

They nodded and left.

Hank turned back to me. "Have you seen Kit?"

I shook my head slowly. "No. She's working on a case for my uncle, and as usual, he hasn't told me squat."

He frowned. "Okay, let me know the moment you hear anything. And I do mean that very moment," he emphasized, and then disappeared into the billowing black smoke.

I got in the hearse and fired up the engine again.

"You did some pretty serious tap dancing back there," Dana said humorlessly.

"Yeah," I mumbled. "I can't stand that guy."

She grinned for the first time since we'd popped back there. "Diaz seemed like such a peach to me."

"You're a real comedian."

"So, where are we going?" she asked.

"A place where we can suck down a few stiff drinks. Any objections?"

"None."

We arrived at my beloved Wolfsbane bar on Central Avenue in Orlando. The name was ironic, because it was actually an herb poisonous to werewolves in ancient times, though modern science proved that to be merely a myth. But I stay clear of the stuff just the same.

Kirby Gallagher was the owner, and he was not only old and wise, but equally strong and mean when riled. He was a wealth of information about supernatural goings-on in the Orlando area, so I made it a priority to stay on good terms with him.

Even though the bar was "officially" closed for remodeling, there were numerous cars parked in front and along the street. The joint was jumping. I parked across the street and walked Dana to the new, unpainted front door. The old one had been destroyed during my last investigation.

The brick façade had recently received a fresh coat of white paint, while the redwood trim below the two grimy windows had been replaced. The neon beer signs in the windows were turned off, and a sign taped to the door read "Closed." Like all Kirby's regulars, I knew better.

After informing Dana that this was a werewolf bar, she stepped inside without reservation. That was a shocker, because most of my non-werewolf acquaintances were hesitant to enter.

The place was packed to the rafters. The jukebox blared out '60s tunes, while a variety of football games appeared on Kirby's four new flatscreen TVs. His replacement tables and chairs, though, hadn't arrived yet, so he constructed makeshift furniture from two-by-fours and plywood. Not the most comfortable way to spend an evening, but what the hell. Any port in a storm.

The barstools had survived, and two of them were empty at the moment. We sat down and Kirby appeared quickly like a genie. I introduced him to Dana.

"Now what can I get you two?" he asked in a booming voice that could be heard above the rowdy din.

Kirby Gallagher was taller and broader than I was. Scars lined both cheeks below his genial umber eyes, but if someone yanked his chain, that benign look changed to brimstone in a heartbeat. The thinning gray hair was the only sign of his advancing age, which I guessed to be seventy-something, but he was still fit and intimidating.

I ordered my usual pint of draft beer, while Dana ordered an Absolut and tonic with lime. He returned with our drinks in a flash. We toasted to Kirby's favorite, getting laid, and then our conversation turned serious.

"I heard via the wolfvine that you've been up to your ass in demons, Joe," he said somberly.

How did the guy find out that stuff? "Yeah, it's true."

"Tell me about it. When did it start?"

"My favorite Uncle Jess volunteered me for guard duty at *Ghostworld's* grand opening, and it's been downhill from there," I replied, throwing back a slug of beer.

He chuckled. "I heard that Kit Wilson and Martha Gibbons went missing that night, too." He leaned across the bar counter. "Know anything about that?"

Kirby was a person to be trusted, so I told him about the attempt on Martha's life, the appearance of the Emerald Zone, and the mysterious tearoom lady supposedly transporting them somewhere safe. He mulled my story over for a while before reacting.

Finally, he took a long swallow of ice water—he never drank alcohol on the job— and looked at Dana.

"So what's your role in all of this, Dana?"

She was caught off guard by his directness, and nearly spilled her drink. "I . . . I was sent here from Washington to help Joe," she replied uneasily. She wasn't as confident about trusting Joe as I was.

His eyes narrowed. "And have you helped him?"

"I think you'd better ask him."

Kirby switched his gaze to me. "Well?"

"She's been a big help," I reassured him.

"And you trust her implicitly?"

What was Kirby driving at? "If Uncle Jess hired her, then yeah, I trust her completely. What are you driving at?"

He bent over across the counter until his square jaw almost touched the rim of my beer mug. "Because I know where Kit and Martha are, and I don't want the wrong people finding out. It would cost them their lives."

46

I couldn't believe my ears. *Why hadn't someone told me where Martha and Kit were hiding?* I was much closer to both women than Kirby was.

"Come again?" I asked dumbly.

"You heard me," he shot back. "Now do you want to know what I know, or are you going to play dumb all night?"

"Sorry, but after what I've gone through the past two days, my brain is oatmeal."

He jerked his thumb at Dana. "I? Don't you mean *we?*"

What a nit-picker. "Yeah, *we.*"

"I can't blame you for being tired, Joe, but this is important." He lowered his voice until it was nearly inaudible in the noisy atmosphere. "Maya told me that she transported Kit and Martha to a different country."

Maya again. I didn't trust that South American teabag as far as I could throw her.

Dana spoke up and arrested my musing. "From what we've seen so far, our suspect could capture and torture her for the information pretty easily."

"Martha and Kit are as good as dead if that happens," I added gravely.

Kirby shook his head. "Maya's in hiding, too. From what I understood, our friends are not only in another country, but in another dimension as well. That was Martha's doing, so if Maya was captured, she wouldn't know exactly how to locate them."

Dana nodded. "Thank God Maya's knowledge isn't the sole connection to their whereabouts. I'm breathing a lot easier now, Kirby."

"Me too," I threw in.

Kirby straightened and thrust his chest out. "This calls for another round of drinks." Without waiting for our agreement, he lumbered away to refill our drinks.

"From what Kirby said, I'd say your friends are safe . . . for the time being, anyway," Dana said. "That ought to take a load off your mind."

A few ounces, maybe. "Yeah, I suppose you're right, but I'm still . . . ."

"Worried about Kit," Dana finished for me.

"Oh yeah, I forgot you could read my mind," I lamented.

She laughed. "Relax. I can't read it now. Only when we're actually working our mission together. This is playtime."

I figured now was as good a time as any to picture her naked, but my imagination was too pooped to pop. Just my luck. I have a pretty good imagination, too.

Dana curled her hand around mine. "Hey, keep the faith. Things'll work out for the best with Kit," she reassured me.

Kirby returned, and we toasted Martha and Kit.

I brushed the foam from my upper lip. "What gets me is why someone wants Martha dead. She talks a tough, but she really wouldn't hurt a fly." I buried my mug in the frosted beer mug, drained it, and burped quietly.

They both agreed.

"Just among the three of us, I'm thinking about bailing on this case. I've gotten beaten up, unofficially killed, and I'm still wearing a big bull's-eye on my back for the killer. And, the kicker is that my magic is no match for his."

Dana was so taken aback that she was about to fall off her stool.

"Suck it up," Kirby growled. "Don't be such a chickenshit about this. You're one of us . . . a werewolf in good standing. I'd hate to lose you for a customer, but I'll banish you if you call it quits on this case."

"You won't have to if I'm dead, Kirby," I volleyed.

"You won't die," Dana pointed out. "You've got me to protect you."

They laughed, but I didn't find her remark particularly funny, and I've got a decent sense of humor.

Kirby smacked me on the shoulder. "Besides, Joe, that's why your Uncle Jess pays you the *big* money. He wants some bang for his buck, old buddy," Kirby said.

Big money. What a joke. "Thanks a lot, Kirby." Boy, he was as funny as rubber crutches in a handicap ward.

The big bar owner shook his forefinger at me. "Don't throw that nasty sarcasm shit at me, son," he warned. "I brought you the beer to drink, not to cry in."

I sighed and forced a slim smile. "I know. It's just I'm at my wits' end with this damned investigation."

"Well, you've got bigger fish to fry than worrying about who wants Martha and your *Ghostworld* buddies six feet under."

Another fish to fry—I don't even like fish. "And what would that be?" I grumbled, gruffly scraping the ice coating from my empty mug.

Dana leaned closer.

His glare lightened a few notches when he switched his gaze to my partner. I didn't blame him—she *was* a looker. "I'm talking about why your suspect wants *Joe and you* dead."

My self-pity instantly evaporated. Kirby was right. I was a werewolf in good standing, and it was about time I acted like one.

Or die.

47

"Any ideas?" I pressed them, having contemplated that enigma a few times in the past two days. I reviewed the vicious attacks on my life. The giant below the Mansion Macabre, the three thugs in the police tent, the giant again outside Martha's shop, the two demon assassins, the vampires in the storm, the pop-ups by the cemetery, and the Emerald Zone giant lying in wait for us outside my farm. Quite a few murder attempts for a measly forty-eight hours. *When would the killer strike next?* Probably as soon as we left the bar.

"There must've been a reason why only certain people were chosen for that first Mansion Macabre ride," Dana suggested. "Possibly the killer saw into the future and knew Joe was going, too."

I snapped my fingers. "You know, I've been wondering about that. I was a last- minute addition to the group, but maybe not an unexpected one."

"But what the killer didn't see ahead of time was you saving the others from the giant," Kirby chimed in.

Dana brightened. "Yeah. Now he might assume that you know too much about his plans to let you live."

"That's gotta be it," Kirby said. "From what you told me, Joe, you're the only one who knows his targets. He's probably afraid that'll you'll stop him along the way."

"Like you did under the haunted mansion," Dana added. She gestured to Kirby for a refill.

Me, I'd had my limit. A couple beers. Too much alcohol made me dizzy. Unable to focus. Blame it on my wolfen genes. What could I say? I was a cheap drunk.

I ordered water on the rocks, and Kirby nodded his understanding. When he returned, he propped his elbows on the bar.

"Somebody who's well-connected locally sicked those three vampires on you two. Those three bloodsuckers weren't out-of-towners and couldn't be conjured," he said thoughtfully.

"I suppose, but that doesn't narrow the field," I lamented.

"And he knew Martha, too," Dana pointed out. "She's local." The ice tinkled in her drink as she sipped it.

It all made sense, but none of their speculation was a compass needle pointed at the guilty party.

Dana switched gears. "What about Jeffrey Stanton's strange last word before exploding. It sounded like a name to me."

My eyes narrowed. "Yeah, I remember now. It was something like 'Wayland' . . . I think."

"There's no thinking about it," Dana said. "That's exactly what he said."

"I don't know anyone or any place called Wayland."

Dana turned to Kirby. "Can you help us out?"

He hesitated. "Maybe." He looked over my shoulder and motioned to one of the customers, who approached the bar unsteadily. His pint of beer sloshed over the glass rim with each step, but he didn't notice.

"Yo, Kirby — what's up, man?"

I acknowledged the tall, skinny, middle-aged werewolf. He climbed power poles for the local utility.

"Well, if it isn't Kevin Williams," I greeted him.

"Long time no see," he replied, shaking my hand. "At least since that horrible fight with the grays."

"This is Dana Drake," I said. I didn't want to go into detail about that terrible fight with the ancient gray werewolves in front of Dana. Frankly, it was none of her business. That occurred during another investigation, *Dead Meet*.

"Okay, knock off the niceties," Kirby growled. "Kevin, didn't you work for a guy named Wayland a while back? Out at his house or something?"

He beamed. "Hell, yeah — I did, but it wasn't no house. Try *mansion*." He paused for effect. "And the guy wasn't just any guy, Kirby. He was Wayland Reynolds, the movie star. Boy, that's one to tell the grandkids about."

The name immediately struck a chord. His too-handsome face was plastered all over the supermarket magazines and movie posters.

"Where's he live?" Kirby posed, glancing hopefully in our direction.

"His place's on the beach in Indialantic. Why?"

"Did you actually *see* Wayland Reynolds?" I asked, ignoring his question.

"Sure. Plenty of times. Coming and going like the muckety-muck he is. I also saw his great-grandfather, too. God, what a hideous mug, and all crippled up in a wheelchair. Looked half dead."

"Did he have any guests who you recognized?" Kirby asked.

Kevin scratched the back of his head. "Not that I remember . . . hey, wait. I did see Senator Kane enter the house. He didn't stay long, and he looked pissed when he left."

My ears perked up at the name. The senator had visited Reynolds; the senator was dead. Hmmm. *Any correlation?* I planned to find out.

"How long ago did you do that side job for Reynolds?" Dana asked.

He screwed up his face. "Let me think . . . now if I remember right, it woulda been two summers ago."

"About the time they started construction on *Ghostworld*," Kirby noted.

Another coincidence? I doubted it.

I looked at Dana. "Anybody else there that summer, Kevin?"

"Nah, that was it. There were a lot of chicks that dropped by for a swim, but hell, I never seen 'em before." He lowered his voice. "And they swam *naked*."

Dana chuckled behind her hand and quickly sipped her Absolut.

"I hope you didn't fall on your ass eyeballin' them titties," Kirby teased.

Kevin reddened, but didn't respond.

"So what kind of side work were you doing for Reynolds?" I pressed.

"Puttin' up some poles and runnin' some electric wires around his estate—lots of wire. And he paid me in cash for the job."

"Isn't installing utility wire without the power company's consent illegal?" I noted.

"Nah. The wires weren't connected to the electrical service or anything."

Kirby and I frowned at each other.

Dana broke into the conversation. "Then what were they connected to?"

"Uh, nothing."

"Then why'd he want the wires strung?" Dana persisted.

Kevin shrugged. "Got me. He'd paid me good, so I didn't ask no questions."

"That was sure an odd request," she said thoughtfully.

Kevin agreed. "He wanted 'em strung in the shape of a star . . . for movie star, I guess. So I set them poles and strung the wire. Nothin' illegal about that."

Kirby refilled Kevin's mug and shooed him away.

"You got something on that pretty little mind of yours?" Kirby asked Dana.

"I'll bet that star shape doesn't have a thing to do with *movie stars*."

"I thought a star was a star," I argued.

She swallowed the last of her drink. "Not if it's a *pentagram*."

48

Kevin wasn't bright enough to fabricate a story that good about Wayland Reynolds' elaborate utility-pole star, so I believed him. Pentagrams were really bad news; they were the subjects of my first magic lesson as a home-schooled kid. Call it Sorcery 101.

A pentagram was employed as a magical or symbolic figure, mostly by the black magicians throughout history, from ancient Greece and Babylonia to the present day. The five-pointed star represented the four primal elements (earth, air, fire, and water) as well as a fifth, called spirit. The circle bound them together to create life. When pointing up, the pentagram's meaning was benign enough, representing spirituality's dominance over the material (pentagram) bound inside the laws of the cosmos (circle).

But it was the upside-down-facing pentagram that spelled trouble. It represented the physical world ruling over the spiritual, creating a coupling with dark magic. I tightened my hand around my glass of ice water. *The reversed pentagram*, with two points projecting upwards, was an outright evil symbol that attracted sinister forces, because it overturned the correct order of things and demonstrated the victory of matter over spirit. Sometimes a drawing of a goat appeared inside the pentagram with its two horns spiking upward, symbolizing antagonism and fatality—the goat of lust attacking the heavens with its horns.

I pensively sipped the water like it was a fine wine. The slight trembling of my hand caused the ice cubes to clink together. If Dana was right about Kevin constructing a pentagram, then Reynolds must control a vast amount of evil energy at his beach house—energy that could easily reach Orlando and . . . *Ghostworld*.

What was Reynolds up to? Maybe nothing, but I'd check him out just the same.

"I think we've gone as far as we can tonight with this case," I stated, stifling a yawn. It had been a very protracted few days, and I needed some serious shuteye.

Kirby nodded. "One for the road, Joe?"

I held up my hand. "Not tonight. I'm driving."

He pointed to Dana. "Your partner can drive you home," he proposed.

"No way," I argued, yawning the yawn of all yawns. "Nobody's driving the Silver Wraith but me."

"Typical *man*," Dana laughed.

Kirby tapped my forearm. "You oughta call glamour boy and set up an interview. You know, tell him that you need his advice on a case. You're good at bullshitting. Make it sound convincing."

I glanced at my watch. It was past midnight. Not exactly a sociable time to phone people for appointments.

"I'll call him tomorrow," I said.

Kirby frowned. "Never put off tomorrow what you can do today."

"Thanks for the sage advice." My words were double-dipped in sarcasm.

I stood and watched Dana down her one-for-the-road drink. She extended her hand to Kirby.

"It was a pleasure meeting you. I'm sure our paths will cross again," she told him before joining me at the front door.

I waved to several friends as we exited into the humidity. The weather never gave us much of a break in Orlando. Hot. Hotter. Hottest.

The traffic was heavier than before, no doubt attributable to the downtown nightlife a few blocks over at Church Street Station. Dana dropped her arm in front of me like a crossing guard and pointed down the street. Several punks had set-up camp around and on my prized black beauty. My blood pressure spiked.

I ran up to them with Dana trailing behind. The eight punks greeted us with sneers beneath the streetlight's pale glow.

"Get off my damned car!" I growled, catching my breath.

"You know what, mister? We're going to take this piece of shit off your hands," a burly Latino said, his body a solid mass of intertwining tattoos.

"Oh, is that how you see it?" I retorted, my arms tensed for some butt-kicking.

He slapped the driver's door twice. "Yeah, that's right. How about we make a trade—this piece of shit here for your lives—and call it even?"

Dana stretched up to my ear on her tiptoes. "Don't attract the cops. Use your magic."

As much as I hated to admit it, she was right, but I was really psyched up for a fight. Oh well. That was life in the big city.

I shut my eyes and conjured a simple spell that wouldn't harm them, but would chase them away nonetheless. I opened my eyes, waiting for the spell to work, but nothing happened. *Dammit!* My magic powers were still MIA after the incident in the Ghost Town butcher shop. I tried again with the same non-results.

"Well, we ain't standin' here all night waitin' for an answer," the leader threatened, and his big, bad buddies added simultaneous "yeahs."

I turned to Dana and shrugged my shoulders. "Zippo."

An ominous grin curled the corners of her mouth. "This one's on me."

I was puzzled. *Why had she regained her magic before I did?* Strange, but that wasn't exactly a news flash in this case.

Now, I'd given a lot of school bullies hotfeet while I was growing up, but I wasn't prepared for Dana's version. Within seconds, each boy's zippered fly burst into flames and ignited the fabric surrounding it. I laughed out loud as our would-be murderers hopped around, hollering and pounding their groins. Double pain.

My partner was even more devious than I was, and I loved it.

"I think I'll pass on your deal, buddy," I shouted at the retreating gang members, who were busy dodging honking cars and putting out fires. I slapped her a high-five, and we sped away toward the farmhouse before any cops showed up. I'd had my quota for the evening.

I finally stopped laughing and wiped the tears from my eyes. "Nice work."

Dana brushed her own tears away. "They were a sight, weren't they?"

"You can say that again," I said, jumping on I-4 and heading north.

We rode along silently, each engrossed in our thoughts. When our Sanford exit came into view, Dana stirred.

"So far, so good," she stated, watching the countryside whiz by.

"What do you mean?"

"Only that if we're attacked before we reach your farm, we'd be in big trouble."

That was a sobering revelation. "I catch your drift. Me and no magic equal big trouble for the two of us."

"That's about the size of it."

I fought escalating paranoia the rest of the way home.

49

Without my magic, I couldn't conjure an opening in the barn for the Silver Wraith, so I had to park my pride and joy outside—where it was at the mercy of the elements, pollen, and especially the birds.

Dana retrieved a second larger suitcase from the back of her government-issue Yukon before we trudged wearily into the farmhouse. It had been a long tumultuous day.

I excused myself while Tillie fixed a midnight supper and rehashed our butcher-shop adventure. I entered my bedroom, sat my small desk, and punched in Uncle Jess's number on my iPhone. His ever-ready assistant, Beth, answered on the first ring.

"It's *you*," she snorted like the bull she was. Beth considered me the vilest person on the face of the earth, and to this day, I don't know why. We'd never even met. Our relationship was strictly a long-distance enmity.

"Very astute," I retorted. "I need all the phone numbers you have on record for one Wayland Reynolds of Indialantic, Florida. The actor."

"And I need a million bucks," she snapped. "Do you know what time it is?"

"Sure do. It's time for you to get me those numbers . . . and quick."

I immediately found myself slammed into that vast black hole of silence aptly labeled "on hold." I realized that my request might take awhile, so I switched on the TV. The "Breaking News" flavor of the night was still *Ghostworld*.

"... too hot for firemen to search for victims. Jeffrey Stanton is believed to be one of the victims in this horrible tragedy, but we won't have any more information about that until tomorrow noon at the earliest. This is Amy Courtland of Central Florida News 13 reporting live from this disastrous scene at *Ghostworld*," the young reporter declared with over-the-top melodramatics.

I pulled off my shoes and pitched both toward the open closet door. I avoided further melodramatic claptrap by muting the TV, so I could concentrate on the video of the flaming administration building. The sorcerer had done an effective job starting the blaze. Nothing would be left to incriminate him.

The phone clicked on the other end, and I was finally through the black hole. But the voice didn't belong to "Beth-the-Horrible."

"Joe, tell me what's going on? Why on earth do you need Wayland Reynolds' phone numbers?" Uncle Jess asked in his typical callous style. He sounded wide awake, too. A man his age should get more sleep.

"I have my reasons," I said vaguely to prevent a heated, late-night discussion on the matter. Or at least try.

"They'd better be damned good ones," he snorted. "I've got Reynolds' FBI file on my computer screen as we speak, and I don't like what I'm seeing."

"That doesn't surprise me," I interjected.

Dear uncle discounted my remark and continued. "Reynolds was charged in a land-swindling scheme twenty years ago in Wyoming, but the witnesses and victims mysteriously vanished before the case was brought to trial."

"You mean they weren't ever seen again?"

"That's what I mean."

"And no one suspected him in their disappearances?"

"Suspecting is one thing, but proving it is quite another. Now let me continue. Uh, there were, let's see, one . . . two . . . three rape charges against him, but all three young Hollywood starlets were killed in separate accidents before his trial. Again, that's just a little too convenient in my book."

I held my tongue and let him go on.

"One of the starlets was burned to death in a house fire, another in an accident where her car lost control and plunged off a cliff on Palisades Highway in California, and the third was crushed when a movie-studio crane backed over her. To say this Reynolds is bad news is a vast understatement. Think he might be the *Ghostworld* murderer?"

"He might be. I'm going to check him out."

"Alone?"

"No, I've got Superwoman to cover my ass," I indicated with a hint of scorn.

"From what I've heard, it's a two-way street," he chuckled facetiously. He had spies everywhere.

"I think it's time that we met face-to-face, so I can size him up."

"If Reynolds is your man, he gets it honestly. I have similar reports that his father, an earlier stage actor, was a suspect in various New York crimes, but those witnesses vanished or were conveniently killed, too. Hmmm."

"What?" I prompted him.

"It says here that his grandfather, an old traveling vaudeville comedian, was tangled up with some shady characters in the late 1800s and early 1900s."

"I heard that his grandfather lives with him."

Uncle Jess paused. "I think your source has it wrong. Old Grandpa passed away thirty-two years ago."

I arched my brows. "Really? From what?"

"Like most coroners' examinations in the old days, the cause of death is merely listed as old age."

"My reliable source swears that he saw a wheelchair-bound guy at Reynolds' place who looked old enough to be his grandfather."

"No, the documentation is all here. The guy's dead."

I whistled. "He must've been important to rate that kind of detailed record- keeping."

"I see your point."

"So I wonder who the wheelchair guy is," I pondered, more to myself than Uncle Jess.

"He could be Wayland Reynolds' dad," he said.

"When was he born?"

"Let me see . . . 1941."

"Kinda young to look *that* old."

"I agree, but check it out. I presume that's why you want his phone numbers."

I held the phone away and yawned. "Absolutely."

He texted me the list as we spoke, and I watched the message pop up on my iPhone. "Are you sure you don't want me to hand this case over to another agent?"

"We already discussed that, and I'm sticking by my decision to stay on the case, at least until I hear that Martha and Kit are safe." That was my out, and I blew it again. Loyalty and pigheadedness could get a guy killed.

"Have you heard anything from Martha and Kit?"

I massaged my forehead. "Not a word." I didn't mention Kirby's revelation.

"That's too bad." He shuffled some papers. "How's Dana working out?"

"She was a little shaky at first, but I think we're coming together as a team."

Uncle Jess chuckled, which was the first sign of humanity he'd displayed tonight. "Personally or professionally?"

I bristled at his remark. "Professionally," I answered coldly.

"That's what I kinda figured. I've heard from other agents who've worked with her that she's not the, uh, amorous type."

"That's okay with me. This case is too dangerous to be fooling around."

"Gotta stay on your toes, eh? Glad to hear it, Joe. Call me after you've met with Reynolds. Good night." With that, he hung up.

I suffered another jaw-busting yawn before dialing one of Reynolds' four FBI-listed home phone numbers. It was late, sure, but those Hollywood types had a reputation for partying hearty till dawn.

A voice abruptly answered "Hello," and somehow I knew that it was Wayland Reynolds' voice.

My bravado waned, and I was tempted to hang up. Maybe it would be smarter to scout out his place first, then schedule a meeting.

"Anyone there?" he asked. "This better not be a damned prank."

He sounded like a prick. One who needed a good jaw busting.

My sudden dislike for the actor incited me to action. I lifted the phone back to my head. *What the hell?* Nothing ventured, nothing gained.

50

"Wayland Reynolds?" I asked. I figured out why I recognized his voice—from the movies.

"The one and the same," he replied evenly. "What's on your mind, Joe?"

How did he know who I was?

"Joe, you there?" he asked.

"Yeah, sorry. I had to yawn."

"It has been a long night for you, hasn't it?"

The only way he could've known that was if he was the Ghostworld murderer.

"You might say that," I agreed cautiously. I supposed it was possible that he was only fishing for information and didn't actually know what happened to me at *Ghostworld*. But that was a long shot. "I wondered if I could drop by your place tomorrow morning and consult you about a case. It involves a Hollywood actress," I lied.

"I'm busy the next few days, but Friday would be fine," he said.

Friday? That was Halloween. I didn't like the sound of that.

But my mouth moved faster than my brain. "How about morning?"

"Morning here begins at noon. We'll have brunch," he said with a humorless chuckle that iced my skin.

I quickly agreed. My appetite might not be there, but I would.

"I have to hand it to you, Joe."

"About what?" I ventured nervously.

"Going out on Halloween without your magic. Kinda dangerous, isn't it, with all the ghosts and demons prowling the earth."

I gasped involuntarily. He knew everything, and it spooked me to the core. "I, uh, yeah, it is dangerous," I faltered, "but hopefully I'll have it back by Friday."

"Oh, I think you will. Check inside that beautiful Silver Wraith hearse of yours after I hang up," he said mysteriously.

Before I could ask him why, he was gone.

I sat in my chair for a while, pondering whether I should tell Uncle Jess about our conversation, but he would just recommend that I drop the case again. I nixed that idea.

I sneaked down the stairs, out the front, and around the house to the barn. I didn't want to explain Reynolds' offer to Dana and Tillie. They'd only worry. Hell, I was worried!

I warily approached the hearse. Its waxed finish reflected the full moon like a polished mirror. I stopped ten feet from the Silver Wraith and thoroughly scanned the area with my wolfen senses for signs of a trap. Nothing. I relaxed.

I advanced and peeked inside the hearse . . . and spied my staff propped against the passenger seat. *How did Reynolds manage to put it there? Or had the staff returned on its own?* Difficult questions. I suspected a trap, but I wrote it off to paranoia.

Next, I carefully examined it. Every nick. Every scratch. Every talisman. It was mine, all right. I opened the door and snatched it.

Shadowy figures erupted from the blackness and charged. I held my staff in front of me, but it crackled and hissed like a statically charged viper. Before I could drop it, blue energy raced up the wood and jolted me. I vibrated uncontrollably, like a can of paint in a mixer. My attackers paused a safe distance away, dumbfounded by what was happening to me. I tried to pitch the staff, but it stuck like it was glued to my hands.

I smelled burning hair—*my hair*—and figured I was a goner. Tricked again. For the last time.

A wedge of light appeared over the back porch and another silhouette ran toward me. Dana! I wanted to warn her about Reynolds' attackers, but the intense vibrations shook my breath away. I thudded to my knees on the driveway and slumped forward on my trembling forehead.

A frigid gloom mingled among my conscious thoughts. *Death.* I was about to become another Reynolds family *accident victim.* I imagined the gossip at the Wolfsbane tomorrow: *Poor Joe. Killed by his own mage staff. A more experienced agent took over the case.*

Suddenly, I was tossed into a turbulent black ocean. My thoughts ceased.

51

Suffocating blackness and silence enveloped me like a medieval dungeon, confining me in a torturous limbo between heaven and hell. Any hope of my continued existence as Joe Luna, sorwolf, vanished with the light, and now I awaited Act II of this gruesome scenario. The intermission between acts was merciless agony.

I tried my damndest to drift off into sleep, but it wouldn't come, no matter how many sheep I counted. I was bored. Scared. Impatient.

Without warning, another presence appeared on little cat feet and invaded my personal space. *Was it God?* I couldn't see my visitor.

"Hello, Joe," a female voice greeted me telepathically.

God was a woman? "Back atcha," I thought, and immediately regretted my gruff response. I should have shown more respect. I quickly amended my error. "I mean, hello."

"Is that you, Joe Luna?"

If I still had eyebrows, they would've shot sky high. That voice . . . was so familiar. *Or, was it my distraught imagination playing tricks on me?*

"It's me, Joe."

My brain spun like a hamster caught in a runaway wheel. I knew that voice, but from where?

"God?" I ventured.

A giggle. "Not quite, but close. I'm a *G* word, too."

Now I recognized it. "Gwendolyn!"

Another giggle. "Yup, that's me," she said, her tone buoyant.

"What are you doing here in my . . . head?"

"I'm not in your head," she replied. "I'm visiting your soul."

I gulped. I *was* dead. "My . . . soul? If we're dead, why haven't we moved on to . . . you know?"

"Heaven?"

"Yeah . . . or that other place down south."

"You just don't get it, do you?"

"I just got here. Get what? Dead is dead," I huffed, irked by her haughty tone. "What else is there?"

"Limbo."

"Where the hell — er, heck — is limbo?"

"I don't know, but someone put me here."

"When?"

"There's no clock," she snapped. "And if there was, we couldn't see it. It's too dark."

"No, I didn't mean *exactly* when. I meant what were you doing at the time someone sent you here?" I cringed at the bloody, gruesome image of her exploding head.

There was no response for a while, and I thought she had vanished. During the interminable silence, I regretted asking her the damned question. I wasn't in the mood to relive her story of her burst brains. Watching it had been disgusting enough.

"The last thing I remember was seeing Jeffrey's car come up from wherever we were, like, below that haunted place. I was so happy, and tears, like, ran down my face, but I didn't care. I loved Jeffrey, so it was okay to let my feelings show, wasn't it?"

I hesitated at his name. "Uh, sure. Why not." I wasn't about to drop the bomb that ole Jeffrey made a bigger splash than her brains. It would probably traumatize her for life, uh, forever.

"And then, just as I was, like, going to run and hug him, I blacked out and, like, found myself here," she narrated in a faraway voice.

"And you have no idea where 'here' is?"

"Not a friggin' clue."

"But you leave here periodically to visit me," I reminded her.

"Yeah. You know, that's weird. A voice in my head tells me what to say to you, and then, like, I suddenly show up wherever you are and pass along the message."

"Well, you looked pretty damned real to me when you showed up."

"Real?"

"Yeah. You had a real physical form. You touched me once," I pointed out.

"That's right," she said, sounding a bit more cheerful. "So, like, maybe I'm not dead."

I'd been wondering the same thing myself, but after hearing her repeat it, the concept sounded . . . well, pretty lame. My spirits sank. We were dead as doornails, and that was that.

"Joe?"

She startled me out of my reverie. "Yeah?"

"I have that strange feeling again, but this time it's about you. You're going . . . ."

I didn't catch the rest of Gwendolyn's strange feeling and how it concerned me, because the blackness vanished and I found myself skimming the cloud tops. *Where was I going? Were Gwendolyn and I some kind of angels who helped people?* That wouldn't be so bad, but I didn't have a voice in my head telling me what to do. *Was I a freelance angel?*

There was one major question I needed answered: *Where was I going?*

Because like Dorothy in *The Wizard of Oz*, I knew I wasn't in Kansas anymore.

52

My eyes refused to focus.

For some reason, the clouds were blurred. Rubbing my eyes didn't accomplish a thing . . . since I had no hands! In fact, I had no physical form at all, and it seemed to me that I was *seeing* with my entire being. This was too bizarre. Too alien a concept for me to grasp, even as a sorcerer.

Perhaps my soul was truly on the road to the hereafter and not simply traveling on an earthly mission. After all, the ancient paintings depicted Heaven's angels lounging on puffy clouds. *Who was I to doubt their validity? Maybe those painters had inside information.*

Without warning, I nosedived through the thick clouds, and jerked to a stop above a hazy landscape. From my bird's-eye view, I noticed several indistinct structures immersed in a sea of green. Seconds later my descent resumed, and I drifted lazily like a down feather in a spring breeze. My next stopover occurred above the largest building.

I didn't know how long I floated there, because in my new world there was no time. And I didn't have any idea how far I'd traveled, either. There were no landmarks on my journey. No odometers. *But* I was acutely aware that I had no control of my actions, and that helpless sensibility was infuriating.

The landscape remained fuzzy. *Was the building below a warehouse, airplane hangar, or a big-ass mansion?* Again, my attempts to focus my vision were thwarted.

However, I *was* aware that the landscape had brightened dramatically while my soul levitated above the earth, but with my sight directed earthward, I couldn't discover if the sun was the sole reason for this anomaly. My range of vision was reduced to an inanimate camera in a fixed position.

Without warning, I plummeted toward the building like the proverbial rock. My screams were locked in my mind as the roof rose to greet me. My efforts to disable my view of the inevitable crash were rebuffed, and all the while my practical side shouted *cool it*. I was already dead and couldn't get much deader. Sound logic. Hard to swallow.

Thankfully I fell through the roof and landed gently on what must have been a shaded porch. Gradually, my surroundings grew crystal clear, and I identified the building. From the gold scrolled address to the massive double-door entrance, I realized that I had materialized on Wayland Reynolds' doorstep.

I instinctively checked the time on my watch out of habit—I did have an appointment with Reynolds at noon on Halloween—and to my utter amazement, I saw it strapped to my wrist. A real, honest-to-goodness wrist with flesh and blood. It was a start. I slowly examined the rest of me and . . . Joe Luna was back. Halleluiah! This sorwolf was ready to rock and roll again.

I felt a resurgence of self-confidence and punched the gold doorbell. I half-expected my finger to continue through the doorbell, but I was relieved when I heard melodious chimes resound throughout the interior.

As I awaited my number-one suspect in the *Ghostworld* murders, I scanned the meticulously landscaped gardens, trimmed shrubs in clichéd animal shapes, and an elaborate fountain that floated serenely on the surface of a large pond north of the mansion. Beyond its rainbow mist stood several stone statues of Roman figures. Maybe gods. Strange. Although they were sculpted in various modes of dress, they all had identical faces.

Wayland Reynolds.

He wasn't too narcissistic, was he? But this wasn't the time and place to ridicule the Hollywood star. I was here to determine if he could be the *Ghostworld* sorcerer, although my strategy for friendly interrogation was still unclear. But I would come up with a viable way. I always did.

Reynolds took an inordinate amount of time to answer his door. Maybe he was letting me stew out here, fearful of his magic advantage. If that was his intent, it was a damned good plan. Coupling his magic edge to my total lack of magic powers increased my anxiety exponentially. It was tough to imagine a worse scenario, but my dead-or-not-dead issue sent my apprehension spiraling over the top. *Which one was I?* I swallowed repeatedly, trying to generate saliva, but my throat stayed dust dry.

My cowardly streak returned. *Or was it my survival instinct?* I decided that it would be better to leave now and live to return another day. I chanted my teleportation spell, and presto . . . I hadn't moved an inch! I tried again and again, but my feet remained firmly anchored to the porch. I tried running for my life, but my shoes refused my command. Finally a terrifying revelation slapped me like a cold hand to the face.

I wasn't in control of my movements. I was a puppet, like Gwendolyn.

Panicked, I checked my belt for my wand, and then remembered that it had been torched. My ring finger was empty, too. No magic protection today. This entire situation felt like a set-up. I was being used, *but why?*

I heard steps inside approaching the door. I guessed that I wouldn't have to wait long for my answer. The door cracked open and an all-too-familiar face greeted me with a frosty grin.

What a day this was turning out to be.

53

There was a brief flicker of surprise in Reynolds' lucent violet eyes when he saw me standing there—surprised that his mage-staff booby trap had backfired? I desperately wanted to change into my werewolf persona and tear him apart, but I seemed to have misplaced my wolfen genes, too. I really was up a creek without a paddle.

"Afternoon, Luna," he managed. "You're right on time. I like punctuality in a person." He eased the door back and waved me inside.

I wanted to say *hello* or *call me Joe* or *anything*, but my vocal cords seemed petrified. Finally, I heard myself saying as I walked past the door, "Surprised to see me?" My mind definitely did NOT create that belligerence. My handler was working overtime behind the scenes to get me killed!

Reynolds crinkled his perfectly unblemished forehead. My retort caught him off guard. "I, uh, didn't think you'd actually come out here, unarmed so to speak. Especially on Halloween. But then you have a reputation for being reckless, don't you?" His intonation was gruff and menacing—quite the opposite of his super-hunk on-screen dialogue.

Before my handler stuck my foot in my mouth again, the actor whisked me inside to the grand foyer. Deep snarls knotted my muscles, and I noticed three huge Rottweilers standing five feet away, their skewer-ready fangs bared and dribbling saliva. Like a puppet, my hand was manipulated out toward the jaws of death and re-formed into a finger-thumb gun. The thumb went down, and *Bam*, the canine bullies shrank into Chihuahua-sized Rottweilers.

"Bang!" I hissed at them. They immediately yelped, turned tail, and raced from the foyer, their tiny nails clicking on the marble floor.

Reynolds smiled unevenly and clapped. "Bravo. You're certainly full of surprises, Mr. Luna."

Mister Luna. Hmmm. I was moving up the list in Reynolds' respect department. "Sometimes I surprise myself," I thought, but this time I voiced that sentiment. *Was I back in control of myself again?* I seriously doubted it.

He magnanimously waved me toward the back of the house. "Well, let's have that lunch I promised, and afterward you can fill me in on that case of yours. I'd love to help out, if I can." He paused. "Perhaps you prefer teleporting yourself back to my patio. Oh, excuse me. I forgot you'd lost your magic."

I was so enraged that I shook, but my unseen handler restrained me. *And* muzzled me. I helplessly followed Reynolds like an obedient pet walking on eggs. He cocked his head once, amazed that I didn't have a retort for his taunt. That made two of us, buddy.

He strode casually through the opulent interior like a king through his kingdom. I didn't know Reynolds' exact age, mostly because I wasn't a movie buff, but he looked about my age—thirty-one. No wrinkles. A flawless complexion. About my height. Muscular. Compelling presence. His light-brown hair contrasted with his bronzed skin, and the mansion skylights underscored his surreal, frigid expression. In my present physical state, whatever *that* was, I was unable to detect his aura, but I presumed it was hellish black.

The back patio overlooked the crash-and-hiss of the Atlantic surf, an immense turquoise-pavered deck, the shimmering water in his Olympic-sized pool, and the bevy of topless, sunbathing beauties in search of a Hollywood career at any cost. A slight sea breeze fluttered the fronds atop two dozen tall and bowed poolside palms.

We sat at a wicker table centered on the wood-plank patio. I was impressed with the fancy tablecloth and the silver-and-china place settings until the Maine lobster and crepes-to-die-for were served. Then I was flat-out intimidated by his vulgar display of wealth. We chased down the cuisine with a suitably aged white wine. For a dead guy, I was in heaven. So to speak.

We exchanged polite chit-chat during lunch. My words were my own during that span. My animated host spoke of the current Florida draught, the failure of the local high-speed rail project again, the up-and-coming breed of no-talent actors, and his disgust for the corporate bean counters who constantly trimmed film budgets and salaries. I responded appropriately with grunts, nods, and yeahs.

Reynolds offered me an after-lunch Havana cigar, and I accepted. *Why not?* Now that I was dead, I didn't have to worry about lung cancer. I puffed repeatedly as he held the lighter flame to the tip of the cigar, and for a brief moment, his face vanished behind the cloud of smoke, but the sea breeze quickly whipped away the veil.

We pushed away from the table, crossed our legs, and deposited an occasional ash in our ashtrays.

He released another puff of tobacco fog. "Now, about this case of yours . . . ."

I propped my cigar in the ashtray, leaned back with my fingers woven behind my neck, and was about to narrate the perfect pseudo-case when my plan was pre-empted.

"I'm here to find out what you know about the *Ghostworld* murders," I growled.

Oh my God! *What happened to discretion?* If I didn't know better (and I didn't), it looked like my handler was deliberately provoking Reynolds, with my neck on the chopping block.

The wicker creaked as I squirmed uneasily in my chair. I sensed that all hell was about to break loose.

And come crashing down on me.

54

Reynolds was taken aback. "How dare you!" he exploded, his tone glacial despite the sweltering heat swirling around us.

"You heard me," I fired back, and my handler jerked me toward him.

The movie star's smug violet eyes momentarily flashed yellowish-red hellfire, and for a fleeting instant I saw—or thought I saw—a grotesque face, clawed hands, and a misshapen frame beneath Reynolds' pretty-boy appearance. An iceberg sailed up my spine, and I blinked. *Did I imagine his inner violent appearance, or was it stress playing tricks on my eyes?* If my vision were legitimate, then Reynolds was something other than what he appeared to be.

Man, I wanted out of here in the worst way. Even though I was dead, I still didn't feel safe from the movie star's malevolent reach.

He stood abruptly and glowered at me. "I think you'd better leave now, Luna. You've outstayed your welcome," he declared stiffly. Without waiting for an objection, he led me through a different door than we'd used earlier.

I double-timed it to keep up with his brisk pace as we entered a long chamber devoid of skylights. Pale lit sconces separated a series of murky oil paintings depicting gruesome night landscapes. Dozens of them. They were all expensively displayed in scrolled and gilded frames.

But upon closer inspection, I cringed. Each painting was a hellish landscape. Purplish-black skies were the backdrop for fiery mountains and desolate, scorched terrain . . . and a single, screaming person. The unfortunate loner in the painting in front of me was the horribly distorted form and visage of *Senator Justice Kane*.

I backed away. The poor guy was engulfed by bluish-black flames. Burned alive. A human torch.

I checked the next painting. Jeffrey Stanton. He was in pieces. A freeze frame the instant after his dynamite vest had been detonated in the Ghost Town. Only the corporeal Stanton wasn't there any longer.

His memory had been banished to that forlorn painting. *Or was it more than just his memory?*

How many others had been painted into these sordid oil paintings? I was terrified as I scanned Reynolds' chamber of horrors. *Why had he painted these grisly scenes? And what was he planning to use them for?*

My handler forced me to move on. The next painting was like the others, except for a full moon rising over the mountains and a vacant spot in the foreground for a victim. *But who?* While I stood there gawking, a faint shadowy figure materialized in the vacant area of the painting. I strained to make out the new person's identity. Flames suddenly flared around the figure like fiery cowlicks and revealed the victim's face.

A werewolf.

I studied it closer.

The supernatural beast reproduction was . . . *me.*

A chilling breeze swept through the chamber, but I barely noticed. My flesh was already iced numb. A sudden movement ahead caught my eye and I glanced at Reynolds.

He stood there, hands clasped behind his back and malice contorting his face. "Admiring my collection?"

I waited for my mouth to say something clever, but my handler was obviously asleep at the switch. "Uh, I . . . ."

My entire body was wrenched to the left, and I reluctantly observed another series of grotesque oil paintings, but the panoramas were unlike the others. Their skies were ominous swirls of filthy charcoal smoke, and the landscapes were flat and barren, decimated by four savage black tornados. The gloomy, yellowed painted surfaces were cracked in numerous places, creating raised mosaic images, indicating to me that they were much older than the ones on my right. But, as with the others, each displayed a single tormented victim who gazed dolefully at me from his eternal oily prison.

Except for one painting. I blinked several times. Standing in torturous poses were the three goons who had jumped Kit and me inside the police tent the other night. Shorty, Lenny, and Pug. *God, what was this place? Had Reynolds released them from this painting to do his bidding?* I was convinced that I didn't want the answer to that one.

Another ancient painting hung alone at the far end of the ghastly room in the shadows and snagged my curiosity. This one was really an antique—the puckered oil blisters were more pronounced. I shuddered. The canvas was completely white, dappled with dirty smudges. I moved trance-like toward it and gasped. The smudges were actually ghosts swimming in an alabaster vacuum. Unblemished white. My hands trembled. The shocking landscape reminded me of . . . .

An elderly man riding an electric wheelchair appeared from another doorway, and his unexpected emergence bulldozed my stupor. His countenance was swamped in a sea of sallow wrinkles, and wintry wisps of hair vacillated above his hollow eyes in the breeze. His emaciated body was horribly deformed, like the Hunchback of Notre Dame. His baggy tailored slacks fluttered loosely around his stork legs.

"Leave the boy alone!" the old man commanded in a frail but firm voice.

"Not a chance, Brice," Reynolds growled. "Luna's been a thorn in my side since the beginning, and you know it. Now it's time for him to go away."

"I won't permit it," the old man argued, his words cracking.

The movie star laughed. "He got what he wanted. Now it's time to pay the piper."

"Then take me, and let Joe Luna walk away."

Reynolds grunted. "That would only prolong the inevitable, Brice, and cause me a great deal of hardship. It took considerable effort to lure him here."

"Then I'll have to make you go away where you belong," the old man persisted, guiding the wheelchair closer to Reynolds.

Without my magic powers, I was relegated to a spectator's role. I didn't understand how the decrepit old man could frighten Reynolds, a powerful sorcerer. But then again, how good could he be if he couldn't figure out that I was already dead?

The old man pulled a fishing knife from beneath his lap blanket with his knobby arthritic hands. He raised the thin blade until the point hovered over his heart.

"Time for *you* to go," Brice threatened the movie star.

I was amazed that Reynolds actually backed away from Brice, but that was the last thing I saw. I was suddenly whisked away. The men blurred, then vanished, and I was flying high above the mansion once more.

I really wanted to see how the confrontation worked out, but my handler had other ideas. But I was satisfied. I now knew for certain that Reynolds was the *Ghostworld* killer, not that I'd ever be able to tell anyone.

I was still dead.

I kept gaining altitude. *Was I finally headed to heaven?* I certainly hoped so. I needed to eventually put this case behind me, kick back, and sample some of that eternal peace.

55

This time around, the grimy cotton-candy clouds seemed to stretch on forever. I waited to break free and rocket up and away from the gloom into the warmth of the sunlight. But I couldn't pull it off. *Was I one of those lonely souls that rode the proverbial bubble between heaven and hell, awaiting a final verdict on my future?*

Suddenly, an indistinct shadow popped into the clouds directly below me, and my placid puffs of charcoal abruptly became roiling black thunderheads. The bloated mass below reeked of evil. I sensed it throughout my being.

I involuntarily re-formed into an ethereal ball, uncertain whether that was my doing or not. A deep resonant voice whispered inside my head with the subtlety of an axe murderer. *Kill Joe Luna.* What a sweet sentiment. I felt tingly all over.

Despite the message's crude brevity, it impacted me like a sledgehammer to the crotch. I didn't need three guesses to figure out who was behind this latest assassination attempt. *Wayland Reynolds.* As skilled a sorcerer as he was in the black arts, ole Wayland had shit for brains. Someone should have clued him in that it was impossible to kill a dead guy.

Wicked lightning bolts split the ebony storm clouds with their crooked, toothy grins. Their tongues snapped at me like cruel bullwhips and released roaring belches that threatened to shake me to death. Hurricane-force gusts knocked my airy soul from cloud to cloud like a powerless pinball, while the ominous *thing* continued its speedy ascent.

Being a dead guy, I realized that I should've been laughing my ass off at the situation, but instead I was inflated with fear to the point of a blow-out, like an over-inflated tire. *So why wasn't I yukking it up?* That was the sixty-four-million-dollar question, and there was only one answer. My handler knew something that I didn't, and he was transferring his feelings to me. Fear. *Panic.* But again, why? I was a goner. Untouchable to earthly powers. Let Reynolds do his worst. I was invulnerable.

Unless . . . .

Oh God, it couldn't be.

My own horror welled within me and crowned my handler's fear like the second scoop of a double-dip ice cream cone. Only this was the ice cream cone from hell.

The evil entity's grotesque silhouette finally caught up with me, but its features remained blurred. Its scorching breath agitated the storm clouds to greater fury, and its eyes burned through me like I was glass.

My being shrank to the size of a beach ball, and the creature reached for me with hazy claws the size of a pick-up truck. Without warning, the bottom scoop of my fear cone melted away, leaving me with my terror and the insane answer to my own question. I dodged the swiping clawed hand like a clever, nimble fly and retreated briskly. There was no more angelic drifting. The storm vanished behind me, and I thought I'd finally ditched my assassin, but I was wrong.

In the fuzzy light, the devil-creature swooped in for the kill. Did I have enough energy to sustain my present velocity? If I didn't, I was a . . . .

Goner?

I wanted to laugh.

Hell, I was dead. *Wasn't I?*

I immediately regretted thinking of that dreadful eternity.

God, I was dead.

There. Much better.

But there was something peculiar about my handler's reaction to the storm and Reynolds' killer that stuck in my craw. His feelings were illogical. Unless . . . .

I was still alive.

I felt the sinister creature's breath blister my entire being, and I attempted to will myself to greater speed. It didn't work. The killer kept toying with me. Closing. Falling back. Reynolds was having his fun.

What if I were really alive? What if Reynolds were smarter than I gave him credit for? What if, what if, what if. There was only certainty.

In my "alive" scenario, if the ruthless assassin caught me, I really would be dead. No doubts. Amen.

In my current semi-crazed mental state, that outcome didn't sound half bad.

56

Without warning, the murderous hellion vanished with the light, and I found myself immersed in pitch blackness again. Alone. No Gwendolyn.

But I found that I wasn't quite as alone as I thought. I heard distant, urgent voices, and they definitely weren't angelic. They sounded familiar, not heavenly.

Where was I? What was I? Dead, alive, or in limbo?

My ethereal existence was frustrating, because I had zero control over my movements. Only my thoughts were my own, but the decision to voice them was left to the discretion of my handler. Anger coursed through me like so many sizzling electrical charges, and I vented it like an old steam locomotive releasing shrieks of steam.

I wanted my life back!

Suddenly, the impenetrable darkness fractured like a black mirror, and a wave of blinding brilliance washed over me. I shrank away from the startling light, and shielded my eyes with my hand.

Hand? Eyes? Where did those come from?

Warm tears slid down my cheeks. *Cheeks? Was I really alive again?*

"Wake up, Joe!" a woman demanded gruffly.

I knew that commanding voice, but I couldn't summon up her name or face.

"Joe, come back to us," a second woman said evenly, and I recognized her voice, too. But again, I couldn't muster a name or visual recollection. *Was I experiencing a post-traumatic hallucination, or was I really alive?*

A hand squeezed my arm and bullyragged it, causing my teeth to click like breaking pool balls.

"Quit messin' around, Joe. Wake up!" a third voice exclaimed. "You're scarin' the bejesus out of us!"

My eyelids fluttered like malfunctioning theater curtains. I very much wanted to be alive and open my eyes to validate that desire, but I hesitated. *What if I were wrong? What if I really* were *dead?* At this point, I didn't know how I would cope with such a devastating letdown.

"Open your eyes, Joe," the second woman pleaded. "You're safe . . . at home . . . in your bed."

Did I hear that right? Did she speak the truth? Or were her words meant to deceive me?

Oh well, it was now or never.

I opened my tearful eyes.

I *was* in my bed.

57

I was as happy as a clam.

My reunion with life was put on hold while I showered, shaved, and made myself generally presentable. I descended the stairs with a little pep in my step and wished the three women awaiting me a hearty good afternoon. It was great to be alive.

I plunked into a kitchen chair at the table and feasted my eyes on the roast beef dinner sitting before me. I was ravenous. It felt like I hadn't eaten in days, and I said so.

"You haven't eaten in days," Martha Gibbons reminded me. Tillie and Dana agreed.

I dug in. "So where have I been?" I managed between mouthfuls.

"In another dimension," Martha replied without elaborating.

"I thought you and Kit were in another dimension," I said, confused. At least that was what Kirby told Dana and me.

"We are."

My fork froze in front of my mouth. "Is Gwendolyn Stockard there, too?"

Martha nodded. "For safekeeping."

I dropped the fork onto the plate. "But the whole world saw her die."

"Not her. Her doppelgänger. I switched them inside the Mansion Macabre before she made contact with Jeffrey Stanton. I saw that Reynolds planned to use her to murder her father, so I pulled a last-minute switch," Martha explained. "There was nothing I could do to save him. Reynolds would've been successful with his second try on the sheriff's life, so I figured — why bother?"

"So I was one of those bee swarms for a while, too?"

"Oh, yeah."

I nodded. It was all coming together for me. "Gwendolyn was the woman sitting with you in the back of the tearoom. She had her head down."

"Very good. I made her do that. I didn't want anyone knowing that she was still alive — including you, Joe. You might've let it slip in front of Reynolds, and he'd pull out all stops to find us."

"So why did you conjure me into that other dimension?" I asked, picking up my fork.

"Because if Reynolds' imitation mage staff hadn't killed you, his army of demons would have. So I swept you away."

Martha was *my* guardian angel. "Why'd you send me to Reynolds' place today?"

"To convince you once and for all that he was your *Ghostworld* murderer. And now you have some idea how he does it," Martha answered.

Martha's voice faded, and she vanished without saying goodbye. Weird. I looked back at Tillie and Dana standing behind me, and they were missing, too. *What was happening?*

Suddenly, the entire kitchen blinked out of existence. I would've thrown my chair to the side, but it was gone. I closed and massaged my eyes as I tried to wrap my thoughts around this peculiar enigma. When I re-opened them, the kitchen was back, and so were Tillie and Dana. I breathed a deep sigh of relief.

"What happened to you guys?" I asked.

Tillie shrugged. "I reckon when Martha returned to her hideout dimension, we got taken along for part of the ride," she speculated, appearing concerned.

Dana smiled and patted my shoulder. "We were just as scared as you were, but all's well that ends well."

I didn't want to frighten them any more than they were, but the new kitchen and their appearances seemed . . . surreal after our partial journey with Martha. Including the food on my plate. But I chalked it up to stress fatigue after my harrowing escape from Reynolds' mansion. I finished my early dinner.

Tillie turned, sashayed to the stove, scooped a gooey substance from a pan, and plopped it into a dessert bowl. I had a shrinking feeling that that blob was meant for me. When she plunked the bowl in front of me on the lace tablecloth, I was sure of it.

"Can't have a dinner without dessert," she said. "It's a new recipe I found in one of them magazines you brought home for me last month."

I peered into the oatmeal-like mess and cringed. No more magazines for her. "What's it called?"

"I forget. It's some kind of pudding. I tasted it and loved it. Don't worry, it tastes better than it looks. There's supposed to be whipped cream on top to dress it up, but we're all out."

My stomach and throat tightened into defensive stances, and even my lips balked at plowing that awful-looking stuff into my mouth. But somehow I found the fortitude—or insanity—to do the right thing and eat it. I didn't want to disappoint her. I shoved a skimpy spoonful past my lips and began chewing. It tasted — well, terrible.

I glanced up at Tillie. "I don't suppose I could wash this down with a beer?"

She crossed her hands across her chest. "Not a chance. You drank the last one a couple weeks ago. Remember?"

I actually didn't remember, so I washed the pudding sludge down the hatch with water. It sluiced down my throat into my protesting stomach, which gurgled like a witches' bubbling caldron. *Double . . . double . . . toil . . . and trouble . . . .*

Spoonful after spoonful, I grudgingly fueled my digestive frenzy until the bowl was relatively clean. Tillie and Dana remained strangely silent while I ate.

"Thanks for going to all this trouble for me," I said.

"You're very welcome." Tillie planted a kiss on my forehead, but I recoiled slightly at the touch of her icy lips. I shouldn't have been surprised. After all, she *was* dead.

I wrung my hands. "So what's next?"

Tillie and Dana eased into chairs across the table. "I'd say it's about time we swapped information about what happened the past three days."

I couldn't have agreed more. "You first."

58

They appeared reluctant to begin our exchange of info.

Dana spoke up. "I guess I'll go first, since I was the one who heard your screams and ran outside to see what was the matter. I saw you struggle with your magic staff, and it looked to me like it was electrocuting you. Your hair was a frizzed out like some hippie lunatic," she began. "Then Tillie came out, and before either of us could help you, you dissolved into a black cloud of bees and drifted away over the house."

Her description matched what happened, but why did I get the impression that she was concocting a whopper of a fish story? Maybe my paranoia had returned with me.

"Your magic staff fell to the driveway and crackled and hissed for another five minutes before it finally stopped," Tillie added. "I picked it up and put it in your barn office."

That didn't jive with what Martha had just told me. She said it wasn't my staff. It was a fake that Reynolds had conjured. Now I was suspicious again, and it wasn't paranoia.

"What about the demon army?" I asked, as if I totally believed them.

"I, uh, we didn't see them," Dana said, and Tillie nodded her agreement.

"And that's our story," Tillie concluded. "So what about you? How'd it feel to be turned into a swarm of bees?"

I sighed. "Lonely. And dark." I slowly proceeded to narrate my eerie existence, but I left out the part about Gwendolyn. I also condensed the details of my visit with Reynolds. No oil paintings. No Brice. No wild chase through the storm clouds. Just lunch and topless babes.

"And that's it?" From her cynical tone, I got the feeling that she knew I'd omitted a few details.

I smiled. "Yep, that's it."

There were several seconds of digestive silence before Tillie spoke.

"So what does it all mean?"

"You got me," I declared, this entire situation clinging to me like frost.

"What do you think, Dana?" Tillie asked.

Dana shrugged. "I don't have a clue."

Tillie's eyes narrowed. "Liar."

59

I waited for the fireworks to start.

Dana wasn't the type of woman who would take Tillie's boorish claim calmly, so I wasn't surprised when she stood abruptly, knocking her chair over in the process. Tillie, though, remained unperturbed and merely stared at Dana and the overturned chair. A slightly amused grin curled the corners of her mouth.

Dana's reaction was nothing like I imagined. My partner's flesh cracked like Humpty Dumpty's shell, sloughing away both patches of human skin and her clothing. My jaw dropped as an amber demon with curled horns, fire-green eyes, a pitted complexion, a double row of sharp yellow teeth, and a lipless mouth confronted me.

I leaped up and felt my wolfen genes start to kick in. Reddish-gray hair sprouted along my arms as I witnessed "Tillie" transform into a white-robed witch who looked nothing like my housemate. Her black hair plunged over her shoulders, and she stared at me over her hooked nose with ruthless coal eyes.

Before my frame completed the transformation, my body started to disintegrate—to break into a bee swarm. Once. Twice. Three times without success. After failing to split me like the atom, the extrication attempts ceased.

My two captors merely watched in amusement.

The witch chuckled at my confusion. "You're not going to get away that easily again," she announced. "That pudding you ate was really a potion to prevent you from splitting into that annoying bee swarm. I call it my glue brew."

The demon bent over laughing.

My suspicion was confirmed, though not exactly the way I'd envisioned it. They'd tricked me. "Where are the real Tillie and Dana?" I demanded, as I became totally human again.

"Your friends are back in their world where they belong," the witch cackled. "We're your new friends, Joe."

Their world? Egg beaters churned my emotions into a blend of pure terror. "Then where am I?"

It was the demon's turn to dole out the next bit of bad news. "In the Emerald Zone. Look out the window."

Alabaster ghosts, thousands of them in every shape and size, flitted in the air outside the glass, their scowling, murderous expressions targeted at yours truly. Instead of my farmscape, there was an infinite sea of dazzling white. If the ghosts hadn't been a slightly darker shade of white, like the smudges in Reynolds' Emerald Zone oil painting, they would've been invisible. But something was missing . . . .

"Where's your demon giant?" I asked.

The witch's amusement vanished. "Your partner killed our pet."

So that's where Dana got those bruises and cuts that night outside my farm. *Damn!* That girl was something else. There was a lot more to her than met the eye.

"But the master will make her pay," the witch promised.

Master? My eyes narrowed. "What master?"

She cackled again, and it was getting under my skin. "You met him, Joe. Don't you remember?" That was her big clue? Obviously she wasn't going to speak his name.

The demon closed in on my left as the witch held my attention, but my peripheral vision was second to none. I wheeled on the demon with both fists raised.

"Back off," I threatened.

My threat sent them into another fit of uncouth laughter before the demon recovered and seized my arm.

"Don't threaten your superiors, Luna!" It tossed me over the table like a sack of feathers. I slid across the linoleum floor and crashed into the cupboards beneath the counter. My shoulder ached, and my wolfen genes went critical this time.

I wished they hadn't. Instead of changing me into a werewolf, the genes misfired and changed me into a yipping Chihuahua. Before I knew what hit me, the amber demon strode across the floor and kicked me hard into the cupboards again. I rebounded off the wooden surface like a china cup. Every bone in my wimpy canine body had splintered like dry wood.

My body reversed the process, and soon I was agonizingly human again. Naked, but human. I laboriously retrieved my shredded pants that lay beside me and painfully slipped them on. My shirt went on next, followed by my socks and shoes. Fires sprang up inside my bones and joints with every movement, but modesty was a strong motivator, and I wasn't about to display myself to those two malicious creeps.

"This is the Emerald Zone, Joe," the witch sniggered. "Your special powers won't work here."

I snuck a peek at my regenerated magic wand tucked under my belt, and I painfully reached for my magical surprise. My bones screamed in protest as I twisted my hips.

The demon snarled, but the witch merely chuckled. "Remember what happened to you when you touched your magic staff a few days ago?"

Boy, did I. That unfortunate incident was what triggered this whole bizarre chain of events.

"Your magic won't work in the Emerald Zone, but go ahead and try casting a spell on us if you don't believe me." She paused to wait, but I left the wand where it was. "On the night your staff went berserk, you weren't on your farm."

"I hate to disagree, but I think I know what my farm looks like," I countered sarcastically.

"The area *looked* like your farm, but in reality we had surrounded your farmhouse with the Emerald Zone."

"If that's true, why wasn't the night white?" I argued.

"The master altered the scenery. He's very powerful."

The witch almost had me convinced, but she was mistaken about my magic not being effective inside the Emerald Zone. The wand worked just fine when I cast my dark flashlight beam at the white giant below the Mansion Macabre. But I kept that knowledge to myself. It might help me escape later. *Might* was the key word.

"And why won't my magic work here?" I asked, stalling until my bones were mended. I felt my wolfen genes at work, but this was a major repair job and would take some time. So, I sat on the floor like a limp dish rag and learned everything I could from the two deceivers that I might be able to use against them later. *Give them enough rope, and hopefully they'll hang themselves.*

The witch shot me an offended glare. "In the Emerald Zone, everything is the reverse of your world. If you sic your magic on us, it will backfire into you. Do you understand what I'm telling you?"

"Loud and clear," I muttered, and turned my head. I was really up to my ass in alligators this time. *Why hadn't I accepted Uncle Jess' offer to resign the case?* My pigheadedness, that's why.

"So do you plan on killing me? Is that the idea?"

The demon growled. "We'd love to tear you apart right now, but the master won't have it. He's saving you," it replied regretfully.

"Saving me for what?"

"For himself," the demon spat.

"Oh." *That was thoughtful.* "So where is your precious master?"

"The master has unfinished business, and you're a big part of it," the witch said. "But he'll be here soon. If I were you, I wouldn't be so anxious to see him."

"I'm a big part of his unfinished business?" I glanced around to make my point. "He hasn't even started with me, as far as I can see."

Both of my Emerald Zones hosts grinned—horrible savage grins.

"Oh, you're already serving him well," the demon said.

"Oh yes, definitely," the witch agreed.

"How? By sitting here like a bony beanbag?" I snapped, tiring of their yuks at my expense.

"Hardly," the witch replied, sobering.

I rolled my eyes. At least *they* didn't hurt. "You two don't know, do you? I'm talking to his lackeys."

The demon seethed with anger at the insult. "Lackeys, huh! I'll teach you a thing or two about respect!" She stomped toward me, ready to break a few more of my bones.

The witch cast a quick spell that transported the demon back to her original position. "Knock it off!" the witch ordered. "If the master finds out you killed Luna, you'll never return to this dimension again. Got it?"

The demon grunted and sneered at me. "The master's using you as bait, and his plan is working like a charm."

Bait? Bait for what? Or worse yet, for *who?*

60

The demon ignored the witch and lumbered toward me again. It back-handed me across the jaw. *Man, that hurt!* The side of my head thumped against the cupboard doors, and I saw murky stars.

"Knock it off, Zela!" the witch shouted, raising both her arms, preparing to cast her demon comrade into another dimension. For good.

Zela shrugged. "I didn't promise you and the master what shape this piece of shit would be in when he returned to finish him off," she snapped gruffly.

The witch lowered her arms, but her expression was wary. Obviously she didn't trust her Emerald Zone cohort. "Okay, but no more physical stuff. Luna's half-dead already."

After minutes of sustained silence, when a torturous dull headache displaced my twinkling, spinning stars, I slowly glanced up to see if my tormentors were still in the room. They were.

My curiosity overruled the severe pain. "You mentioned that I was . . . was being used as bait. For who?" Blood leaked out the corner of my mouth as I spoke, and dribbled down my chin. I couldn't move my broken hands yet to wipe it away.

The two exchanged anxious glances, and finally the demon nodded its hideous head.

"I guess it won't hurt for you to know, since you're not getting out of here alive," the witch said thoughtfully, but I could see that she wasn't too keen on the idea of divulging secrets. Especially her master's secrets.

"The master sure has played you for a fool, Luna," the demon added meanly.

I couldn't disagree with Zela's assessment. Obviously, I had been their master's investigative jester since day one. I wasn't embarrassed by my failure. *I was mortified.*

And now my conscience had to bear the weight of another death. But who was his next target?

"The master wants your Uncle Jess."

Oh, my God! I nearly passed out from shock. It was true that I deeply despised my uncle, but I never wanted to see him die for being such a schmuck. I was at a loss for words. Thoughts. Emotions. I guessed it showed.

The witch chuckled. "Surprised, huh Joe?"

No words came.

"You see, it's such a simple plan. Since you went missing a few days ago, your uncle flew down to Orlando to lead the search for you, and in doing so, he exposed himself to the master. No more hiding in Washington DC where he was protected day and night," the witch explained a little too willingly.

Hiding? Another shocker. I didn't know he was a hunted man . . . er, werewolf.

"And his search is going to take him to *Ghostworld* tonight when all hell breaks loose—literally." She glanced at Zela. "He'll have a ghost of a good time."

The pair laughed heartily as I shook my head to clear away some of the mental sludge clogging my thought process. Now I would be forced to escape by tonight to save Uncle Jess. *Talk about pressure!* I examined my right hand and moved my fingers up and down. No more pain. They were healed. Now my wolfen genes needed to play Florence Nightingale on the rest of my broken body.

I had a pretty good idea who their master was, but I was reluctant to ask them again. They might clam up, and then I wouldn't learn anything valuable that would help me trash his plans for Uncle Jess.

"So what kind of hell is breaking loose tonight?" I asked as casually as I could.

Zela grunted. "It speaks again."

"Let's just say that *Ghostworld* will live up to its name," the witch replied evasively.

"Why there?" I pressed, "unless your master is planning to release all the ghosts from the Emerald Zone into our world."

"You're pretty clever, Luna," Zela said.

"Shut up, you fool!" the witch rebuked the demon. "No more information. We've told him enough."

"But we're going to kill him, so what's the big deal?"

"The big deal is that if the master finds out that we've been shooting our mouths off to Luna, he might kill us both."

The demon backed off. "I still don't see what harm it'll do. If we aren't allowed to kill him, I don't see why we can't torture his mind—drive him insane. Like I said, he's a dead man . . . sitting," Zela muttered beneath its breath.

"So your master built *Ghostworld* as a cover," I said to no one in particular, purposely thinking aloud. "That means that he had a stake in the theme park, personal and probably financial. But why murder his partners?" I attempted to bait them into revealing their master's purpose for constructing *Ghostworld* as a cover.

But neither nibbled, so I sweetened it.

"So why would he murder his partners, and then purposely destroy the theme park? He'd be ruined, unless . . ." I let my incomplete thought dangle in the electric air for a few moments. I noticed that they were paying attention now. "Oh, of course! Unless he wanted to cash in on the park's insurance!" I declared triumphantly.

"You fool, he doesn't care about the money," Zela exclaimed. "The master used the park as a cover to amplify his . . . ."

The demon never finished. The witch cast Zela back into the underworld.

But Zela had revealed just enough of the puzzle for me to insert a few more pieces. I recalled the pentagram-shaped wires surrounding his Indialantic mansion, and now I knew what to research about *Ghostworld's* construction site. I had a good idea why that particular site was important, but I had to escape to prove it. I scanned the kitchen for any object I could use to overpower the witch, but there was nothing at first glance.

My plight appeared hopeless until I did a double-take at an object on the counter. An idea dawned. A damned good one. *Why didn't I think of it before?* The item had been in front of my face the whole time.

Now if I could only pull it off without getting killed.

I wriggled my toes and nonchalantly stretched my left leg. Painlessly. I slid my hand closer to the wand at my waist. My healing had escalated. *But could my wolfen genes restore me to full strength before the master arrived to finish me off?*

That part of my plan required a miracle.

61

The witch looked jittery. Tense.

Her master must have been delayed. She periodically split the curtains, peered outside, frowned, and looked away from the window. The ghosts now swam together so tightly in the Emerald Zone that they resembled nebulous sardines in a white tin can. I couldn't have squeezed my arm between them.

"Your master late?" I pried.

She shot me a withering glance. "*Hardly*. I'm just watching his progress with the others. His final victims are falling nicely." She huffed at my mystified look. "I have the ability to see outside the zone."

"Final victims?" I winced, and suddenly her magic gruel gurgled loudly in my stomach.

"Yes, *victims*. He needs them to finalize his black-magic grid to open the gate to your dimension. Your Mayor Ellis just caught a train—on the tracks. So much blood."

She paused for effect, but I didn't let my revulsion show. Disappointed by my lack of response, she continued. "And Governor Branch will be the master's final target. He should be history within the hour." She smiled horribly. "You know, murdering your uncle has nothing to do with the ritual. You might say it's a fringe benefit for the master. He hates Jess Luna, but I don't know why. What I do know is that the master has held that grudge for more than twenty years."

I was surprised that she decided to tell me so much, since she'd zapped Zela into another world for letting his secret slip. After watching Branch bite the dust, she must have figured my death was a sure thing, and I wouldn't be around to tell anyone.

I ticked off *Ghostworld's* victims on my restored fingertips. Victim number *one*: Lance Stockard, who was involved up to his sheriff's badge in the *Ghostworld* project. I didn't know how, but I vowed to find out. The poignant irony of *his* gruesome murder was that his own daughter was the murder weapon.

Victim number *two*: Senator Justice Kane. The human torch. Victim number *three*: Jeffrey Stanton. The human bomb. Victim numbers *four* and *five*: from what the witch just told me, Orlando Mayor John Ellis caught a train to hell, and Governor Branch Tucker was an hour away from joining the *Ghostworld* Five. Uncle Jess wasn't in that group. He was a Lucky Strike extra.

So what did the five corpses represent? Why were they so critical to the master's plan tonight? My gray cells were slowly catching fire and functioning again now that my body was ninety percent repaired. Before long, the explanation appeared amid a marching band and fireworks. The *Ghostworld* Five neatly fit a diabolical pattern that spelled calamity for the entire world.

Five. The ominous black magic sum. The propitious number for wizards who dabbled in the black arts. In this case, there was one murder victim for each point of the evil pentagram. I had to hand it to the *Ghostworld* murderer—the master bastard had orchestrated his wicked scheme to a "T." What I didn't understand was how each victim contributed to the pentagram's power. But at least I knew where to find their souls—in the gruesome paintings displayed in Reynolds' art gallery for the rich and morbid.

I mentally shoved this train of thought aside (no pun intended, late-mayor), because it was time to get my escape in gear before I became another *Ghostworld* casualty. I chanced another glimpse at the counter, stood, and stretched.

"Your wolfen healing system worked damned fast," the witch observed, her suspicious gaze tracking my exercise movements.

My left hand drifted toward my wand as I slipped my right into my shredded shorts' pocket. As I hoped, she focused solely on my left hand. Big mistake. Really big.

"As I told you before, your wand won't work here, but if you're going to be your typical stubborn self, then by all means give it a try," she cackled.

In the Emerald Zone, everything is the reverse of your world. The witch had unwittingly handed me my plan on a silver platter.

"I might at that," I shot back smugly, as I aligned our reflections in the vanity mirror on the counter. A rivulet of sweat trickled down my forehead. I was placing all my eggs in one basket with this trick. If it didn't work out, I'd be a bucket-kicker.

I nonchalantly withdrew my right hand from my pocket while my left closed around the wand. Timing was critical.

Suddenly, her vigilance flipped to fear. "Get your hand away from your . . . ."

With my right hand, I flung my magic dust at the witch's reflection in the mirror, and her image became covered in the sparkling white powder. *In the Emerald Zone, everything is the reverse of your world.*

For a change, the expected happened. The actual witch standing in the conjured kitchen hacked blue smoke like a supernatural asthmatic. The spasms grew worse, and she wilted to her knees. Finally, her entire spasmodic body crumpled into a smoking heap on the floor. In her dying throes, she looked at me through filmy eyes with a combination of bewilderment and shock. After her head thumped to the floor, the witch melted into a steaming puddle of blue ooze. Good riddance.

Instantly, the Emerald Zone vanished, and I found myself lying on a country road about a mile from my farm. Although I was healed, the oppressive Florida air sapped my reserve strength, making it difficult to stand. When I finally climbed to my feet, I lurched forward like a binge drinker in the general direction of my farm.

A pick-up truck roared up behind me, blaring a twangy country-music hit from a super-bass sound system. I staggered off the pavement onto the slender ribbon of grass and waited for it to pass. It didn't.

"Hi, Mr. L," Jason Hollinsworth hailed from the driver's seat. He was a big boy, about my height, with broad shoulders, muscular arms, but shy several pounds. His expression was always the same—jovial sincerity. "Need a ride?"

"Oh, yeah," I said breathlessly. With considerable effort, I climbed aboard.

"If you don't mind me sayin' so, you look like you just played in a football game without pads," Jason declared lightly. He switched off the music and put the truck into gear, and we sailed down the road at twice the posted speed. Oh, to be young and invincible again.

"Good analogy," I replied. "Where were you heading?"

The seventeen-year-old chuckled and patted down a stubborn cowlick in his wavy, sandy hair. "I'm going over to see my girl. She lives just past your place," he replied.

"She wouldn't be Samantha Capshaw?"

He smiled like the cat that swallowed the canary. "Yep. She's the one."

"She's a real looker."

"Oh yeah. And popular at school. I'm pretty lucky," he added. "Here we are, Mr. L." He pulled off the road in front of my driveway gate.

"Thanks. You saved my life." I slid down off the worn cloth seat. "Have fun with Samantha, but remember one thing."

Jason frowned, anticipating a lecture.

I was glad to disappoint him. "You've got things backwards. Samantha's lucky to be with *you*."

Jason grinned broadly. "Thanks, Mr. L. Thanks a lot."

I quickly entered the security code and wobbly-walked through the opening gate. As I approached the front porch, Merlin did his watchdog thing and came flying through the door. I gave him a weary smile and shooed him off to play with the squirrels.

Dana and Tillie ran out the front door to greet me, but I was standoffish. I'd already been duped once today, and I wasn't going for a second. *Were these two my real friends? Was I really out of the Emerald Zone?*

"Wait right where you are," I shouted, extending my open hand. I closed my eyes and leveled a spell at them, and presto, each held a fall bouquet of mixed flowers. My magic had returned! They froze and swapped puzzled but pleased glances.

"Landsakes, what's the matter with you, Joe?" Tillie demanded in her typical not-so-subtle tone. "Thanks for the flowers, but . . . ."

"No buts, Tillie. Just Happy Halloween," I concocted on the spur of the moment.

Dana looked amazed. "No one's ever given me flowers before," she sighed.

That I found hard to believe. "Well, there's a first time for everything, Dana. Excuse me, but I've got to grab a catnap—lion-sized. I'm beyond bushed."

On the way up the front walk, I gave them a quick run-down on my bizarre experience in the Emerald Zone. Dana tore her eyes from her bouquet and listened intently. Tillie just stared at me as if I'd lost more than a few marbles, and nearly tripped on the first porch step.

When I finished my incredible tale, Tillie squeezed me for all she was worth on the porch. "Good to see you back safe and sound, Joe," she sniffed, dabbing the tears at the corners of her eyes. "We wondered what the hell happened to you earlier when you vanished from the kitchen."

Dana sniffed her flowers for the zillionth time. "It's good to have you back."

Tillie merely folded her arm around mine. "You look like something the cat dragged in. Before your nap, how's about some food?"

I cringed, recalling that horrible pudding. "I'm still kinda full."

"From that witch's potion. You know, evil witches give us all a bad name," she sputtered, stomping her foot on the threshold as we stepped into the house.

I patted her arm. "Don't get yourself worked up. Witches like that just make me appreciate you more," I said, trying to mollify her.

"Why that's right nice of you to say," she said, her ire ebbing.

Before ascending the stairs, I stopped. "Uncle Jess hasn't been around here today, has he?" I asked, cloaking my urgency with casualness.

"Oh yeah, he was here," Tillie replied. "That man's a real sweetheart," she added with a double dose of sarcasm.

My stomach knotted. My captors had been telling the truth. I was the bait who flushed him out of his safe haven. "Where's he now?"

Dana stepped around in front of me. "Where else? *Ghostworld*."

My heart sank like a lead balloon. Uncle Jess and the governor were as good as dead unless I warned them of their impending doom.

"I'm headed out to the barn to phone Uncle Jess and tell him that the killer's after him and the governor," I exclaimed, limping past them toward the back door.

"Stop!" Dana shouted behind me.

"Not now. I don't have a minute to waste," I yelled back from the back porch.

"It's too late," she said.

I stopped on a dime. "Too late for who?"

62

Dana accompanied me to my barn office and made me sit down. Tillie appeared beside the chair, and the next thing I knew, I was waking out of a deep sleep.

I glanced around the office, trying to get my bearings, and found Dana sitting next to me. "What happened?" I asked amidst a jaw-splitting yawn.

"Tillie put you to sleep. She said that you needed that more than you did my news," she replied with a grin.

I stretched wordlessly, feeling more energetic than I had since . . . before my initial visit to *Ghostworld*.

"How long have I been out?" I asked.

"About twenty minutes."

"That's impossible," I argued lightly.

Her smile broadened. "Not if a witch puts you under with her sleeping spell."

Hmmm. Tillie and her magic had been at it again. She'd whipped up a twenty-minute power nap for me. Now if only I could bottle that spell, I'd be a billionaire.

Suddenly, the importance of Dana's news struck home. *Could both my uncle and the governor be dead?* I figured that Tillie put me to sleep because there was nothing I could do to change the outcome. That had to be it.

"So what happened to . . . ." I choked up. Even though Uncle Jess treated me like the black sheep of the world, I was still emotionally devastated by the loss.

"Joe, it's not what you think."

"Just tell me. My uncle's dead, isn't he?"

She cleared her throat. "No, he's not dead, Joe."

"But . . . ."

"If you *listen* for a minute, I can explain."

My heart hammered my ribs. "I'm listening."

"Governor Tucker died about a half-hour before you came home.

There was a horrible head-on collision between his sports car and a dump truck on the Beachline. His car was crumpled like an accordion and burst into flames. I'm afraid that there wasn't much left but bones and ash." Dana paused, her hands clenched white. "His wife was interviewed briefly on TV while you slept, and she told the reporters that he had been on his way back to Orlando after visiting Wayland Reynolds."

The *Ghostworld* Five were now living in Reynolds' oil paintings. "So Uncle Jess is okay?"

Tillie materialized by the desk. "Right as rain, the last I saw him," she replied. "Acid rain, that is."

Uncle Jess was alive to torment me another day.

"I've got to get a hold of him and tell him about Reynolds' plans," I announced, reaching for the government phone.

Tillie shook her head.

"What's that supposed to mean?" I carped, standing.

"You can't get a hold of your uncle. Dana tried after you fell asleep. Your new-fangled cell and sat phones aren't working inside *Ghostworld* today," she pointed out.

I looked at Dana.

"I called DSI in Washington, and that's what they told me. They haven't spoken to him since noon today, and that was from your farm," she said, worry creasing her forehead.

"Dammit! What next?" I groused. "I suppose we'll have to drive down there."

Another Tillie headshake.

"Now what's the matter?" I barked in annoyance.

"You're not using your noggin. While Uncle Jess is the focus of your killer, you and Dana should be sneaking up on Reynolds and ambushing him from behind."

I rocked in my chair. "And just how do you propose we do that?"

"You're the one getting paid for this cloak-and-dagger stuff. You two put your heads together and figure it out." Tillie vanished abruptly. *Women!* They could be so exasperating at times. Umm, *most* of the time, really, in my experience.

I grabbed Dana's hand and we teleported to Tillie's favorite haunt— the kitchen.

"You're not getting off that easily," I said sternly. "You're in this, too. So help us."

I believe Tillie was impressed that we followed her into the house and needed her input. "I don't have much else cookin' around here, so why not? I'm in."

"So do you remember what I said Reynolds is planning to do tonight?"

Tillie scowled at me. "Of course I do. I can listen as well as the next person. You told Dana and me that son-of-a-bitch was going to unleash the ghosts from the Emerald Zone into this world, right?"

I backed off some and chilled out. "Yeah, that's what I said."

She wagged her finger at me. "Those ghosts are real bad ones, Joe. It'll be like emptying the prisons into innocent neighborhoods. Those ghosts were sentenced to the Emerald Zone as a punishment — *forever*."

They must have been hard-core, soulless devils. "So how can we stop Reynolds from succeeding?"

"I don't have any experience with ghosts, but I know who might."

"Who?" I implored her, my impatience showing again.

Her gaze narrowed and her arms intertwined over her chest. "I won't answer anyone who uses *that* tone of voice with me."

She was right. I was a little over the top. "Sorry. It's just that I'm feeling so helpless. My magic skills are far inferior to what's in Reynolds' bag of tricks."

"That's no excuse for being rude, Joe."

I felt like I was ten again, suffering my mother's scolding. "Okay. Would you *please* tell us who we can consult about those ghosts."

"Much better." Her arms dropped to her sides. "First of all, you're going about your problem from the wrong angle. Don't be concerned with Reynolds' magic."

She had me there. That was the *only* element that I was concerned about since my charming little beachside luncheon with Wayland.

"Then what should I be worried about?" I prodded.

"Your real problem is stopping the ghosts that'll escape into our world," she continued.

I was skeptical to say the least, but I tried not to show it. I wasn't fond of Tillie's patented tongue-lashings.

"So you're telling me that we really should focus on the ghost invaders?"

"Bingo! Give that boy a medal." She slapped my shoulder. "So, bright boy, who do you think you'd see to work out your ghost problem?"

I raised my hands in surrender. *Ghostbusters?* "You got me," I admitted reluctantly. I hated playing the part of *Dummy* to her *Genius*.

Tillie chuckled in that annoying, know-it-all manner that drove me up a wall.

"Joe, think. If you need to fix a ghost problem, then consult a *dang-burned ghost!*"

I was speechless.

63

Why hadn't I thought of that? Must have been my bee-swarm hangover blocking my common sense.

I thanked Tillie, slipped past Dana who was speaking into her cell phone (an odd-looking cell phone at that), and walked out to my barn office again. Even though the phones were out of service inside *Ghostworld*, including Uncle Jess' new and improved anti-block sat phone, I dialed his number to leave a message. Hopefully he'd get it sooner than later.

To my surprise, he picked up on the first ring. "It's about time you contacted me," he grumbled.

Some things never changed. He was still the warm and fuzzy guy I loathed.

"The whole world's been trying to contact you at *Ghostworld*, but I was told the phones aren't working there. At least until now," I said.

"So I've just seen on my voicemail record. We drove out to get lunch a couple minutes ago, so that's how you were able to reach me now. I presume that you're back in this dimension and going to stay for a while."

"How'd you know . . . ?"

"I have agents staking out Reynolds' place in Indialantic. So did you learn anything about him?"

I shouldn't have been surprised that Uncle Jess suspected him, but I was. "How'd your guys know that I was in another dimension?"

"They saw you materialize in front of Reynolds' place from a bee swarm." He chuckled. "And I got a voicemail from Martha telling me all about it and your visit to the mansion."

"Did she fill you in on my conversation with Reynolds?"

"Pretty much."

"Why'd you suspect his involvement with the *Ghostworld* murders?"

"We've been following his movements for decades. The murders just sounded like his ruthless style. You remember. Accidents. Fires."

"I remember."

"Gwendolyn Stockard's exploding head was a new one for him, and it's got the press stumped. They've been interviewing doctors for the past several days on TV, but all they ended up with were ridiculous theories. No actual causes."

That was typical media. I changed topics. "Then you know about Reynolds' gallery of death paintings."

Uncle Jess stiffened at his end of the connection. "*Death* paintings?"

"Yeah."

"No, Martha didn't mention them in her voicemail."

I briefly described the victims and scenes in the ghastly oil paintings, and mentioned that I didn't get the chance to see them all.

"That's serious black magic," he muttered.

"Well, hold on to your hat, because that's not the biggest shocker."

"Don't keep me in suspense."

"Reynolds used my disappearance to lure you out of Washington, so he could murder you tonight," I told him bluntly.

"Hmm," he said.

Not quite the reaction I expected. "Do you know why he hates you so much?"

"I can think of at least twenty reasons—he was a suspect in twenty murders I investigated, but there wasn't enough evidence to arrest him. But I tried. Of course, it wasn't hard to understand how he pulled off those murders. Reynolds is a first-class sorcerer," Uncle Jess explained angrily. "Make no mistake about it, Joe, he's an unconscionable killer."

"So he wants revenge?"

After a moment of silence, Uncle Jess finally spoke. "More than likely, yes."

"I saw that old man in the wheelchair I spoke to you about before. It was a strange situation. Reynolds actually appeared to be afraid of him." I paused. "If the geezer hadn't shown up when he did, I would've ended up in one of those awful paintings. There was one reserved for me."

"Really?" Uncle Jess murmured. "What did the old man look like?'

My memory took a stroll down Nightmare Lane. I told Uncle Jess about the geezer's waxen wrinkles, the sparse white wisps of hair, and the camel hump for a back. I couldn't wait to click my mental delete command and lose that horrible image.

"What about his face? Did he look familiar?" he prodded.

Look familiar? Hell, I'd never even met Reynolds before, so how could *anyone* look familiar? "What are you fishing for?" I demanded brusquely.

"Just try to picture his face, and then I'll answer your question."

Like a police artist, I mentally pealed away those massive Shar Pei wrinkles, but it was slow going. Uncle Jess remained patiently quiet for a change. When I finally finished, the old man's face stood out very clearly. I was stunned.

"Oh my God!"

"What's the matter?" Uncle Jess asked excitedly.

I cleared my throat several times before the frog died. "He looked a lot like—you won't believe this."

"I *will* believe it when you get around to telling me," he blustered.

"Okay, okay. The old man could've been Reynolds' identical *twin*, except for their absurd age difference."

"Hmm."

That *hmm* again. "I told you that it was pretty farfetched."

"No, Joe, it's not that. If Reynolds is a soul-stealer, like his paintings suggest, then the old man *could* have been . . . ."

I waited. This had to be good.

"Been his *son*."

I nearly laughed. "C'mon, that's impossible."

"Or his grandson."

I was beginning to believe that Uncle Jess had lost his marbles.

"I'm telling you, the guy looked to be a hundred."

"Looks can be deceiving. You ought to know *that*."

Sure I did, but I didn't think that phrase applied in this case. "Okay, let's say that hypothetically the old guy was Reynolds' kid. How's it possible for a kid to look older than his father?"

"Simple. Reynolds uses his magic to feed off his kid's life force to preserve his own youth. Which probably explains why Wayland Reynolds hasn't aged much in nearly fifty years," he explained.

"Here I chalked it up to good genes."

"It's more than that, trust me."

"So the bastard stays young. How does that help us defeat him?"

"I don't know. I just don't know," Uncle Jess replied, as if he were daydreaming. "*I'll* figure it out, though."

I was fit to be tied! He implied that I *couldn't* come up with a sound strategy from that single detail. His tedious arrogance had reared its ugly head again.

Instead of using my time wisely to develop a plan, I wasted it by trying to knock Uncle Jess down a peg. "I wouldn't put too much thought into your energy-stealing theory. After all, we're only speculating here," I reminded him. "Your primary goal should be self-protection."

"Sure. Right. When are you coming out to *Ghostworld?*"

I was on to his tricks. Whenever he dropped a subject like a hot potato, it was to diminish its importance. In other words, he didn't want to discuss it any further with me. He'd run the subject by his other agents. *Full-time agents.*

"Later tonight."

"Why not sooner?"

"I've got an appointment in . . . ." I glanced out the window at the retreating sun. ". . . in about thirty minutes."

"What kind of appointment?" he probed.

"I have another angle I'm working on to stop Reynolds," I answered guardedly.

"Care to tell me about it? I'm only your superior on this investigation!" he growled.

I grinned. Score one for the home team. "Later," I said and hung up.

Before meeting with some old and dear friends, Dana and I were going to have a little heart-to-heart chat.

64

I contacted Dana on the barn-to-house intercom, and she showed up in five minutes, wearing khaki shorts and a tight coral knit top. Her Florida-ish fashion certainly displayed her curves and legs nicely. I was all for that.

But her mood didn't reflect her cheery clothing. Her face was drawn, as if she'd lost her best friend. I asked her about it.

Dana sat heavily in the chair across from my desk. "We're losing the battle with Reynolds," she replied bitterly, her hands clenched on the chair arms. "And there's not much the two of us can do about it without waging a full-scale war with the bastard."

I rocked my weight back in my office chair; I was taken aback by her response. *Reynolds?* He wasn't why I had summoned her, but it was an intriguing digression.

"Silly me, I thought we *were* waging a war with the ruthless killer," I contested.

She shook her head. "An all-out battle requires more magic than you and I have combined," she lamented. "Since the beginning of man, there have been forces at work behind the scenes that have prevented power-hungry tyrants like Reynolds from destroying humans, but even these ancient forces can't rein him in him without basically laying waste to our planet and its inhabitants."

I whistled. I didn't realize that she was such a supernatural historian. "Aren't you being a bit melodramatic?"

She shook her head. "I wish I were."

"Shit the bed, Fred!" I exclaimed breathlessly and scratched my head. It sounded like Reynolds was going to destroy the earth, and there was nothing we could do to stop him. That was encouraging.

"And who are the mighty guardians that have protected us all these centuries?"

Dana appeared horrified. "It's better if I don't say."

"Then I'll say it for you. The *Gorgons*. Right?"

Her hands trembled, and she quickly folded them in her lap. "Yes."

"So if they're not getting involved in our defense this time around, then why'd they send that creature into Martha's shop and have it draw their mark on the wall? It seems to me they wouldn't have done that if they planned to hide behind the scenes."

"They had their reasons," Dana declared softly.

"Is that a fact? How would *you* know?" I pressed.

"I just know. You'll have to trust me on that for now," she said apologetically.

Trust! She was asking a lot. In this investigation, I was learning that trust could get me killed.

"Whatever," I groused. "So we're doomed. We might as well take a trip to a nice island beach and live it up till we die. How about it?"

"You're being ridiculous," she snapped.

"Hey, you're the one who came in here preaching gloom and doom. If we can't defeat Reynolds, there's no use trying. Make the best of what little time we have left. I don't find that so ridiculous," I argued. I hated giving up, but if I were forced to, I damned well planned to do it in style.

Dana remained mum while my temperature spiked. This was getting us nowhere.

I finally cooled down. "Do you really want to quit?" I asked.

Determination radiated from her gaze. "No."

"Okay, then we won't."

"I like that plan," she said. "I believe in us as a team. We can nail Reynolds. You and me. Forget the . . . *Gorgons*."

My plan sounded a lot like a suicide mission. Me and my big mouth. "Nice discussion, but I called you here to find out if you made any progress on our case while I was buzzing around Reynolds' place. I guess I already know your answer."

She dropped her head.

"You know, I get the feeling that you and my uncle knew the murderer was Reynolds all along. Am I right?" I drilled her.

"I can't speak for Jess, but I guess I blew it, huh?" she muttered.

"Blew what?" I pressed, unprepared for her candor.

She sighed, and her hands reappeared. They weren't trembling any more. "I was instructed to help you bring Reynolds down," she admitted evenly.

"Yeah, I know; Uncle Jess asked you to lend a hand."

Dana shook her head. "Not directly." She paused, carefully choosing her words. "You see, your uncle was ordered to send me down here to assist you. Watch over you."

"Well that didn't work out so well," I asserted. "In fact, I saved your life once, and then Tillie and Merlin saved it another time in that ghost butcher shop."

My partner held up a hand. "I know, I know, I failed you there. I apologize."

"Why didn't your handlers come to our rescue?"

"They couldn't. I . . . we're expendable."

"We meaning you and me?"

She nodded.

"So who are these swell guys who think we're pawns in this fight?"

She shifted uncomfortably in her chair. "This is strictly confidential. Not even your uncle is to know. Agreed?"

I almost balked at leaving dear old uncle in the dark on this one, but then he's been doing that to me for years. Paybacks are a bitch.

"Deal."

She rose from her chair and planted her face so close to mine that I thought she was going to kiss me.

"The *Gorgons* sent me, Joe."

65

Now I was totally baffled.

How had Dana managed to get hooked up with the mythical snake ladies that turn people to stone?

I asked her.

She exhaled sharply. "They're my . . . aunts, if you have to know."

I felt my jaw drop to the floor. "That would make you over a thousand years old!"

She smiled and stepped back. "Not really. I am one in a long line of human descendants. I'm actually twenty-nine, and not a year older," she said.

"So these aunts of yours don't care if you die bringing down Reynolds?"

"Oh, they care, but they realized that you and I are their best chance of stopping Reynolds without destroying earth in the process."

"I feel like we're a couple of a misfit toys. My magic can't stand up to Reynolds' power, and I doubt that yours can, either. So what makes us so special — besides that critical handicap?" I demanded.

"We work well together, and my aunts seem to think that we're both cleverer than Reynolds. That's what makes us the perfect team to bring him down," she replied without an ounce of modesty. "If my aunts get directly involved, our case will escalate into that full-scale war I told you about."

My kind of girl. Cocky. Confident. Cute.

"So we've got to outsmart him and dazzle him with bullshit. Right?"

She chuckled. "That's one way of putting it."

"What about your guardian angel? Is she real?"

"Oh, yeah. That's my grandma, and she's got magic powers, too."

"So where was she when we needed her?" I pressed again.

"She can interfere only when my aunts sanction it. Grandma's old and vulnerable, so they don't send her on too many errands unless they know she can handle them," Dana replied.

I felt like I was living a fairytale without knowing the rules.

"Did she bump off the demon giant in the Emerald Zone?" I knew Dana had done it, but I wanted to hear it for myself.

She winced. "Sorry for lying to you a few nights ago, but I'm the one who took it out. It almost killed you in *Ghostworld* and in front of Martha's shop, and I didn't want to give it a third chance."

"I'm impressed," I said somberly, and meant it. This girl was full of surprises. "So how many aunts do you have?"

"Two."

I knew of Medusa, but I couldn't think of her two sisters' names. "So it's safe to say that Medusa's dead."

"Yeah, it's safe to say that."

"And your aunts' names are . . . ."

She leaned close to my face again. "Aunt Stheno and Aunt Euryale," she whispered.

"I can't believe that they're still hanging around after all these centuries," I marveled. "It's too bad that they can't just zap good ole Wayland into oblivion or turn him into stone or something."

"As I said, he's too powerful. It would take an all-out effort."

"Just who is Reynolds, if he's that powerful? A god?"

Dana lingered close to me as she whispered, "He's not a god."

I turned my bottom lip into chewing gum. "Then where does he come from?"

"I'm not allowed to tell you," she answered fretfully. Before I could complain, my extraordinary partner, niece to the *Gorgons*, kissed me. The sensuous, passionate, tongue-on-tongue variety.

The desk lamp flickered, and the office door slammed shut.

And still our lips were locked.

I hoped her aunts wouldn't turn me to stone.

66

That was one sweet kiss.

Although I feared the *Gorgons'* wrath, I refused to quit on the kiss of all kisses. For some curious reason, I was irresistibly drawn to her, unwilling to end our embrace and call it a day.

Suddenly, a feral orgasmic force excited my senses beyond belief. The sensation spread rapidly from my energized lips to the tips of my toes and fingers. The passionate force agitated my wolfen genes into a frenzied stampede, and boosted my magic way beyond its prior limitations. I felt like a superhero, at once indomitable and vulnerable.

And still we kissed.

Although my eyelids were pressed down, I experienced an exhilarating phenomenon. My spirit separated from my earthbound body and soared above my barn, past my workshop and pond where the cantankerous crocodile, Ole Luke, basked in the bright sun, through the lofty pines, and over the quaint and quiet cemetery where the GPS resided. But my remarkable journey didn't fizzle out there.

I zoomed past the boggy Moccasin Wallow and picked up so much speed that the disparate topography below became a gray blur. The land didn't come back into focus until I heard the thunderous hiss of the Atlantic waves smacking the sandy shore.

My exhilaration died when my revelational flight ended in front of Wayland Reynolds' mansion. I now floated six feet above the bastard's meticulously mowed lawn and ten feet below the pentagram wire configuration. The black-magic wire hummed and crackled, generating a skyful of billowing black storm clouds. Forked lightning tongues licked the gunmetal ocean and the shadowy shore, and then exploded angrily.

A sixty-foot yacht fought the building swells as it entered the bay half a mile down the shore. The sizeable craft bobbed like a buoy until it slipped past the rocky walls into the inlet, where its nodding motion calmed.

I sniffed the air — which, when I thought about it, was all but impossible in a vision. But then again, so was sound. This trip was remarkable beyond belief.

I inhaled the briny ocean breeze again, but this time the smell was different. There was an odd assortment of scents, and they triggered a recent memory. Brimstone, saline, dune grass, and motor oil. *When had I experienced these smells before?* It didn't take long to isolate the place.

In Martha's storeroom. The odd collection of smells had wafted from the dimensional rift where the devil dogs emerged. My discovery was another nail in Reynolds' coffin. The devil dogs' rift had been conjured right here—beside the ocean, and the Intercoastal Waterway across the road where he docked his boat. One mystery solved.

I found myself moving again. I drifted through one of the mammoth paned windows, and continued through the spacious living room and past an impressive stone-hearth fireplace. But there wasn't time to marvel at its grandeur. I was whisked into Reynolds' repugnant gallery of horrors. Like my first tour as Martha's puppet, I wasn't in control of my actions. This peculiar dream-like state compelled me to relive the terrors of my previous visit, whether I liked it or not.

Dana's rapturous kiss softened the terror this go-round, so I grew composed enough to objectively examine the room. Reynolds had made one major alteration. Five of the portraits had been rearranged to form a pentagon in the center of the chamber, and each portrait was angled so that it was parallel with the corresponding side of the wired pentagram outdoors.

I didn't need to inspect the paintings' subjects. I knew them by heart. Orlando Chief of Police Lance Stockard. US Senator Justice Kane. Jeffrey Stanton the Fourth. Orlando Mayor John Ellis. Florida Governor Branch Tucker.

The Ghostworld Five.

Click! The lights went out. Total blackness! The portraits and gallery vanished in a blink. I was reconnected with my body, wondering who had pulled the plug on the vision. Then I knew. Dana. Her lips had separated from mine . . . and that was that. To hell with the vision. The only fitting adjective in Webster's for that kiss was *Wow!*

Dana's eyes glittered like opulent diamonds as they gazed deeply into my own, and I noted that her tanned skin now had a reddish tint to it. An unmistakable blush.

"That was . . . um, interesting," she purred, her sweet breath fanning my face.

I was thunderstruck. "*Interesting?* Is that all you felt?" I asked, my body still tingling like a pincushion.

Dana's mouth widened into a smile, and she laughed. "Let me try that again. I thought our kiss was . . . *exciting*," she stated.

"Much better. You're the best kisser I've ever . . . well, kissed," I laughed.

"Really?" She appeared thrilled by my compliment. "Not bad for a beginner, huh?"

"C'mon — you're kidding, right? That couldn't have been your first kiss," I countered.

She awkwardly shifted her gaze to the carpet. "As a matter of fact, it was," she replied softly.

How could a sensational woman like Dana make it twenty-nine years without sharing a lip-lock with a guy? The answer was beyond reason.

"That was by far the best kiss I've ever experienced," I said. I saw the closed door and remembered its slamming shut when our lips first touched. "What was the door trick all about? Was that your aunts' way of showing their disapproval?" I asked nervously.

"It had nothing to do with my aunts. It's all about us. The force was created by our kiss," she said without hesitation. "Seriously, Joe, don't be concerned about my aunts. I'm a grown woman, and they pretty much leave me alone in the relationship department."

Not only grown, but electric.

I hated to diffuse our euphoria, but I was puzzled by my vision. "While we were kissing, I experienced something . . . strange. A vision of some kind."

Her smile flattened. "I had it, too. I was afraid to mention it, because I thought it only happened to me."

I was relieved. For a few minutes there, I thought I might be losing my mind.

"Have you ever heard of a vision with sound and smell? When you think about it, the entire concept is contradictory."

"Yeah, that was strange all right, but then again I haven't experienced many visions."

She sat on my desk and looked at the picture of my late parents attending Jill's and my high school graduation. Those were happy times.

"Your parents?"

I nodded.

"They look like fun. You must really be proud of them."

"*Was* proud of them. They were murdered five years ago," I said, feeling a lump rise in my throat.

"I'm so sorry," she said, and pecked me on the lips. There was just enough contact to reignite my full-body prickles.

"Thanks. In your vision, did you travel to Reynolds' oceanside mansion, too?"

"Yes, I was there, but I wish I hadn't been. I was enjoying our kissing so much, and . . . ."

I gripped her shoulders. "What is it?"

She gnawed the corner of her lip and rolled her eyes toward the ceiling. "It was like we were both under a spell."

"Well, I guess it was like that. To tell you the truth, I wasn't really thinking much at the time."

"Oh my God, I've got it! It had to be my aunts who cast the vision spell on us," she fumed, furious that they'd interfered during an intimate moment.

"Your aunts can do that?" I asked nervously.

"Oh yeah, they can. No one else that I know of has the power to pull a stunt like that," she added bitterly. "How dare you interfere with my personal life!" she shouted upward, as if they were celestial dwellers.

I waited a moment for her anger to ebb. "Why would they put us through that?"

Her annoyance gradually subsided, and she pondered my remark. "I hadn't figured it that way. You're saying that my aunts had a reason for taking us to Reynolds' place?"

"It crossed my mind. Got any ideas?"

"Maybe it was to show us those five paintings."

"Could be, but why?"

"We'll have to think about it some more," she suggested.

I checked at my desk clock. "Dammit!"

"What's wrong?"

"I'm late for my meeting," I muttered.

"I'm sorry I've kept you too long. Go ahead. I'll wait in the house."

I grabbed her hand. I trusted her beyond a doubt now. "Oh no, you won't. You're coming with me."

She looked completely mystified. "Where to?"

"It's a surprise."

"Oooh, you can be so exasperating."

Some things never change.

67

The tall ragged pines reminded me of my last visit to the cemetery where the pop-ups nearly killed us. If it hadn't been for that mysterious yellow light . . . .

We stopped short of the white picket fence enclosing the modest graveyard, home to the Ghoul Philosophers Society—Tillie's friends and relatives from the good old days. Mockingbirds flitted among the live oaks, palms, and pines, raucously tweeting their imitations of other birds' calls. The sky was mottled with sooty puffballs as the sun started its descent behind the jungle.

Dana and I anxiously surveyed the area, specifically looking for more pop-ups, but the coast was clear. I breathed a lot easier.

I looked at my partner. "There's something that's been eating at me since our near-death experience out here the other morning."

Dana fidgeted with her fingers. "Yes?"

"Level with me. Did you see who healed me in the meadow? There was definitely someone or something in that yellow light," I asked.

Dana emptied her lungs. "I'm not sure, Joe, but I suppose it might've been one of my aunts. I don't know anyone else who could destroy the pop-ups, except maybe for Wayland Reynolds," she replied thoughtfully. "And I'm sure he didn't save you."

I nodded. "Yeah, me too. He was probably the one who sicked them on us in the first place." I paused, vividly recalling Dana hunkered down beneath that monstrous fan palm. "If one of your aunts healed me, why didn't she heal you at the same time?"

"You know, I've wondered that myself. I was pretty pissed, until I realized that you could heal me. I'm certain that they knew that, too."

"It was pretty cruel to make you suffer like that."

She smiled weakly. "No pain, no gain, they say."

"Whatever." I shifted my attention to the shadowy shroud slipping over the cemetery. I pushed the gate open and motioned for Dana to step inside.

Captain Harley Watterson, the grizzled sea captain, rose from the grass until he was fully revealed, and stretched. "So what brings you two back here?" he barked. "I thought the pop-ups would've kept you away for good."

"We don't scare that easily," I shot back.

He sneered. "I hear ya, but I ain't buyin' it."

Dana tugged my arm and motioned for me to cool it. She was right. We needed information, not discord.

Watterson gestured in the direction of Moccasin Wallow. "Have a look-see."

Black storm clouds roiled on the horizon.

"Just like we saw in our vision," Dana reminded me. "You'd better make this a short meeting."

"You bet," I agreed as I watched the other residents appear.

Rupert O'Neil, Tillie's brother, rose next, followed by his wife Lavinia. She regarded me with her ice-blue eyes—minus their usual twinkle.

"I knew you'd visit us tonight, being Halloween and all," she declared. "What can we do for you two?"

Captain Watterson opened his ethereal trap to say something, but Lavinia beat him to the punch. "You just pipe down, Harley, and let these nice people have their say without you adding your two pence worth," she admonished him. Her stern countenance reinforced the threat. He muttered to himself, but instantly backed down.

I organized my thoughts before speaking. "We need your help."

Dana stepped in and brought them up-to-date on our investigation, including my swarming experiences and Reynolds' appalling art gallery. The ghosts listened intently. Tillie, back in her ghostly form, and Merlin the Wonder Dog materialized at her brother's side.

"You say the guy's name is Wayland Reynolds?" Rupert asked, his eyes narrowing.

"Yes," Dana replied.

Rupert exchanged uneasy glances with his friends. "Got a picture of your suspect?"

I didn't, but I magically produced one and held it up for them to examine.

Lavinia's hand flew to her mouth. "Oh dear."

"*That* sea snake!" Harley huffed.

I was beyond incredulous. "You know this creep?"

"Yep," Rupert answered tersely. "Only he called himself *Wilton Reynolds* back in our day."

"Wilton?" Dana exclaimed. "That's when my aunts lost track of him."

"What's the matter with everyone?" I demanded. It looked like I was the only one who didn't see the connection between Wilton and Wayland Reynolds. Dana looped her arm through mine and pressed her trembling body against me. "Wilton must be Wayland's great-great grandfather or something," I offered.

Lavinia shook her head. "They're one and same, Joe. Wilton merely changed his name, but it's him. Scar on the left cheek and all."

I studied the picture and the saw the scarcely perceptible scar.

I was flabbergasted. "How is that . . . *possible?*"

"Trust me, it's him — but that's not the worst news," Dana said softly. I knew then that she wasn't trembling because she was frightened, but because she was incensed.

We all stared at her.

I gasped. "What could be worse than this guy being immortal?"

She hesitated.

"Go on, dearie. Tell us," Lavinia prompted.

Dana squeezed my arm tightly as she gathered her courage. "He's not immortal, folks."

I was completely lost. "Then how can he still be alive?"

"He's an extremely powerful sorcerer."

I gazed down into her cocoa eyes. "How *extremely powerful?*"

Her nostrils flared like an angry bull's. "He's my aunts' long-lost nephew. He's a . . . a *Gorgon.*"

68

We could have heard the proverbial pin drop in the silenced cemetery. The stupefying news brought out the entire GPS clan for the first time in months. In addition to Lavinia and Rupert O'Neal and the irascible sea captain, Harley Watterson, Emma Sullivan, a former neighbor of Tillie's who was hanged for witchcraft as well, and her husband, Francis, both drifted into sight. Tillie's sister, Freda Shanahan, and her husband, York, burst from their graves like Jack-in-the-boxes, as did Robert and Ida O'Reilly, friends of the hanged witches. The last to appear was Robert's cranky mother, Margaret O'Reilly. The cemetery certainly got its Irish up that afternoon.

"Did I hear right, young lady?" Margaret O'Reilly snapped. "That son-of-a-bitch Wilton is really a Gorgon?"

Dana nodded. "Medusa's son."

"Does he have snakes for hair?" Freda Shanahan asked.

"Course not, you fool, or we would've seen them," Margaret retorted.

"Dana, you said earlier that he wasn't immortal," York Shanahan plied. "I thought all the *Gorgons* were immortal."

"Medusa's sisters are, but not her. That's probably why her son isn't," Dana explained.

"Wasn't he born when Perseus decapitated her?" I said, faintly recalling the story from my old mythology class.

"That's the way the stories go, but I'm not sure. My aunts won't talk about it."

"Then what's Wilton's given name?" Lavinia queried.

"Chrysaor."

"Odd name," York muttered.

"Well of course it's odd, you blunderhead," Harley barked. "The guy's Greek, and them names are all a mouthful."

"Oh," York said voiced softly, drifting away from the captain.

"My aunts call him Chris," Dana offered.

"So what's he want after all these years?" Lavinia asked.

Silence.

"I'd guess revenge for his mother's death," I said finally, glancing at Dana.

"That's our guess, too," she agreed. "After all, Perseus was human, so I guess the entire human race is on Chris' revenge list." She smiled grimly and gestured at the GPS. "I meant the living ones."

"So cuttin' the Emerald Zone inmates loose from their prison is supposed to satisfy Chris' vendetta against you folks?" Harley growled, doubling his airy hands.

"From what I've seen inside the Emerald Zone, I'd say 'yes.' Those ghosts are killers," I said.

"Well I got news for ya," Harley continued. "Those Emerald Zone escapees will murder us and all the other ghosts on earth first. We can't die, but we can cease to exist . . . anywhere."

"Why would they do such a thing to us?" Margaret demanded.

"I betcha dollars to doughnuts that they'll see us as a threat to their domination and wipe us out. They've got the numbers, so we'll be easy pickings for them." Harley paused to allow his revelation sink in. "So since we've got personal stakes in Joe and Dana's investigation, we'd better put on our damned thinkin' caps and come up with a plan they can use to kill that scurvy varmint."

Old Margaret's mussed blue-gray hair suddenly shot straight out like she'd been electrocuted. "Murder us! Well, I'll be go to hell! The very idea that our own kind would . . . ."

Her son, Robert, interrupted her. "Now, Mother, calm yourself."

"Don't you be a-tellin' me what to do, Robert. I'm still your ma, and don't ever forget it!"

Robert rolled his gauzy eyes. "How could I?" he commented quietly.

His wife elbowed him in his airy ribs. "Now don't go startin' something," she warned him.

"Knock it off, all of you," Tillie hollered. "Didn't you listen to a word Harley just said? These two need our help to stop Reynolds, if for nothing else than to save our musty backsides. Harley and I aim to see that they get it, and anyone with different ideas can return to the grave."

She shot everyone her dour *I-dare-you-to-cross-me* expression. Nobody did it better than Tillie. Trust me.

A hush fell over the ghostly group. Even Margaret managed to keep her venomous mouth closed. Every member of the GPS exchanged reproving glances, but they all remained topside.

Satisfied, Tillie turned to us. "Well, what do you and Dana need?"

I hugged Dana to my side, and she casually slung her arm around my waist and squeezed. *What did we really know about Reynolds that would help us defeat him, and what he had he been up to the past thousand years or so?* I gawked at the dusky horizon and the nasty tempest blowing our way.

I shuffled my feet before addressing the small specter gathering. This rag-tag bunch was our last hope, unless Dana's aunts decided to throw their considerable magical powers into the ring. Fat chance.

"For starters," I began, "tell us everything you can remember about Wilton Reynolds."

69

Every ghostly head turned in Tillie's direction.
"Dang it, whatcha all lookin' at *me* for?" Tillie protested.

"You know damned well, Tillie O'Neal!" Rupert exclaimed, wagging at finger at her. "You . . . ."

"All right, all right," she surrendered, cutting him off.

I was amazed at how small a world it really was. "You *knew* Wilton personally?" That gal certainly got around in the old days.

Lavinia laughed. "Course she did," she added, as if the connection between the two were common knowledge. "Tillie was quite a coquette back in the day, and wherever a handsome man turned up, you'd find Tillie nipping at his heels."

"Now, Lavinia . . . ." Tillie started to object again.

"Tsk, tsk — you know it's true," Lavinia persisted with a gleam in her eye.

"Can you get on with your story, Tillie?" Dana asked, nervously eyeing the approaching storm clouds. She moved closer and whispered in my ear. "You don't seriously believe that Reynolds will let us stand out here in the open much longer without making another attempt on our lives, do you?"

She had a point. I checked out the rapidly advancing storm and felt the evil energy approaching.

"Okay, enough with the bickering, Tillie. If you know something about Reynolds, please spill it," I urged her.

"Okay." Tillie sighed. "I met Wilton in St. Augustine one summer afternoon. He was walking his German Shepherd and talkin' to some Apache along the bay by the fort, and I just happened to be strolling along in the opposite direction . . . just minding my own business." She shot the others a stern look, daring them to dispute her claim. When no one did, she continued.

"I complimented his dog, and before you knew it, we were sipping café de olla and sharing some pan dulce in the Planters Hotel. He told me that he came to Florida twice a year to check on his real estate investment outside Orlando, and was even forthright enough to describe its location. Anyway, he promised to look me up whenever he was down my way.

"Wilton was as good as his word, and he courted me for a couple of weeks before disappearing without so much as a *goodbye*." Tillie wrinkled her brow in annoyance. "It didn't dawn on me till a few weeks passed that while he was down here, four local farmers had gone missing. Their bodies were never found.

"Curious, I convinced Rupert that we ought to have a look at Wilton's property. So one fall day, we hitched up the horse to my buggy and found Wilton's so-called real estate investment. The place was nothin' but a rundown shack built on a few hundred acres of swampy land. Despite dear Rupert's objections, I hightailed it over to the shack and pounded on the door.

"Maybe I expected to find those missin' farmers' bodies inside. I don't rightly remember now. Anyway, no one answered, so I was about to skedaddle when a wisp of a woman opened the door. She was badly hunched over and looked half-dead.

"I sensed she was a witch right off, but her magic was pretty well drained from age . . . or so I thought at the time. After what Dana told us about Reynolds' paintings, I'm not so sure anymore. I asked her why she lived way out there in the middle of nowhere, and do you know what she said?"

Nobody, except Rupert, had a clue, and he knew not to spoil his sister's story.

"We don't have time for twenty questions," I reminded her sharply.

"Well, you'd better make some time, *Mister Impatience*," she snapped, "or these lips will clam up quick."

Dana shot me a *don't-piss-her-off* glance, so I grudgingly backed down.

I hated guessing games. "All right, let me guess. Uh, did the old witch tell you that she was . . . *the guardian of Wilton's property?*" I proposed.

"Very close, very close," Tillie said, a grin creeping across her mouth.

"C'mon, Tillie, don't keep us waitin'," Lavinia carped.

"Oh, hold on to your knickers, Lavinia." After torturing us long enough, Tillie finally graced us with the witch's revelation. "The poor woman told me that she was Wilton's *daughter*, and that he moved her out there so's she could keep an eye on his investment."

We all inhaled sharply. *Wilton's daughter looked older than he did?* Reynolds had been draining his offspring even back then.

"Did she say how long she'd been stuck out there?" Dana asked, as she exchanged a worried glance with Harley Watterson.

"For seventy-two years and countin', she said. That would put her back to the Indian wars and swamp fever," Tillie replied. "Obviously, Wilton's daughter protected the place with her magic when she was younger. When I saw her, she was in no condition to fight off lizards, much less Indians."

Why did he purchase that particular piece of worthless land and protect it with magic? And why did it need protection?

"I wonder who Wilton replaced her with after she died," I ventured.

"For all I know, she could've been living in that shack until Stanton started construction on *Ghostworld*."

It was obvious that Wilton didn't trust anyone but his family with the job, but *what did he have out there that was so valuable?* It certainly wasn't the swamp land.

"*Ghostworld?*" Dana repeated, echoing my own thoughts. "Just where was his property?"

Before Tillie answered, Merlin growled.

In the deepening dusk, I spotted dozens of obscure shapes camped out around the cemetery. Their coloring blended well with the gloom.

The shadowy figures slowly closed in on us. I peered through the deepening twilight with my wolfen vision and identified their tall bony black frames.

Dana hugged me. "What are they?"

"*Demoids*, not be confused with hemorrhoids, although both are a pain in the ass."

These demons were killers of the first order and could be conjured only from the blackest recesses of the underworld by the most skilled sorcerers. It didn't take a rocket scientist to figure out that Reynolds had sent them to murder Dana and me, but it might take one to figure out how to get rid of them.

"Got any bright ideas?" Dana hissed.

"Do you?"

"No."

Damn! As I followed their nimble movements, I wracked my brain trying to recall my childhood paranormal lesson about those rarely seen slayers.

Finally, I hit pay dirt. *Demoids* were nearly invincible, but there was one way to send them packing to the underworld. Of course, I'd conveniently forgotten that part of the lesson. *Talk about brain lock.*

I looked at Dana's expectant face and did what any red-blooded sorwolf would do in this situation—I lied.

"I've got one idea, but it's a long shot at best," I told her.

70

I cringed inwardly.

Dana looked anxiously at me for a sure-fire Demoid cure, and all I had to offer was a lie and a bad memory. I was about to let both of us down . . . down as in *pushing up daisies*.

When all else failed, I tried my common sense. Demoids were used to fire on their home turf, so using that as a weapon against them was out of the question. Suddenly I had an idea. Whether it was a bright one was yet to be proven.

"Head back to your graves!" I shouted at the GPS members, and then turned to Tillie. "You and Merlin take a hike. There's nothing you can do to help us."

Before I could say *boo*, Dana and I were alone with the scourge of the underworld.

"Staff, appear!" I commanded, and my mage staff appeared in my right hand. "Dana, jump on my back and don't let your feet touch the ground until I tell you otherwise. Okay?"

"Got it," she whispered, as she leaped up and wrapped her arms around my neck.

"Not too tight," I warned her.

I tapped the staff on the ground five times and recited a familiar spell chant under my breath so as not to alert the Demoids to my intent. The Demoids had been steadily approaching the picket fence, and now they were close to striking distance. As I waited for the spell to manifest itself, I gave the merciless killers the once-over.

They were nearly five feet tall, with skulls shaped like upside-down spade shovels—pointed chins and flat brows. Twin arrowhead horns sprouted above their high foreheads, deep-set eyes burned maize and crimson, pointed ears were flush to the skull, and their broad thin-lipped mouths were packed to the max with hedges of ebony teeth. Black leathery hide tightly draped their lean frames, and splayed fingers and toes were tipped with lethal curled nails.

My memory recalled another scrap of information from my childhood Demoid lesson. They were quick. Forget about using arrows, bullets, or clubs. So it was up to my spell to do the trick, or Reynolds won.

The cemetery trembled, and I fought for balance as a blue ring appeared in the ground around us. As it brightened, its size swelled as well, but a very small area remained dark below my feet.

"What's happening?" Dana whispered.

"My spell," I replied quietly.

The eerie blue light cast long shadows behind our would-be assailants and reduced the swaying palm fronds, fluttering live oak leaves, and bobbing timothy grass and weeds in the background to silhouettes. The flickering lightning from the distant storm added the perfect ambience for a horror-movie set.

I glanced down and watched the radiant spell pulse when it reached the cemetery boundaries. Dana and I remained stationary within the dark doughnut hole, safe from the spell's effect. There was no alternative. We were hemmed in by fierce, cat-quick Demoids that would slice and dice us before we reached the gate. Even my wolfen genes were unusually dormant, sensing death in a physical battle with the killers.

Without warning, the motionless Demoids sprang to life. Releasing high-pitched, ear-splitting wails, they bounded over the low fence into the cemetery. Dana's arms constricted around my throat, but my muscular neck prevented her from accidentally crushing my windpipe, sending me to the ground, and terminating the spell.

The underworld killers landed lightly on the blue iridescent earth and slashed at us with their menacing nails. The thought of being skinned alive and eaten was enough to shake my resolve, but I stayed the course. I had Dana to think about. No time for cowardice.

The advancing fiends were so close now that I smelled their hellish cologne . . . I wish I hadn't. The stench was a pungent mélange of a heavy European musk and good old US of A pig shit.

Their fleet assault decelerated, and they appeared to be bounding in super-slow-motion. The spell's supernatural luminescence crept over their curved toes, but the blob didn't stop there. It steadily climbed up their legs, past their torsos, and shrouded their hideous visages.

Their progress stopped. The spell had changed the brutes into frozen Demoid-sicles.

I practically jumped out of my shoes at the spell's success. We were saved, despite my memory's failing. Dana flung herself off my shoulders and landed unceremoniously on the grass with a sickening thud.

Outside the doughnut hole. Onto the blue grass.

I panicked and grabbed at her before she was frozen, too, but thankfully the ring faded the moment she landed. My partner was sore, but at least she was safe. Dana stood stiffly, massaged her backside, and dusted off her shorts.

She looked at me with a gargantuan smile. "You did it, Joe!" she squealed and threw her arms around my neck again and . . . kissed me. This kiss, though, was a shorter affair with brief orgasmic side-effects.

"You okay?" I asked after we came up for air.

"My butt's a little tender, but that's all. At least I'm alive." She closed in for an instant lip-lock replay, but I retreated a step.

"Later," I said regretfully. "Business before pleasure. We've got to put an end to that cousin of yours, Reynolds." I studied the approaching storm. "And we're running out of time."

Her eyes suddenly ballooned to melon balls. *What was the matter now?*

"Oh God, look!" she said, jerking her head to her right.

I did and immediately wished I hadn't.

"Son-of-a-bitch!" I exclaimed in utter shock and disbelief.

We were done for.

Dead in the water.

The blue ice was crumbling away from the Demoids like melting ice. Fast.

71

So much for common-sense solutions to supernatural problems.

The radiant blue coating melted like warm candle wax from the Demoids' ebony bodies and puddled at their feet. I stood there, horrified and speechless. My spell had dissipated, and with it, our sole chance to survive.

Dana was awestruck that my spell failed to permanently purge the Demoids from the cemetery. I couldn't bring myself to confess that *I* was the one who went wrong, not my spell.

Dana snuggled next to me and hugged my waist. "The spell didn't work," she whispered. "We're as good as dead, aren't we?"

The Demoids shimmied the last of the coating from their skin like wet dogs.

"It looks that way."

Like a doomsayer, I felt like marching around the cemetery holding one of those handwritten signs proclaiming the end of the world. It was the end of our world, anyway. We stood there, waiting for their attack, but they didn't rush us. Instead, they gazed eastward in unison, their twin tongues flicking crazily like they were afraid of the impending storm. A strong gust of cool air buffeted us, and the Demoids moved back a few steps toward the fence. Rainbow lightning repeatedly stabbed the distant horizon and colored the jungle, followed by faint thunderclaps, but Reynolds' wicked storm didn't bother me in the least. We'd be dead before it arrived.

I saw Dana's face turn eastward. "Look at that!" she cried out, and clapped a hand over her mouth.

I pried my eyes from the Demoids and took a look. I didn't gasp—I *cringed*. A massive black bee swarm fought the gusts as it descended toward the cemetery. *Was it one of Martha's swarms, or one sent by Reynolds to trick us?* We'd know in a few seconds.

The Demoids warily watched the swarm touch down in front of us and slowly materialize into a human form. I raised my staff overhead and prepared to club our unknown visitor, but Dana held me back.

"Take it easy. It might be a friend," she declared.

It could be an enemy, too.

The buzzing shape grew refined, and there stood Martha! She immediately took hold of my mage staff and shook it to gain my full attention.

"Joe, we have about ten seconds to live unless you repeat after me."

I shed my astonishment and listened.

"*Dalluh*," she shouted against the rising wind.

I repeated the magic word while the Demoids grew restless and eyed us hungrily. They screamed again and charged.

"Sahlumma."

"Sahlumma," I shouted.

The Demoids were three yards away and about to spring when my pathetic memory recalled the rest of the Demoid extermination spell.

"*Reflectum!*" I roared triumphantly, surprising Martha.

A mirrored, cylindrical wall appeared around us as the Demoids sprang. Caught in the air, it was too late for the fiends to retreat. In a split second, they vanished in mid-air before colliding with the mirrored surface. Their reflections frightened them back to the underworld. Their tormented wails filled the cemetery and gradually faded away.

Before Dana and I could express our gratitude to Martha, her solid form dispersed into the bee swarm again and rose skyward.

"Hey, wait!" I shouted.

"Run!" Martha's voice pleaded.

"Why?" Dana hollered.

Her voice was nearly lost amid the loud buzzing.

"Blizzard . . . ."

The bee mass quickly disappeared into the escalating clouds.

"What did she mean by that?" Dana shouted into the wild wind.

"How do you feel about building a snowman together?" I turned and jogged toward the barn for shelter.

72

A six-foot chain-link fence suddenly appeared in front of me and bounced me to the ground. Puzzled, I looked back at Dana, who hadn't budged from the cemetery.

"Not so fast!" she called.

I rubbed the tip of my nose where it hit the fence. "What was that for?"

"Joe Luna, you're the most impetuous man I've ever met," she harrumphed, hands on her hips. "You're not leaving here until you get what you came for, and that was a plan for defeating Reynolds."

Oops. She definitely scored a point there. I was so worried about the snowstorm that I temporarily lost sight of the big picture. Shit happens.

I ambled back. "You're right," I admitted sheepishly. Shelter would have to wait. "Okay GPS, c'mon out," I called out to my ghoulish friends.

Dana's irritation with me subsided. "That's better."

By now, the gale force winds nearly swept Dana into the closest tombstone. I caught her elbow, and she shivered. The temperature had dropped precipitously in the past several minutes, but I hadn't noticed. I was too busy eating humble pie. I conjured a thermometer and checked the temperature. It read thirty-nine degrees. For Central Florida, that was *cold*.

One by one, the ghostly contingent re-emerged from their graves and nervously surveyed the area.

"Those damned Demoids gone?" Harley growled uneasily.

"All the way back to hell," Dana assured him.

"The bastards can stay there for all time as far as I'm concerned!" he bellowed, his gravelly outburst slicing the wind.

Lavinia spoke up. "Joe, Dana, you need to find out what Wilton's hiding on his property. That might give you some idea as to what he's up to tonight."

Tillie and Merlin returned. "If it's a treasure, take it and use it to bargain with him."

"I hardly think it's a treasure, like gold and jewels," Margaret piped up.

"Why's that?" I asked.

"Because he built *Ghostworld* smack-dab in the middle of his property — didn't he, Tillie?" she replied.

Tillie nodded while Dana and I tried to hide our shock. He owned that piece of land? Unbelievable.

Margaret faced me. "Would you want thousands of people tramping over your gold and jewels every day?"

"No," I said thoughtfully. "Then what could it be? It'd be nice to have some idea before we search the place." I held out my hand and caught a whirling white dot.

"Snow!" Dana exclaimed.

Tillie wrinkled her brow. "First time I ever laid eyes on the stuff."

"Snowing in Orlando? This has to be Wilton's work," Margaret huffed.

"But why make it snow in Florida?" Dana asked. "It doesn't make any sense."

I recalled my visits to the Emerald Zone. "Maybe it does."

The others turned to me.

"The ghosts I saw in the zone were immersed in a cold white environment, so it stands to reason that they might need a frigid atmosphere to survive when they first cross over into our world."

"Hold on!" Dana cried out suddenly, startling me.

"You don't agree with my theory?" I said defensively.

"No, it's not that."

"Then what is it?"

Dana had to cup her hands around her mouth and shout to be heard above the howling gusts and the clapping palm fronds. "It might be that his so-called treasure is really a magical item that he needs to increase his own powers, so that he can keep the Emerald Zone gate open for all time," Dana ventured.

"Hell, that could be anything," Harley snapped sourly.

A few others nodded their assent.

"That's not necessarily true, Harley. That item would also have to be something that prevented my aunts from interfering with his plans," Dana yelled.

"That narrows it down, all right, but we don't know enough about your aunts to make an educated guess," I lamented.

"But Dana does — don't you, dear?" Tillie said, a sly grin creasing her cheeks.

Dana nodded indifferently. I got the feeling that she dreaded what she was about to tell us.

"The only thing that fits both scenarios would be . . . ." She paused and looked around.

I had no idea how she was going to finish her statement, but I was positively certain that I wouldn't like it.

73

Tillie and the other ghosts drifted closer to hear what she was going to say.

"...would be his mother's . . . *head*," Dana revealed.

"Oh, great. Not the snake lady," I groaned, but my reaction was lost to the howling gusts.

"Makes more sense to me than anything I've heard so far," Tillie said. "If you're right, Dana, then Medusa's head would not only give her rotten-apple son extra magical powers, but it would also have been the ideal guardian for the Emerald Zone portal all those years. If anyone got too nosy, he would be turned to stone."

"So Reynolds' daughter was really safeguarding Medusa," Margaret surmised.

"That's the way I figure it," Harley chipped in.

I winced. "Which means if we find Mama Medusa, we might end up as garden sculptures."

Margaret chuckled facetiously. "But it *also* means that you and Dana got lucky, because Tillie knows exactly where that shack was — right, Tillie?"

Tillie's normally pallid spectral complexion blanched even whiter. "I suppose you could say that," she admitted grudgingly.

"So here's what we do," Harley barked, seizing control of the meeting. "Us ghosts will do the searchin' for Medusa's head, so's you don't have to run the risk of being turned to stone. When we find her, we'll let you know where she is and how to get to her."

"Being ghosts, you can't be turned to stone. Harley, you're a genius," Dana exclaimed.

"That I am," Harley agreed with a pompous flair.

"So what do we do with her head when you find it?" I asked.

"Why, you destroy Medusa's ugly noggin," Harley blustered.

"That's easier said than done," Tillie added.

"We'll cross that bridge when we come to it," Dana said.

Me, I'd rather not cross that bridge.

Tillie addressed the other ghosts. "Let's get crackin', folks. A little snow's not going to slow us down."

"Thank you all for doing this," Dana said approvingly, tightly gripping my arm against the furious white wind.

The GPS vanished into the blizzard. I noticed that the accumulating snow made my farm look like the Emerald Zone, and that daunting sight chilled me from the inside.

"So what do we do while they're out searching for Medusa's head? Freeze our asses off here in the cemetery?" I griped.

Dana poked me hard in the ribs. "I've got an idea."

"I'm listening."

"I'll give you the details when we're on our way," Dana replied ambiguously, to keep me guessing. I deserved that. Turn-about was fair play.

Dana's hand skated down my snow-covered arm to my hand and tugged me toward the barn. "We've got a lot to do and precious little time to get it done."

Wearing shorts and short-sleeved shirts, we were a couple of outlandish snowmen treading between the pines and across the wooden bridge. But our appearances weren't important. What mattered was Dana's plan . . .

. . . of which I didn't have a clue.

Was I nervous?

You bet.

74

Brrrrrr. I didn't realize northern winters could be *that* cold.

We stepped inside the kitchen, shivering and brushing the clingy wet stuff off our exposed skin and summer clothes. Dana swept the snow from her glittering black hair with both hands, creating a blizzard at her feet, and then fluffed the drooping strands.

I got a couple of bath towels out of the linen closet and tossed her one. "So what's your plan?" I shrugged. I was champing at the bit to find out what card she had up her sleeve—an ace . . . or deuce.

She took my hand with her icy one. "For starters, let's go up to your bedroom."

We ditched the wet towels, shoes, and socks, stopped by the guest room to pick up some dry clothes for Dana, and climbed the stairs, hand-in-hand. My worries thawed. It looked like a hot time in the ole bed tonight. I already loved her plan.

Sadly, I was way wrong about the *loved* part. There were no sexual shenanigans. We showered and dressed separately, and then she described her scheme to outwit Reynolds. My libido was deflated big time.

A half hour later, we sat in my snow-covered Silver Wraith outside the barn. I definitely balked at this part of the plan, because it called for Dana to drive the hearse. I never imagined letting someone else operate my black beauty, but like most everything else in this investigation, I was taken by surprise.

Dana disguised herself as *me* . . . a decoy for yours truly. After all, it *was* Halloween—but her costume was all trick and no treat. The masquerade was a critical part of her ingenious scheme, and I supported it one hundred percent.

When she first tried on my outfit, she looked like a dwarf in giant's clothing. After sharing a few laughs in front of the mirror, I magically sized them to fit her. Her disguise included one of my black werewolf rip-away Spandex outfits, an ebony trench coat, and a black wool fedora.

Meanwhile, I sported the dapper GQ look—baggy gray sweatpants, a hooded UCF football sweatshirt, my beat-up gray New Balance running shoes, and my plum-diamond protective ring. I never left home without it. My mage staff lay angled against my right leg in the hearse, and my trusty wand was tucked into the elastic waistband.

"How do you start this thing?" she asked, searching for the ignition switch.

I was offended. "*Thing?* This marvelous machine is a genuine antique that . . . ."

"Cut the crap," she said sharply. "We don't have time for lectures. Just show me how to crank up this thing . . . er, marvelous machine."

"It starts only for me. I specifically programmed it to respond to my magic." I chanted a few words beneath my breath, waved my hand over the spot where the ignition switch had been, and presto, the engine sprang quietly to life.

"Easy now . . ." I cautioned her, but my advice was ignored.

Dana floored the accelerator and flattened me against the back of the leather seat. We barely cleared the front gate before she swerved sharply to the left, disregarded the wild fishtailing, and somehow avoided the grand-canyon ditches bordering the snow-covered road.

When the Silver Wraith finally stabilized, I shook my head at the falling snow. Orlando had never experienced a blizzard before, and the local meteorologists had to be going crazy trying to explain it. I imagined that the Weather Channel had already sent Jim Cantore down here to cover the freakish anomaly.

"You're a maniac behind the wheel, do you know that?" I griped.

Dana grinned cheekily. "Tell me something that I don't know, Joe — but like you told me earlier, time is of the essence."

"If we're dead, it isn't," I grumbled, my concern equally allocated to the Silver Wraith and myself. I had to relax for the mission ahead, so I gave us an edge over the inclement weather. I cast a spell that dissolved the snow on the pavement ahead of us and eliminated our skidding and fishtailing.

"I bet the kids are bummed about the snow messing up their

Halloween," Dana said, making small talk.

"Yeah, but I won't miss the pranks."

"Don't be such a killjoy. Let the kids have some fun. I'll bet you pulled your share of pranks," she reminded me.

"Probably, but I don't remember," I lied, hoping to end this ridiculous conversation.

She took the hint and we continued in silence.

Once we arrived downtown, Dana stopped in the alley behind Maya's Tearoom. Earlier, she had suggested that we get as much information as possible about Reynolds before heading out to Indialantic, and she was certain that Maya was in cahoots with the *Ghostworld* killer. Me, I didn't have an inkling of a clue about Maya. Dana added that her aunts had cautioned her to beware of Maya, so here we were. Snow everywhere and the world about to end, and we're taking time out for tea.

"Don't be late." She kissed my cheek, and then pulled the fedora low over her forehead. "I can't handle Maya alone."

"I'll be there," I promised. I quickly shoved the door open and slid out.

She planned to park on Pine Street and go into the tearoom through the front door. Meanwhile, I used my mage staff to magically break into the tearoom's heavily bolted rear entrance.

Employing my preternatural wolfen night vision, I vigilantly navigated the labyrinth of dark shapes that populated the storeroom. As I entered the hallway and its maze of turns that led to the restaurant, I heard clinking cups and saucers and female chit-chat. Sounded peaceful enough.

Suddenly, those pleasant sounds were supplanted by breaking china, scooting chairs, and hysterical shrieks. One of those shrieks belonged to Dana.

I darted recklessly into the hall, and that was my undoing. I failed to detect the hollow section of flooring halfway to the restaurant, and a trapdoor vanished beneath me.

I tumbled helplessly into a seemingly bottomless black abyss.

75

I cursed my carelessness.

I was headed toward oblivion when I was suddenly jerked to a stop, jolting every fiber of my being. The tremendous braking force almost ripped my left shoulder from its socket. A tidal wave of acute pain rippled along the strained muscles to my fingertips, temporarily stunning me. I dangled in the black silence and wondered what had arrested my freefall. Moments later, the feeling came back in my fingers, and I knew how I'd been saved.

My mage staff.

I was still holding on to it, and I nervously tightened my grip on the invisible staff. It must have been longer than the trapdoor's width, and when I dropped over the edge, the ends hung up on the edge. Talk about lucking out!

But I wasn't out of the woods yet. Not by a long shot. Now I had to climb out of there and get to Dana. Hopefully she was still alive.

I became weightless and easily leveraged myself over the staff and into the hall. I kissed my ever-ready staff and listened. The shrieks had died—all was quiet. Too quiet. I tried to blot out hostile thoughts of the tearoom customers dying, but the grisly images of slaughtered women refused to fade away.

I stepped over the opening in the floor and tiptoed toward the restaurant light ahead. I slowed as I reached a corner by the two back doors I'd seen before, and cautiously peered through a potted fern into the candle-lit area. *Was Dana still alive?* A growl rumbled in my chest. She had better be, or there'd be hell to pay.

She was. Barely.

Dana was unceremoniously sprawled on the harlequin tile floor near the front door, among broken and splintered tables, chairs, china . . . and my flattened black fedora. *I loved that hat.* She stared toward someone in the center of the room, but I couldn't see who it was. The damned fern blocked my line of sight.

Dana appeared stunned or in a trance. She just lay there staring with unblinking eyes. Terror parted her lips in the midst of a silent scream, but there was no sound. I stepped out into the restaurant area and saw a terrible creature poised to leap on my partner.

Horrific fiend was a more apt description. It was hideous. The sinister mutant menace that cornered Dana and knocked her mind into the stratosphere had a very muscular velociraptor body, but that's where the dinosaur resemblance ended. At seven feet tall, the thing towered above Dana. Its head was forged from a longhorn steer with wickedly curved horns that could easily shish-ka-bob its enemies. A battery of armored reptilian scales swathed its skull and surrounded its malevolent black-pearl eyes. The most intimidating of this abomination's animal parts was its long crocodile mouth, displaying vicious protruding fangs.

The creature hadn't seen me yet, so I crept along the back wall toward Maya's office. I figured that she must have conjured the hideous thing and was manipulating it from someplace in the tearoom. I needed to neutralize her, and her office was as good a place as any to begin my search. I readied a mage-staff spell and warily entered the office, but it was empty. Back to the drawing board.

As things stood now, it appeared I would have to tackle both the Raptor-Croc and Maya—two against one—which definitely reduced my odds of success. Nothing ever seemed to come easy.

I tapped my staff on the floor to draw its attention from Dana. For a large creature, it moved fast. It pivoted on a dime and studied me with its shark-like eyes. The terrible crocodile mouth opened wide and generated a grating roar before it charged me, trampling more tables, chairs, and china along the way. My trembling hands held the staff out as I conjured my spell.

I prayed that I didn't skip any magic words this go-around. There wasn't time for a repeat performance.

Raptor-Croc was on me.

76

But I messed up again.

No spell.

I used the staff to fend off the ominous jaws closing in on my head, and the lethal chompers snapped like a bear trap on the staff and missed severing my fingers by mere inches. The staff's unyielding composition of eucalyptus and haugtrold woods was unyielding and unharmed from the attack, but I was a different story.

The Raptor-Croc bully-ragged me and the staff back and forth so violently that I nearly swooned. I held on for as long as I could, but eventually the room blurred, and I went flying with the greatest of unease toward Dana.

Our looming collision appeared unavoidable, but to my surprise, I crashed into a protective force field before I landed on her. I hit the floor with a mind-numbing impact. My consciousness whirled like laundry trapped inside a spinning washing machine tub. My thoughts were not only jumbled, but disabled. I was incapable of counting to ten, much less casting a coherent magical spell.

Escape was futile. So was self-defense. My total lack of attention to detail when chanting spells would cost me everything this time. My vulnerability was showing. I was trapped between a croc and a hard place.

The Raptor-Croc sensed my helplessness and dropped my staff. It clattered uselessly to the floor. The mutant creature paced the room in front of me, terrorizing its next victim—me. It was working. But then again, I saw four ugly Raptor-Crocs instead of the one after my concussive collision with Dana's invisible force field.

I turned to Dana. She was still in that trance-like state and couldn't help me take this thing down. I glanced up at one Raptor-Croc the next time, and saw that playtime was over. It roared and rumbled toward me again, but before it had covered half the distance between us, a brilliant purple radiance saturated the tearoom. The creature slowed considerably.

Its brawny legs trudged forward, inch by inch, as if stuck in quicksand.

My protective ring had come through for me again.

My runaway-carousel mind finally eased to a stop, and my wooziness dissipated. I jumped up and was about to retrieve my staff, when I noticed that it had already appeared in my hand. It was trained better than a homing pigeon.

The enchanted talismans no longer dangled loosely from the tip—they extended toward the Raptor-Croc. Puzzled, I studied their independent movements. I hadn't given the staff a command. *Or had I?*

My purple defensive shield vanished simultaneously with the appearance of a blue energy cage around the Raptor-Croc. I pumped a victory fist into the air. I hadn't fouled up my spell after all. Apparently, there hadn't been enough time for the staff to execute my command before the fiend sank its teeth into it.

The arcing blue bars of the cage sizzled and popped each time the creature contacted them. Unlike the more familiar electrical jolts, my magical ones were ten times more excruciating. The Raptor-Croc thrashed about my supernatural cage, and hideously buckled with each contact with the blue force.

Refusing my repeated entreaties to lower the shield, Dana just sat there like a bump on a log and was unable to tear her unblinking eyes from the captivating spectacle. When I glanced back at the cage, the Raptor-Croc was reduced to a nebulous image, like an indistinct apparition, and then transformed into a miniature Brahma bull. I scratched my head. *What was up with that?*

The muscular bull repeatedly attempted to ram the blue arcing bars, but to no avail. Ear-splitting bawls rent the air after each failed attempt at escape. Finally, the stubborn creature lay quiet in the center of the cage, its body smoking and near death. Extraordinary. The fiends, like Demoids, were difficult to kill in our dimension. The most we sorcerers could hope for was to send them packing back to the underworld.

But it wasn't a fiend. The bull blurred into wavy heat lines like a desert mirage, and quickly changed into . . . .

Maya!

So that was how the Raptor-Croc became a Brahma bull. The tearoom owner was a *shapeshifter*. *Who would've known?* Now Maya appeared to be dying, and I realized I didn't have much time to question her.

"Tell me what you know about Wayland Reynolds," I demanded firmly, shaking my staff at her.

"Go to . . . hell!" she wheezed. "I'll die before I betray the master."

I launched a thin lightning bolt into her gasping body, and she writhed like a headless snake. "Tell me about Reynolds," I shouted.

Her gaze widened. "About . . . *what?*"

I grasped at straws. I had no idea what specific information Dana needed from Maya. "We're, uh, paying him a visit tonight and plan to shut him down. Anything you can tell us about his mansion?"

Maya managed a few breathless chuckles before they escalated into a coughing fit. "I wouldn't . . . count on . . . it, Joe Luna. It's a . . . ."

"It's a what?" I pressed.

She clearly had only seconds to live.

"It's a what?" I repeated, threatening her with another jolt from the staff.

"Trrrap," she rasped, and her body shut down. For good.

The energy cage vanished, and my talismans resumed their usual dangling positions. As I gaped at her smoking form, Dana came up beside me and looked none the worse for wear.

"You feeling okay?" I asked her.

She shrugged and gazed at Maya's corpse as I scrutinized my partner's appearance. Dark bloated pouches shadowed her red-rimmed eyes, but other than that, she appeared animated and rational.

"That was some magic shield you erected around yourself. You'll have to give me the recipe sometime," I said lightly.

"I'd be glad to, but I wasn't the one who conjured it."

"Then who . . . ?" I stopped myself in midsentence. *Her guardian angel? Her aunts?* "Uh, your employers did that for you?"

"My grandma," she replied weakly. "Look."

I did and spotted the empty space where Maya had died seconds before. Her body was gone without a trace. No ash residue. Nothing to indicate that she had ever existed.

"Odd," was all I could muster at the moment.

"Maybe she wasn't completely dead."

My brows shot up. "Really? Mind explaining that one?"

"Shapeshifters can hibernate in the face of death. Maybe that's what she did."

"So? That doesn't explain her disappearance, unless she's a witch, too."

Dana rubbed her eyes. "I have a sneaking suspicion that my aunts removed her before she could cause us any more problems."

Got to love those aunts. "I hope you're right about that. I wouldn't want to tangle with Dino-Croc again, that's for sure."

"Me either."

A familiar bee swarm buzzed its way into the tearoom near the rear. Dana inched closer to me as we kept an eye on the pair of materializing figures. Martha must have brought a friend along, and I could only hope that *she* was . . . .

Kit, not Gwendolyn.

77

Kit appeared alongside Martha.
I rushed over and hugged her. "It's good to have you back," I exclaimed. I felt like a cad greeting Kit like that after Dana and I had shared such wonderful kisses, but I had to pretend everything was status quo between us—we were kind of a steady item.

Kit backed off and gave me a half smile. "Good to see you, too, but we've got business to attend to."

Her tone iced me. *What had I done to deserve the brush-off?* I looked at Dana, and she served me up an iceberg expression, too. I felt like Robert Peary at the North Pole.

"Right . . . business," I repeated with as much gusto as a dead horse.

Martha felt the friction in the air between the two women and gave me a warm hug. "I hope you have a plan," she said softly.

No plan for my women problems, but one for Reynolds. In this case, one out of two was bad.

"Yeah, we do." I studied Martha. "Why'd you come out of hiding so soon? Reynolds wants you dead."

"I know, Joe, but I knew you'd need our help."

"Absolutely," Dana chimed in. "Back-up support is essential to our plan."

"That includes me, too," Kit bristled. "I didn't come back here for nothing."

Dana never mentioned anything about back-up support before, but I had to agree. "That'd be great," I said, trying to keep the peace between them. My hunch told me I was failing.

Dana bailed me out by tapping her watch crystal. "Time's a-wastin', Joe. We've got to get cracking on plan B if we're to have any chance of succeeding."

I gestured toward the escapees. "But what about them?"

"We can handle ourselves, can't we, Kit?" Martha smiled at her surly companion, who left the question unanswered. "Besides, we've got some clean-up work to take care of before we meet up with you two at *Ghostworld*."

Kit was not at all excited about Martha's indefinable *clean-up work*.

"I want to tag along with you two," Kit asserted, her jade eyes wide and expectant. "I've been stuck in that hellhole coma while you two were having all the fun, and now it's my turn."

I averted Kit's gaze, but Dana merely grinned. "There is something you *can* do."

Kit perked up. "Name it."

"Stick around *Ghostworld*, but stay out of sight until we give you the signal," she explained, hinting that Kit's assistance would be vital to our success. "And bring your gun along."

"What's the sign?" Kit asked, her depression lifting. "And what do I do once I see your signal?"

I was elated when Dana fielded Kit's request. In all probability, I would have botched the situation and offered a clumsy excuse why Kit couldn't tag along with us. I was well aware of my personal limitations.

"I can't tell you exactly, because he might be listening to us right now," Dana said, and Martha nodded her agreement. "Trust me, you'll know the signal when you see it," Dana added secretively, then waved at me. "Let's go."

Kit was definitely not placated by Dana's ploy. She wanted to ride with us now. If looks could kill, Dana and I would have been goners. Murder in the first degree.

I picked up my flattened fedora, reshaped it the best I could, and gave it to Dana.

"We couldn't leave without this. It's a critical part of your disguise," I declared.

Dana raised one brow. "Really?" She stuck it on her head. "And here I thought you just couldn't bear to part with it."

Ouch. Nailed again.

After wishing Martha and the incensed Kit good luck with their mission, we hurried outside. I looked back at Kit through the foggy window to see if she had calmed down yet. She hadn't.

"Are you going to stand here all night?" Dana quipped, breaking my reverie.

"Uh, no. Sorry." I magically swept the five inches of accumulated snow from the Silver Wraith, and we climbed inside. With a brisk wave, I started the engine.

"Damn, it's cold," I complained, vigorously rubbing the chill from my hands. I was glad to be wearing the trench coat. It was the warmest coat I owned.

Dana grinned. "I take it you're not a big snow skier." She put the hearse into gear and sped away. My prior spell continued working to clear a path through the mounting snow in front of us. Dana navigated the downtown streets with the skill of a NASCAR driver and steered the Silver Wraith onto the entrance ramp to the Beachline toll road.

"It's now or never," Dana muttered. "We either bring my cousin down, or humans will be his to command and destroy as he sees fit."

I was mesmerized by the sheets of blowing snow flying across the twin headlight beams and nodded distractedly.

Dana frowned. "You're still game for our operation at Chrysaor's place, aren't you? No second thoughts?"

"No, I'm good with it." I wished I could have mustered more enthusiasm for my response, but I realized that the odds were against us. Even with Martha and Kit as our back-ups, I still harbored doubts.

It seemed that the powerful Chrysaor and his demon minions had the deck stacked in their favor.

78

The storm escalated into a complete whiteout when we neared the coast, and continued its relentless glacial assault on Central Florida's tropical environment. Lightning cast multi-colored reflections in the opaque curtain, adding to the blizzard's menace and eeriness. The magical tempest piled the snow into monstrous drifts that buried the ghostly parade of stalled cars along the Beachline's shoulders. Ole Wayland had certainly cooked up one helluva iniquitous ploy to cloak his vile scheme.

The Silver Wraith raced ahead at over 100 miles an hour, untouched by the abominable precipitation, but that wasn't what concerned me. I had a hunch that Reynolds knew we were headed his way, so I fully expected an indomitable line of defense to impede our invasion of his Indialantic property. Outwitting him was my department.

My prediction was right on the mark. As soon as we passed the Indialantic exit sign on I-95, an enormous blazing hoop, larger than the one lion tamers used in their cage acts, appeared in the snowstorm and blocked the exit ramp. Dana slowed the Silver Wraith to sixty miles per hour. She squinted at the shadowy objects leaping past the fire into the deep snow.

"What are those things?"

I was very familiar with them. Devil dogs. Dozens of them. I told Dana how they had attacked Martha in her storeroom.

"Damned pests," she retorted.

"You've seen them before?"

"Oh yeah. Want to toss a few fireballs their way?"

I wished she'd been around when I battled the demon assassin inside Senator Kane's home. "No time. Let's just stick to the plan."

She looked at me like a kid with a popped birthday balloon. "You're the boss, boss. What do you want me to do? Drive around the ring?"

I could've done without the naked sarcasm. "Sure. Skirt the fire and run 'em down if they get in our way," I replied confidently. "The spell that repels the snow should do the same with the damned demons."

Dana looked skeptical. Her poise faltered. "Are you sure?"

"Sure I'm sure. Now hit the accelerator."

Dana deftly maneuvered around the flaming hoop, plowed through a half-dozen devil dogs, and raced up the exit ramp. The rear end fishtailed like a belly-dancer's hips when Dana stood on the brakes to navigate the twenty-five-mile-an-hour curve. I didn't panic. My resolve held firm.

Fortunately, there was just enough pavement to hold the Silver Wraith as it skidded around the sharp curve. The alternative would have been to plow through the steel rail and plummet into a mountain of snow, leaving us at the mercy of the devil dogs. But we weren't out of the woods yet. I peered into the sideview mirror and spotted a couple dozen snapping, howling hellhounds bounding after us.

Dana noticed them, too, and floored the accelerator, leaving our pursuers in a whirling snow wake. But we knew those demons wouldn't quit. Those green emaciated canines would hunt us to the ends of the earth, or Reynolds' place, whichever came first.

Dana shot me a quick glance. "Well, you ready?"

She referred to my upcoming solo performance. "It's going to be close, but I'm ready."

"You sure?"

I envisioned the Emerald Zone's ghostly killer horde running amok on earth. Wiping out our species. Not on my watch.

"Do it."

Dana appeared both relieved and frightened at my response. "As soon as we reach A1A, you bail—like we planned."

"Good. His mansion's about two miles up the road." I'd had a great aerial view of his estate's layout from my unorthodox approach as a bee swarm.

"Right."

Dana kept checking the sideview mirror. The dogs were a hundred feet back and closing. "I hope you can pull this off without them seeing you," she said, worry scrunching her forehead.

"You and me both." I wasn't worried. If they spotted me, I was dead. If I didn't try the upcoming maneuver, then the world died. Hope was the only answer.

"A1A's coming up in less than a mile." She goosed the accelerator pedal, urging more speed from the hemi-engine.

I grabbed my mage staff and a small Nike backpack loaded with goodies, and I don't mean picnic food. My other hand curled around the door latch.

"I'm as ready as I'll ever be."

"Meet you later."

I studied her. "Having second thoughts about your plan?" I asked.

"No. Well, yes. I didn't expect the hellhounds."

"But we expected something. We knew Reynolds wouldn't just let us walk into his mansion without a fight."

"I know, but . . . ."

"But nothing. We stick to the plan, and that's that."

"Okay," she said softly. "Good luck."

"Good luck to you. Your part's risky, too."

"I've got it handled."

"At least your aunts can come to your rescue if things get out of hand."

She shrugged. "I wouldn't count on it."

"Keep the faith."

"We're here," she announced, kissing her fingertips and touching them to my cheek. "Be careful, Joe, and I mean it."

"Aye aye, Captain." With that, I yanked the door lever, leaped from the Silver Wraith, and hit a bank of snow at fifty miles an hour. Talk about a rush.

Dana wildly spun the hearse to the south on A1A, the opposite direction from Reynolds' mansion, while I burrowed into a snowdrift to cloak my scent from the approaching hellhounds. Their paw-pounding was muted beneath the snow, and I held my breath, hoping that they'd continue past and follow the Rolls Royce.

I waited a full minute before I crawled out from my hideaway. I stood there waiting, collecting snow like there was no tomorrow. But the hellhounds were gone. Maybe they'd like it down in Miami Beach.

I brushed the snow off my raggedy clothes and checked the ground for tracks. They were faint because of the blowing snow, but they were there and following Dana. I breathed a little easier and turned north toward the mansion.

Before I trudged a hundred feet through the knee-deep drifts, I stopped. There was a low growl behind me. A savage, hellish growl. A hellhound. Their pack leader must have left one behind to secure their flank . . . or it was a straggler that got lucky and spotted me? Whatever the scenario, this one was about to throw off our schedule.

I spied the underworld canine ten feet behind me. Too close for comfort. Under normal circumstances, I would have heard its approach, but this howling blizzard made it all but impossible to detect anything visual or auditory. The soulless killer's beady, unblinking eyes zeroed in on my throat like menacing black laser beams.

This was definitely a *good news-bad news* state of affairs.

The *good* news was that I had to contend with only one of the damned demons. The *bad* news was that I was forced to contend with one damned demon.

Before I knew it, the hellhound launched itself at me through the gusting whiteout.

Fangs first.

79

My mage staff glowed and transported me six feet to my right, avoiding the snow-glittering green form that whizzed past. *What can I say?* Occasionally, my staff had a mind of its own. Before the devil dog turned, the staff re-formed itself into a lethal spear. I couldn't use fireballs to slay the creature, because the noise and light might alert Reynolds to my presence—with Dana cleverly disguised as me, I had to assume that he didn't know I was anywhere near his mansion yet.

The demon charged again, but I stepped back and lopped off the killer's rear quarters with the staff's ultra-sharp blade. The twitching legs and thighs dropped into the snow, burst into flame, and vanished. The rest of the canine dragged its body into swirling blizzard.

Without the back half of their bodies, most violent predators would slink away and die. But they weren't devil dogs. It would continue to execute its prime directive — namely, dispatching me — until its head was separated from its body. Even in its severely crippled state, decapitating it would not be a walk in the park.

I scanned the endless white landscape for the damned thing, but it was no use. Even after amping my wolfen sight, I could barely see the tip of my nose. As a last resort, I conjured a snow-free zone in a ten-foot radius around me, but there was still no sign of my attacker.

When magic failed, my combat choices were narrowed to one: werewolf.

I quickly used my wand to remove my disguise, and my ratty clothes vanished. I dropped the mage staff and wand into the snow and started the transformation into my seven-foot alter-ego. My mind dulled as my wolfen instincts gradually cloaked my human reasoning capabilities. My emerging, singular directive became *kill or be killed*.

I swatted at the falling snow in frustration. It blinded me and blocked my sense of smell, leaving me vulnerable. My savage mind was wary of the situation. And waited, unwilling to risk a blind search. Let the devil dog come to me.

My attack-impaired enemy slyly tunneled beneath the snow like a mole, rose up, and buried its red-hot fangs in my calf. I howled my pain, but swiftly clamped my muzzle, remembering that I didn't want to alert Reynolds to my presence.

A hellhound's bite didn't spread rabies or other diseases—it doled out an unhealthy dose of hell's fire. If its fangs stayed embedded in its victim for too many seconds, then the victim burst into destructive flames.

My enormous paws burrowed furiously into the snow and grabbed the demon's neck. Sensing defeat, it tightened its bite to hasten the barbeque process before I could break its neck. But the devil dog ran out of time. I tore its snarling head away from its abbreviated body and pitched into the whiteness. With a brilliant yellow flash, the demon head exploded.

I breathed a lot easier.

Until I heard two snarls in front of me.

I bent forward and growled menacingly at the new four-legged arrivals, but my intimidating sounds didn't deter them. *Where did they come from? Could the rest of the pack be far behind?* Things didn't look good for the home team.

One of the brutes charged through the mounting drifts, kicking up the white stuff like a gas-powered snow thrower. The devil dog leaped for my throat, but I snagged its shoulders in midair. We went tumbling into the drifts along the road until we resembled marshmallow deli wraps. Its fangs clacked together inches from my muzzle as I struggled to gain the upper position and rip its throat out. But the brute was too wiry, and I ended up on the bottom.

That wasn't my only fatal disadvantage. My peripheral vision was glued to the second hellhound waiting patiently on the sidelines. If it joined the fray, I'd be fighting an uphill battle for survival.

A vicious fiery crunch into my right shoulder bone brought my full attention back to the fight. My head shot up, and I sank my sharp teeth into its exposed shoulder, but that had little effect on my supernatural enemy. I increased jaw pressure and tugged with all my wolfen strength. The ragged shoulder and convulsing leg came away in my mouth. I quickly spit out the sour-tasting appendage and slid my left paw past its vacant shoulder to its exposed neck.

My own shoulder smoldered like a green-twig campfire. I roared angrily and plunged my keen claws into the glossy green neck. They curled around something hard, and I yanked fiercely, launching spine, bone, flesh, and gristle at the feet of the hellhound's partner.

The devil dogs didn't have a pack attack mentality; they were basically loners. One for one, and none for all.

The third demon charged. I ripped the second attacker's mouth from my shoulder and heaved the head at the new attacker in town. It ricocheted off the third's side and exploded, but the demon barely flinched.

By the time I pitched the rest of the dead devil dog's carcass away and watched it flash into oblivion, the third one was airborne and targeting my uncovered throat. I elevated my one good arm and both legs, and snatched the skyrocketing creature from the air like a circus bear catching a ball, and tossed it over my head.

Out of the corner of my eye, I saw a fourth demon party crasher bound through the snow in my direction. The gods weren't smiling on me tonight.

The demons had me outnumbered, and despite my primal strength, I was sure I couldn't defend myself on my back. Maybe if I reminded them that wolves were on the federal endangered species list, they'd leave me alone.

But I got a distinct feeling that these two were poachers.

80

While the third hellhound struggled in the snow to right itself, the fourth pounced in my direction with its claws extended, but an enormous shadow glided above it and snatched its back a second before it flattened me. Their momentum carried them through my snow-free zone and into the blizzard. I didn't take the time to speculate on my savior's identity; I leaped up and met the third's charge head-on.

Catching the growling beast by its slender shoulders, I lifted its wriggling body high over my head and drove it down hard into the snow pack. I realized from my previous encounters with devil dogs that my body slam wouldn't knock the wind out of it; the damned things didn't breathe to begin with. I merely stunned it long enough to execute my next maneuver.

Howling, I swung my good leg crossways high atop its bony chest, slipped my paws to its neck, threw my head back, and wrenched its head off. Then I did my ecological bit by disposing of its head and body with a couple of long throws before giving myself one or two victory chest thumps. The celebration was brief, because I was acutely aware that there was another supernatural entity out there somewhere.

I sniffed the area where the fourth attacker and my savior had vanished, but my nose was as useless as before. I stood in the center of my snowless area and waited for the outcome of their battle. *Would it be the devil dog or my enigmatic savior?* Time would tell.

Except for the rustling snow and whistling gusts, the road was silent. No howls, yowls, or terrible wails, which I expected from a death battle. I prowled the edges of my circular zone like a caged zoo animal. After several minutes of vigilantly awaiting the victor, a hulking shadow appeared at the periphery of my zone. It hesitated before entering like a timid boxer climbing into a boxing ring.

The daunting black panther's 500-pound physique moved with the grace and balance of a predator ballerina. The cat's iridescent jade eyes met mine, and my trepidation withered a few degrees. The monstrous cat growled softly and playfully, and I responded to its affable greeting with one of my own. I immediately recognized the werepanther's familiar scent and wholly relaxed.

But I was hopelessly behind schedule. I should've been at the mansion by now, executing Dana's plan. I scooped my wand and staff from the snow and motioned for my ally to follow. It did.

We found it hard going against the brutal Atlantic winds. Blinded by the snow, we had to proceed cautiously so as not to collide with any object and injure ourselves. We loped around stalled snowbound vehicles, fallen oak limbs, and live utility lines along the deserted stretch of A1A. By the time we reached the outskirts of the immense seaside estate, I wasn't certain whether we had time to pull off the mission and stop Reynolds.

The werepanther nudged me hard before we vaulted the seven-foot bricked fence enclosing the southern portion of the property. She pawed the icy brick-and-mortar surface while nodding upward. The gist of her crude charade finally penetrated my thick werewolf skull—she wanted me to scout ahead so we both didn't rush into Reynolds' trap. Maya had mentioned a trap with her dying breath, so I growled my agreement. I stretched beyond my full height on my clawed toes, and peered over the wall.

The entire property was snowless . . . and *warm*. A full blood moon shone down through a round break in the racing clouds and cast a sinister glow on the estate. Overhead, black energy sizzled and crackled as it surged through the pentagram-shaped power grid that Kevin Williams had installed. Somewhere, Wayland Reynolds, aka Chrysaor, was extracting intense black-magic power from it.

I scanned the meticulous landscape and spotted four beefy, no-nonsense sentinels, armed with what appeared to be AK-47s. They patrolled the mansion's eastern and southern perimeters in teams of two, but there were no doubt others patrolling the west and north sides of the vast house. Their expressions were granite, and their eyes murderous. Probably ex-Navy SEALs. Or ex-Army Rangers. Or even ex-cons.

They weren't my principal concern. Our major problem was getting across the broad expanse of open ground between us and the mansion, unseen. We'd be sitting ducks if we attempted to charge the house from here without cover.

I eyeballed the grounds for the safest path to the mansion, and then the werepanther and I stealthily moved down the wall toward the pool deck where the lawn and shrubbery were cloaked in moon shadows. We both cleared the top of the fence with one leap, and after landing quietly, we zigzagged toward the looming mansion and the first pair of hardboiled sentinels.

As luck would have it, someone alerted the sentinels to our approach, and they opened fire. Reynolds must have installed security cameras around the place. The rapid gunfire chewed up the St. Augustine lawn faster than a battalion of chinch bugs. I wasn't running at full speed, because my left ankle was gimpy from the hellhound's vicious bite. Thankfully, the werepanther hit the guards first, knocking one of the GI Joes down and ripping him limb from limb. He never knew what hit him.

Three bullets made the acquaintance of my body before I reached the other one, but since the lead intruders weren't silver, they didn't slow me down. I leaped on the stone-faced sentry, forcing the tip of the AK-47 barrel into his ribs. The impact of our collision forced his curled finger against the trigger, and he basically blasted every organ inside his muscular body to bloody pulp.

The werepanther joined me and we loped toward the front corner of the mansion in anticipation of the next group's appearance. They didn't disappoint us. As they sprinted around the corner, they saw us and started shooting. Their hurried aim was atrocious.

I took a few more insignificant hits, but their guns went quiet in seconds. The werepanther severed the first one's arms with two quick swipes, and then I waded into the other panicked gunman, clawing and ripping him apart as if he were a straw man. Soon, both were reduced to ragged sushi on the blood-dappled lawn.

I didn't wait for her to rejoin me. I bounded on all fours back to area above the pool deck, hid in the tall shrubbery, and anticipated the arrival of still more guards from the estate's north side. Additional mercenaries skulked into view, and I allowed them to pass before jumping out and smashing their heads together. Their skulls caved in with sickening thuds, like over-ripe melons hitting the sidewalk from a ten-story drop.

Without warning, another pair of guards got the drop on the werepanther while she was watching me, and carved her back like it was a Thanksgiving turkey. They were much cleverer than their cohorts. They had used their coworkers by the pool as expendable decoys, so they could ambush the werepanther from behind. She dropped from the intense blood loss. She desperately needed time to heal so she could defend herself.

I roared furiously and charged the merciless pair as they laughed at their suffering prey. They swiftly raised their AK-47s and peppered her legs from point-blank range. The bullets couldn't kill the werepanther, but they could immobilize her.

A massive amount of blood streamed from her numerous wounds and discolored the grass around her legs. I arrived just as they paused to reload. When I finished with them, they weren't laughing any more. I kicked their mutilated corpses aside and then heard the words every werebeast dreaded.

"Larry, load your sidearm with the silver bullets Reynolds gave us and let's finish this ugly cat off. I'm past ready for a goddammed beer."

"Make it a six-pack, Jim."

"You're on."

The two new arrivals clicked their cylinders into place and pointed their gun barrels at the werepanther.

"Sweet dreams, asshole."

81

I appeared in the nick of time.

Larry was about to adorn my partner with silver and damn it to werebeast eternity. As his pudgy forefinger slowly, torturously applied pressure to the trigger, his cruel expression collapsed faster than you could gargle into a werewolf's mouth! I cuffed the side of his head with my paw and knocked it into the shrubbery bordering the mansion.

Jim turned to unload his silver dispenser at me, but I batted it into the left field bleachers. The rest of Larry fell flaccidly atop the AK-47 beside his partner.

Jim reached for his scabbard and yanked out his serrated military knife. He took one swipe at me before I seized his knife hand and twisted his wrist until it cracked and his hand drooped uselessly. The knife bounced harmlessly on the lawn.

Swearing loudly, Jim drew his automatic weapon with his surviving hand and fired point-blank into me. I whipped my paw around with such force that it shattered the bones in his forearm and dislocated his elbow.

Jim's face became a contorted mask of anguish and rage. Despite the futility of the situation, he ran to the werepanther and kicked her bleeding legs as hard as he could.

Big mistake.

I tilted my head back and roared angrily, my orange eyes blazing, before I charged the scrawny assailant. I buried my long teeth in Jim's midsection and bit down hard. My formidable jaws crunched his torso and splintered his hips, while his organs, veins, and arteries erupted through his torn flesh like blood bombs. His dazed eyes popped out of their sockets and dangled over his bruised cheeks on stringy fibers as his spine snapped like dry wood. I stepped back, punched my nails and fingers through his chest, wrapped them around the ribcage, and yanked it out. I released Jim, and his amorphous, unrecognizable form dropped lifelessly to the blood-puddled grass.

I strode over to Larry and dropped Jim's ribs on his bloodied corpse. *There's your six-pack, buddy*, I thought.

I returned my attention to the werepanther. Her perforated legs continued to leak blood at an alarming rate, and despite her ability to self-heal, with such a debilitating injury, that process might take a week. I simply didn't have that much time. In a week, the world as I knew it would be depopulated and trashed by the Emerald Zone's ghostly inmates.

The werepanther glanced once at me, sadness and pain reflected in her jade eyes. I looked away toward the blizzard raging beyond the wall, and an idea formed in my primitive mind. I bounded away toward the spot where we breached the security wall and hoped that the werepanther didn't think that I was abandoning her. I kept one eye on her and one on the wall ahead.

Panting hard, she suffered mightily as her werepanther genes began ejecting the bullets from her legs, one at a time, so she could begin the lengthy healing process. It was impossible for her to return to her human form at that juncture, because the human body was too frail and would succumb to the injuries. End of story. End of my friend.

I swiftly reappeared with my mage staff and magic wand. I dropped them beside her, knelt, and sniffed her damaged legs. Her wide glassy eyes rolled toward me, and she whimpered her thanks. I growled compassionately in return.

I glanced up at the pentagram's lone electrical wire and sighed. Even my small animal brain recognized that unless my mage staff functioned beneath Reynolds' black-magic force field, I couldn't instantaneously heal the werepanther.

I retrieved the staff and glanced around to see if there were any more guards, but none were in sight. Still in my werewolf form, I quickly conjured the most powerful healing spell in my magical arsenal.

And held my breath.

A feeble white glow radiated from the talismans at the tip of my mage staff before fizzling out. Undaunted, I squeezed my eyelids shut and attempted the spell again. And again. Same glow. Same results. Zippo. I peered at my mammoth ally and shook my head. No go. The black energy humming and crackling overhead was too potent for my white magic to surmount.

Not exactly a big surprise, but it was a bitter disappointment.

I hammered the ground with my immense fist, leaving a shallow crater. I was frustrated to the max. I'd have to ditch my ally and complete the mission. Too many people depended on me, starting with Dana. If I failed her, Reynolds would kill her.

The ridge of black hair along the back of the werepanther's long neck abruptly stiffened, and she roared raucously at the mansion. I shielded my eyes from the harsh glare of the floodlights that had just been turned on and spied a male silhouette seated inside a first-floor window. *Was it Reynolds? Who else would it be?*

I glanced down at the werepanther's crippled legs and snarled angrily.

This was just what we didn't need.

More damned trouble.

82

I couldn't believe my eyes.

The silhouette in the window waved at us. *Waved!* Talk about strange. *What did he expect? A couple of werebeasts to wave back?*

As it turned out, that *wasn't* the most surprising thing to happen to us during that brief span.

Out of the blue, my mage staff commenced glowing in my paw, just a smidge whiter and brighter than before. The werepanther lifted her head and whined, bobbing her muzzle toward the radiant staff. Werewolves aren't the greatest at playing charades. We're slow-witted at problem-solving, unless it involves survival. Hmmm, survival. I glanced at the glowing staff, and the werepanther's meaning became clear. Repeat my healing spell.

I conjured the curative spell once more, and to my gratification, the staff brightened and directed its healing brilliance on her chewed-up legs. Immediately, the bullets dislodged from the muscles and oozed through the ruined flesh. The werepanther growled and whined in agony, but at least she was healing. The bullet holes steadily sealed, and her jet-black hair regenerated over the multitude of restored lacerations. I bent and nuzzled her grimacing face.

After the healing process was completed, a myriad of red-stained bullets framed her reanimated legs, and the mage staff's glow waned, then faded out. She stood shakily on her four legs, and I regained my human form and conjured the return of my clothes. As I dressed, the werepanther regained its . . . *her* human form, too, but sans clothes.

"Good to see you alive, Kit," I said with relief, having recognized her werepanther identity from the get-go. She had disclosed her surprising supernatural alter-ego to me during our last investigation together and swore me to secrecy.

"You mean you're glad to see me *naked,*" Kit fired back. She stood there, declining to conceal the most intriguing parts of her divine anatomy. I wasn't shocked by her behavior. I'd seen them all before on numerous occasions.

After giving those parts the twice-over, I grinned. "Well, there is that, too."

"C'mon, Joe, use your magic and dress me," she demanded, keeping her voice low so as not to attract any sentinels we hadn't met yet.

"Casual or combat?" I asked, prolonging her discomfort.

Her eyes were spitfire green. "Dammit, quit horsing around. You know damned well what styles I wear."

Against vociferous objections from my male libido, I waved the tip of my wand at her and said *Sayonara* to her exquisite body. For now. Instantly, Kit was fully clad in black jeans, a tight-fitting black top, and black socks and running shoes.

"That's better," she huffed, "but the top's a little tight."

"That's gratitude for you," I quipped, and then glanced toward the mansion window to signal thanks to her magical savior, but the window was vacant.

"Who was that guy?" Kit asked.

I shrugged. "It certainly wasn't Reynolds. The only help we'd get from him would be personal fittings for coffins."

"Let's get a move on and sabotage Reynolds. That was your plan, wasn't it?"

"Yeah," I replied suspiciously. "As I remember, you weren't invited to the party."

"Yeah, well I sorta invited myself when I saved your ass back there from those scrawny attack dogs." She tapped her shoe on the grass and dared me to fault her logic.

I wasn't biting; at least not yet. "All right, then tell me this. How'd you just happen to show up forty miles from home in a blizzard?"

Her cheeks flushed, but she refused to answer.

"I don't know how you did it, but you followed us, didn't you?" I pressed.

"Yeah, so what? Martha thought you could use my help on your cozy mission, and she used her magic to send me to that exact point where you were attacked. I wasn't about to let you and that . . . that Victoria's Secret model have all the fun. I earned the right to be included."

I didn't have time to argue any longer. "Okay, you can tag along, but under this condition: what I say goes. Agreed?" Kit detested taking orders, especially from Diaz and me, and I fervently hoped that she'd refuse the attached string and bail out.

"It's a deal," she concurred through gritted teeth.

So much for logic. "First, we arm ourselves." I waved my wand again, and my bag appeared. It was filled with automatic weapons, C-4 explosives, knives, and grenades. That might have seemed like overkill to Kit, but after what those sentinels had done to her legs, I planned to be ready for anything.

"Around back," I said with a quick nod toward the ocean.

Before I turned, Kit seized my arm. "And the next time you dress me, conjure me a bra, too. Savvy?"

"Sorry for the oversight."

"Right. Oversight, my ass," she muttered.

"What was that?"

"Never mind. Let's roll."

Crouched low, we darted along the beautiful landscaped gardens that led to Reynolds' lavish oceanside pool and deck. The plush furniture alone must have easily set him back a hundred grand. Despite the blizzard outside the property, several topless young ladies seemed oblivious to it as they cavorted in the water. *Were they blind? Didn't they ever question Reynolds about such extraordinary phenomena?* I chalked it up to vapidity and dropped that futile train of thought. I had more to worry about than a gaggle of gigglers trying to score a moontan. *Much more.*

I waved and smiled like we were invited guests who had just arrived, and we continued past the pool and up the steps to the patio where Reynolds and I had shared lunch. If the ladies were that naïve, then I was certain they'd ignore the arsenal we carried.

Kit and I had climbed half the steps when she tapped me forcibly on the shoulder. *What now?* Time constraints had a way of stressing a person. Irritated, I swung around.

She nodded at the pool. "We've got company."

I looked, and what I saw sucked the wind from my sails. "Shit!"

Those beautiful, giggly poolside bunnies no longer frolicked in the pool. And, they were no longer beautiful . . . or women; each resembled a hideously charred skeletal figure with banana breasts, lifeless coral eyes, nasty-looking claws, and thin elfin horns that sprouted from their foreheads.

Our wannabe escorts squatted on their haunches, ready to spring up the steps after us, and I was pretty sure they weren't planning to extend us a warm welcome.

"What *are* they?" Kit whispered, leaning firmly against me. She was tough, but the sight of those gruesome stick figures would unnerve anyone.

That was a fair question, but one I couldn't answer. "Run!" I whispered.

We scampered up the remaining steps like mountain climbers on speed, but the zombie matchsticks closed fast.

We made it halfway across the patio before our escape hit a solid roadblock: three of the matchsticks vaulted us like Olympic high jumpers and blocked the mansion entrance. When the others showed up, they circled us like Indians around a wagon train. Their toothless mouths spat and hissed at us.

"What now?" Kit demanded tautly.

"Start shooting?" Desperate, but not necessarily brilliant.

Kit was skeptical. Hell, I was too. "So you really believe our bullets can kill those things?"

I kept a wary eye on our repulsive visitors. "Maybe. It's either that . . . *or* teach them how to bunny hop."

A low-pitched feminine voice spoke to me inside my head. *Was I hearing things now?* The name of our charred friends suddenly was *implanted* inside my head.

Corfu Bloodsuckers.

Weird name. *Who was feeding me this information? And why?* Identifying our enemies didn't help me get rid of them.

Guardians of the Gorgons.

Oh great. Another useless scrap.

Do nothing.

That voice again. Do nothing? *Was this a joke? Were we supposed to let these things kill us?*

Have faith.

At an early age, I discovered that I'd been genetically deprived of *faith*, especially in situations where I was armed to the teeth for battle and told not to use them. I noticed Kit studying me. She probably thought I was nuts. Maybe I was.

"Still want to shoot our way out?" she asked quietly.

Tough question. Around and around the *Corfu Bloodsuckers* danced, drawing closer to us with each orbit. It was either act now or die.

Have faith.

The voice was more insistent this time. Against every instinctive fiber in my being, I made the margin call.

"Don't shoot," I replied, amazed that I'd spoken those words aloud. "Do . . . nothing."

She regarded me quizzically.

"*Nothing?*"

I nodded as if in a dream. "Nothing. Have . . . faith." *Was that really me telling someone else to have faith?* Unbelievable.

"They're going to kill us, you know, if we don't do *something!*" she persisted.

"Trust me. Keep the faith."

She reluctantly lowered her automatic rifle. "You're insane."

Bingo.

83

The overhead floodlights softly winked out.

The black matchsticks appeared more sinister beneath the eerie red moonlight. Kit and I exchanged troubled glances. Losing the lights couldn't be good a sign for our survival. I reprimanded myself believing in that faith stuff. In hindsight, which is always 20/20, blowing those *Corfu Bloodsuckers* away with our automatic weapons appeared to have been a wiser course of action.

I had previously considered the moonlight too pale, but I wasn't prepared for the alternative: total darkness. A dense black gauze drifted across the doughnut hole in the storm clouds and snuffed out the moonlight. I tightened my grip on the handgun as a pinpoint of light appeared in the blackness and swelled into an ethereal humanoid form. A ghost. *The ghost.* That metal-winged visitor that had sketched the *Gorgons'* symbol on the back wall of Martha's shop during the blackout.

Its radiance intensified, and the *Corfu Bloodsuckers* ceased their movements, ostensibly mesmerized by the brilliance. Within seconds, the circling matchsticks leaped away, presumably retreating to the pool below to resume their defensive posts.

The apparition directed its blinding radiance toward us, and we shielded our eyes.

"The *Corfu Bloodsuckers* have been the *Gorgons'* bodyguards at their Corfu Island home for many centuries. Chrysaor kidnapped several of his aunts' protectors long ago, but they forgave him for his impudence and consented to let them watch over him. However, his aunts maintained ultimate control over these protectors and can cancel Chrysaor's authority when the situation warrants it. I am but their magical messenger ordered to act in their absence," it said.

"The all-wise and merciful *Gorgons* have chosen to spare you and Kit from death at the hands of the *Corfu Bloodsuckers*. Only the *Gorgons* themselves have the power to destroy these wondrous warriors. They have also instructed me to deliver a warning to you, Joe Luna. Once you enter Chrysaor's home, you are on your own. There will be no assistance from the *Gorgons* and their appointed emissary, Dana Drake. None will intercede on your behalf against Medusa's son. Is that understood?"

"Look, we're just carrying out Dana's plan here. I can't let her down," I reminded it.

The ghost remained silent.

"I understand your warning, so if you're finished here, we've got work to do. We're wasting time talking," I pointed out. *What did the Gorgons expect me to do? Turn tail and run? Let Chrysaor destroy mankind?* Not a chance.

"Then good luck, Joe Luna," it said, and vanished.

The moonlight reappeared, as did the floodlights. Kit turned and faced me, her mouth gaping in amazement. She was totally floored by the messenger's revelation.

"*Gorgons? Can you believe it?* I always thought they were mythological creatures."

"We'll they're not," I said, and paused outside the back entrance. I cautiously studied the ominous blackness inside the patio door. The *open* patio door.

Kit moved to my side. "No lights."

"Yeah," I said pensively, wondering what awaited us inside. *More monsters? AK-47 toting sentinels?* I was tired of dealing with both of them.

"So what do you think?"

I amped my wolfen sight and peered through the glass, but I couldn't see anything but murky shapes. "About what?"

"You know, going in there after Tinker Bell's warning."

I sighed. "I'm going inside and finishing this, but you can wait out here if you want."

"Not on your life. Let's go."

We stepped past the open door together into the noiseless gloom. Our guns were out and ready for any surprises Reynolds might have rigged expressly for our personal demise.

84

The outdoor floodlights dimly illuminated the marble floor, but the rest of the interior was pitch black. Kit quietly slid the door shut behind us, and we cautiously advanced into the gloom.

Suddenly, lights sprang to life ahead of us, and we both ducked in the shadow behind an overstuffed Queen Anne chair.

"Welcome," a thin, unseen voice hailed us from the large chamber straight ahead—Reynolds' macabre art gallery.

I nodded for Kit to follow me toward the light.

"Wait here," I said as we reached the arched pass-through. I held my finger to my lips, and then I charily stole into the chamber.

The same ancient man who had threatened Reynolds during my previous visit sat calmly in his electric wheelchair. It looked like Reynolds was already at *Ghostworld*, ready to pull the portal plug and let those ghostly criminals into our dimension. He had left the old man behind as our official greeter.

"Hi, Brice," I said as if we were meeting in a casual social setting.

"Tell your young lady that she may enter, too. I mean you no harm," he declared weakly.

Kit poked her head around the wall, and I motioned her in.

If anything, Brice appeared longer in the tooth than before. His sallow wrinkles were deeper, his recessed eyes darker, and his shoulders and upper back more stooped. The thin white wisps of hair stood straight up from his speckled scalp, like a balding Albert Einstein. To me, he had one foot in the grave, with the other soon to follow.

"Thanks for saving Kit's life." I said. "It was you, wasn't it?"

"Guilty as charged," he chuckled, but his laughter was rapidly swallowed by a phlegmy coughing fit. After he caught his breath, he added, "Great-grandfather would kill me if he found out that I helped you."

"So why did you help us?"

Tears washed his eyes. "Because the son-of-a-bitch is going to release his pet ghosts on earth, and . . . he murdered my twin brother, Basil."

I felt his anger. His need for revenge. "Then you know why we're here, right?" My eyes roamed the great expanse. The five portraits sat in the middle of the main aisle in the same formation that Dana and I had seen during our kissing out-of-body experience.

The old man composed himself and nodded like a turtle with its head fully extended from its shell. "You want to destroy his art, which you think will release the poor souls trapped inside."

"Those five over there?" Kit asked me.

"Yeah." Something struck a sour note — the way Brice said *think*. "Are you implying that destroying these portraits won't release those people's souls?"

He scowled at the portraits. "Oh, they'll be released all right, but I don't see how that will help you stop Great-grandfather. And I want him stopped."

You could have knocked me over with a feather.

"It won't weaken him?"

He shook his head. "It'll save those souls, but it won't save *you*."

"I thought he used these portraits for a magic power boost," I managed, panic welling up inside.

"He does, in a way, but not for magic. They help keep him looking young. I think he left you a red herring on your prior visit," Brice explained, then succumbed to a brief coughing spasm. When it ended, he looked at Kit. "Who are you, young lady?"

"Lieutenant Kit Wilson. It's a pleasure to meet you, Brice."

"Likewise."

"Your great-grandfather looks a lot younger than you do. How's that possible?" Kit asked.

He wrung his withered hands. "He's been draining his kin's life force and others' for centuries, including Basil and myself."

Kit wasn't privy to the case information, so she didn't know about Chrysaor's murderous ways. "Centuries? Then he's the *original* movie star, Wayland Reynolds?" Kit gasped.

"Yep."

"Do you know his true identity?" I asked Brice.

"Wayland Reynolds?"

I shook my head. "He's Medusa's son, Chrysaor, and like his long-dead mother, he's not immortal. That's why he needs to feed off your and rest of his family's life force to stay alive . . . and young."

"A *Gorgon?*" Brice rasped. "I didn't know. That's hard to believe."

"Believe it. He wants to avenge his mother's murder by wiping out the human race," I enlightened him.

"Perseus was mortal, wasn't he?"

"Pretty much," I said.

"So that's what he's been up to." Brice scratched his head. "So how do you plan to kill him?"

"If I can find a way to weaken him and put his magic powers on par with mine, I can do it," I replied. The butterflies in my stomach suggested that I'd squandered too much time here. My portrait theory was a bust. Our magic would never be equal.

"There is a way, but like I said, destroying those damned pictures won't do it." Brice went into another coughing fit, and this one lasted too long. His pale complexion flushed blue, and his head sagged close to his blanketed lap. He was plainly dying.

I ran to his side and lightly slapped his frail back in hopes of stemming the fit, but my effort failed. It continued unabated.

He clutched my hand and tried to speak, but the coughs mangled each word. Finally he exhaled loudly, and I thought he'd bought the farm right then and there. His head slumped forward, his filmy eyes wide open. The coughs ceased, too.

I laid his hands in his lap and closed his eyelids. Whatever he wanted to tell me had died with him, and so did my chance to stop Reynolds. I turned and looked at Kit.

"I guess we're wasting our time here," I lamented. "We'd better head over to *Ghostworld.*"

I started walking away when I heard Brice gasp. I swung around and knelt at his side.

He stared at me with those large dead eyes and motioned me closer. I craned my neck so my ear was close to his trembling lips. His breathing was shallow as he tried to speak again.

"The . . . fountain . . . ."

His head tumbled forward, and I thought that was finally it, but then it jerked up.

"Garden . . . *him* . . . ."

His voice faded, and his life was close behind. That was the end of his miserable existence.

"The fountain garden?" Kit repeated behind me. "What's it mean?"

Him? I stood. "I don't know, but we're going to check it out right now."

85

With snow swirling around the estate, the unlikely heat and humidity slapped our senses as we strode outside and headed for the garden. I had fleetingly observed it during my prior frenzied visit, but I couldn't recall any specific details. The garden rested on the north side of the mansion, and when Kit first caught sight of the colorfully lighted floral showcase, it took her breath away.

The pond and disk-shaped fountain were centered among hundreds of colorful blooms and ornamental shrubs. A red-brick walk contained the crystalline pond where the fountain spewed water twenty feet into the air, only to be recaptured below and tumble down four levels into the pond.

"Oh my God, it's beautiful," she exclaimed.

I hadn't realized that Kit was into cultural stuff like that. She broke away from me and hurried toward the steps that descended three feet into the garden. Evil permeated its splendor, and quickly I caught up with her and pulled her back off the first step.

"What are you doing?" she protested, yanking her arm from my grasp.

"Saving you. The place reeks of evil, and I'm certain that it's well-protected against uninvited guests."

"You're paranoid, do you know that?" she huffed, and started for the steps again.

"We've got a riddle to solve out here. There'll be plenty of time for you to visit some other day . . . if we survive the night," I reminded her.

Her temper cooled from a boil to a simmer. "Fine. Here's the *garden* and there's the *fountain*. So how do those clues help us discover how to weaken Chrysaor's powers?" she asked belligerently.

I studied the layout of the extensive garden. There were the garden and fountain as Kit had just said, but where did *him* fit into the total clue? I vaguely remembered seeing something odd out there, but what was it?

I scanned the layout of the flowers in case the diverse colors conveyed a message of some kind — but if they did, I didn't see it. Then I studied the fountain for any special shapes or symbols in its design, but again I came up empty.

"Is this supposed to be a Roman garden?" Kit asked.

"Uh, what?" I replied, lost in thought.

"Is this supposed to be a Roman garden?" she repeated.

"I honestly don't know. Why'd you ask?"

"See those statues around the garden? They're all dressed like Romans or Roman gods," she pointed out.

Statues. That was it! I recalled thinking how every one of them had Reynolds' face. "You're a genius!" I exclaimed.

"But I . . . I didn't say anything," she protested, though mildly.

I showed her how each of their faces resembled Reynolds.

"They do," she agreed, amazed.

"Brice's clue, *him*, fits that scenario perfectly. That was what he was trying to tell us."

"And like the important portraits, there are five of them."

"Representing the five points of the pentagram," I muttered.

"Pentagram?" she asked.

"I'll explain on the way back to *Ghostworld*," I said, unzipping my black bag and pulling out five bricks of C4 explosive, detonators, and identically numbered cheap cell phones. I quickly planted the explosives and detonating devices at the bases of the statues. Before leaving, I made sure that I had their collective number in my phone. I did.

"Now for the pièce de résistance," I remarked, grabbing the black bag. "C'mon, follow me."

"But I wanted to walk through the garden. It won't take me more than a couple minutes. You can spare that amount of time, can't you?" she asked cynically.

Dammit. Not really. "Look." I marched to the edge of the garden drop-off, fished a spare detonator from the bag, and threw it onto the pathway encircling the fountain. The skipping detonator clinked across the bricks. Four asps slithered from their hiding places and converged on the detonator, striking it several times.

Kit's hands flew to her mouth. "I didn't know . . . ."

"But *I* did," I rebuked her. "You've got to have a little faith in me."

Kit looked at me strangely, as if to say, "Since when are you so hyped about faith?" But she didn't vocalize her sentiments. She merely followed me around to the south side of the mansion, which was peppered with sentinel corpses.

"Hop over the wall, and I'll meet up with you in a few minutes," I instructed Kit. "I've got to shut down this black-magic generator, so I can use my magic to take us to *Ghostworld*."

"What are you planning to do?"

"You'll see. Now vamoose."

I raced to the closest utility pole and planted the C4 explosive on the side facing the mansion, to protect us from the blast. I retreated swiftly to the wall and phoned in the explosion. It ruptured the pole's middle section. As the top fell away, it pulled the wire with it, but the wire didn't split when the pole buried itself in the ground.

I ran back, conjured wire cutters, and sliced the stubborn wire. The hissing and snapping ceased immediately. His magic amplifier was permanently out of order, and our odds of defeating the mad *Gorgon* had just been upgraded.

I leaped over the wall and landed beside Kit. Reality greeted me with pelting snow and an incredible wind chill. I shouted at Kit to move next to me, and I tapped my staff twice into the snowdrift. The two of us vanished.

Our next stop—*Ghostworld*.

86

We materialized inside my Silver Wraith, half-buried beneath a snowdrift near the Wraith Water Park at the south end of *Ghostworld*. Beside the fire-gutted Ghost Town. I landed behind the steering wheel, and Kit appeared on the passenger's seat. I was a happy camper. I was back in the driver's seat once more.

"Now what?" Kit asked impatiently.

"We wait."

She folded her arms, and scowled at the swirling snow. Inaction wasn't her thing.

A cacophony of gunshots and shouts erupted inside the park, so I waved my wand in front of the glass windshield and transformed it into an HD television screen that magically picked up any activity inside *Ghostworld*.

Dozens of cops were firing at a giant of man, all decked out in gold armor and a helmet, over by the The Raving Revenant Coaster. He brandished his supersized gold sword at the cops and used his shield to deflect their puny bullets.

"Who's that? The Jolly Green Giant?" Kit quipped.

"That's Chrysaor, Medusa's kid."

"Reynolds?"

"Yep."

"Where's he heading?"

I mentally manipulated the screen to zoom out. I should have guessed as much. "He's headed toward the Mansion Macabre."

"Where this whole damned case started," Kit murmured.

I had vowed to stay away from that haunted attraction, but some promises were made to be broken. "Yeah."

"Isn't there anything you can do to help out the cops? Like magic?"

"Not until I hear from Dana. We're not going out blind in that blizzard, because we could zap one of your buddies by mistake," I spelled out as delicately as I could.

Kit bristled at the mention of Dana's name, like I knew she would. "Who's your new partner, anyway? FBI? CIA? Superwoman?" she growled.

"Let's just say she's very familiar with this situation and leave it at that."

But she didn't want to retire the subject. "Let's be honest here. Do you have a hard-on for . . . this . . . *Dana* person?"

Her question blind-sided me. "*Hard-on?* Are you kidding me? Our relationship is strictly professional." I paused. "Sounds like you're jealous."

She harrumphed. "Dream on. I could care less who you slept with while I was recuperating with Martha. I just don't want your bedtime activities to affect your professional judgment, especially when my life's on the line. Got it?"

Kit was lying through her teeth. She was so jealous that her breath was smokin' green.

"Kit, I swear that there's nothing romantic going on between us." From Dana's one and only trip to my bedroom, I stated that with confidence. "And you can trust me with your life."

Glancing at the screen, I saw that the cops scattered across the slick snow-covered concrete walkways, trying to dodge the lethal blows from Chrysaor's sword.

The ones who slipped and fell didn't make it. Their neatly severed bodies bloodied the snow beneath many of the ghost-shaped sidewalk lamps.

"I suppose you want me to have a little faith in you," she snapped facetiously.

"Just a little?" Dana appeared behind us.

"Dana!" I exclaimed. "What's Chrysaor doing out there?"

"Killing cops, what else? He's even transformed some of them into sheep and ponies."

"I blew up Chrysaor's wired pentagram at his beach estate, and when you give the word, I'll cripple his strength as well," I reported.

She nodded. "Then your part of the mission was a success. I ditched the devil dogs and got back here a half-hour ago. I was beginning to worry that you didn't make it."

"We were late, but as usual, there were complications."

"Tell me about them sometime over a drink at the Wolfsbane," she said, needling Kit.

"Sounds good. I'll be there," Kit piped up.

Dana's grin turned south again. "Did the GPS find Medusa?"

"I haven't seen them to ask," I replied.

"They're a great bunch of ghosts, by the way," Dana added.

Kit rolled her eyes. "How nice."

Right on cue, Captain Harley Watterson appeared beside Dana, spooking her—literally. "There's a problem."

I groaned. "What else is new in this investigation?"

"Sorry about that." The ghost didn't look one bit sorry. "Medusa's head is guarded by the *River Styx Bone Slayers* from Corfu, underneath that haunted house."

"Of all the rotten luck," Dana groaned. "They'll attack us from anywhere in the park if they sense a threat to Medusa or Chrysaor."

"What are they . . . exactly?" I asked.

Dana took a deep breath. "From what little I know of them, the Bone *Slayers* come from the island of Corfu. They're skeletons armed with sabers, as well as bone and flesh shields made from the offspring of the Nemean Lion."

"The *what* lion?" Kit pressed.

"The Nemean Lion. In mythology, this enormous beast was strangled by Hercules, because no weapon could penetrate its skin. At the time Hercules killed it, he didn't realize that it had offspring, which Medusa and her two sisters transported to Corfu and raised until they were fully grown. After that, they slaughtered the lions and crafted shields for their undead army," Dana explained.

"So where does the River Styx fit into the picture?" I asked.

"The River of the Dead," Dana murmured, as if she feared it. "The *Slayers* are skeleton corpses of the great warriors who drowned crossing that horrible river. The *Gorgons* reanimated and armed them, so the *Slayers* could defend them."

"I hope I never run into one," Kit said.

"So how'd Chrysaor gain control of the *Slayers*?" I asked.

"Chrysaor took them centuries ago, and they've been his to command ever since."

"Like he did with the *Corfu Bloodsuckers*," I lamented.

"You saw them?" Dana exclaimed.

"Oh yeah. Live and in person," I said. "But your aunts bailed Kit and me out."

"Thank heavens. Only my aunts can kill them."

"That's what the good fairy messenger told us," Kit submitted.

I shook my head. "Why don't your aunts reclaim those *River Styx Bone Slayers* from Chrysaor like overdue library books?"

Dana shrugged. "Ask them yourself. *But,* slayers can be destroyed by anyone."

Finally, some good news about them. I twisted the conversation back to Medusa's head. "So the Mansion Macabre was the previous site of Reynolds' old shack, and underneath it, he had Medusa's head guard the portal to the Emerald Zone."

"And his daughter protected Medusa's snake hairdo," Harley added.

I nodded. "Makes perfect terrible sense."

Kit leaned close to me. "How do we defeat Chrysaor while he's doing his *knight-in-shining-armor* bit?" she whispered.

"A tank might do the trick," I proposed, half serious.

Dana shook her head. "The armor's protected by his magic, too."

"Then I guess we'll have to neutralize his magic," I speculated, patting the phone in my pocket. One call, and the statues and his extra magic source would be history.

"The gang and me are ready to help neutralize them Emerald Zone ghosts. Just tell us when," Harley said.

"Just keep an eye on the mansion, and you'll know when," I told him.

"Aye aye." He popped out of view.

Kit's jaw fell open. "Do you think those old ghosts can really help?"

"We'll see. It's a tall order," Dana replied.

"Where do we start out there?" Kit asked, pointing into the blizzard.

"The Mansion Macabre, I'm afraid," Dana answered, watching for my reaction.

I forgot that she could read my mind while we worked together, so she already knew about my promise to myself. I stayed quiet, mulling it over.

Dana patted my shoulder. "C'mon. We can't do this without you."

What the hell. Feeling like a lamb being led to slaughter, I flung my door open and reluctantly climbed out into the blizzard. Medusa, here I come.

My mother would have been proud.

My father would have thought I was nuts.

87

We trudged through the foot of Central Florida snow toward the Mansion Macabre and didn't encounter any resistance until we reached the chaos outside the gloomy attraction. The whipping snow swallowed the immense attraction and the dim sidewalk lamps bordering the walkways up to its entrance. The thinned ranks of cops were badly outnumbered by the crowd of bleeding corpses.

"So how do we get inside?" Kit asked, her biting sarcasm forgotten.

"Through him," Dana answered, pointing at Chrysaor. "He's cast an impenetrable defense spell around the building, so we can't reach the portal and Medusa's head while it's activated."

Tillie O'Neal materialized beside us, wearing her standard cotton and lace dress. The cold didn't bother the dead.

"You guys stuck on how to get inside?" she asked.

I nodded, but it went unnoticed in the blinding snow.

"We need to get past his defense shield," Dana replied.

"I can help you do that," she stated boldly.

"How?" Kit asked.

"You see, I can enter the place in my ghostly form anytime I please," she explained.

Dana snapped her cold red fingers and winced from the sharp pain. "I get it. You just turn us into ghosts and away we go."

"That's it, Dana. I'm still a powerful witch."

Kit appeared worried. "I think I'll stay out here and help my cop buddies," she said.

"We'll need you inside sooner or later," I reminded her. "You can't help if you're dead."

Before she replied, I heard a loud swish headed our way. "Duck!" I yelled, and everyone but Tillie did. Chrysaor's monstrous sword passed over our heads, missing by mere inches, but sliced right through Tillie's airy form.

"He's found us," Dana cried.

But those were her final words before a huge hand swept her away. Chrysaor's booming laugh reverberated throughout the park.

"Got you at last, Dana," he told her, and backed away toward the entrance.

"Not yet!" she screamed down at me, referring to blowing the statues.

I raised my mage staff and readied a spell, but Dana shouted into my head for me to back off. Save my magic until it would be effective. I reluctantly complied. She added that she would be fine. Don't worry— be clever. I planned on it.

I wondered how Chrysaor was going to enter the attraction, when the doors were much smaller than he was, but he showed me a minute later. The three of us watched Chrysaor's armor melt from his body, convert to steam before it touched the snow at his feet, and vanish, leaving the soul-stealing actor clothed in a sweater, jeans, and deck shoes. Next, he shrank his form to its normal size, but he still possessed enough strength to hold onto the writhing and kicking Dana.

"C'mon, let me change you now!" Tillie screamed into the wind.

I shook my head. "I've got to check on Uncle Jess first. Meet us back here in twenty minutes," I explained.

"Whatever you say."

"*Us?* What about me?" Kit asked.

"You're coming with me, so I can keep an eye on you," I responded.

I took her hand and guided her back toward the center of the park, where I was certain Uncle Jess and his agents were orchestrating the cops' demise. It was slow going, tramping through a foot of snow that got deeper by the minute. Kit slowed, her body weakened from her Emerald Zone episode.

"Try to keep up," I shouted. "We're running out of time."

She looked around at the frosted corpses. "And running out of cops."

But Chrysaor wasn't done with us yet. I spotted several balls of light heading right at us. As a parting gesture, the bastard heaved boulder-sized fireballs to kill us once and for all. I raised my staff and fired my own fireballs, which intercepted the incoming ones and exploded them halfway between our position and the mansion.

Chrysaor's angry bellows dwarfed the storm's gusts, but there were no more fireballs.

We cranked up our speed a notch and advanced as fast as the snow allowed. I just hoped that Uncle Jess was still alive.

Why, I wasn't quite certain.

88

U ncle Jess and his agents stood huddled in a circle at the center of the park, where I had predicted they'd be. When Kit and I closed to within ten feet, the agents took notice and drew their guns. I waved my hands over my head and shouted to my uncle. He waved back and ordered his people to lower their weapons.

"Where in the hell have you been?" he shouted, hands stuffed in his overcoat.

"Out at Indialantic sabotaging Reynolds and his plans," I replied, dusting the snow from my brows.

"How?"

"No time to explain," I said.

"Kit? Glad to see you alive," he said and shook her hand. No handshake for me, though.

"We've got to go," I told him. Stay back here until you hear from me," I explained.

"Back here?"

"Yeah, where it's safe. There might be a lot of magical fireworks in the Mansion Macabre, and I don't want you and your men caught in the crossfire."

He nodded pensively. "Good enough. We'll stand down . . . for now."

Kit and I plowed our way back toward the mansion. Suddenly, glowing lights flew through the blowing snow overhead, and I yanked Kit down and created a purple protective dome over us with my ring. More fireballs. Chrysaor wasn't finished with us.

But the fireballs sailed over our heads and exploded near Uncle Jess and his agents. The conflagration towered above us, devouring every snowflake in its fiery path. The heat was tremendous and changed the surrounding drifts to steaming ponds.

Warm tears clouded my vision and streaked down my cheeks. I turned to Kit.

"Check on my uncle, will you?"

"Where are you going?" she asked, but I think she already knew.

"I've got a score to settle." With that, I marched toward the son-of-a-snake-woman who had murdered my uncle—my family. It was times like this that I was grateful to Mother for drilling those chivalric notions into my psyche. Putting an end to that mythological bully was going to make me feel all warm and fuzzy inside.

As I neared the haunted attraction, I saw him. Dana was helplessly pinned to the wall next to the entrance by green energy manacles. Chrysaor hadn't seen me yet, and I was thankful, because I had time to adjust my plan of attack. A direct assault didn't seem like the smart approach any longer. Too dangerous. So I altered my strategy to a sneak attack from behind. Much better.

I created my never-miss *implosive* fireball that wouldn't harm Dana when it hit Chrysaor. I quietly prowled the edges of the snowy landscape along the entrance wall behind him. I looped the end of my mage staff toward Chrysaor's back and hurled my silver-fire orb. It was like lobbing a lacrosse ball. It made contact between his shoulder blades and ruptured, capturing his form in a silvery net.

Chrysaor arched his back and screamed at the unexpected impact. He twisted and wrestled the burgeoning energy as it spread like a spider's web to every inch of his anguished body before it imploded.

My instinctive reaction was to step back and wait for the fireworks, but my feet didn't budge. I smacked my forehead. Dammit! My fireball hadn't penetrated the defense shield enveloping his body.

With a mighty scream, he wriggled out of his protective shield and dived headlong away from me. The protective shell stood there, still molded in his shape. The fireball implosion detonated before he hit the snow, attracting all the white stuff within a ten-foot radius and annihilating it. The inferno came close to dragging Chrysaor into it, but missed. At least it fried his deck shoes. A small victory, but satisfying nonetheless.

I didn't hesitate. *Kick 'em when they're down.* A sound philosophy when fighting for your life . . . and your family's honor. I fired off another of my Jim Dandy fireballs at close range. He threw his hands up and stopped its progress in mid-air with his magic. With considerable effort, he stood as he controlled my fireball, and his face hideously contorted as he tried to repel it back toward me. I employed my magic to prevent that from happening, and like a game of hot potato, the hissing burning ball traveled back and forth between us.

It was a losing proposition. His magic strength was dominant, and soon my hopes of killing him were deflated as the fireball inched steadily in my direction. Its intense heat melted the falling snow and changed it to rain. In a minute, we looked like two wet dishrags playing freeze-frame volleyball. Except that our game was for keeps.

The acrid odor of my burning hair sickened me, as did the prospect of dying. I thought of using my cell phone to destroy his statues and reduce his strength, but I needed both hands on the staff to delay the fireball's arrival.

A fast-moving silhouette appeared in the whiteness beyond our battle zone and bounded toward Chrysaor. With a soaring leap, it crashed into him and sent him splashing through the melted snow. I quickly redirected the fireball away from us and toward the ruins of the administration building, where it imploded harmlessly. When the silhouette strode out of the blizzard into the rainy area, I was both stunned and relieved. I recognized the reddish-gray werewolf—Uncle Jess. He had somehow survived the fireball blasts.

But he was no match for Chrysaor's strength and magic. The sorcerer tossed Uncle Jess aside and raised his arms to cast a killer spell, but he never got the chance. Another hostile shape moved in like a speeding locomotive and blindsided him. The werepanther! Kit had joined the fray after all, bless her cantankerous heart. She inspired new hope for the home team.

My uncle quickly recovered and pounced on the struggling Chrysaor after he flung the 500-pound werepanther away like a yippy toy poodle. He then deflected my uncle's leap, which sent him rolling over and over in the snow. The werepanther shook the snow from her fur and advanced again, more deliberately this time.

"Kit, jump him — quick!" I shouted, but my advice came too late. The sorcerer swiftly extended his arms and propelled a fireball at her. The explosion launched the flaming werepanther toward Ghost Town's blackened shell, and out of sight. Before my dazed uncle could get his act together, Chrysaor spun and blasted him over the Mansion Macabre.

He redirected his malevolence at me. "Now, back to you. You're finished, Luna." He glanced at Dana. "And so's she."

I spread my legs shoulder-width and held my staff horizontally in front of me.

"Go ahead — do your worst, Chrysaor," I challenged.

My use of his real name momentarily caught him off guard, and he raised his brows. "Well, well; so you know who I am. Good detective work, Luna, but I'm afraid you're going to take that knowledge to the grave."

A slender rubicund beam flew from his fingertips, but my staff deflected it to the side. The snow hissed and burst into a mini-geyser, forcing me to shift before the steam scalded me.

Unfamiliar with failure, the *Ghostworld* killer sent a more imposing beam my way, but my staff deflected that one, too. The impact, though, sent me flying backward, and I landed on the seat of my pants, my staff still held in front of me.

Infuriated, Chrysaor discharged a heavy-duty magic beam that I instantly recognized to be much more powerful than my staff. I grudgingly heaved the staff at the beam and dived out of the impact zone.

The third time was the charm for Chrysaor. This dynamic collision produced a blackish-yellow energy burst that fractured my staff and created an even larger geyser between us. The scalding spray blistered my right side as I scrabbled away.

He laughed raucously, apparently believing that he had me cornered.

"So long, Joe. I wish I could say that it's been nice knowing you, but we both know that'd be a lie." His eyes rolled white as his fingers discharged another of his lethal beams.

Despite the searing pain, I jerked my ring hand up and the purple diamond flexed its supernatural strength and met the beam head-on, stopping it in its tracks—*a nerve-wracking foot from my face.* Chrysaor bent toward my prone form, forcing the beam forward, and to my horror, it slowly, steadily advanced.

Desperate, I scanned the area for signs of help, but we were alone with an audience of one. Dana was imprisoned, and her aunts voluntarily sat this confrontation out.

Chrysaor's beam progressed to within an inch of my chin. I closed my eyes, and the image of my late parents appeared with vivid clarity. They weren't thrilled at the looming prospect of a family reunion. Frankly, neither was I.

89

Just as my chin was about to receive the closest shave ever, a dazzling alabaster ray united with my purple ring's power and forced Chrysaor's murderous beam back at him. The black-magic energy flared as it struck Chrysaor and chucked him like a wobbly Stinger missile into a nearby sidewalk lamppost. The glass ghost globe shattered and showered the staggered sorcerer with splintered shards. The badly dented post snapped and collapsed on his head, knocking Chrysaor for a loop. The blizzard and its accompanying gale-force winds abruptly slowed to a light dusting seen in Norman Rockwell winter prints.

I presumed that my savior was Tillie, but when I craned my neck and looked up, Martha Gibbons stood over me. Always theatrical, she blew on her crooked dogwood wand like it was a smoking gun barrel, and smiled grimly.

"You get yourself into the damnedest messes, Joe," she chastised me, although by the twinkle in her one good eye, I knew that she was pleased with my initiative, if not my results.

"Tell me about it," I grumbled, standing. I pointed to the motionless Chrysaor. "Now what?"

She adjusted her eye patch, and then shook her head. "Look for yourself," she snapped with her customary crankiness.

I looked back at the fallen lamppost, but Chrysaor was gone. He now glided above the snowpack toward the Mansion Macabre like a Hollywood superhero wannabe strapped to a pulley. Only he wasn't using a pulley.

He grabbed Dana off the wall and vanished through the entrance doors.

I wisely decided against rushing the place. For one thing, the building was still protected by his spell. And for another, Tillie had promised to get us safely inside. Although I was worried what that madman might do to Dana, I was waiting for reinforcements this time.

I bent and inspected my ruined mage staff. I brushed the thin veil of snow off its two jagged lengths and tried to cast a simple spell. Nothing happened. There wasn't one magic blip in either piece. The talismans dangled flaccidly, unresponsive. The staff was stone-cold dead. No spirited magic would ever stimulate its grains and knots again.

I dropped the lifeless sections onto the snow. It was irreplaceable. From now on, it was me and my wand against the baddies.

Martha shook her head. "Too bad."

"Yeah."

"Well, we can't stand out here crying over spilt milk. We've got to get inside that place and free Dana," she said sternly.

"Got to wait for Tillie. She can get us past the spell," I informed her.

Martha adjusted her eye patch. "Then where is she?" she asked, irritated by the delay.

"She'll be here soon." I was even more anxious about Dana's safety than I had been earlier, especially since she hadn't spoken to me telepathically for quite some time. *Had Chrysaor blocked her communications?* I checked my phone, and it still worked even though it had experienced a good soaking. It could still play its part in blowing the statues.

Martha frowned and glared silently at the haunted attraction. After several moments, she grabbed my wrist and checked my watch. "Time's a-wastin'," she muttered. "Tillie was probably late for her own funeral."

I stayed quiet. I wasn't going to win that argument.

"Joe! Wait up!"

My neck snapped around toward Ghost Town. I immediately spied Kit, who was hobbling on one of the icy sidewalks connecting Ghost Town and Mansion Macabre.

I smiled and rushed to meet her. "I'll be damned. She's alive."

"She is, and you probably will be damned," Martha called out behind me.

That woman had a sick sense of humor.

"Martha Gibbons? Is that you?" a male voice shouted from the side of the mansion.

Uncle Jess! He'd survived Chrysaor's spell, too, although he walked with a more pronounced limp than Kit. But I wasn't overly concerned. He and Kit both possessed werebeast recuperative powers.

We reunited around Martha and planned our next move. Time, of course, was the critical factor, and that brought our conversation around to Tillie again.

"That danged witch will be the death of us all if she doesn't shake a leg," Martha grumbled.

"Martha, give the ghost a few more minutes. I'm sure she has a good reason for being late," Uncle Jess suggested.

"I doubt it," Martha muttered, but she fell silent again. We were all grateful.

Sirens whined and blue lights strobed as several police and SWAT vehicles drove through the park's entrance and plowed through the drifts toward us.

"What the hell . . ." Uncle Jess boomed.

"Oh no," Kit cried. "They'll ruin everything. We can't change into ghosts in front of them."

"Is that what we're doing?" Uncle Jess posed.

"Yeah," I snapped. "That *was* the plan."

When the vehicles arrived at the spot where I'd found my uncle and his agents, countless patches of snow exploded into the night air throughout the park.

"Oh my God!" Kit shouted.

Eyeless, fleshless skulls emerged and glared sightlessly at the approaching cops and . . . the three of us. *The River Styx Bone Slayers.* Chrysaor's last line of defense.

90

I'd forgotten about those boneheads.

The dotted snowscape looked like an Alaskan prairie dog city. The armed skeleton warriors kept surfacing until our odds dwindled to slim and none. The OPD vehicles stopped, and the cops piled out, but they were no match for the *Bone Slayers*. The killers had fully emerged from the snow with shields and sabers and attacked. Bullets against invulnerable shields. Sabers against flesh and blood. It was a slaughter.

Several advanced toward us, but I wasn't concerned, because Martha and I could zap them with magic. Unless they blocked our magic with their invincible shields. Worry crept into my consciousness and lopped off a chunk of my confidence.

The *Bone Slayers* ceased fighting when a cacophony of savage roars echoed throughout the park. We stared at the entrance and saw a mob of what looked like tall people and . . . Tillie!

Her distinctive animated gestures stirred her followers into a riotous frenzy until the mob began snapping, leaping, and howling wildly. Moments later, Tillie motioned for them to charge *Ghostworld*, and she flew ahead and guided the stampeding silhouettes to the *Bone Slayers*.

Tillie quickly abandoned the violent werewolves and joined us. They assaulted the skeleton killers, throwing shields into the snow, ripping away sabers, and cracking skulls. The tide had turned. The *Bone Slayers* left us and ran to help the others. We were safe. For now.

Tillie landed beside us. "Sorry I'm late. I thought you could use some help with those skeleton swordsmen," she said with a wide grin. "I took a detour over to the Wolfsbane and rounded up Kirby and his regulars."

"Great idea," I praised her.

"You figured right, Tillie," Uncle Jess asserted. "Good work."

Martha remained quiet while Kit expressed her sincere gratitude. No sarcasm.

"Where's Dana?" Tillie asked.

"Inside," I replied. "We've got to get in there now."

The others nodded.

"Then what are we waiting for?"

Before Tillie changed us into ghosts, a teeth-rattling explosion rocked the Mansion Macabre. The tremendous shockwave blasted the roof into the next county, and sprayed deadly bricks, splintered beams, and plumes of choking dust everywhere.

"Hurry," Martha cried. "Dana's in big trouble. I can feel it."

The ghostly transformation was painless, but controlling our movements was awkward at best. Tillie instructed us to join hands, and then she guided us through Chrysaor's spell and the outer wall into the chamber with the holographic portraits and the infamous fireplace. I shivered in spite of my airy form. This place was loaded with bad memories.

We materialized in the physical world again and advanced toward the lighted crater where the fireplace *used* to be. Heated voices erupted from the vast hole and created a greater sense of urgency in us. We half-jogged, half-ran to the edge.

"Don't look down," Martha warned. "If Medusa is out, one look at her and you're stone."

We did a quick-step away from the crater. Martha conjured hand mirrors for us to use so we could take a look.

"Her reflection can't hurt you, but I wouldn't stare into her eyes just the same. You never know," Martha explained.

Dana screamed, and I rushed to the edge, leaned over, and beheld the terrifying scene below.

Dana was again magically manacled to a wall, but this time she was face-first against the rough rock. Arrow-headed vipers swarmed inside the hole in the center of the crater, and Chrysaor stood looking at Dana, his back to me.

"I am done with your impertinence, Dana. You will suffer while I release the ghosts from the Emerald Zone, and then you will become their first victim," he snarled.

"Joe, Maaaaaa . . . oooow!" she screamed, as Chrysaor extended his hands and shot green lightning bolts from his fingertips into her back. She thrashed against the black-magic manacles and shrieked from the mind-bending pain.

Tears pooled in my eyes and anger flushed my entire body. The bastard! Suddenly, Dana's whimpers were inside my head. It couldn't be. I had to be hearing them with my ears, not my mind. I tucked the mirror in my waistband and plugged my ears. The sounds were still loud and clear.

"What do you want, Dana?" I asked mentally.

More sniffles. "Make . . . make that call."

I didn't need to be told twice. I stepped away and punched the speed-dial number. After the connection was made, I visualized the statues exploding to pebbles, and I hoped their destruction devastated Chrysaor's magic ability, as planned.

I laid the phone on the floor and looked down into the crater again. Dana didn't move. My grip tightened and nearly crushed the mirror's handle. Chrysaor now held the snakes in one hand, but they were attached to Medusa's dangling head. I hated snakes.

Neither mother nor son had spied me. Yet.

"Well done, son," she growled hoarsely with an inhuman voice. "Now finish it."

Her son nodded and directed a magical surge at the large flat rock inside the hole. The rock vibrated, then gradually levitated upward. Three ghosts stuck their cruel faces through the widening crack and growled like wildcats. Chrysaor grinned as the rock continued to climb.

"Noooo!" Dana screamed, suddenly alert.

The three ghosts grunted as they tried to squeeze through the narrow gap and free themselves, but the aperture wasn't wide enough.

Suddenly, I was aware that I wasn't alone. I looked away from the crater and noticed the entire GPS crew standing beside me.

"You take Chrysaor and his mother, and we'll take the three ghosts," Harley whispered.

I nodded.

"Us first," he reminded me, and the group vanished.

When they reappeared, I nearly fainted. I couldn't believe my eyes, and I doubted whether my memory would believe it later, either. The entire group had forged one single monstrous ghost, as fearsome-looking as I've ever seen, and I've seen some uglies in my young life.

The monster ghoul descended into the crater toward the hole, and

I curiously watched the expressions of the three would-be escapees. Their violent scowls quickly flipped to hideous masks of terror. The three strained until they vanished back into the Emerald Zone. His concentration was broken, and the rock crashed down over the portal.

"What the . . ." Chrysaor barked, until he glanced up and saw the GPS monster ghost. He was speechless, but his mother wasn't.

"Send it into the Emerald Zone," she ordered sharply.

Dana started laughing. At least, I thought it was laughter. She might have been crying. I was too far away to be certain, and the sound wasn't in my head.

Chrysaor yanked Dana's head back by the hair and stuck Medusa's head in her face. "Look and die!" he screamed.

She opened her eyes and . . . *lived.*

I couldn't believe it, and neither could her cousin.

"That's . . . that's *impossible!*" he shouted at the top of his lungs. "You should be stone by now."

Dana's voice was strained, but then again her head was pulled back. "No, it's not impossible. I'm your distant cousin," she said. "Your mother's curse doesn't affect us *Gorgons.*"

"You're what?" he gasped. "This can't be."

Medusa chuckled humorlessly. "I suppose my sisters put you up to this?"

"They did," she managed.

"Kill her now before they show up. We've got to find another hideaway," she directed her son. "I won't spend the rest of my days living with those two."

He released Dana's hair and stepped away to electrocute her with his lightning.

"Not this time," I yelled. "You're going down, Chrysaor."

He swung his mother's face toward me, but I didn't turn to stone, either. I saw their reflections in my mirror, instead.

"Turnabout's fair play," I shouted, and then zapped his reflection with the lightning bolt of all lightning bolts.

He held up his arm to deflect it, but my magic struck through his weakened defense and pummeled his chest. He stumbled back against the rocky wall and dropped his mother's head. It rolled thumpity-thump into the portal hole. Face down. Eight ball, corner pocket. Perfect.

I ditched my mirror and leaped into the crater. Chrysaor's manacle spell dissipated while he examined the smoking hole in his chest, and I gingerly helped Dana down to the floor. His chest wound was cauterized by the lightning, but blood leaked from his nose and mouth. His body slowly wilted, and he finally collapsed, head-first, onto the floor of the crater.

"Can you save him?" I asked Dana, but she shook her head.

"That wasn't part of my aunts' plan. If he lived, so be it. If not . . . ."

A pair of fierce, creaking, metal-winged creatures descended from the sky and glided down through the attraction's roofless space. They dwarfed Dana and me.

The new arrivals possessed a live-snake hairdo like Medusa, and serpent scales covered their golden wings and bodies. There was no doubt about their identity. They were Medusa's sisters. The resemblance was striking. They were just as, ahem, ugly as their sister.

Both aunts appeared pleased at the outcome. The larger one conjured a black silk bag and addressed me.

"Look away while we pack our sister for her long journey home."

I did. No complaints.

The other *Gorgon* sister stepped up to me. "You kept your word to me, Joe Luna. I will grant you one wish, within reason."

I thought about it for a millisecond. "Thanks, but I'll take a rain check, if that's all right with you." We Lunas earn our own way in the world. No hand-outs.

She/it laughed. At least I hoped it was laughter, but it sounded an awful lot like a braying jackass.

"I understand," she said.

Once Medusa was safely tucked away, Dana introduced us.

"These are my Aunts Euryale and Stheno."

Shaking their clawed hands demanded a monstrous dose of courage, but I rationalized that there were worse things in life. Like being turned to stone.

The *Gorgons* flapped their metallic wings. "Dana, come visit when you have time," Aunt Euryale said, glancing at me. "We are done here."

And thankfully, so was this case.

With imperceptible nods, they soared into the clearing sky on their golden wings. Uncle Jess, Kit, and I waved from the edge, and my uncle even gave me a thumbs-up. That was as sentimental as he'd ever be, so I relished it. When I glanced up through the roof, the *Gorgons* were already out of sight. I sighed and threw an arm around Dana. With a quick chant, we joined the others up top.

Right then and there, I washed my hands of mythological beings.

Except for certain distant cousins.

Epilogue

I could have slept for a week, but there I was sitting on my front porch with good ole Uncle Jess, who had a penchant for rising with the chickens. His agents sat inside the black Navigator in the driveway, drinking coffee while they waited for their boss.

Dana was inside packing. She decided to fly back to Washington with Uncle Jess, much to my chagrin. There was another bizarre case pending that needed her attention. I really wanted to experiment with those killer kisses some more, but she politely declined. *Business before pleasure.* I rationalized that her leaving was probably for the best. I was too pooped to pop anyway. But that was the worst rationalization I'd ever heard.

Holding his Tillie-special Irish coffee, Uncle Jess swayed placidly in the webbed rocker. My coffee was straight black. No alcoholic additives this morning. I might slip into a coma.

"So what's going to happen to Gwendolyn Stockard?" I asked casually, watching the dawn peek over the trees across the road. "About a zillion people saw her die on the news."

He sipped his coffee. "Witness Protection Program and a touch of plastic surgery," he replied.

Well, at least she wouldn't be buzzing back into my life any time soon.

We fell silent again and listened to the birds singing in the trees. A slight breeze moved the palms and shook off the remaining snow. The temperature was back in the low eighties, and the snow was melting fast. The news people around the country were having a hell of a time explaining our weather anomaly. Some blamed it on global warming. Others pinned the blame on the coming ice age. Only a handful of us knew the truth, and we weren't talking.

Kit predicted that she'd be locked away in her office for a week catching up on her paperwork and caseload. That was fine by me. After her bitterness toward Dana, we needed some time apart to reassess our feelings and relationship.

Ghostworld was in shambles, and I doubted that it would ever be reopened. The attractions would be mothballed until Tandy Stanton could find a buyer, and then the entire park would no doubt be razed to make room for another tourist-convention hotel. Before we left Mansion Macabre last night, Dana sealed the portal to the Emerald Zone forever with a spell her aunts had taught her.

My hearing perked up when the back door slammed, but then I relaxed. My curiosity was too exhausted to check it out. Probably Tillie taking out the trash. It didn't concern me. I was between cases at the moment, and I liked that state of affairs. I planned to kick back and smell the roses before getting involved with another one.

"So why do you think Chrysaor wanted to kill Martha?" I asked.

Uncle Jess finished his coffee and placed the mug on the wicker table between us.

"Martha's too powerful, and can see into the future. Once the *Ghostworld* killings started, all she had to do was look into the future and see that he was the murderer. I'm sure that he didn't want to be exposed so early in the game," he replied soberly.

"So he went after her," I muttered.

"And you," he added.

"Yeah. I guess he wanted me dead, because my funeral would draw you away from Washington."

"That's about the way I figure it, too."

Dana walked onto the porch, her overnight bag in hand. Tillie was with her. They hugged, laughed for no reason I could see, and then it was my turn for my good-bye act. No kiss. Just a firm hug that actually felt damned good.

Uncle Jess stood and shook my hand. "I'll have my staff overnight your paycheck. You've certainly earned it."

I waited for him to add *this time*, but he was too mellow for sarcasm. "I appreciate it," I said simply, and walked Dana and my uncle to the SUV. The agents stuffed their cases into the back and climbed in after Dana and Uncle Jess were settled.

I waved, but no one in the car reciprocated. Oh, well. *Business before pleasure.* What a lousy motto.

I entered the house and found Tillie watching TV in the kitchen. She looked up at me and frowned.

"I heard some noise earlier out back past the pond, but I didn't see anything when I went out to look."

So she was behind the slamming door. Mystery solved.

I yawned despite the coffee. "I'll go out and take a look."

"Better take your wand. You never know what you might run into back there."

It was my turn to frown. "Like what?"

"Like snakes."

"Good idea." I grabbed my wand and walked across the slushy grass toward the pond. Tillie was right. There was nothing there. I continued across the pond bridge and headed for the GPS cemetery.

I stopped suddenly. There was brilliant light on the other side of the pines. It had to be bright to outdo the intense Florida sun. I tightened my grip on the wand and cautiously crept along the path splitting the pines.

After I passed the trees, I saw that the light came from the pop-ups' meadow. Taking a deep breath, I jumped from cover . . . .

And felt like a fool.

Dana sat on a picnic blanket within a snow-free, dry magical zone. She wore a string bikini and was in the process of opening a bottle of wine. A picnic basket lay open beside her, with a feast fit for a king spread around it. Tillie had been busy in the kitchen early this morning. She was a witch, but she was really a matchmaker at heart.

Did I mention the string bikini?

"I thought you . . . I mean, I saw you get in the car," I stammered, totally bewildered *and* pleased.

"I changed my mind. A girl does that from time to time, you know?"

"I know."

She smiled seductively. "Wine?"

I shook my head.

"No? Food then."

I shook my head again.

"You're hard to please this morning. What exactly do you want?" she asked.

"You," I replied and joined her on the blanket.

CPSIA information can be obtained at www.ICGtesting.com
Printed in the USA
BVOW011259270912

301382BV00006B/1/P

9 780578 108537